MW01387989

THE FIND

A NOVEL

by

James J. Valko

Fireside Publications
Lady Lake, Florida

James J. Valko

This book is a work of fiction. Names, characters, businesses, events and incidences are either the product of the author's imagination or are used fictitiously. Any resemblance to actual persons, living or dead, is entirely coincidental.

Published by:

Fireside Publications
1004 San Felipe Lane
Lady Lake, Florida 32159

www.firesidepubs.com

Printed in the United States of America

First Edition: August 2009

ISBN: 978-1-935517-03-0

"Some of the biggest men in the U.S., in the field of commerce and manufacturing, are afraid of somebody, are afraid of something. They know that there is a power somewhere so organized, so subtle, so watchful, so inter-locked, so complete, so pervasive, that they had better not speak above their breath when they speak in condemnation of it."

—President Woodrow Wilson

"Part of me suspects that I'm a loser, and the other part of me thinks I'm God Almighty."

—John Lennon

"The truth shall spring from the earth."

Psalm 85

"The most dangerous enemy is the one that is not perceived, yet whose presence is everywhere."

The Ancients

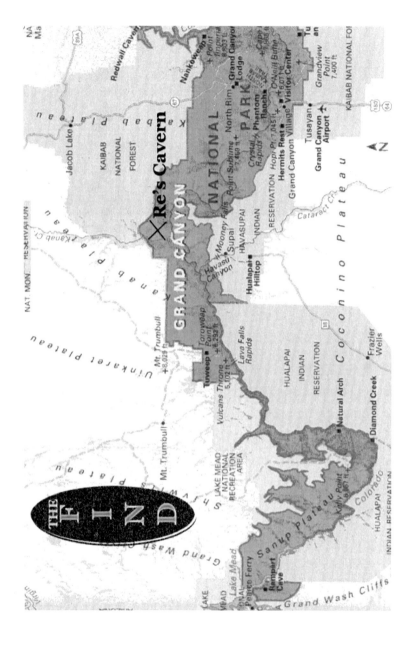

PROLOGUE

The Grand Canyon
4784 feet below the South Rim
Present day. Dawn

Dr. Jensen Reinhardt awoke in his sleeping tent, his head pounding and a sharp ringing in his ears.

This was unusual. He rarely got headaches, and had never experienced ringing like this before. Not that he could ever remember.

He sat up on the air mattress and rubbed the grit from his eyes. *My God.* It felt as if a cactus had sprouted inside his skull during the night, with needle-sharp spines knifing the backs of his eyeballs.

A harsh, metallic taste lingered in his mouth. *Is it from something I ate last night?* He tried to remember what he and his crew had eaten for dinner.

Tried. But nothing came to mind. Strange. The pain was clouding his thinking. *Did I have a stroke in my sleep? After all, I'm . . . I'm . . . how old?*

He sucked air deep into his lungs, trying to clear his head. The polyester tent smelled like tar. He never noticed this smell before. It made him dizzy. *How old am I?*

Canned black beans. Millet. And tuna fish.

That was a relief. He'd remembered what he'd had for dinner. But for the life of him he couldn't remember his age.

Numbers flicked through his mind: forty-four, fifty-three, forty-eight . . . Intuitively, he knew none were his current age.

He hoped like hell it wasn't a stroke. The archeological camp was situated in an isolated, dried-up basin, a mile below the rest of the world. There'd be no calling 911 down here.

He slowly rose from the air mattress. Put one bare foot forward. Same foot back. Stood on one foot. Waved his arms. Wiggled his fingers. Probably not a stroke.

A sudden dark intuition clawed at his chest. *My crew. Something is wrong with them, too!*

Ignoring the pain in his head, Reinhardt thrust his legs in his pants, and yanked on his boots.

The gun. I should bring the gun.

He always carried a gun on archeological digs. Snakes, hungry animals, and other undesirables were a given. He reached under his backpack, felt the leather holster, and ripped his Ruger from it. Turning toward the exit, he caught a glimpse of himself in the small mirror Velcroed to the tent wall. His eyes were a mucousy web of bloodshot veins.

My God. . . What's happening to me?

Gripping the gun in his fist, he stepped outside. Shrouds of dreary gray mist encapsulated the campground, and black granite buttes rose skyward on either side of him like walls of a great medieval fortress. The wind whistled in his ears, down from the Colorado River valley not too far off.

Or is it the ringing?

He headed out and lumbered past the gaping mouth of Re's Cavern. For the past three weeks, he and his crew had been conducting their excavation deep within the limestone cave. They had been searching for . . . for *what?*

Fifty-five. No. Fifty-six. I'm fifty-six years old.

His pace quickened as he passed in front of the three sleeping tents for the crew. But as he drew closer to the larger, yellow-domed excavation tent, his coordination waned. Just putting one foot in front of the other became a challenge. Everything seemed to happen in slow motion: his breathing, his thinking, his movements . . . Becoming desperate to reach his team, he forged clumsily ahead, ignoring the spastic movements of his legs. The crew would be in the tent, making plans for the day. After all, today was *the* day. All they had done over the past three weeks would culminate in today's activities. In fact, everything Reinhardt had done over the last six months—no, over his entire professional life—would culminate today. He knew this to be true. Yet for the life of him, he couldn't remember exactly what they were scheduled to do.

As he approached the main tent, the ringing intensified: an endless, high-pitched shriek that scratched at his eardrums.

Re-gripping the cold handle of the gun, he entered the large excavation tent. As he'd anticipated, the others were there. What he didn't anticipate was that they'd be stumbling about like tranquilized animals, their eyes void of life, saliva dribbling from their mouths.

What the . . .

By now, he had lost his ability to form logical thoughts. Within moments, he, too, started dribbling from the mouth. A feeling of utter hopelessness and desperation spread through him like a deadly virus. He suddenly had an insatiable craving for death—his own.

A voice commanded Reinhardt to release the gun. It hadn't come from outside him, but inside. Someone else's dark booming voice in *his* head: *Release the gun, now!*

The weapon fell from his fingertips.

Suddenly a handful of men wearing black helmets with reflective silver eye protectors entered the tent. He wanted to fight them but was helpless. In his futile mental state, he held only one desire—that they kill him and the others. Death didn't represent an end but a new beginning. But the men didn't kill him. Instead, they gagged and handcuffed him. Drove a stake through the tent floor, then another, and yet another. They tightened a chain around his neck, attached to the stakes. A helmet was thrust on his head. The world darkened through the silver glass, and the feeling of desperation left him. His coordination returned. The headache disappeared, as did the ringing in his ears.

He began to think straight again.

What madness is this?

He struggled to break free. But his movements worked only to tighten the chain, cutting off his air.

He coughed, and out of the corner of his eye caught a man entering the tent, carrying a cooler. He hauled it up onto a table and starting filling Styrofoam cups from the spigot. Handed the cups to his crew. *Dear Lord.* "No," Reinhardt cried. "Don't drink it!"

Only two heads turned toward him: Din Morton and Karen Stoltz. They looked at Reinhardt with deadened eyes. Like the others, they seemed to follow the orders of an invisible dictator. They each took a cup and drank, as if obeying the same internal commands—*the voice.*

One by one, his crewmembers collapsed to the floor like puppets whose strings had been cut. At first, Reinhardt thought—hoped—they had only passed out.

But they weren't just unconscious. Bodies convulsed on the floor, and death rattles filled the air. The cups from which they drank obviously contained poison. He was witnessing the mass murder of his archeological crew.

Rinehart's trembling body jangled the chains. His eyes burned tears under the helmet.

These were student archeologists who had volunteered for the dig. He pictured their mothers and fathers getting the news of their children's deaths. Saw their grief-stricken faces and terrorized eyes. Heard them cry, and heard their endless questions:

How? Who? Why?

What unseen force had seized control of their children's minds?

Reinhardt's blood boiled, and again he struggled to break free. The soles of his shoes skidded on the canyon floor. The chain tightened around his neck, and everything started to go black. He fell to the rock-hard ground, gasping for air.

Who were these men?

And why? W-h-y?

He knew the answer.

He remembered now. Remembered what he and his team had excavated from Re's Cavern, only three days ago. This is what had brought these men to their campground. It's why they had killed his crew. They had come for the find.

ONE

Greenwich Village, NY

Bruce Brackin sat on the sofa, his long legs draped over the edge. He clutched a Walther handgun in his fist. The fingers of his other hand choked a bottle of Jack Dean whiskey.

The loft apartment smelled like liquor and aged wood. Knotty pine bookshelves overflowed with vintage rock record albums, compact discs, and photograph albums. A camera sat atop a tripod between two tungsten lights set in reflector umbrellas. A partitioned-off workspace contained two computer workstations and a printer. Behind yet another partition, Rachel's art tools— colored pencils, dozens of horsehair brushes alongside calligraphy pens, and an airbrush—lay, everything perfectly placed, just as she liked it. The loft was a picture of simplicity. There was no television, only a Bose audio system that he exclusively used to play his classic rock collection.

Brackin brought the bottle of Jack Dean to his lips and threw it back. The sharp barley fluid bit his throat. He gasped. He lowered the near-empty fifth on the end table, but caught only its edge, sending the bottle tumbling to the floor, where it landed with a dead thud. He watched the amber liquid gurgle from the neck and pool around his bare feet.

"Good-bye, Jack," he whispered sadly. "I'll miss you."

He reached for the framed photograph of Rachel sitting on the table and lifted the picture before his swollen eyes. He had taken it eight years, three months, and two days earlier. Rachel was wearing only a blue pinstriped shirt, leaving bare her supple, bronzed legs. She had tossed her raven hair over her shoulder and smiled for the camera.

Bruce had first spotted Rachel a decade earlier in an espresso bar in Tel Aviv. She sat in the corner booth, drawing. Her eyes, like droplets of dark chocolate, studied her subject in the

5

distance, while her silky, olive fingers guided her pen as if it were a fine musical instrument she was playing. He had to approach her.

"*Haeem Ata oman mikzoee?*" he asked, nervously struggling to get the Hebrew words right. "Are you a professional artist?"

Rachel's gaze remained on her subject. "*Ani Mekave lehyot oman mikzoee,*" She answered in her lilting Israeli accent. "I hope to become one."

Thrilled that she engaged with him, Bruce said, "*Haeem ani yachol leknot lach cos tzeva?*" "May I buy you a cup of coffee?"

She looked at him for the first time and started laughing.

"*Haeem amaerti machehoo mazhik?*" he asked. "I said something funny?"

"You asked if you could buy me a cup of *paint*," Rachel returned, struggling to enunciate each word.

He glanced away to hide his blushing face, but quickly returned his gaze, not wanting to keep his eyes off her for long. "You speak English?"

"About as good as you speak Hebrew." Her eyes glistened.

"I meant *coffee*. May I buy you a cup of coffee?"

"Since you put it that way. . ."

He sat down, and as they talked Rachel seemed to look directly into his soul, stirring awake some past life where they'd made a sacred promise to recognize each other again, should they meet. A week later, he told her she would be happy with him in New York. They would work in advertising as a team— she the artist, he the writer/photographer. They'd be successful and grow old together. She left her family and joined him. Innocent and childlike, she trusted him. She had always trusted him.

Now a different image superimposed itself over the photograph of Rachel in his hand—one of his wife's face, gaunt and pale, as she lay in a steel box. A solitary teardrop fell from Bruce's eye and dotted the glass covering the picture.

Goddamn, how he wanted the tears to flow. They were like hot acid dammed up in his eyes. But he was beyond tears. He was an emotional runaway train, motivated only by a longing to be with her. Even more maddening was his desire to punish himself for allowing her to die.

He carefully placed the picture back on the end table. Then he tightened his grip on the handgun and directed it at his temple, forcing his quivering finger to the trigger.

Don't be a pussy, he thought. *Do it just like you planned it. Do it fast.*

His sweaty finger tightened on the cold trigger.

Just fucking do it!

Another picture flashed to mind: his brother, Peter, finding Bruce's dead body lying face down in its own blood. Bruce was nine years older than Peter and had helped raise him from birth. He'd always thought of Peter more as a son than a brother. But Peter wasn't a baby anymore. He was in his twenties now, and perfectly capable of taking care of himself.

Bruce thrust Peter from his mind. *Damn it. It's my body. I have a right to this!*

He sucked in his last breath. *Don't be a pussy!*

But Peter wouldn't go. He defiantly stood there, the little shit, looking down at him, crying. *How could Bruce have done this*?

Suddenly, Bruce was out of his head, gawking down at his body from above. It wasn't his imagination. He was out, way out. Pressed to his skull, the gun barrel shook violently. His legs jumped like a jackrabbit's. A river of tears started flowing from his eyes. The dam broke. He watched his body cry as if watching someone else. It moaned like a child, although as a child he had never cried like this.

He suddenly realized that even if he pulled the trigger *he*—the guy on the ceiling looking down—wouldn't die. He'd probably just remain there and cry for the next thousand years, a tormented, sorry-ass excuse for a spirit. *Even death won't release me from this hell.*

The phone rang.

He jumped back into his body.

The gun fell to the floor, and he collapsed on the sofa. He curled into a fetal position. It was his fault Rachel was dead.

The phone rang several more times before the answering machine picked up. Rachel's voice greeted the caller with a prerecorded message:

"Bruce and I aren't here right now. He's washing the car, and

7

then he's going shopping for us, then he's going to paint our bathroom, then he's going to take me out. Me? I'm napping. Leave a message. *L'Chaim!*"

"Hello, Bruce, this is Murdock Collier from *American Times* magazine. I've got an assignment for you at the Grand Canyon. Call me ASAP."

TWO

Bruce wasn't dead yet.

He'd stayed on the couch for a long time before dragging himself into the kitchen, where, while sipping a day old cup of Colombian coffee, he returned Murdock Collier's call. The conversation was short, not with Collier, but his secretary, who told him Mr. Collier would fill him in about the assignment in person.

Two-and-a-half hours later, Bruce sat in the managing editor's office of the *American Times* magazine.

Collier's secretary smiled at him from behind her desk. He tried to smile back, which was amazingly difficult to do. It hurt to look at her bleached white teeth, even through his dark glasses. A thought skittered around the edges of his aching head: *You're not up for this. Leave now before you make a fool of yourself.*

Before leaving home, he'd perceived Rachel's presence—again. *How many times had it happened since her death?* It wasn't just a faith-induced concept of her. He actually *felt* Rachel near him, hovering. Reaching out to him. For a month, he had sat in his apartment trying to reach back, and drinking himself numb in the process. He could do it no more. He decided if he wasn't going to off himself, he needed to interact with people again. But could he act normal—*pretend* to act normal?

The phone rang at the secretary's desk and Bruce jumped in his chair. She frowned at him. Picked up the handset. "Yes, I'll bring him in." She hung up.

"Mr. Collier will see you now," she announced. She slipped out from behind her desk and moved to a ten-foot Gothic-looking door. Wearing open-toed high heels, Bruce noticed her ruby-red toenails matched the color of the carpet, the same color scheme as *American Times* magazine.

"Please hurry. We don't want to keep Mr. Collier waiting."

He crossed the room to her.

She stared at him.

"You doing okay?" she asked.

"Fine."

"You look like Tom Cruise with those glasses on."

"I think I'm taller than he is—and younger."

"I think you should take them off. Mr. Collier doesn't like it when people don't look him in the eye. He's very direct, you know."

"But I scratched my eye. The doctor said I have to wear them." Even he was impressed by how pathetically wounded he sounded.

She bit her lip, thought for a moment, and then opened the door.

They entered the managing editor's office—a palace of an office with dozens of glittering gold-leaf-framed *American Times* magazine covers adorning the walls.

A rail of a man stood behind a desk, gazing out the window with his back to them.

"Bruce Brackin is here to see you, Mr. Collier."

Bruce had never met Murdock Collier in person, and when the old man turned around, Bruce was shocked. With pallid, wafer-thin skin stretched over bony cheekbones, Murdock looked like half man, half cadaver. Just the act of standing seemed painful to him. This was the famous news magazine mogul he'd heard so much about over the years?

"They say at the end of your life, it's not the things you did that you will regret, but the things you didn't do. What do you think, Brackin?"

"In my case, I'd say there'll be plenty of both."

Murdock Collier laughed, which quickly dissolved into a coughing fit.

For a moment, Bruce thought the man might choke to death. But Nina gave Bruce a sidelong look that seemed to indicate this was nothing unusual.

Collier finally hacked up a wad of phlegm, laid it into a Kleenex, and disposed of the tissue beneath his desk—in a wastepaper basket, Bruce hoped. "Please sit," Collier said.

Bruce sunk down in the burgundy leather chair in front of Murdock's desk and heard a toilet flush. A man exited the john across the room, while rubbing his hands on his pants.

"This is my son, Seth Collier," Murdock informed Bruce.

Unlike his father, Seth's skin was a perfect tanning-booth bronze. But like his father, Seth's cheekbones rode high on his face, reminiscent of a hammerhead shark.

Bruce extended his hand, but Seth didn't seem to notice. He took a seat.

Murdock also sat.

There was an awkward moment of just looking—the two men at Bruce, Bruce at them.

"He scratched his eye. Doctor's orders," Nina informed the Colliers and left the room. Seth retrieved a hand-exerciser from his silver sports jacket. The springs squeaked as he started pumping it.

Bruce didn't like being dwarfed by Murdock's desk. The thing was bigger than a king-sized bed, for Christ's sake. He straightened his six-foot-two frame in the chair and slid forward; it sounded like gas expelling.

"I have a little assignment for you in the Grand Canyon," Murdock said.

Wasn't that why he was here? "What is it?"

"Got an e-mail yesterday morning," Murdock said. "A team of archeologists were on an expedition, and something went wrong."

"What went wrong?" Bruce asked.

"The e-mail didn't give many details. We know someone was killed. We suspect murder." Murdock's eyes showed no emotion.

Bruce shrugged. "Murder happens every day. Why not just let the local papers cover it?"

"The leader of the excavation is a strange bird," Murdock said. "Our source tells us he was involved in some pretty bizarre activities."

"His name is Reinhardt," Seth chimed in. "Dr. Jensen Reinhardt."

Squeak . . . squeak . . . squeak . . . went the hand-exerciser in Seth's grasp.

Murdock shoved a manila folder across his desk's vast surface.

Bruce caught it. Inside was a newspaper article written two years earlier from the Medill News Service, a Chicago news service of the Medill School of Journalism at Northwestern University.

Jensen Reinhardt, professor of archeology at Northwestern University, was terminated from his teaching position yesterday morning. Dr. Reinhardt had taken eight students on a "field trip" to Zihuatanejo, Mexico, to learn remote viewing (out-of-body-seeing) techniques taught by a local shaman named Emilio Mandes. Some archeologists claim to use remote viewers to discover the whereabouts of ancient cities and artifacts. An unnamed mother of one of the students on the field trip claimed her daughter "was forced into cult-related rituals that had nothing to do with education."

Other parents complained as well.

NU's Dean of Humanities, Marion Keating, expressed his deepest apologies to the victims of the misguided field trip. He assured everyone concerned that the school did not sanction such activities, and that the severest discipline had been administered. Dr. Reinhardt was immediately relieved of his teaching responsibilities.

When asked about his termination, Dr. Reinhardt's only comment was, "Witch hunts are alive and well in northern Illinois."

There was a photograph of Dr. Reinhardt. He had a thick black beard with a small patch of gray below his right cheek. His eyes were like black onyx. They had a sort of hypnotic, drawing effect. *I know this man*, Bruce thought. *But, from where?*

He lowered the paper to see Murdock's contrasting ice blue eyes staring from across the desk.

"There's a press conference at the Grand Canyon park headquarters tonight," Murdock said. "Our source tells us the FBI is involved. We want to send you to cover it. Your flight leaves in a little over three hours."

Huh? "The FBI?"

"Yes."

"But I don't get it. Why me?"

"I have a gut feeling about this," Murdock said to Bruce. "Normally I'd send Joshua Quint or Madeline Nelan to cover such a story, but they're both in Washington. All my other freelancers are tied up with projects. To be honest, you were the last on my list. If the story turns out to be major, I'll pull Madeline and send her in behind you."

"Maybe I should rephrase my question, Mr. Collier. How come *you're* talking to me? You're the managing editor of the country's leading news magazine. I'm a nobody. A beginner. I've only done a handful of magazine articles in my life, and only one for *American Times.*"

Murdock intertwined his bony fingers on the desk. "That little human interest story you wrote for us."

"'Things Overheard in New York,'" Bruce reminded him.

"Yes. Clever little piece."

One day last winter, Bruce had been in a Starbucks jacked up on java. On his right had been a woman talking about her hysterectomy on a cell phone and on his other side was a group of students reading erotic poetry. He wrote a humorous article about them and sent it to the *American Times.*

Squeak . . . squeak . . . squeak . . . Seth pumped the hand-exerciser.

Murdock smiled at Bruce but didn't look happy. "You can make a lot more money writing advertising copy than magazine copy. You *do* know that, don't you, son?"

At first, the statement surprised Bruce. But as he looked around the room at some of the gold-framed *American Times* covers—the Great Depression, the housing market crash, global warming, and the end of the world—it started to make sense. The reason a nobody in journalism like him was summoned to Murdock Collier's office was because *American Times* was feeling the brunt of him not writing advertising copy anymore.

Bruce had been the top copywriter at the Chapman/Wallace Advertising Agency. When he quit the company last year, they lost business, which apparently had a ripple effect. *American*

Times lost business, too.

And so it was. Murdock started to ramble on about how valuable Bruce had been to the Chapman/Wallace Advertising Agency—a place he'd worked for six years.

"I think you should consider going back—"

Bruce cut Murdock off. "Things have changed in my life, Mr. Collier. I'm not interested in advertising anymore."

The capillaries in Murdock's cheeks flashed red. He obviously wasn't used to being interrupted. "Do I have to spell out for you what's going on here?"

Though Murdock Collier looked like a rickety bag of bones, he possessed an intimidating, "I-shit-bigger-than-you" presence that was, no doubt, designed to make writers and other minions in his publishing empire squirm.

Not today. Being suicidal and depressed had its upside—you just didn't give a damn. Who could intimidate someone who'd blow his own brains out? Bruce almost felt liberated.

"No, Mr. Collier, you don't have to spell out what's going on. I'm through with advertising."

"Yet you're willing to do freelance magazine work? That doesn't pay for shit!"

Bruce doubted a man like Collier could conceive that anyone would do anything that wasn't for money. Fine. The truth was, advertising had offered a way for Rachel and him to work together. With her gone, it just didn't matter anymore.

"Does this conversation have anything to do with the Grand Canyon?" Bruce asked.

He noticed Murdock's right hand quivering. The old man quickly dampened it with his left. He looked up at Bruce and said, "Have it your way, son. I need a story along with photographs. The gig pays sixty dollars a day, plus ten cents a word. You in?"

Having traveled most of his life, Bruce knew the therapeutic benefits of getting away. God knows, he needed some form of therapy. Besides, he'd never been to the Grand Canyon before. A little R&R. A vacation . . .

"I'm in."

Murdock gave him a nod and stabbed the intercom on his desk. "Nina, please give Mr. Brackin his plane tickets and

14

itinerary on his way out."

Seth stood up, towering over Bruce. "Since you're not a real investigative reporter, I'll have to guide you. E-mail me a rough draft by tomorrow morning, and call me at two o'clock, EST. Any questions?"

Bruce noticed the biceps flexing beneath the sleeve of Seth's silver jacket as he pumped the hand-exerciser. *Squeak . . . squeak . . .squeak . . .*

"No questions," Bruce said, rising to his feet. He bid them farewell, and left.

Back in reception, Nina handed him an envelope with an electronic plane and hotel reservation in it.

"Don't let Seth bother you," she said. "He resents many decisions his father makes. Hiring you just happened to be the latest."

She'd obviously been listening to their conversation through the intercom.

Nina smiled at him with those blinding teeth and then pushed a business card at him. "I wrote my cell number on the back if you need any help."

As Bruce took the card, Nina touched his arm with a warm palm.

He quickly pulled back his hand, thanked her, and bolted.

Relieved to be out of there, he took the stairs. He'd rather walk six flights down than chance Nina catching up with him at the elevator. He stopped on the first landing and checked the time of his flight. It departed at four-thirty, which meant he had about three hours to stop at home, pack some things, and get to Newark Airport. He excavated a pint of Jack from his coat pocket and took a long swallow.

Then it hit him. . .

He remembered where he'd seen Dr. Jensen Reinhardt before:

"Peter."

THREE

Sitting on his front porch in his wheelchair, Peter spotted Bruce's silver Jeep coming down the street. Bruce had called him and said he was dropping by the house on the way to the airport. It was the first conversation they had in nearly two weeks and Peter was relieved to hear his voice. With Bruce not returning his calls, he was starting to think crazy thoughts—after all, Rachel had been murdered in cold blood.

The Jeep turned into the driveway, stopped, lunged forward, and stopped again. Bruce stepped out and crossed over the front lawn. He wore dark glasses, the same ones he'd worn at Rachel's funeral. Peter wasn't sure if Bruce was hiding his eyes from the world, or the world from his eyes. In either case, Bruce had become a shadow of the man he'd been before her death. What Peter would give just to see his brother smile again.

Bruce mounted the porch steps. "The landscaper on strike?"

Peter looked over the weed-infested lawn. "I found him passed out on the Lawn-Boy and fired him. The guy was a drunk. Here, have a beer."

Peter excavated a green bottle from the ice chest beside his chair. He unscrewed the cap, handed it to Bruce,

"What's this?" Bruce asked, inspecting the bottle.

"Kingfisher. 'World's number-one Indian lager.'"

Peter's new pastime was taste-testing foreign beers. Being relegated to a wheelchair twenty-four/seven, it was a good hobby.

After Bruce gulped down some beer, Peter extended his arm for a shake and said, "I've been worried about you, you fuck head."

Bruce gripped his hand, and a wave of emotion washed over Peter. He pulled his brother into an embrace and patted him on the back. They broke apart.

Peter watched Bruce wipe away a tear, as Peter did the same. It had been a rough month. Bruce visibly lost weight too, down from two hundred to probably about one-ninety. The same weight as Peter only Bruce was seven inches taller. Not a pound of fat on him.

"Been spending time at the dojo?" Peter asked. Bruce had been doing Brazilian jujitsu for years. Maybe he'd stepped it up since Rachel's death, that's why he'd lost weight.

Bruce shook his head. "Nah. Haven't been there in weeks." This was unlike Bruce. Not working out. Losing weight. "Want some Molinari salami? I ordered five pounds online. It just arrived yesterday."

"I really can't stay that long."

"You said you have a plane to catch?" Peter took a swig of his Kingfisher. The coldness bit his throat.

"*American Times* magazine is sending me to the Grand Canyon to cover a story. A paid vacation. Do you believe it?"

Pete didn't believe it. "What kind of story?"

"Someone was murdered there."

"Murdered?" He knew Bruce had done minimal freelance work for *AT* in the past, but nothing like this. "*You're* going to cover a murder story?"

Bruce shrugged. "They have to send someone. The press conference is tonight, and I'm the note-taker. They think a guy named Dr. Reinhardt is involved. Name sound familiar?"

"Dr. *Jensen* Reinhardt?"

"Yeah. That's him. You had Rachel check out a video of him online a while back, right? I remember seeing her watch it."

Peter had forgotten all about that. "Yes, I believe I did tell her about him, if we're talking about the same guy." A few years back he attended a 9/11 conspiracy convention, and Dr. Reinhardt had been one of the speakers. Peter liked what Reinhardt had said and learned he had some lectures posted on YouTube, which he told Rachel about.

"What do you know about him?" Bruce asked. He started pacing in circles, making the floorboards creak.

"He's an anthropologist, I believe," Peter said. "But he was talking about conspiracy stuff. You don't like conspiracy stuff. Rachel was interested so I told her about him."

17

Peter was getting dizzy watching Bruce pace. "Why don't you sit down?" He motioned toward the wicker chair opposite him.

"Actually, I gotta go."

"Already?"

"No. I mean to the bathroom. Be right back." He ran into the house.

"Conspiracy stuff" was an ongoing point of contention between them. As far as Peter could remember, it had started after their father, an Air Force engineer, was killed in a plane crash. Military records stated a fuel tank explosion caused the accident. Major Paul Brackin had been engaged in Top Secret activities relating to the Iraq War, if you can even call it a war. On their mother's deathbed, she more than hinted that the crash had been no accident.

"Your father was dangerous to those who employed him," she'd whispered to Bruce and Peter. *"He knew too many of the government's dirty, stinking secrets."*

Neither Bruce nor Peter had ever heard their mother talk this way before. While Bruce was content to let the comment die with her, Peter dug into every conspiracy book ever written to discover exactly what she might have been referring to. Although he never directly learned the "*dirty secrets*" behind their father's death, Peter's research opened his eyes to the covert conspiratorial forces at work in this world.

How many times had he and Bruce argued about 9/11 since it happened all those years ago? While Bruce echoed the standard government PR line, Peter always challenged him with any number of big, unanswered questions: Why did WTC 7 collapse in a free fall *exactly* like the Twin Towers had, *even though it wasn't even hit by a plane?* Why had the *The 9/11 Commission Report* totally ignored this anomaly? Why was molten metal found at ground zero, when the *only* thing that could cause metal to burn that hot was thermite, the explosive used for demolitions of buildings? Why had two of the hijackers' *paper* passports survived the aircraft crashes and been found in the rubble, when everything else had *burned like a fireball?*

Peter's blood ran hot just thinking about it even now.

And Bruce's answer was always the same: "If 9/11 was an inside conspiracy, too many people would've had to know about it, and people can't keep secrets. Someone would've spilled the beans."

Peter doubted he'd ever convince Bruce that he and the rest of the American population had been duped. Peter had talked to too many other "non-believers" not to notice a similarity among them. They saw the world in black-and-white—black hats and white hats, good guys and bad, terrorists and us. This was the mentality the *real* conspirators had banked on to pull off 9/11. And this was Bruce. He believed in the supreme righteousness of Captain America, Indiana Jones, and Uncle Sam. Bruce wasn't naïve and didn't wear rose-colored glasses; he just believed in the black-and-white goodness of people. But if he ever did cross over to your side, forget about it, he'd fight to the death to defend your position. You'd never have a more committed teammate.

Bruce stepped back on the porch. Took another swallow of his Kingfisher and said, "So, what did Reinhardt talk about on that video?"

"About how societies have been controlled throughout history—always by small groups of royalty or whatnot—by the manipulation of the same specific control points—*including our present society!*"

Bruce said nothing.

"Reinhardt called them the Ms," Peter said.

"The Ms?"

"The four areas that influence our present society the most. Control these areas, and you control the population." He listed them, emphasizing the "em" sound in each word.

"Media. Military. Money. Mental health."

Bruce absorbed this. Glanced at his watch. Looked back at Peter. "Media, military, money, and . . ."

"Mental health."

"I got the first three, but why would anyone want to control the crazies of the world?"

"Mental health isn't just about crazies. Today, shrinks and Big Pharma are in bed together working to get as many people on psych drugs as possible. It's all part of their master plan to dumb down America."

Bruce nodded. "Uh huh. Well, maybe Dr. Reinhardt is crazy himself; he might be wanted for murder."

"Really?"

"I gotta go, or I'll miss my flight. Do you have the necklace?"

Peter leaned over the side of his wheelchair and picked up the small jeweler's box next to it. He pulled out Bruce's necklace, and handed it to him.

Bruce yanked gently on the lock, which Peter had repaired for him, then turned over the Star of David pendant. *Anie Oevet Otha Leolam,* it said, I love you forever.

Peter had engraved the words four years ago at Rachel's request. He watched Bruce delicately hang the chain around his neck and tuck it under his shirt.

Then Peter handed Bruce a small gift-wrapped package. "Picked these up the other day for you."

Bruce tore into the wrapping paper. It was two classic albums by Jethro Tull on CD: *Aqualung* and *Stand Up.*

Bruce was a classic rock 'n roll aficionado.

Peter wasn't really into classic rock. These albums had received good reviews on iTunes so he bought them. "I was surprised it was classic rock," Peter said. "Thought a name like Jethro would be a bluegrass band, which didn't add up because I know you're not into bluegrass—"

"Except for Alison Krauss."

"Right. So what instrument does Jethro play?"

Was that a genuine smile that crossed Bruce's lips?

"Jethro Tull isn't the name of a real person. It's the name of the band."

"Ohhhh. I didn't know that." Peter grinned.

Bruce started laughing, genuinely laughing, and it warmed Peter's heart. Of course Peter knew that Jethro Tull was the name of the band.

Bruce drained his bottle of Kingfisher, and kissed the top of Peter's head. "Thanks for the CDs. Gotta fly. Be back in a couple of days." He turned on his heel and descended the steps.

Crossing over the lawn, Bruce shouted back to Peter, "The landscaper may have been a drunk, but he was still good enough for Mom to keep all those years. Might want to give him another chance."

Technically, they both owned the house. After their mother died, they'd inherited it equally, but Bruce had insisted Peter live there and continue to run his jewelry repair business from home.

"I'll think about it," Peter shouted back. "Hey. If you run into Reinhardt, don't mess with him!"

"Why's that?"

"Dude's about six foot eight inches tall!"

"I'll keep that in mind."

Peter watched Bruce get into his Jeep and back out of the driveway. But as he did so, a cold chill washed over Peter—a feeling that he might not ever see his brother again.

FOUR

Bruce slept most of the flight from Newark Airport to Phoenix. Actually, it was more like a state of suspended animation. After the plane landed, a flight attendant shook him to consciousness. With her big brown eyes staring down at him, she looked hauntingly like Rachel.

"Time to wake up."

In a daze, he half expected a kiss, maybe even some coaxing with her hands downstairs, like Rachel used to do. "Thank you," he said. At least his headache was gone.

At the terminal he claimed his reservation on a small Saab aircraft, which jounced most of the way to Grand Canyon Airport, where it landed just past seven o'clock Mountain Time. Relieved to get his feet on solid ground, he procured a Nissan Maxima and a handful of tourist maps at the Hertz Rent-a-Car station, and headed down Route 180.

After passing through the tiny town of Tusayan, he would have liked to snap a few shots of the towering ponderosa trees edging the open road, but time didn't allow. The press conference was scheduled to start in less than an hour.

Several miles later he entered Grand Canyon Village, described on the map as a small community on the South Rim of the canyon consisting of hotels, restaurants, and novelty shops. He followed South Entrance Road through the park to a lot near the Grand Canyon park headquarters where the press conference would be held.

Funny thing about a canyon; when you're near it, you can't see it. Not like mountains. According to the map, the rim was about a half-mile north. Short on time, he'd have to check it out tomorrow.

He grabbed his camera and a notepad, slipped out of the car and headed toward the park headquarters.

The descending sun cast a crimson glow over the landscape, and, as he strolled over the parking lot, he could feel the heat of the day rising from the pavement. He thought of how excited Rachel would be if she were here with him.

Like the time they'd visited Masada, the ancient ruins of a Hebrew fortress in the Judean Desert. Reportedly, in about 70 BC over nine hundred Jews took refuge on the mountaintop. With the Roman army closing in, the Jews were said to have chosen death by their own hands rather than being captured or made Roman slaves. He remembered Rachel telling him the history at the ruins. Her words had stuttered from English to Hebrew and back. She did that when she got excited. God, he missed her.

The dry air here at the Grand Canyon even smelled like the ancient rock of Masada.

As he approached the designated press conference area, he was surprised to find a large crowd of people milling about.

A stage was set up in front of the park headquarters with a bundle of microphones gathered before a lectern. Behind the lectern was a large silver screen. Cables snaked along the pavement from under the stage like a gathering of boa constrictors.

Media people swarmed, about two or three hundred of them, Bruce estimated. There were rows of wooden chairs in front of the stage, and behind them another stage with dozens of cameras on it. Obviously there was more to this murder scenario than Murdock Collier had thought—or had let on.

Working his way into the crowd, Bruce got caught up in a wave and was swept to the back, where he fell into an empty chair.

A man gawked at him from the seat next door.

"Nothing but assholes and elbows around here, eh?" the follow said.

A cloud of white, curly locks covered the old guy's head and warm glow radiated in his tawny brown eyes. He was a half-foot shorter than Bruce, even sitting down.

"Hi," he said.

"Howdy."

"You've never been to a press conference before, have you?"

"Is it that obvious?"

The little guy extended a hand. "Dillon. Dillon Waterford. I'm out of Toronto."

He wore a gray tweed suit jacket that looked like he had rummaged it from a Salvation Army store. Where his left arm should have been was a free-hanging sleeve. Bruce shook Dillon's right hand. "Bruce Brackin, out of, ah, New York."

A voice screeched over the PA system: "Ladies and gentleman, can I please have your attention."

A stately looking man stood at the lectern.

"Who's that?"

"Bob Milliken, the governor of Arizona," Dillon replied.

"Thank you for coming this evening." The governor addressed the media, his tone somber. "I regret to inform you that two days ago a dreadful tragedy occurred in the Grand Canyon. Thirteen people were found dead."

Thirteen people?

Murmurs rippled through the crowd of reporters, many of whom were still vying for seats.

"Grand Canyon National Park is managed by the National Forest Service, not the State of Arizona," the governor said. "For reasons you will learn today, the Forest Service has solicited the help of the FBI to deal with this situation. That said, to brief you, I would now like to turn the microphone over to Special Agent William Pittman."

A man wearing a concerned frown took the stage. He had a massive neck and wide shoulders. Even seated fifty feet away, Bruce could see his face was badly pitted. His jawbone worked a wad of gum in quick, even chomps. He set some pages on the lectern and then stared out over the crowd of reporters. Bruce heard the clicking of cameras, and it occurred to him that he should do the same. He stood up, got the FBI man in his viewfinder, and snapped the shutter.

The agent said, "About thirty-two hours ago, on June the eighteenth, at approximately two-thirty p.m., a Grand Canyon park ranger discovered a group of bodies in a tent at an excavation site. We delayed informing the media until all the relatives of those found had been notified. That goal has been met. We have expressed, and continue to express, our deepest condolences to the families of the victims."

Bruce slid forward on his chair.

"On June the fifth, a group of fifteen people arrived at a cave in the Grand Canyon for the purpose of an archeological excavation. Their leader was a man named Jensen Reinhardt. That's R-e-i-n-h-a-r-d-t. Dr. Jensen Reinhardt . . ."

Bruce jotted notes on his yellow pad as Pittman told the crowd that Dr. Reinhardt was a doctor of phenomenology, a type of philosophy, as well as an anthropologist and teacher. "Reinhardt has led expeditions all over the world—some anthropological in nature, while others would have to be classified as spiritual or mystical."

The agent placed his hands on either side of the lectern and leaned into the microphones.

"Reinhardt held two teaching positions in the past—one at a small college, the other at a major university. He was dismissed from both for subjecting students to what has been described as 'unusual metaphysical activities,' or rituals.

"Reinhardt had obtained a permit from the Grand Canyon Park Geological Society to conduct an excavation at Re's Cavern, a large cave just beyond the park's main area."

A map of the Grand Canyon appeared on the screen behind Pittman. He directed a laser pointer to the Colorado River.

"The excavation took place here," Pittman said. "At Re's Cavern."

The screen switched to a picture of a gaping black hole in the face of a cliff wall. A man standing in front of Re's Cavern was dwarfed by its vast size.

"Reinhardt and his crew set up camp at the mouth of Re's Cavern, and for almost two weeks they involved themselves in the excavation, or so it seemed. On the thirteenth day, there was an impending threat of a severe thunderstorm, which prompted a Grand Canyon backcountry ranger to radio Reinhardt to warn him of the approaching storm. Reinhardt had been previously given strict instructions by the ranger to leave the radio lines open, especially in the presence of bad weather. I'm told lightning and flash floods can be dangerous in this area of the canyon. When Reinhardt didn't respond, the ranger went to their campground.

"On the afternoon of June eighteenth, the ranger found thirteen dead bodies in the main tent situated outside Re's Cavern. A rescue unit arrived yesterday morning at seven thirty a.m. Bad weather and nightfall prevented the team from getting there any earlier. The bodies were removed by helicopter."

A picture of the interior of a large, yellow tent appeared on the screen. Dead bodies scattered haphazardly on the floor were mostly face up. All wore short-sleeved shirts and shorts. Bruce craned his neck to get a better view. *What the hell?* He saw no signs of violence on the bodies. Some had bloated torsos, blown up like balloons, but most just looked peaceful, as if they were sleeping. His breathing labored. They were younger than him; barely out of their teens, for Christ's sake.

He heard Dillon sigh.

The screen switched to a new image, a cluster of brown glass bottles sitting on a table.

"Cyanide." Pittman's voice hissed through the PA system.

The audience was as quiet as a praying congregation. The sky had now darkened, and a gust of wind swept through the crowd like a sigh of death creeping up from the canyon itself.

The screen changed to a picture of a group of FBI men, wearing face-masks and rubber gloves, lifting black body bags into large wooden crates. Agent Pittman advanced to another picture showing the crates being hoisted on to a helicopter. Bruce took several shots of the screen and scribbled, "wooden crates put into helicopter," on his notepad.

"The cause of death was the same with each person," Pittman said. "According to forensic and autopsy reports, it was potassium cyanide poisoning. The cyanide was mixed with apple juice."

Pittman enunciated the next words slowly and distinctly. "There were originally fifteen people involved in the excavation. Thirteen were found dead. Two are missing—Dr. Jensen Reinhardt and his assistant, Megan Eastwood. Next."

The silver screen showed the same photo of Jensen Reinhardt that Bruce had seen in Murdock Collier's office that morning. It had a profoundly different effect on him now, however.

26

Reinhardt's eyes were darker, his expression cold and distant. Bruce recalled what Peter had said about Reinhardt, giving a lecture about the "Ms." *A conspiracy nut? A murderer?*

The screen switched to a close-up of Reinhardt's assistant, Megan Eastwood.

She had short red hair and sea green eyes, slightly big for her face. Her lips arched into an alluring smile for the camera.

Bruce took a picture, wrote "Megan Eastwood" on his notepad, and underlined the name.

The photograph of Reinhardt appeared back on the screen and stayed there. His bearded face stared coldly at the audience while Pittman continued his briefing.

"The bottles of cyanide had Reinhardt's fingerprints on them. Also, a plethora of mind-altering drugs were found in the sleeping tents. These included peyote, psilocybin mushrooms, and LSD."

The audience rustled in their seats.

"Ladies and gentlemen, it is the belief of the FBI that Jensen Reinhardt and Megan Eastwood contributed to the deaths of thirteen individuals, and then fled the scene. There are warrants out for their arrests I will take your questions now."

Pittman showed no emotion as he gazed out at the audience. He began working his chewing gum between his teeth.

A man near the stage jumped to his feet. "Is it your belief that Reinhardt and the girl forced the students to drink the cyanide?"

"At this time, there is no evidence of compliance by force. It appears the members of the group swallowed the poison of their own free will."

A female voice shouted from the back, "Are you suggesting assisted mass suicide?"

If Pittman answered her question, Bruce didn't hear. Dillon was grumbling too loudly. "Another Jonestown. Another stinking Jonestown!"

Bruce remembered reading about Jonestown years ago: Reverend Jim Jones and the Peoples Temple. Under pressure from Jones, the members of his sect had participated in a voluntary ritual mass suicide. Now that Bruce had become more intimate with suicide, he wondered how one man could possibly con a thousand people into taking their own lives.

Suicide just ain't that easy.

A man with bleached blond hair stood up.

"Forest Gray, NBC News," he announced. "What types of artifacts were they digging for in Re's Cavern?"

Pittman said, "I'm told they were digging for American Indian artifacts."

Bleached blond said, "According to the information you presented, it appears that Dr. Reinhardt was on a legitimate excavation. Why then would he—"

Pittman interrupted. "It seems Dr. Reinhardt had other intentions that were not scientific in nature."

Pittman clicked the projector button. The newspaper article Bruce had read in Murdock's office that morning appeared on the screen.

Pittman read aloud how Reinhardt was fired for bringing students into what were described as cult-related rituals, and that Reinhardt had a history of involving students in occult practices, such as telepathic experiments and other psychic phenomena.

Bleached blond pressed on. "You're suggesting a college instructor and his partner assisted in the suicide of thirteen people. What would their motivation have been?"

"We don't know what motivated Reinhardt. Just as we do not know what motivated Jim Jones or David Koresh."

Several more questions bombarded Pittman. Dillon jumped to his feet to get Pittman's attention, but the agent pointed to a woman wearing a red dress.

"In the pictures, there were several tents and many tools," she shouted. "You said the group river-rafted to Re's Cavern. Did the equipment also come by raft, or was it flown in?"

"I'm told that flying in and out of the canyon can be dangerous due to uncertain wind conditions," Pittman said. "Normally it is done for emergency purposes only. All the equipment was brought to the campsite by raft."

Dillon's voice suddenly rose above the crowd. "There are many unanswered questions about Jim Jones and David Koresh. In each of their cases, there is, in fact, evidence that suggests they themselves were victims."

The audience craned their necks to see who was speaking. The old man stepped up on his chair to be seen.

"Do you have any inclination to pursue the possibility these people were murdered by an outside agency?" A gust of wind flagged the empty sleeve of Dillon's jacket.

"We pursue every angle, sir. This case is no exception. However, murder by an outside agency seems highly unlikely at this time."

"Instead, we are to believe that thirteen people on an excavation just woke up one morning and drank themselves to death?"

"Admittedly, there are many unanswered questions. As I said, the investigation is ongoing."

"Yes, it is a mystery." Dillon pressed on. "Yet it seems to me, Mister 'Pitt Man,' that you may have issued warrants for the arrests of two people who are possibly being held hostage by the murderers themselves."

The agent grimaced. "The name is Pittman. And yours?"

"Dillon. Dillon Waterford."

Bruce had the urge to grab the back of Dillon's jacket and yank him down into his seat. Why was he being belligerent with Pittman?

"You ask an important question, Mr. Waterford," Pittman admitted. "But if you've ever tasted cyanide, you'd know it is impossible to drink without knowing it's poison. These members drank the liquid willingly. Even if they were held at gunpoint, at least *some* would have fought for their lives. There were no recent cuts, bruises, or abrasions on any of the bodies, except for that of a young lady, which we believe was caused by a fall. There's not another campground within twenty miles of Re's Cavern. The killers would have had to hike down a trail, walk twenty to thirty-five miles, murder everyone, and then hike back out of the canyon. Or perhaps they river-rafted to and from the crime scene. But any rafts or dories that are launched at Lees Ferry must register with the park. The murderers would have had to launch at night. Experts tell me it's impossible to run the river at night. But, indeed, the main question here is motivation: why would someone murder a group of people digging for artifacts?"

"You just referred to the victims as 'members,'" Dillon protested. "But these people were not together as members of anything. They were a team of archeologists. This wasn't a church. This was not a cult."

"As you saw in that newspaper article, Dr. Reinhardt has a questionable past. Our investigation shows he once started a cult called the Holy Reincarnation of the Albigenses."

"Eh?"

"The Holy Reincarnation of the Albigenses," Pittman repeated. "Reinhardt began the sect while in the employ of Northwestern University. He apparently is a very charismatic man, as most cult leaders are, and reportedly got many of his students involved in activities such as levitation, psychokinesis, and séances—activities that fall outside the framework of archeology. They more closely parallel behavior found in secret cults. Considering the event that took place at Re's Cavern, we must assume Reinhardt's motives were related to more than archeology."

Another reporter stood up and asked if the members had been under the delusion that Re's Cavern might be a place where they would rendezvous with a supernatural entity or even an alien spacecraft.

Pittman did not deny the possibility. He simply said, "We don't know what they believed."

"Did they find any artifacts?" someone shouted.

"No artifacts were found that we know of. This leads us to question what they were really doing down there. Inside Re's Cavern, we found hand-drawn paintings of the sun, on paper as well as on the cavern wall."

"What does that mean?" another reporter queried.

Pittman didn't answer. He thanked the group for coming and bid them good night. A barrage of questions continued as he gathered his notes. He ignored all but one. It came from the back of the audience, and by its very nature, it had to be answered.

Bruce was standing. "Why were wooden crates used to remove the bodies?" he shouted.

Pittman craned his neck to get a glimpse of who asked the question.

"Bruce Brackin. *American Times* magazine," he announced and elaborated on his question:

"The picture on the screen showed each body being placed first into a body bag, and then into a box crate that was much larger than the body. I was thinking that probably not a lot of those big crates could fit into that small helicopter. Which meant the helicopter would have to make several trips to fly all the bodies out of the canyon. Or several helicopters would be needed to take all the bodies away. And since flying in and out of the canyon is dangerous, as you pointed out, I was wondering why all the body bags weren't piled into one helicopter minus the wood crates? That way it could be done in one or two trips."

Pittman cleared his throat. "Those crates were made specifically for that helicopter. They fit four across and can be fastened down. The body bags by themselves would have slid around inside, perhaps causing physical damage to the corpses, possibly altering the structural state of the bodies, thus tainting the autopsy results."

Dillon stood up. "So the coroner did not determine the cause of death until the bodies had left the canyon?"

"The final verification of cause of death was via autopsies done in a lab. This couldn't be accomplished at the campsite."

With that, Pittman said good night for a second time and stepped down.

A pale and thin woman quickly took the stage.

"My name is Debra Hammond," she announced into the microphone. "I will answer your questions about cults."

"Come on." Dillon Waterford nudged Bruce with his arm. "Let's get out of here before I get sick"

31

FIVE

Bruce suspected Dillon's distain for the press conference ran deeper than the news about the deaths of the archeologists. And as they walked away from the gathering under the light of the pale blue moon, it didn't take long to find out he was right.

"That was a well delivered script," said Dillon.

"How so?"

"Pittman spun the story."

"What makes you think that?"

"When you've been in this business as long as I have, you develop a sixth sense for press manipulation."

"The FBI is lying?" Bruce asked.

"Half truths."

"What half wasn't true?"

"That's exactly what I aim to find out."

Moving down South Entrance Road, Dillon's armless jacket sleeve swayed freely as he took two steps to every one of Bruce's.

"But Pittman did present a lot of facts," Bruce said.

The old man looked up at him. "Facts aren't the truth, though they do impress people. Pittman knows we're all pressured to get a story out quickly. None of us will have time to investigate any of his claims." Dillon shook his head. "Hell. Nowadays, practically everything is reduced to quick-hit sound bites and shock-infused video clips."

Bruce couldn't argue with that. He hated sensationalism, and for that reason he could never be a serious journalist. Even as a copywriter, he'd gone to great pains to be truthful about the products he'd represented. He'd always felt that advertising was the most honest communication that existed in the media. At least the audience *knows* it's biased. Journalism, on the other hand, gives the illusion of impartial reporting, which it isn't. But that was the media; he expected more from the FBI. He couldn't imagine they had a hidden agenda in this case.

32

Why would they?

Dillon kicked a stone on the payment. "Even if the scenario Pittman presented is later discovered to be untrue, it'll forever be imprinted on the minds of the public. First impressions stick. You can bet that he structured his story with that in mind. Where you staying?"

"Holiday Inn," Bruce said as they reached his rent-a-car. He stopped and turned to the old man." I still don't understand *why* you think Pittman manipulated the press."

"Why? Because he was too eager to position the deaths with cult suicides."

"But there was a lot of evide—."

"Like Jonestown, right?"

Before Bruce could answer, Dillon began laughing while scratching his curly locks. Bruce liked the guy. Wasn't sure why. Wasn't sure why he was laughing either. "I said something funny?"

"The people at Jonestown didn't commit mass suicide. They were murdered."

Uh oh.

"And the CIA had a hand in it."

Oh brother.

Dillon stared up at Bruce. "When Jonestown happened, the American media had run the cult suicide story, which was a fabrication forwarded by CAC, the Cult Awareness Committee. Same group Hammond is with."

"Hammond?"

"The girl who started talking about cults at the press conference when we left."

"Right."

"The U.S. media ran with CAC's story, because they didn't know anything about cults back then and assumed CAC were the experts. Jonestown was a lie."

Bruce didn't like where this conversation was headed. His brother supplied him with enough conspiracy theories to last a lifetime. Besides, the bottle of Jack was calling his name from the car. "Well, okay. It was nice meeti—"

"Dr. Leslie Mootoo," Dillon interrupted, "was the chief medical examiner of Guyana. He inspected the bodies at

Jonestown. Most of the members had received cyanide injections in places they couldn't have reached themselves. Many had been shot with guns. In his official report, Mootoo concluded the majority of the deaths were murders, not suicides. Later, in a court of law, a Guyana jury made the same conclusion: members of the Peoples Temple were murdered. You'd never know that by listening to the U.S. media back then, eh?"

Bruce didn't need to hear this. "Look Dillon, I was just a kid when Jonestown happened. I read about it years later."

"You asked why I thought the FBI was lying."

That was true.

Dillon continued, "All one has to do is say the words 'cult' and 'suicides' to a group of reporters, and they're electrified. Jonestown set the precedent. Tomorrow morning, the world will read how Reinhardt brainwashed kids into doing bizarre 'cult activities' that resulted in suicides. Truth is, we don't know what happened yet."

Bruce thought about giving Dillon Peter's number. They'd both be in conspiracy heaven. But it was getting late. Bruce was still on EST and he had a story to write before packing it in.

"Good meeting you, Dillon."

The old man looked a tad rejected.

"I've had a really strange and long day," Bruce explained. "I gotta get some sleep."

Dillon nodded. "Forty years in journalism and I'm still searching for the truth. You'd think I'd learn by now, eh?"

Bruce said nothing while Dillon reached into his back pocket and slipped a card out of his wallet. Bruce took it.

"My cell number is on the back," Dillon said, returning his wallet. "If you need anything, let me know. I'll be poking around here for a few days."

"Searching for the truth?" asked Bruce.

Even in the dark, Bruce could see the old man's eyes sparkle under frost-white brows. "There's *always* a story behind the story," Dillon said, and extended his arm.

Bruce shook his tiny hand and said goodnight. He got in the Maxima, followed South Entrance Road to Route 64, and drove about two miles to the Holiday Inn where he had a reservation.

He checked into the hotel, found his room, gathered some ice, and unpacked his laptop. After dropping a couple of cubes in a glass, he added some Jack Dean, and did exactly what Dillon said he and the other reporters would do; he wrote an article based on the FBI presentation. At four in the morning, he burned the document to a CD with the photographs he had taken and e-mailed all of it to the *American Times* from the business center in the hotel lobby.

Back in his room, Bruce studied the photographs on his laptop more closely. Earlier, something had caught his eye. The men carrying the bodies to the helicopter wore white face-masks. Having once written copy for Proctor & Gamble, he knew something about face-masks. He was sensitive to chemical fragrances, and while touring their plant had to keep the chemical odors to a minimum by wearing the correct mask. A single-weave cotton keeps out dust particles. A triple cross-weave nylon inhibits odors. He zoomed into the photo. The thin rubber bands from the mask to the ears showed these were not odor masks, which required a tighter fit and used wide rubber bands wrapped around the head, not ears.

Why would the FBI be wearing dust masks?

He was just too exhausted to tackle the problem now. He stripped off his clothes, and collapsed on the bed. Within moments, events of the last day flashed through his fading consciousness like bats in the night: Murdock's quivering hand, dead bodies sprawled inside a tent, a gun at his head . . . Rachel's beautiful eyes.

"All is not what it seems, my love," she whispered.

SIX

Bruce woke up not knowing where he was and what the hell was blinding him. He sat up in the bed, shielded his eyes from the onslaught, and looked around the room. Besides being disoriented, he had a nagging feeling he had done something wrong . . . no, that he had missed something.

Then he remembered where he was.

A hotel room near the Grand Canyon. He'd left the curtain open a crack the night before, allowing the sun to laser through it. He looked at the clock on the nightstand: 2:30 PM. One thing about depression, you get plenty of sleep.

He got up and yanked the curtain shut.

That nagging feeling . . .

"Damn."

He'd missed his two o'clock appointment with Seth Collier. He dug in his jeans pocket and found Seth's phone number, and then punched it in on his cell. Nina, the receptionist, picked up. She told him Seth wasn't there, gave him Seth's cell number, and slammed the phone in his ear. Bruce called Seth's cell.

"Hello."

"Seth, this is Bruce—"

"You're off the story," Seth announced.

"What do you mean?"

"We've got a real story so we need a real reporter. I've arranged for Madeline Nelan in Washington to arrive at the Grand Canyon tonight. From now on, your job is to just take pictures." Seth was short of breath.

"But I was hired to write the story."

"Ehhhhhhh!" Seth made a buzzer sound.

Bruce yanked the receiver away from his ear. He heard Seth say from a distance, "You were hired because my father promised David Chapman he'd talk you into writing copy for the agency. The Grand Canyon story was just an excuse to get you into the office. *Comprendo?*"

"Fine."

"I'm glad you understand. I read your e-mail. This is major. We need someone who knows what they're doing."

On the night stand, Bruce noticed the business card Dillon had handed him last night. He could hear grunting and shouting in the background.

"Are you in a gym?"

"Dojo," Seth said.

"Dojo?"

"I teach karate."

"I see."

The comment Dillon had made after the press conference about the FBI spinning the story had started to sink in more during the night. Bruce didn't buy it completely but didn't disregard it, either.

"You saw in my report that the FBI arranged for a woman from the Cult Awareness Committee to speak at the press conference."

"Debra Hammond."

"I think they're pushing the cult angle too hard."

Seth grunted. "This is exactly why Madeline is going to write the piece instead of you. It's the cult angle that gives it teeth."

"Teeth? How about truth?"

"Our job is to report news of public interest. It's the FBI's job to find the truth. They think it's cult-related—we go with that. I need a shot of the campgrounds, the tents inside and out, the cave inside and out, the river, the cups they drank the poison from, the rafts they came in on, Grand Canyon headquarters, and scenic lookout points. Use film, not digital. FedEx each roll to me as it's shot. Deadline is Friday. Call me in two days. And—" He caught his breath. "And don't tell anyone you're from *American Times* magazine."

Seth hung up.

Bruce stabbed END on his cell. Reminded himself he'd had no expectations when he came to the Grand Canyon. As much as he hated to admit it, Seth was right. He wasn't an investigative reporter, and didn't care much about becoming one.

Although the press conference had taken his mind off his miserable life for a while, he was okay with not researching the alleged cult-related murder story. Taking pictures only would be just fine. Let Madeline what's-her-face from Washington cover the rest. In truth, another murder story was the last thing he needed; he'd had enough of one with Rachel.

He showered, got dressed, and headed downstairs to grab something to eat.

The waitress directed him to a window booth, where he ordered a bacon, lettuce, and tomato sandwich. While waiting, he studied a Grand Canyon tourist guide.

Taking pictures of the canyon from the rim would be easy; dozens of lookout stations were listed. But, to get shots of Re's Cavern he'd have to travel *into* the canyon. He had three choices: go down by mule, by river-raft, or on foot. Although riding the back of an ass didn't exactly excite him, it was more appealing than going by foot.

And forget about river-rafting. Aqua phobia was the technical term—the fear of water. Per the clinical definition, he didn't entirely have aqua phobia; he feared only one type of water: rapids. When he was eleven-years-old, his father had taken him whitewater rafting on the Hudson River. Being the defiant kid he was, unbeknown to his father, he hadn't fastened his life preserver, and just had it draped over his shoulders. The raft had banged against a swell with such ferocity that Bruce bounced out of the raft into the drink, the impact ripping the life preserver right off him. The undertow instantly sucked him in. He could feel it in his stomach even now: the sensation of being pulled down, down, away from the raft, his father, his life. . . sucked into a churning hell devoid of oxygen. His young muscles strained to reach for the fast departing surface.

Suddenly, the same power that had dragged him under reversed and catapulted him back toward the surface. His father had grabbed him by the scruff of the collar and pulled him into the safety of his arms. Ever since, Bruce avoided rapids or even rivers, for that matter.

He made a few calls on his cell to those places listed in the guide and learned that all the mule rides were booked up months in advance. Looked like he'd be hiking down.

The waitress delivered his BLT.

"Have you ever hiked into the canyon?" he asked her.

"Dear lord, no. But my boyfriend has."

"How long does it take?"

"Depends which trail you use, but usually an entire day, I think. Supposed to rain today." She looked out the window.

Bruce followed her gaze. It wasn't raining yet, but it was overcast. He thanked the waitress and bit into his BLT. The tomatoes were soggy, and the bacon was lifeless and brittle. Memo to self: *Don't eat here again.*

Nevertheless, he forced down the sandwich, while circling a couple of the foot trails with a pen that looked like possibilities, specifically Bright Angel and Kaibab Trail. Getting to Re's Cavern once he got down there would be another problem. He decided to tackle that later. The first order of business was to take pictures from the rim.

Before leaving the restaurant, he fetched his camera from the bag, along with the Tetra underwater casing. If it did start raining he didn't want to chance getting his Nikon wet. After securing the waterproof casing, he slung the camera around his neck and left the hotel. Back in his car he drove to Grand Canyon Village, parked, and went to the Yavapai observation station.

It was the first time he'd ever viewed the canyon, and when he looked into it, the air got caught in his throat.

Golden shafts of light poured into a vast stone universe below him. Massive buttes, like thrones of gods, cropped up from the depths in an array of colors—gold, auburn, crimson—misty prehistoric earth tones that blurred into each other in the rising heat.

A few stray clouds floated overhead, and shadows slithered across the sea of stone like black-winged dragons.

In the past, others had told him about the magnificence of the Grand Canyon, but that was just talk. *This . . . this was beyond words.* The sight of it triggered some primordial emotion in him that he hadn't expected . . .

Then a voice whispered in his ear, "*I miss you.*"

He turned and saw Rachel next to him, olive skin glowing and black satin hair tossing in the wind. Her eyes, normally brown, were now the color of the ocean. Her lips parted, and Bruce wanted to feel their softness with his fingers. A gust of wind swept up from the canyon and fanned her hair out away from her shoulders like angel wings.

"Rachel?"

"*I miss you,*" she whispered again.

She reached out her hand to him.

He reached back, but as he touched her skin, it turned to vapor.

She was gone.

He wiped the wetness from his eyes with his hand, and then he yanked the pint of Jack from his pocket, and took a hit. *Gone.* He gasped sorrowfully and slipped the bottle back into his pocket. They had traveled so much together. She would have loved this place.

He retrieved his camera from its case, pointed it at the canyon, and adjusted the aperture.

Just keep going. Keep working.

He snapped a couple of wide establishing shots he would need later, but quickly looked for tighter, more interesting ones.

A particular butte caught his eye in the distance. Bruce thought it looked like an Indian face. He captured its stone cheeks and chipped nose and clicked the shutter. Then he zoomed in on its angry, rain-stormed eyes. It was a face sculpted by the Colorado River, the wind, and the rain. He felt a connection with the stone face, as if on some level he was shooting a self-portrait. *I am a rock, I am an island,* he heard Simon and Garfunkel sing in his head. *If I never loved, I never would have cried.*

After taking several more shots, he packed up his gear and went back to his car.

He followed the map to Hermit Road, which took him to Hopi Point, Powell Point, and Maricopa Point, all of which offered gorgeous views of the canyon. Over the next three hours, he took more than a hundred and fifty pictures, shooting anything and everything that caught his eye. He doubted if many of the shots would be useful to the magazine, but at least he was keeping busy.

Shortly after the sun went down, he headed west on Hermit Road, passing a homey-looking place called Bright Angel Lodge. He'd always found rustic interiors had a calming effect on him. If the inside looked anything like the outside, he'd be staying for dinner. He did a U-turn, parked in the lot, and went inside.

The interior of Bright Angel Lodge was a picture of charming simplicity—like stepping back in time a hundred years. Sections of the wooden floor even creaked underfoot as he strolled toward a fireplace near the center of the lobby. It was shaped like an igloo made of stone blocks, with the square hearth as its door. Square and simple, the way things should be. He decided that, after dinner, he'd grab his camera from the car and take a few pictures of the lodge.

Over a basket of fried chicken and a beer, he again studied a map of the interior of the Grand Canyon and tried to figure out how to get to Re's Cavern. Talk about going at it blind. There were no marked trails, no signposts or landmarks that said, "This way to the murder site." How in God's name was he going to get to this place to take pictures?

Tearing into the last remaining leg, he had an idea. In the movies, there were always guides to take people to desolate regions of jungles "where no white man has ever gone before." Certainly there must be a guide he could hire who could lead him to Re's Cavern.

By the time he left the lodge, night had fallen. In the parking lot, he noticed several policemen poking around. The beams of their flashlights played off the pavement and parked cars. Bruce thought it would make a good picture. He hurried to the Maxima, jumped in the front seat, and pulled the Nikon out of his bag. After checking the strength of the battery and seeing that it was fully charged, he paused a moment, realizing that maybe things were going as he had hoped they would out here in Natureville. Since waking up that morning, and all day, he hadn't thought of killing himself even once.

Of course, the day wasn't over yet.

He reached for the car door, and a cold object pressed against the back of his head.

"Don't move!"

Bruce's heart lurched in his chest.

"I won't hurt you." The voice quivered. "*If* you do exactly what I say."

In the shadows in the rearview mirror, he saw a woman who wore a cap with a visor holding a gun to his head. She leaned forward, slipping one side of her face out of the shadows. A remarkable green eye stared at him.

"I want to help you, Bruce. But we have to move fast."

Rachel used to admonish him about not locking the car door. He wished now that he'd listened. He'd seen this woman before—just last night in fact, on that big silver screen at the press conference.

Did she say she wanted to help me?

SEVEN

Her eye was like a cold, polished emerald, glaring at him.

From outside the car, a light got Bruce's attention. Nearby, a cop shone his flashlight into the parked cars.

Her gaze flitted out the car window, momentarily capturing the cop, then back to Bruce. Beads of sweat rimmed her lips as she tightened her finger on the trigger.

"Drive now," she ordered.

Bruce recognized the gun as a Walther. Not unlike the one he held to his skull yesterday morning. He had originally bought it for Rachel. With her exceptional looks, walking alone at night in New York City was not advisable. She'd taken shooting lessons, and he'd requested she always carry the gun in her purse. If only she had listened. If only she'd had the Walther that night. If only he'd been with her . . . they had fought earlier . . .

"Back the car up now, or I'll shoot you!"

She really looked scared. *What was her name? Whatever.* The situation was almost poetic. Yesterday he couldn't kill himself, and now this woman was offering to do it for him.

"What are you smiling at? This isn't a joke!" she growled.

Again, the light caught Bruce's eye. The cop was moving closer.

Suddenly her name came to him. *Megan Eastwood.*

"What do you want from me?" he asked.

"I told you—I want to help you."

"Call me stupid, but I think *you're* the one who needs help here."

The eye grew more intense. "You deserve to know the story. You were on the right track at the press conference. You were the *only* reporter on the right track. Why did the FBI use oversized wooden crates to carry away the bodies, one body per oversized crate?"

"The agent said the helicopter held four crates and—"

"Oh please. You know better than that. That's why you asked the question. They used the oversized crates because they had to smuggle *other things* out of the canyon. They put those other things in the crates alongside the bodies. They took out of the canyon what we excavated. No one committed suicide—they were all murdered!"

"The FBI stole what you excavated?" he said. "Why? What did you find down there?"

She bit her lip. "You'll learn every last detail. But we have to go now!"

Seth Collier had pulled Bruce off the story earlier that day because he wasn't experienced. Yet, out of the hundreds of "real" reporters who were at the press conference, this woman— one of the people the entire press conference revolved around— had sought him out. More poetry.

But did it really matter? Did he really give a rip? Hardly. He'd come to the Grand Canyon for a little R&R. He'd be damned if he was going to end up in jail for helping someone on the FBI's Most Wanted list. He'd rather be dead than locked up. At least her shooting him would be a noble way to die.

"Sorry," he told her. "I'm not going anywhere."

The eye narrowed. The gun began shaking in her grasp.

"Well, aren't you going to shoot me? You said you'd shoot me."

She clenched her teeth.

On cue, the memories that had haunted Bruce since Rachel's death roared to life. Uninvited and unexpected they arrived, as always, like the grim reaper in the night, coming to claim his soul: *The call requesting he come to Precinct 49, the cold, fluorescent-lit room with the wall of steel drawers, one stuffed with the woman he'd loved more than life itself, the razor-tipped dagger that plunged into his heart when his burning eyes took in Rachel's ghostly skin, and the lips he'd kissed so many times. The lips now sealed forever.*

Eastwood said something but Bruce didn't hear a word. He grabbed the gun barrel and pressed it against his own forehead. Closed his eyes.

"Pull the fucking trigger!"

Nothing happened.

"C-o-m-e o-n! S-h-o-o-t!"

He opened an eye, saw the shock and confused look on Eastwood's face, and almost felt sorry for her. She'd gone from perpetrator to victim. He removed the barrow from his brow.

"You're crazy," she gasped.

Just to prove it, Bruce found the pint of Jack Dean stowed in the glove compartment, hefted it to his lips, and took a slug.

"I picked a loon," she mumbled.

Outside, the cop's movement got Bruce's attention, looked like he was about thirty feet away.

Bruce couldn't tell whether or not the dark tinted windows would prevent him from seeing inside the car with his flashlight. He took another slug to calm his nerves. Rolled the situation over . . .

Learning from Eastwood what had really happened at Re's Cavern certainly had some appeal. Once he got her story, the "true story," he could at least rub it in Seth Collier's face.

"Get down," he ordered.

"What are you going to do?"

"Trust me."

"Oh Sure. Why not?" she said, her smirk highlighting the sarcasm in her voice.

Bruce started the Nissan and Eastwood slid down in the backseat. He pulled out of the parking space and waved to the cop as he drove by.

The cop looked at him but didn't wave back.

After he pulled onto Route 64, Eastwood sat up.

Bruce kept one eye on the road and the other on the mirror. He could see her better now, as her face lit up intermittently under the passing road lights. Her eyelids blinked heavily. There were smudges of black dirt on her forehead and chin, and her lips were dry. He wondered exactly what she'd been through. The FBI said Reinhardt had orchestrated the mass suicide. They'd cited his past activities as evidence he was capable of doing such a thing.

But, what of Eastwood? They hadn't said anything about her past, and very little about her relationship with Reinhardt. The FBI apparently assumed she was involved in the crime because she was his assistant and her body wasn't found among the dead. Obviously, there was more to the story, simply by the fact that she'd tracked Bruce down as someone she *thought* was a reporter.

"Listen," he said. "I have a tape recorder in my hotel room. I'll hear your story, but no promises. Truthfully, *American Times* hired me as a photographer, not a reporter." It wasn't the exact truth but close enough.

"A photographer?"

"Yep."

She started massaging her temples with her hand. "But you could write a story and they'd read it, right?"

"Probably. Whether they'll print it or not, I don't know."

"Fine." She heaved a sigh. "We'll go to your hotel room." She leaned back in the seat, seemingly without the strength to say more.

A minute later Bruce heard a police siren. He glanced in the rearview mirror to see flashing lights gaining on them.

Eastwood slid down to the floor of the backseat once again.

She began mumbling to herself and Bruce figured she was probably praying. Not a bad idea.

The siren blared, and Bruce pulled to the shoulder.

EIGHT

Bruce watched the patrol car race past them from the shoulder of the road, not sure whether he should be relieved or disappointed.

Eastwood, no doubt, could rest easier. Her hand covered her heart to slow her breathing as she carefully eased her body up from the backseat.

He half-smiled and glanced at her in the mirror then swung the car back onto the highway. Minutes later he pulled into the parking lot at the hotel.

Eastwood became all business again. Gripping the Walther in her fist she explained in explicit detail the manner in which he would escort her through the lobby. "Put your right hand around my shoulder and your free hand in your left pocket. Look straight ahead. Don't talk to anyone."

He pursed his lips to avoid laughing. She sounded like a bad actor in a B-rated movie. She still didn't get it. The gun was no threat to him. Initially, he wanted to boot her out of the car, but considering her situation a part of him felt sympathy for her. If she'd told the truth, that all her archeology friends had been murdered, it was something he could somewhat relate to. Sympathy aside, his curiosity was piquing; *what did the FBI take from the excavation site?*

"Right O," he said, deciding to play the game.

After she tucked her loose strands of hair up under her hat, they exited the car and entered the hotel. As they crossed the lobby, her body pressed against his side, and the gun jammed into his rib cage, he could no longer hide the idiotic smile plastered on his face. Luckily, the receptionist who had checked him in the night before waved hello, so he nodded and smiled back at her.

They rode up in the elevator in silence. At his unit, he slipped his cardkey into the door, and ushered her into the room. She yanked off her hat, threw it in the corner, and ruffled her sweaty hair into a red mop. Braless, her breasts jiggled under her top with the motion.

"I need a minute to get my bearings," she said looking around the room.

"Take two," Bruce said and plopped down on the bed. He thought about offering her one on the rocks but figured she wasn't the drinking type. With all the traveling he'd done in his life, if there was one thing he was good at it was reading people.

At a glance Eastwood seemed to be a study in contrasts. With her large round eyes and full lips he could easily picture her, with some makeup added, on the cover of a glamour magazine. But at the same time he suspected that makeup was not something often found in this woman's purse—if she indeed ever carried one.

She took a long breath and walked toward the window. Her blocky orange boots had dried mud caked around the edges. She led with her hips, the boots scuffing over the blue carpet as if too heavy for her legs to carry.

She continued to keep an eye on him while she pulled open the drapes and looked out the window.

The edges of her body were finely honed, yet there was a youthful softness to her—a vulnerability in her features, even in the small of her back, which lay bare between the bottom of her tank top and the upper edge of her low riding jeans.

He watched her shoulders rise and fall as she took several deep breaths. She appeared to be in her late twenties, but definitely had the mind of someone far older, or at least the *experience* of someone older. His suspicions that her emotions were not so well developed, and she most likely would demonstrate an element of immaturity, turned out to be right.

With her fists squeezed into tight balls, one still holding the gun, she opened her mouth to speak. Nothing came out. Instead, a tear rolled down her cheek, and she quickly looked away.

Bruce grabbed the box of Kleenex off the nightstand and held it out to her.

"I didn't want this to happen," she stammered, and blew her nose into a tissue.

He sincerely hoped the crying wouldn't last. Aside from having to fight the urge to join her, he was fairly dysfunctional at consoling a sobbing woman. Even during such times with Rachel he'd often say the wrong thing. A friend finally advised him not to say anything.

"When a woman cries," he had said, "just hold her and tell her you love her."

That clearly wasn't an option in this case, so Bruce simply said, "I understand."

"Do you? Do you understand what it's like to find people you love murdered?" She talked with her hands, waving the gun in front of his face.

"Ah, actually, yes."

"Do you know what it's like to spend two days hiking out of the Grand Canyon without food or water, and then when you approach the park headquarters to tell them what happened, you see *your* picture up on a giant screen and learn you're the one wanted for the murders?"

He wished she'd stop waving that gun around.

"You arrived at the press conference while it was in progress?"

She said yes but shook her head the same time, as if not believing it herself.

Bruce was starting to feel her pain, which bothered him. He had enough of his own to occupy him.

"Okay look, ah, Megan, I think we've had enough drama for one night. I'm willing to listen to your story. Just give me the gun. I'll put it in the closet and—"

She stepped back and re-gripped the weapon.

"No. I keep the gun."

Now she was starting to piss him off. How many times would he have to prove that the gun had no leverage with him? As a matter of principle, there was no way he'd listen to her story at gunpoint. Not going to happen. Either she gave up the weapon, or no deal. Those were the terms, and he told her so.

She doggedly shook her head. "I have to trust you first."

He felt an adrenaline rush. Suddenly all the pain and frustration that had been building over the last several weeks exploded in his muscles. He'd had enough.

He leaped off the bed and seized her wrist. Piece of cake, he thought. Three years of jujitsu training made his next move automatic. He forced her arm behind her. Slapped on an arm-lock, what's known in the martial arts world as a *kumora*. Then he applied just enough pressure so she would give up the gun.

Instead she just stubbornly gawked at him.

"Drop the gun," he growled.

She squirmed in his grasp. "Let . . . me . . . go."

"Drop . . . the . . . gun!"

He applied more pressure, and she released the weapon. It hit the floor with a loud thud, causing him to jump backward and relax his grip slightly. Eastwood showed her gratitude by driving her knee into his crotch.

His testicles became fireballs that shot into his stomach. Survival instinct kicked in. He released her arm to protect his genitals. She grabbed the radio clock from the nightstand, and before he could react, whacked him in the nose with it.

"Ahhhh!" It felt like a sledgehammer.

She dropped the clock on him again.

His hands rose from his pulsating crotch to protect his face. Christ, that left him vulnerable down there!

She fell to a knee. Grabbed the gun from the floor. Jumped to her feet and spun to train it on him.

Bruce quickly snatched her arm before she could aim it directly, put her in *kumora* again. This time without mercy, he bent the limb in a direction it wasn't supposed to go. She dropped the weapon and sank to her knees in pain.

He applied more pressure . . . slowly.

Having been on the receiving end many times in training, he knew the arm-lock hurt like hell, but Megan Eastwood didn't scream or cry under the pressure. She just stared up at him defiantly, jaw locked, lips pursed. This was one tough woman.

His crotch pulsated with such intensity that he couldn't keep his body upright for long. He released her arm and shoved her backwards with both hands, sending her tumbling onto her back on the bed. Then he snatched the gun from the floor and pointed it at her.

"Turn over so you're facedown," he ordered.

Through his watering eyes, he watched her stand up, remove the pillowcase from the pillow, and move to the refrigerator. She pulled out an ice tray, wrapped some cubes in the fabric, and placed them on her elbow.

Bruce doubled over from the pain. *God, it hurt!* He swayed like a drunken sailor and again barked the order for her to lie on the bed . . .

"Or *I* will shoot!"

"There's no bullets in it, you fool," she huffed.

Bruce pulled the clip out of the gun's handle. It was as empty as his life had been lately. He stood there in front of her, one hand on his nose, which was swelling before his burning eyes, the other clamped between his legs. He collapsed on the bed.

Megan grabbed the other pillowcase, went to the refrigerator, made another ice pack, and dangled it over him.

"This will help bring the swelling down."

On which body part?

"I didn't kill anyone," she said. "There was no cult. The entire thing was a setup." She handed him the lumpy pillowcase. "Please don't call the police."

He gazed up at the blur that was Megan Eastwood.

I wouldn't sic this woman on my worst enemy.

Oh, oh. Bruce's stomach started to erupt. He jumped to his feet and fled to the bathroom, where he promptly and violently vomited. With his head hanging over the toilet, he heard a knock on the door.

"We must hurry," she said. "The artifacts we excavated at Re's Cavern will change life as we know it on this planet."

Oh, brother. And all I wanted was a little R&R,

He retched again.

NINE

After making that prophetic statement to Bruce, Megan turned from the bathroom door, walked over to the window, and gazed out at the ice-blue moon in the night sky. A gorgeous summer night, lost to the horror she was living. In the last forty-eight hours, she'd gone from thinking she was on top of the world to literally encountering death at the bottom of it. Not only had she lost her friends, but also part of her memory.

That dreadful morning, a blinding headache and loss of coordination had overcome her when she'd entered the excavation tent. At first, she thought it was brought on by the emotional shock of seeing the dead bodies. But in the hours that followed, it became evident that some other *force* had seized her mind and body.

After she left the tent, her dexterity eventually returned. She spent the next two days hiking out of the canyon. But something else was wrong: she had partial amnesia.

Initially, she couldn't even remember why they'd been in the Grand Canyon at all. But as the hours passed, segments of her memory had started to return: a lost hour here, an entire afternoon there, yet specific portions of her immediate past, the days just before finding the bodies were still missing. Including exactly what they excavated at Re's Cavern. But this didn't stop an inner voice from telling her whatever they found it would have great impact on the world. She just knew this to be the truth.

She also knew that thirteen colleagues had been murdered in cold blood—people she'd personally recruited for the excavation. Many were old college friends with their entire lives ahead of them. And then there was Dr. Reinhardt, her friend and mentor, who had mysteriously disappeared. *Dead? Kidnapped?* Megan could hardly stand to think about it anymore.

Her one hope, she'd decided, was to enlist the help of a reporter. If the truth were published, maybe someone, somewhere, would come forward with a clue as to who the murderers were and the whereabouts of Dr. Reinhardt. She also hoped that telling someone what had happened would help jog her memory.

Now she heard the man she had enlisted groaning in the bathroom. And he'd said he wasn't even a reporter, "just a photographer!"

She felt her eyes sting with tears once more but quickly wiped them away. Upset that she'd cried in front of him earlier, she wasn't going to allow it to happen again. *Why did I pick this guy, anyway?*

She'd been at the press conference, hiding behind a TV production van, watching the proceedings on a monitor. Bruce Brackin had begun speaking, and she immediately sensed he was different from the others. Her intuition was validated when he asked the FBI agent the only intelligent question of the evening. At a distance, Brackin struck her as being intuitive and someone not afraid to stand up for what was right. This was why she'd picked him out of the sea of reporters, and tonight slipped into his car when he was in the restaurant, only to learn he wasn't really a reporter but could swig straight from the bottle without the slightest gag. *Amazing!*

She heaved a long sigh. The stress had apparently skewed her perceptions. The man was probably a drunk.

He stumbled out of the bathroom.

"I think you broke my nose!"

Megan bit her tongue to keep from laughing. She recalled that Bruce hadn't been a bad looking guy before their skirmish. Now his nose was swelled up like a potato.

"Let me see," she said. She pinched his nose with her fingers and bent it to the right.

"Ouch! What the hell are you doing?"

"It's not broken."

"God, damn. That hurt!"

"If it was broken, I wouldn't be able to bend it. You said you had a tape recorder?"

53

He crossed the room to the closet, mumbling something under his breath, and then yanked a portable cassette recorder out of a duffle bag. Glaring menacingly at her, he crawled up on the bed, where he leaned against the headboard.

Megan felt so grungy she could hardly stand it. She thought about taking a shower, but decided she couldn't chance his running off. The man had a tape recorder, and he was willing to listen. Now was the time to get it done.

She wrapped two new ice packs in the pillow cases, one for his nose, the other for her elbow. She handed Bruce his, grabbed a chair, and scooted it next to the bed.

Placing the ice on his nose, he reached out to hit the RECORD button but stopped short.

"Like I've been telling you, I'm not a reporter. We'll record this conversation, but I'm not promising you anything." His voice was muffled by the pillow case.

"Fine."

He stabbed the red button, and said, "So what did you excavate that could 'change life as we know it on this planet,' as you put it?"

Megan contemplated this. She couldn't exactly tell him that she knew they excavated ancient artifacts, yet had no memory of what they were. Not yet anyway. He first needed to have some understanding of their archeological mission.

"We'd better lay some groundwork before we get to that."

His blue eyes peeked over the ice pack. "Alright, we'll start with the deaths. If your crew didn't commit suicide at Re's Cavern, how was it they drank poisoned apple juice?"

"Someone forced them to drink it."

"Did you see this 'someone'?"

"No."

"Why are you still alive, when they're dead?"

"Because I wasn't there when they drank the poison. I'd been off taking pictures when it happened. When I returned to the campground, I found everyone—" She stopped short.

"How long were you gone?"

"About four hours. Earlier that morning, I hiked to a place called Edwin Falls."

He lowered the ice pack as a curious eyebrow rose.

54

"And what about Reinhardt? Was he there when you returned?"

"No."

"So, you found thirteen dead bodies and your Coincidence leader was gone. I know what the FBI thinks about Reinhardt. From your perspective what kind of man was he?"

"Was?" she said. "No 'was.' We will discuss him in the present tense, thank you."

"Okay with me. What's your relationship with him? Is it sexual?"

Oh, brother. "You think just because I'm a woman—"

"I'm just trying to establish your relationship."

The thought of Reinhardt as a sexual partner was like . . . incest.

"Dr. Reinhardt is almost twice my age. Our relationship is strictly platonic."

"What about all that stuff the FBI said about him being into the occult?"

She sighed. "That was ridiculous."

"Pittman showed proof of Reinhardt getting fired from Northwestern University because of his occult camping trips. He had to have some connection."

"Dr. Reinhardt had a connection with the occult all right, but not in the way the FBI had made it seem." *Megan remembered seeing Dr. Reinhardt for the first time at Northwestern as a student in his Anthropology 101 class. She didn't know what she wanted to major in at the time, and had taken the class just to get some credits. Expecting to endure dry lectures given by some geek about cavemen she instead got Dr. Reinhardt—looking like a Greek God with Atlas-like shoulders and a presence that filled the lecture hall—talking about the mysteries of archeology.*

That first day, Dr. Reinhardt told how the most important Central American find ever made—a six-foot-high stone head that weighed ten tons—came about because a clairvoyant had led archeologists to it. He told the class how other clairvoyants could, with no prior knowledge, tell an artifact's age just by touching it. They could even describe the culture from which it came.

"Dr. Reinhardt wasn't interested in mysticism for its own sake," she told Bruce. "He was interested in results. He'd witnessed the effectiveness of extrasensory perception relating to archeology and simply sought to use it in a practical way. If a clairvoyant could locate an artifact, then Jensen would use him because it worked. All that stuff about cults they said at the press conference was a lie."

His eyes gave no hint that he believed her, yet he seemed to accept her answer.

"Alright," he sighed," so exactly *how* did the Grand Canyon excavation come about in the first place?"

Staring at Bruce, who at the moment bore a spooky resemblance to Bozo the clown, Megan suddenly had doubts. Could this man even handle the truth? Could she really trust him? If told, was he even capable of *comprehending* why they'd done the excavation in the first place? Megan looked at the red record light on the tape recorder. There was no chance of him leaving now, she thought. He wanted to hear the rest of the story..

"Please stop the recorder," she said.

"Why?"

"I need to use the bathroom."

Bruce pushed the button.

Megan stood up. What she really needed to do was closely examine what she was about to reveal to this Jack-Dean-touting stranger. Their original purpose for doing the excavation—that *truth*—in the wrong hands, could cause disaster. She needed a moment to decide just how much she'd tell him. "I'll be right back."

She went into the bathroom and locked the door.

TEN

The actual start of the excavation had come in the planning stage, six months before they arrived in the Grand Canyon. Megan had received a call from Dr. Reinhardt on a frigid Chicago day in January. She'd just completed her last guided tour at the Field Museum, a temporary job she'd taken to pay the bills. Truth was, she'd been bored out of her mind and yearned for some excitement in her life. Strolling the Great Main Hall toward the exit, she stopped to read the number on her chiming cell phone. The 520 area-code she recognized as being from Arizona. But when she answered, she was astonished to hear Jensen's voice. She had neither heard from nor seen him since he'd left Northwestern three years earlier.

He told her he had been in South America, and that his wife, Helen, had passed away.

Megan knew Helen had been sick for some years. "I'm so sorry—"

"Thank you, Megan." His deep voice rattled her cell phone. "I need you to organize an excavation for me,"

Megan's heart jumped. "Where?"

"The Grand Canyon. A remote cave called Re's Cavern."

"What would we be digging for?"

A stretch of silence. "I can't tell you everything over the phone, but I can tell you this much. I've become privy to an ancient global grid map that shows the location of many of the world's great mysteries in relationship to each other. Re's Cavern is on the map."

"What kind of mysteries?"

"England's Stonehenge, Egypt's El Kula Pyramid, Giza's Sphinx, to name just a few. Ancient mapmakers positioned hundreds of such enigmas at various locations around the planet, using the secret global grid as their guide."

They used a map to position these enigmas?

"Are you saying the Sphinx was placed intentionally in the desert of Giza, because its location relates to other intentionally placed enigmas around the world?"

"Basically, yes."

"And this Re's Cavern, in the Grand Canyon, is located on this global grid?"

Dr. Reinhardt's breathing grew heavy. "We believe there is something in Re's Cavern linked to the ancient world."

Jensen had then explained how the global grid was constructed. The world's geographic coordination system (GCS) consisted of the lines of latitude and longitude used as reference points on a world globe. Greenwich, England, was the current "prime meridian"—zero degrees longitude, the dividing line between east and west. Jensen said that before Greenwich, at different times in world history there had been nine other prime meridian designation points.

"As you know, the prime meridian is just an arbitrary designation," he said.

Megan recalled from her studies that a group of twenty-five nations had declared Greenwich the prime meridian near the turn of the twentieth century.

Jensen said, "If you were to use the Great Pyramid of Giza, Egypt, as the prime meridian instead of Greenwich, you would get an entirely different view of the world."

"You think the Great Pyramid was once used as the prime meridian, zero degrees longitude?"

"Unofficially, yes. The Ancients used a mathematical code system to determine where to place important sites and sacred temples around the world in relation to the Great Pyramid."

Megan's heart began to race.

"Re's Cavern is about a mile below the rim of the Grand Canyon." He continued. "It falls on a key nodal point on the latitude and longitude system, with the Great Pyramid as the prime meridian. We'll need a small crew for the excavation."

"But what will we be digging for?" Megan asked.

"I can't tell you that now—not on the phone. I'll mail you details of the plan and funds to make the necessary preparations. And Megan—"

"Yes?"

"Keep this just between us, okay?"

Megan told him she would. They said goodbye.

And as she washed her face in the bathroom sink, she knew she had to keep the promise she'd made to Dr. Reinhardt: *Keep this just between us.* It wouldn't be easy. She was well aware that her Achilles heel was her compulsion to always be truthful. The *big lie* she'd been told by her mother in her youth had forever forced her onto the straight and narrow. Long ago she decided that lying was cancerous to the soul, and honesty, her lifeline to sanity. Yet this was a time when withholding the truth was obviously the greatest good. For now, she *had* to keep Bruce on a need to know basis only. She'd start with the letter she'd received in the mail a few days after her conversation with Jensen.

Leaving the bathroom, she again joined Bruce by taking the chair next to the bed.

"Are you ready?"

Megan nodded and he started the recorder.

"Six months before we started the excavation," she said, "Dr. Reinhardt mailed me a printout of a microfilm copy of an old newspaper clipping and his notes about an excavation that had taken place in the Grand Canyon at the turn of the century. The microfilm showed that on April fifth, 1909, a front-page story appeared in the *Arizona Gazette* that told of an archeological excavation in the canyon funded by the Smithsonian Institute. The story said a citadel filled with ancient artifacts was found— hieroglyphs, armor, statues of deities, and even mummies—all Egyptian in origin."

"Egyptian things in the Grand Canyon? But how—"

"That's the point. Everyone knows that in our history, the Egyptian culture never spilled over into the Americas. Never. Yet the article declared this find actually had taken place."

"And it was sponsored by the Smithsonian Institute?"

Megan nodded. "That's right, but anyone who contacted the Smithsonian was told no records existed relating to their role in the Grand Canyon excavation. Incredibly, there was no record anywhere of the find other than the *Gazette* front-page story. Dr. Reinhardt's research even revealed that the archeologist who headed up the dig was later killed in a climbing accident, and the excavated artifacts mysteriously disappeared. Nevertheless, Jensen believed the newspaper story was correct, and that the records had been hidden from the public. He believed there were more Egyptian artifacts in the Grand Canyon to be unearthed."

"So you were digging for Egyptian artifacts at Re's Cavern?"

"Yes."

"At the press conference, they said you were digging for American Indian artifacts."

"We lied to park officials."

Bruce swung his legs over the edge of the bed and stood up. "Why?"

"Trade secrets." She shrugged. "Archeology is the act of digging for hidden treasures. If you think you're on to a significant find, you keep it a secret. There are archeologists who have more resources than we did. If they'd known we were planning a dig at Re's Cavern to search for Egyptian artifacts, they might have gotten there first."

Bruce scratched his head. "All right. But there's something I don't understand. If Re's Cavern was already excavated in the early twentieth century, wouldn't the early excavators have already gotten all of the Egyptian artifacts that were there?"

"Probably," Megan said. "But the artifacts weren't found in Re's Cavern."

"But you just said the reason you excavated Re's Cavern was because Egyptian artifacts were found there at the turn of the century."

"The original artifacts were found four miles south of Re's Cavern in a place called Isis Temple. You're right—all the Egyptian artifacts probably were excavated from Isis Temple. But to our knowledge, no other caves in the area had been excavated. Jensen believed Re's Cavern would be a prime excavation site." *Because it was on the global grid map,* she thought, but of course didn't say.

Megan then explained the other reason Jensen had chosen Re's Cavern. He had been working with a remote viewer named Montgomery Mendelssohn who had previously worked for the U.S. Army in the eighties using his psychic ability to help locate Soviet subs. According to Montgomery's "remote view" of the

Grand Canyon region, there were no artifacts in Isis Temple, but "something human and very ancient" was buried in Re's Cavern. Because of Mendelssohn's perception, Jensen wanted to excavate Re's Cavern.

The cassette recorder clicked, indicating the tape had reached its end. Bruce flipped the tape over, inserted it back in the machine, and eyed Megan before hitting RECORD.

"What?"

"I'm assuming you found Egyptian artifacts at Re's Cavern?" he asked.

"No."

"No?"

"We found something totally unexpected at Re's Cavern."

He stabbed the RECORD button. "Tell me what you found."

As Megan tried to remember, an ache started in the back of her head, not dissimilar to the one she'd experienced at Re's Cavern after discovering the dead bodies. She tried to ignore it and closed her eyes, hoping—praying—the memories would come back.

Then there was a loud rap on the door.

ELEVEN

"Mr. Brackin?" An ominous voice demanded from the hallway.

Megan hopped up from her chair and started running in circles, looking for a place to hide.

"Mr. Brackin, this is the police. Please open the door."

She grabbed Bruce's arm and drew her lips to his ear.

"Please, don't. There is so much more to know. I need your help. Make . . . them . . . go . . . away."

She released his arm, dashed to the bathroom, and closed the door.

RAP . . . RAP . . . RAP.

"This is the police. Open the door."

Bruce glanced at the clock on the nightstand—the weapon Megan had used to mangle his face. It read 9:55 p.m. They had entered the hotel over an hour ago. Had someone in the lobby recognized Megan? If so, why had the police taken so long to get here?

RAP . . . RAP . . . RAP.

He unbuttoned his shirt, ruffled his hair with his hand, and opened the door just enough to see into the hallway. Two cops stood there, an Afro-American and a Caucasian. Their bright silver badges read "Tusayon Police."

Bruce yawned. "I was sleeping."

They gawked at him, neither saying a word. The white cop bit his lip as if to keep from laughing.

The black cop chuckled.

It took a moment for Bruce to realize what was so funny: his swollen nose.

"I ran into something at the press conference," he offered, not knowing what else to say.

"You were at the press conference?"

Bruce yawned again, trying to act as nonchalant as possible. "Yeah. I was there. In fact, I saw the police poking around at Grand Canyon Village tonight."

"Who do you work for, sir?"

"I'm a photographer for *American Times* magazine."

"You got a business card?"

"I have a press pass."

"May we come in?" the black cop said.

Bruce swallowed hard. "The place is a mess. I'll get it and—"

"We need to come in, Mr. Brackin."

"Right."

They were about to find Megan. *I should tell them that she's here first*, he thought. He could claim that she'd held him at gunpoint. True. And forced him to listen to her story—almost true.

But he didn't say anything. He just opened the door, allowing the police to enter.

"Something to drink?" he asked, crossing the room to the small fridge.

Both cops declined, but Bruce grabbed a Perrier for himself. He dug his press pass out of his bag and handed it to the white cop. The cop didn't even glance at it. Instead, both just stood there looking suspiciously around the room.

"You know," Bruce said, "if I were Eastwood and Reinhardt, I'd probably be in Barbados by now. Why would they stay around here?"

"Standard procedure," the white cop said. "They've got us searching every hotel in the vicinity."

"They?"

"The FBI."

The black cop was staring at the closed bathroom door. "You alone?"

Bruce didn't answer.

The other cop opened the closet and looked inside.

"Who's in the bathroom?" the black cop asked.

"No one."

Bruce's mouth suddenly felt dry. He nervously brought the bottle of water to his lips and threw it back. The black cop reached for the bathroom doorknob. He was about to find Eastwood hidden in there.

That's it. Game over.

He'd heard Megan's little story and found it interesting, but he was damned if he was going to prison over it.

As he opened his mouth to tell them about Megan, the Perrier went down the wrong pipe. Suddenly his lungs froze. He couldn't find air!

The cop flung open the door . . .

The bathroom was empty.

Bruce flew into a coughing fit.

The cop slid open the glass shower door. Megan wasn't there either.

Where is she?

It wasn't the first time he had nearly choked to death on liquid. When it had happened in the past, he'd closed his mouth and tried to relax and breathe through his nose. With his nasal passages swelled shut, that wasn't an option today. He continued hacking up a storm, desperately trying to breathe.

The white cop slapped Bruce on the back. He sucked in a pinch of air, just enough to keep from passing out. The black cop exited the bathroom. Both cops headed for the main door.

"You okay?" the white cop asked.

Bruce nodded.

He was still coughing when they said goodbye and left.

It took a full minute before he was able to breathe normally.

With a creak, the cabinet door under the bathroom sink opened. Megan climbed out, unfolding her body like a butterfly leaving its cocoon.

How in God's name did she fit in that little space? He tried to ask her, but his damn vocal cords still didn't work.

"Yoga," she said, anticipating his question. She stared at him with her big emerald eyes.

Then she lunged at him, and Bruce shielded his face. But this time she didn't assault him. Instead, she wrapped her arms around him and squeezed.

"You didn't tell them. I knew I picked the right person. I knew it. We are going to make a great team!"

I didn't tell them because I couldn't tell them, he thought sadly.

"It's not safe here," she whispered. "We have to leave."

Bruce waited twenty minutes before departing. As his room was near the end of the hallway on the top floor, he hoped he was one of the last people the police had interviewed, and that they had then left the hotel. First he checked the lobby, then the stairwell and back exit. After seeing no hint of the cops, he slid out a side door, scurried to the front parking lot, found the Maxima, and drove it around to the back of the hotel. Then he returned to the room, got Megan, and together they snuck down the back stairs and out the door. They jumped into the waiting car and headed south on Route 64 toward Flagstaff.

TWELVE

Only after they were on the road for some time with no evidence of anyone following them did Megan start to relax. She slipped off her boots and perched her stocking feet on the dashboard.

Driving into the night, Bruce inspected his nose in the rearview mirror.

"You really clocked me," he moaned.

Megan laughed. It felt like the first time she had done so in years. *You clocked me!* She really had, too!

"You started it."

Bruce wasn't laughing. His hand dove under his seat and came up with the bottle of ...

Oh no, Megan thought. "Please put that away," she reprimanded him. "It's illegal to drink and drive."

"Now that's funny." He pointed at her. "*You're* wanted for murder, and *you're* worried about *me* drinking and driving. Afraid I might get a ticket?"

He took a swig of the bourbon. Megan could smell the toxic fumes from where she sat.

He lowered the bottle, gasped, and hit the RECORD button of the cassette player, which sat on the seat between them. "So, what exactly did you excavate at Re's Cavern?"

While waiting for her answer, he took another hit of the...

"If you are going to insist on drinking that stuff, you could at least offer me some."

Bruce looked surprised for a moment, but nevertheless handed her the bottle.

She opened the car window and chucked it out. Without looking, she could feel him glowering at her.

"I don't owe you a damn thing," he snarled. "You do know that?"

66

Yeah. Whatever. "Sorry," she said but didn't mean it. They had a job to do, and she needed him to be sober. Period.

He turned his attention again to the dark road in front of them. "The tape's running. What did you excavate from Re's Cavern?"

Megan's heart started to race. She closed her eyes and searched for the memories for several minutes. It was like looking into a dark cave. Nothing but blackness.

She finally opened her eyes and faced him.

"I can't."

"Can't what?"

"I can't remember."

"Huh?"

She turned away. "I can't remember what we excavated at Re's Cavern."

"More funny. You're on a roll."

Megan was beside herself. Losing her memory was a frightening experience. She felt a tear roll down her check. *Damn.*

"Oh, Jesus. You're serious?"

She wiped the wetness away with her arm. Told him about how, when finding the bodies, she had experienced some strange electronic sensation in the excavation tent. Said she'd had a slight case of amnesia ever since.

"Electronic sensation?"

"I don't know how else to describe it, almost like I'd been drugged."

He shook his head. "Then you got a 'slight case of amnesia? What does that mean? Back in the hotel room, you told me that what you excavated at Re's Cavern—let's see, what were your words? 'It could change life, as we know it on this planet.' What was that about?"

Megan dreaded this moment. It was true, she did say those exact words, but now she couldn't substantiate them, not exactly. She'd said them mostly to keep Bruce curious and desirous of writing her story.

"Well?"

"That's the crazy thing. I can't remember what we found," she blurted out, "but I *know* about it. I know it was something so important that—"

"Please, how is that possible?"

"I'm . . . I'm not sure. It's like knowing you were born, but not actually remembering being born."

He shot her a questioning look.

"Okay. Bad example." She tried to think of a better one . . . "It's like knowing you ate breakfast but not being able to remember exactly what you ate."

"We're writing a story here right? This is a bit of a hole, wouldn't you say?"

"I thought if I talked to someone, it would eventually come back to me . . . I know it will!"

The tense look on his face told how unhappy he was with her.

She watched as he glanced at his bulbous nose in the mirror again, guessing he probably thought he used to be more handsome than he actually was. His lips moved as he started to say something, but Megan didn't hear a sound. She looked into his blue eyes, but saw a different pair of eyes staring back at her. A woman's eyes . . .

The eyes. Those were the eyes of Karen Stoltz, her friend, a crewmember on the dig at Re's Cavern. A sudden wave of vertigo swept over her and with it vibrations increasing in strength began creeping up her legs. At first, the noise she heard was faint then it turned into a rumbling sound growing louder like a thunderous roar erupting from the Earth's core. The movement startled her as the ground under her feet began quaking. *What is it? What is happening to me?*

Then it started to come back. She was in Re's Cavern . . .

The shaking earth caused a floodlight above her to topple to the ground, and an explosion of silver sparks sprayed into the air, biting into her skin. She heard herself scream. Before the other tripods with floodlights toppled over, she saw a handful of crewmembers jump like rabbits from the excavation pit.

But Megan was stuck in a smaller sub-pit with Karen, who was staring with her mouth gaping and her eyes bulging at Megan. Then in a surreal instant, Karen's blonde hair rose up as the cavern floor gave way beneath them. Megan felt her stomach jump to her throat as she, along with Karen—and twenty tons of earth—began to free fall.

The memory stopped as fast as it had begun, like a movie projector that had suddenly lost power. Megan tried to get it going again, but it was no use.

She reoriented herself to the present.

Bruce was still looking at her.

"There was a cave-in," she told him.

"I don't understand."

"At Re's Cavern."

"So you do remember?"

One piece of the puzzle had fallen in place—the floor of Re's Cavern had given way while they were excavating. She remembered something else about it, too; it had happened on June the thirteenth, *Friday* the thirteenth. She could remember everything leading up to the morning of that day. But what had happened directly after the cave-in? It had been June the sixteenth, Monday morning, when she'd found the bodies. *What happened in the interim? Was the find the result of the cave-in? Of course it was. But what? What exactly did we find?*

She took a breath. "Re's Cavern has six chambers. We had set up shop to do the excavation in chamber C, the largest one. We spent the first week or so digging a vertical cross-section into the cavern floor—I remember all this clearly. I remember digging up a few Indian remains, pieces of shale pottery, slivers of straw weave, stuff like that. I remember that Mendelssohn, the remote viewer, was insistent that something of greater mass was buried deeper in the floor. We kept digging, but found nothing. Then a section of the cavern floor caved in."

She stopped talking.

"And?"

"And the next thing I remember, it's three days later, the morning I find the bodies at Re's Cavern."

He said nothing, and the silence gathered.

She became aware of the tires rolling on the hard asphalt as they drove down the dark highway. She heard the tape player between them squeaking as the tape looped around its wheels. She could still smell the bourbon in the closed interior. She pressed the sunroof button on the dash, and the roof slid open. Fresh air wafted over her.

"I want to revisit the part where you found the bodies in the tent," he said. "You said you were off taking pictures?"

"I had woken up early on the morning of June sixteenth. I hiked to Edwin Falls by myself to take pictures. When I returned to the campgrounds, that's when I found them."

"You think someone came into the campgrounds while you were gone and made everyone drink the poisoned juice?"

"I know that's what happened."

He frowned. "So you *just happened* to be gone when the murderers arrived?"

"That's right," said Megan injecting as much certainty into her tone as possible. She knew this fact seemed awfully suspect, but it was absolutely true. Why was *her* life spared? She'd asked herself this question a hundred times. The only sense she could make of it, the only positive twist she could put on it, was that if she discovered the murderers and brought them to justice, that act, in addition to justifying her existence, would somehow serve the world in ways that she could at this moment not see, for whoever the murderers were, they must have committed many more unthinkable acts against mankind. She *had* to find them

"We'd been in the canyon for almost two weeks, and I wanted to get shots before we left. That's all there is to it," she said.

"Before you said you were gone for four hours. That's a long time."

"Edwin Falls is about three miles from Re's Cavern. The round-trip hike alone took almost two hours."

"What did you do for the other two?"

She shrugged. "After taking shots of the waterfalls, I took a nap."

All this, Megan remembered clearly.

70

The falls were two translucent curtains of water that cascaded off a bronze cliff into a series of three pools, each one tumbling into the next.

She'd taken several pictures before climbing down to a flat rock at the water's edge where she removed her clothes and lay on the cool stone slab. It had felt good to lie there with nothing on, blanketed only by the canyon sun. Her bones seemed to melt into the rock, and she slept.

"I woke up sometime later and hiked back to the campground. When I approached the main tent, I immediately sensed something was wrong."

"What did you see, exactly?"

The words came slowly.

"I went inside the tent, and they were lying on the floor. I checked the bodies to see if anyone was breathing. When I realized they were all dead, I looked for Jensen's body."

"And?"

"It wasn't there, so I ran from tent to tent searching for him, looking for any clue as to how this could have happened."

She shifted in her seat, trying to get comfortable.

"It was unbelievable. Things in the sleeping tents looked normal. I mean, things like clothes, toothbrushes, magazines—they were lying around just like on any other day."

"I see. Then what did you do?"

"I went back to the main tent to radio for help, but I couldn't get the shortwave radio to work. That's when I saw the bottles of cyanide sitting on the benches, and I realized I could be in danger."

"You didn't think you were in danger before that?"

"Sure . . . I mean . . . I don't know. I wasn't thinking—I just reacted."

"Did you touch a bottle of cyanide?"

She thought for a moment. "I don't remember. I went for help."

"Where?"

"Re's Cavern is in one of the most isolated sections of the canyon," she said. "It's like being on another planet. Cell phones don't work. The only communication line was to a backcountry ranger via the shortwave radio, which, as I said, wasn't working.

So I followed a map to the ranger station, which I reached by nightfall. No one was there, so I slept outside. The next morning I waited for hours. Finally, I wrote a note and slipped it under the door."

Bruce cleared his throat. "A note under the ranger's door? What did it say?"

"What I just told you—that someone had come into our camp and murdered everyone."

"The FBI didn't say anything about finding a note."

They sure didn't, Megan thought. She had met the park ranger, Kurt Burney, before they started the excavation. He was a quiet, nature-loving sort of fellow. She wondered if he'd ever found the note in his cabin.

She told Bruce she didn't know why the note hadn't been mentioned at the press conference. Then she told him she had hiked to Phantom Creek Trail and begun her climb out of the canyon.

"Because of the rain, it took me two days. When I reached the South Rim, I went to the park headquarters to report what had happened. I arrived in time to see my face on a screen and hear how Jensen and I were wanted for murder!"

Bruce drummed his fingers on the steering wheel.

"The FBI said the crew drank apple juice laced with poison. You're saying someone came into the campground during the time you were gone and forced them to drink the juice?"

"We've already been over this. It's freaking insane, I know! But that's precisely what happened."

"Okay. Let's pretend for a moment your friends were murdered by someone else. Do you have any idea who might have killed them, or why?"

Megan wished she had the answer.

"For three days, I have thought about little else," she said, "and I don't have a clue who did it. I can only conclude they came for whatever we found."

"But how could they possibly have known about what you found? *You* don't even know what you found."

It was true. The whole thing made no sense, and it would take more energy than she had at the moment to figure it out. The exhaustion had settled in, and she simply couldn't talk about it anymore. Every muscle in her body ached, and she felt like she was getting sick—something she couldn't afford to let happen. She needed to sleep.

"Where are we going?" she asked wearily.

"I'm just driving."

She couldn't keep her eyes open.

"I have more questions," he said.

She told him he'd have to wait until she got some rest, as she couldn't talk about anything more at the moment.

Megan closed her eyes and wondered about Bruce—where he lived, how long he'd been a photographer, what his likes and dislikes were, if he was married? He wasn't wearing a ring. Anyone who drank straight out of the bottle like he did had to be harboring some pretty serious personal issues.

At least I'm not alone anymore. At least he can get my story to American Times magazine, she thought.

She started to drift . . .

Karen's mouth gaped, and her eyes bulged. Suddenly, her blonde hair rose up as the cavern floor gave way.

Drift . . .

Megan felt her stomach rise to her throat as she, along with Karen—and twenty tons of earth—began to free fall.

She was engulfed by blackness. Voices cried out above her.

"Megan!"

"Karen!"

She looked upwards to see beams of light slicing through the air like elongated light sabers. Dust particles swirled in the path of the beams. Grit coated her tongue and clogged her nose.

"Megan, are you all right?"

Just moments before, Megan had been standing near Karen in chamber C. Now she was lying on a bed of rubble staring into the dust cloud above.

Karen stirred in the rubble next to her and sat up from the ruins. Megan sat up, too, ignoring the sharp pain in her back. Light captured Karen's face from above. Strands of her hair were red, as a stream of blood trickled from the right side of her forehead.

Megan placed her hands on either side of Karen's face to get a better look. There was a surface gash in the skin next to her eyebrow. Megan patted the wound gently with her sleeve, absorbing some of the blood.

Bathed in the flashlights, Karen's deep blue eyes began to focus on Megan.

"Are you okay?" Megan asked. She wondered how far they had fallen. Ten feet? Twenty? They had landed in a hidden cavern below Re's Cavern.

"I think so," Karen said weakly.

"Megan?" Jensen's deep voice reverberated from above.

"We're both fine," Megan shouted upwards. Actually, she wasn't sure if she was. She was breathing, but she didn't know beyond that if all her parts were in working order.

Then she noticed Karen staring at her like she had three heads. Something was wrong. Megan ran her fingers over her own face to feel if it was wet with blood. She didn't detect any. Then she realized Karen wasn't staring at her, but over Megan's shoulder.

"What is that?" Karen gasped.

Megan had a sudden feeling something was creeping up behind her. She whipped her head around . . .

Blackness.
And then she slept.

THIRTEEN

"Bruce."

"Bruce."

"Huh?"

"I'm going back into the Grand Canyon."

Bruce forced his eyes open. Megan Eastwood's face was looming over his. Reddish hair hung in curled strands around her forehead. Black pupils dilated in a sea of green as they focused on him. A pendant hung from her neck, dangling before his eyes.

He blinked.

"Wake up. I'm going back to Re's Cavern," she said.

The pendant was black onyx, about the size of a marble. In its center was a white pearl inlay of the Sphinx, and below that a word he couldn't make out, also done in pearl inlay. He had the strangest urge to bite it off the chain.

He was in a foul mood. Lying cock eyed in the backseat of a mid-sized car all night unable to breathe through your nose will do that to you. He'd driven until the early hours of the morning before finally pulling behind an old church on the side of the road next to a hayfield. Megan had already been sleeping in the passenger seat so he just crawled into the back.

And during the night in a sleep-deprived sober moment he reminded himself the woman in front, now leaning over the backside of the seat staring at him, was wanted for murder and quite capable of using him in a plot to—to what? Well, he hadn't figured that out yet. One thing for sure—he suspected she was hiding *something*.

Did she say she was going back to Re's Cavern?

He sat up, forcing Megan to retreat and settle back into the front seat.

"I'm going back to—"

"I heard what you said," he interrupted, swinging open the door. He piled out of the car. Like a flamethrower, the sun cast its rays over the landscape from the eastern horizon. Blinded by the light, and not realizing his right leg was asleep, Bruce took a step away from the car and tumbled to the ground. Cursing, he struggled to his feet and hopped behind the old church on one foot, where he relieved himself. After some degree of feeling returned to his leg, he limped back to the car and got in the driver's seat.

He turned the ignition, noticed the gas gauge was riding on empty, and threw the Maxima in gear.

Heading north on Route 64, he massaged his aching neck with his free hand.

"I have to go back to Re's Cavern," she said for the third time.

Bruce had no idea how to respond. He wasn't fully awake. "We need to get some gas," he said.

"At the press conference, they didn't say anything about the floor of Re's Cavern having caved in. They would have seen it when they found the bodies," she said.

That was true, Bruce thought.

"Why would they withhold that information?" she asked.

"Because it didn't happen?"

"You're doubting me?"

Ah, yeah. "According to you, your memory has been a bit spotty."

"But it's starting to come back. As I told you yesterday, I specifically remembered the floor caving in. I also remembered more before I fell asleep last night. I'm now *positive* there's an underground cave beneath Re's Cavern."

"You're suggesting the FBI is intentionally keeping that a secret?"

"What else am I to assume? If we go to Re's Cavern, and find that the floor is caved in, that will substantiate my story. The story *you're* going to write."

"Has the thought occurred to you that the FBI has set up shop at Re's Cavern? You'll walk right into their hands. You *are* on their Top Ten list, you know."

She smacked her lips, as if his caveat was completely unfounded. "We'll just work the problem." She faced him. "Listen, even if we don't get inside Re's Cavern, just seeing it again may trigger my memory so I'll know what we found there."

We'll work the problem? When *we* get there? *I don't think so.*
Bruce needed coffee before he could even think straight. He
hadn't seen any signs for a service station or a restaurant, so he
told Megan to keep an eye out.

She gazed back out the window while compulsively caressing
her pendant between her thumb and forefinger.

"What's the word inscribed on it?" he asked.

"On my pendant? Leo. It's my sign."

"I see." *Astrology.* He felt sorry for astrology people. They
were so confused they had to look to the stars for an explanation
to their existence.

"It was a gift," she said, fondling the pendant. "It has an inlay
of the Sphinx in it. In the year ten thousand four hundred fifty
BC, if you viewed the Sphinx from the east at dawn on the vernal
equinox, its outline matched perfectly with the constellation of
Leo. It keeps me inspired."

"Inspired?"

"No one knows who built the Sphinx or why. There was a
time when no one even knew of its existence. Thutmosis the IV,
who lived in about fourteen hundred BC, had a dream one night
that something was buried in the desert. He ordered his slaves to
dig where his intuition told him, and beneath the sand, they
found the Sphinx."

Her voice rose. "The Sphinx represents everything I love
about archeology—mystery, romance . . . dreams."

Even at this early hour, Megan spoke with fervor, as if she
was addressing congress, or some other deathly important group.
He hated to admit that he almost found it stimulating.

They passed a sign that said SERVICE AREA 1 MILE. Bruce
drifted into the right lane, took the exit and pulled into the
station.

Megan told him she had to use the restroom. He retrieved the
key from inside the station for her and handed it over.

"I would like some coffee. Cream and sugar, please," she
said. "And I'm starving. I'll take whatever they got." She exited
the car.

Bruce filled it up, paid cash inside, bought two large cups of
coffee, two bananas an apple, and a newspaper. Megan's and Dr.
Reinhardt's pictures were on the front page. That was no

surprise, but what was a surprise was that Megan's picture was a mug shot.

He got back into the car and quickly scanned the newspaper article for an explanation as to why she'd been arrested. Maybe it was something minor. *People do stupid things when they're young, right?* Problem was, the picture looked like it could have been taken yesterday. Finding no explanation, he dug deeper.

The paper contained an entire section dedicated to the "Grand Canyon Suicides." Color pictures of the canyon, dead bodies, and empty bottles of cyanide were scattered across the pages. The caption under the photo of Re's Cavern read, "The Devil's Lair." An entire page was dedicated to "Dangerous Cults in America." There were excerpts from a book written by a psychiatrist, Dr. Victor Ophryon, titled *When a Loved One Has Been Abducted by a Cult: A therapy handbook for recovering cult victims*. All of this but still no mention as to why Megan had been arrested.

An article at the bottom of the page caught his eye: The park ranger who first discovered the dead bodies at Re's Cavern had been killed in a freak accident. According to the story, Kurt Burney's horse had lost its footing while climbing an escarpment. The ranger fell and broke his neck. Last night, Megan had told Bruce that she'd left a note at Barney's station about the "murders." Would his death explain why it had never been found . . . or at least not been reported?

Megan swung open the passenger door, and fell into the seat.

He tucked the paper under his arm and handed her a Styrofoam cup of coffee.

"Have you ever been arrested for anything?" he asked.

She fumbled with the lid, spilling coffee on her leg.

"Why do you ask?"

"Because I'm putting a lot on the line being here with you. I have a right to know the truth."

She glared at him. "You want the truth? We found something buried beneath Re's Cavern. Whatever it was, it was smuggled out of there—I'm sure of it. Thirteen people were murdered as a result." Her eyes widened. "And now there are only three people on this Earth who know what really happened in the Grand Canyon. You, Jensen, and me. *That's* the truth."

He didn't like her answer. The greater truth was he didn't owe her or this world anything. He could walk at anytime. "Let's get something straight. I don't have to prove your innocence or fight for *any* cause."

"But you do have a conscience, don't you?"

"Theoretically."She didn't seem to know what to say.

"You picked the wrong guy. I've got enough problems. I'm not sure if I trust you, and if I were you, I definitely wouldn't trust me."

She looked surprised, wounded. He didn't care.

"Have you ever been arrested?"

"No."

"You're being truthful, are you?"

"Oh, stop."

Bruce swung open the door. With the paper still under his arm, he got out and went around to the back of the car. Bracing himself against its trunk, he considered what his next step should be. In the soft breeze, the sweet scent of the Ponderosa trees lining the edges of the road tantalized his sense of smell. He tried taking deep breaths to absorb their fragrance but all he got for his effort was a high-pitched nasal squeak emanating from his nose. *She did this to me.*

A contrite, child-like Megan slipped quietly next to him.

He obsessed for a swig of Jack Dean. A wave of angry emotion swept over him as he relived the memory of watching her throw the bottle out the window last night.

"I…I need your help."

Megan's usual energetic tone was flat and void of life. He wondered if she was trying to sound deflated only to get his sympathy.

Her shoulders rose and fell, as if the air suddenly got thinner. Then she looked directly at him, her pupils swelled in the early morning light. Her eyes glistened with liquid. "Please don't abandon me," she said.

"Abandon you? Twenty-four hours ago I didn't even know you."

Whatever idealist notion lay in her head, he had to put a stop to it now. He shouldn't have come this far with her. He didn't need, or want, any drama in his life. "I can't help you," he said, bluntly. "I can't help anyone."

He stepped away from Megan, putting distance between them. "I'm not going to Re's Cavern with you."

She pursued her lips and folded her arms over her chest. He could feel anger start to emanate from her. So what? Did he have a conscious? No he didn't, not with someone who so easily lied about her past.

He watched a car pull up at one of the gas pumps. A white curly haired puppy leaped out of the passenger window. A young girl about eight years old shouted after it to stop. Then she piled out of the car, and started chasing the dog toward the highway. A scream came from the mother in the car, ordering the girl not to run onto the road. Bruce took off after the animal, snatched it up before it became road kill. He returned it to the girl, but not before the dog bit his hand.

Chumo Emesto stood inside the gas station. The action outside the window got his attention. A man had just saved a dog from perhaps being run over, and then had returned it to the little girl. When he got back to the woman with red hair, she started shouting at him, shaking the newspaper in his face that he'd dropped, and stomping her heels on the pavement. The man looked dizzy from watching and turned away. She starting marching stubbornly down the highway. The man threw up his arms and got in the car.

Personas locas, Chumo thought. Crazy people.

He reached for his coffee and noticed the photograph of a woman on the front page of the newspaper on the counter—a woman with red hair, not unlike the girl marching down the road. He looked back out the window and saw the car stop. The man got out, picked the woman right off her feet, tossed her into the car, and drove off.

Chumo again took in the photograph. *No hay duda,* he thought. It is the same woman! He barely spoke English and couldn't read a lick of it. Yet he recognized something in the picture: *numbers.* She was wanted for a crime. His son, Jesus had such a picture taken once, for stealing a car in Mexico when he was a teenager.

Chumo helped out in the gas station once a week, cleaning the restrooms. Just grateful to be in America, he was paid in cash, and didn't normally get involved with lives of *gringos*.

But he did need money, badly. *Puede haber una recompensa para la captura de la mujer?* Might there be a reward for the woman's capture?

He folded the newspaper under his arm. He'd bring it home and show it to his son. Jesus could call the officials. Chumo could make *dinero*.

FOURTEEN

It was mostly a biological, male hormonal response. Bruce had no other explanation for his behavior.

While chasing the dog he dropped the newspaper, and by the time he got back to Megan she'd looked at it and was yelling at him, explaining that she'd forgotten about having had a mug shot taken. She told him she'd been arrested for unpaid parking tickets back in Chicago.

"Get real. They don't arrest people for not paying parking tickets."

"They do when you are served and don't show up in court," she shouted back.

He didn't like her making a scene so he'd literally picked her up and put her back in the car. After that, she'd accused him of being "insensitive" and "selfish." Like he really cared. But then she branded him in a way he couldn't ignore.

"You're a failure."

Eastwood wasn't just talking about his wanting to give up on her. The woman sensed he had a festering emotional wound— beyond his bleeding dog-bit hand, which she hadn't seemed to notice—and she had dug her nails in. She was right. He was a failure. His wife had been killed in cold blood on a night when he should have been with her. A man can't fail any more than that. Before Megan's comment, he'd been perfectly content to let her go back into the Grand Canyon alone, as she had threatened. Afterwards, he started thinking like a man jacked up on testosterone. He was suddenly compelled to prove to this woman that, although Bruce Brackin was a failure, he had the potential to be better.

Yet he wasn't an idiot—or at least not a total one.

"They're going to catch you if you go back there," he said.

She waved off the warning, like she'd done an hour earlier.

"The last place they'll expect to find me is at Re's Cavern."

82

She had a point. The FBI probably wouldn't be looking for her there. Only a complete imbecile would return to the scene of the crime, innocent or not—especially a crime scene in the depths of the Grand Canyon.

She finally noticed his wound. "You're bleeding. We'll get Band-Aids and hydrogen peroxide along with the other supplies we'll need for our trip."

She was persistent, he had to give that to her.

Unfortunately he believed her mug shot story and so agreed to accompany her. After all, he did need a guide to get to Re's Cavern to take pictures. Now he had one. Even if they did get caught, she was the one wanted for murder. Not him.

While Bruce drove, Megan made a list of supplies. Her handwriting was perfectly slanted with the ends of the letters curving into fine, almost sexy points. Bruce was surprised her i's weren't dotted with little smiley faces, although a final period at the end of the list was. Her list included a Maglite flashlight, a Bruceman stove, two four-liter canteens, a first aid kit, two Chrysalis down sleeping bags, two Jansport external-frame backpacks, stick matches, a leak-proof kerosene lamp, and a pair of Northern Star hiking boots for him. Bruce added a couple of racks of number 3, round nose, .38-caliber cartridges for Megan's Walther, which was still in his pants pocket.

She directed him to a place called Casey's Camp Fitters. He went inside with the list while she waited in the car.

When he returned, she handed him a grocery list. They stopped at a supermarket, where he got everything she wrote down, mostly canned foods and fresh fruit. He returned to the car with enough rations for ten days. After that, they washed up separately at a gas station and headed to the Phantom Creek Trail.

Megan had suggested Phantom Creek because it wasn't maintained like the other trails closer to Grand Canyon Village. With few tourists traveling the route, it offered a good chance of their being able to hike into the canyon without being seen. They parked about a mile from the canyon's rim, got out of the car, and helped each other strap on the bulging backpacks, finally arriving at the starting point by late morning.

Bruce was already sucking wind by the time they reached the tattered wooden sign at the trail's entrance:

Phantom Creek Trail
Difficulty/elevation change:
Very Strenuous – 3100 feet 745 m

He gazed into the canyon. Embedded deep in the stone universe, the Colorado River looked like a vein of mercury a million miles away. He remembered having read that the canyon extended two hundred miles in length, longer than New Jersey. The depth, he recalled, was about five thousand feet in its deepest section, four Empire State Buildings stacked on top of each other. Scientists say the canyon was created by millions of years of erosion from the Colorado River.

The Hopi Indian tribes that live down there had a different story: God had created the Grand Canyon one day when their people had angered Him and he pounded the earth with a hammer. This explanation seemed more reasonable to him. How could one river possibly create this monster abyss in the earth? He took some pictures, and while doing so the canyon started looking more like a living, pulsating, stone organism that didn't take kindly to foreign invaders. He replaced the lens cap and brought his Nikon to his chest where it hung on the neck strap.

"The hike down—it isn't dangerous, is it?" he asked Megan.

"Always," she said not bothering to look at him while rubbing sunscreen on her arms.

She wore the white cotton T-shirt and tan khaki shorts he'd gotten her, along with the pink socks that were folded over the uppermost edge of her boots. Cleaned up, she didn't look half bad. "What do you mean, 'always?'"

She tossed him the tube of lotion. "Let's hope you don't get Kaibab Shuffle."

"What is *that*?"

She smiled. "You'll find out if it happens," then moved past him toward the canyon's rim.

Bruce looked up at the blazing sun hoping to see a cloud or two roaming nearby. There were none. He wondered if it would be hotter or cooler in the canyon. The bottom was farther away from the sun. It must be cooler, he thought. He gingerly applied some lotion to his swollen nose. His socks had already slid down his sweaty ankles from the heat. He yanked them up then caught up with Megan.

Together they began their journey into the canyon.

For the first hour or so, the trail was easy, as the path was wide and the incline gradual. Megan pointed out the different rock strata along the way.

"That's Supai and Redwall. And see that ridge over there? That's Bright Angel."

She explained that each stratum represented millions of years of history, the result of marine deposits and sand dunes that over thousands of millennia had compacted and hardened into eroded sandstone, shale, and limestone.

Following the direction of her finger, Bruce took pictures as they went.

Then Megan told him about the Great Unconformity, the strata in which Re's Cavern was situated.

"There are about a dozen major strata exposed in the Grand Canyon," she said. "The bottom strata represent the Earth's oldest time period, and the top represent the period closest to present time. The bottom step is the Precambrian strata. Its rock formation is called Vishnu schist, which is about two to four billion years old. The strata up from that is the Grand Canyon series, a group of various rocks that range roughly from two billion to five hundred million years of age. Above that is Tapeats sandstone, the strata between four and five million years old."

Bruce heard her words, but was mostly watching his own baby steps along the trail that was becoming increasingly narrow. He kept wondering if he might get "Kaibab Shuffle."

Megan went on. "Much of the recorded history of the middle strata, the Grand Canyon series, doesn't exist because of erosion. Geologists call it the 'Great Unconformity.' In essence, it's between two hundred fifty million and a billion years of missing Earth history."

"Uh huh."

"The Great Unconformity has no fossils deposited in it. It's like a section of a world history book with blank pages.

Geologists don't know what happened on Earth for that time period."

Walking the narrow trail like it was a four-lane highway, with her red hair bouncing and arms swaying, Megan didn't seem to notice the two-thousand foot drop just to their left. The pale freckles that dotted the backs of her legs were getting increasingly difficult to see. "Not so fast," he said, while practically hugging the wall on his right.

She slowed her steps while continuing to talk. "The geologic environment of Re's Cavern is the Great Unconformity. We don't know what was happening on Earth during the period when the cavern was formed."

Bruce had always assumed that geologists knew the complete history of Earth. Apparently not. He gazed out at the endless, diamond-studded butte walls beyond the empty void of space edging the trail, the geologic history book with its billions of years of "pages." *Billions of years.* If he hadn't already been feeling small and insignificant before he certainly was now. His lifetime—Rachel's lifetime—wouldn't even register as an ink blotch on one geologic page of earth's history. In the grand scheme of things what would be the difference if they existed at all?

Bruce's thoughts were suddenly interrupted by the sound of slashing helicopter wings.

"Come on!" Megan blurted and grabbed his hand. She pulled him and his trembling legs over the narrow path and under a nearby outcropping.

In the shadows, they sank down onto the hard rock and waited for the helicopter to pass over them. When the tail of it came into view beyond the overhang Megan said, "I think it's a tourist helicopter."

"Why?" Bruce asked. From its height and angle, he couldn't see any writing or other distinguishing marks that indicated it was a tourist helicopter.

"Because of the bright red and blue colors," she said.

"Why is it the only helicopter we've seen since we started? Wouldn't tourist helicopters be flying by all the time?"

To this Megan had no answer. Bruce didn't like it. For all he knew it was an FBI helicopter disguised to look like a tourist helicopter.

Finally the machine flew out of sight. Bruce hoped like hell whoever was in it hadn't spotted him and Megan before they'd slid under the shelter.

She suggested they rest for a moment before continuing. Exhausted and thirsty, Bruce didn't argue.

Heat rose from the golden buttes and pressure ridges that surrounded them in shimmering waves. Bruce wiped sweat from his brow and realized he'd gotten the answer to his earlier question: did it get hotter or cooler deeper into the canyon. He was starting to feel like bacterium that the fevered stone organism might expel at any moment.

Megan rose to her feet and gazed outward through binoculars.

"How much further?" he asked.

"A good four hours."

The concept of Megan hiking up out of the canyon after finding her friends dead was becoming more real to him. No wonder she was cranky by the time she got to him. He took a long swallow of water from his canteen.

Megan also took a sip from hers. She then poured some water over her head. He watched it trail down her front and soak into her T-shirt, bonding the fabric to her skin. She pinched her top and pulled it outward, creating a barrier of air.

Gliding the air currents, a hawk swooped toward him, almost close enough to reach out and touch. He watched its black-pebbled eyes gaze down its beak at him, perhaps thinking he might make a good afternoon snack. Then it turned upward, out of sight.

When the bird swooped in close for a second look an unexpected voice said, "Hurry Bruce, take a picture before it flies away."

He looked to his right to see Rachel seated next to him. His wife touched his arm, her skin warmer than the canyon air. He went to place his hand on hers, but she started to dissolve the moment he touched her.

"Rachel."

Megan removed her eyes from the binoculars and looked at Bruce. He sat with his torso slightly twisted to his right, as if facing someone seated next to him.

"Who are you talking to?" she asked.

He looked up at her as if she just dropped out of the sky for a visit. "I…ah…can we go now?" he mumbled.

Shadows darkened his eyes and creases forged into his brow that she hadn't noticed before. He didn't look well. Maybe the heat was getting to him. Or—did he need a drink? Of course, he did.

He stood up, moaning from the weight of his backpack.

Could he be experiencing alcohol withdrawal? What if he went into a fit of delirium tremens?

Megan had an uncle who was an alcoholic. When younger, she remembered stories of his hallucinations when he quit drinking. He kept thinking bugs were crawling on him. What if Bruce started seeing bugs crawling on him? *Maybe tossing his precious bottle of whiskey out the window last night wasn't a good idea.*

He inched up next to her, gasping for air. He was so out of shape. *Maybe insisting he come with her wasn't a good idea.*

They headed out from under the overhang and continued their descent. Had he called her Rachel? Why? *Maybe tracking him down in the first place wasn't a good idea.*

Less than five minutes back on the trail, another helicopter thundered from above. By the sound, it was nearer to the ground than the last. They turned around and shuffled along the trail back under the overhang before it was directly overhead. This one Megan knew wasn't a tourist helicopter, for it was black and silver. True, tourist helicopters were colorful, happy looking things designed to attract attention. This helicopter looked anything but happy.

FIFTEEN

It only lasted a brief moment—a moment where the helicopter was almost directly above them, and they hadn't yet reached the shelter of the overhang. Instinctively, Megan had looked to the sky to spot its location. Her gesture allowed those inside to clearly see her face, if they were so inclined. *Stupid.*

Yet, as Bruce and she slid under the outcropping once more, the helicopter kept right on its path. What that meant Megan wasn't sure. Would the FBI have stopped midflight and hovered? Or kept going only to radio ahead to a team, who would then hunt them down on foot?

Having no choice but to stay the course, after the helicopter was out of earshot they hit the path once more.

For the remainder of the hike down they barely spoke a word, with their ears glued to the skies and eyes continually on the lookout for the next overhang to hide under, if another helicopter showed up. To Megan's relief there were none.

Almost eight total hours had elapsed by the time they reached the bottom of the canyon. It felt good to stand on level ground—well, almost level ground—again. Bruce had held up better than she thought he might. Since his earlier episode, he hadn't babbled to himself, or broke into tremors, nor done anything else unusual.

The sun had dipped below the canyon's rim and twilight shadows were beginning to cool the air. Retrieving the topographical map from her backpack Megan asked Bruce to hold it for her. Studying the document through her magnifying glass, her attention drifted to his fingers clasping the edges of the paper, and the sweat-beaded tiny black hairs on the back of his hand. She thought about how those same long fingers had wrapped around her arms at the hotel. Regardless of the pain he'd inflicted upon her during their skirmish, there was something oddly *caring* about his touch. Or was it just her imagination? *Because death makes you crave human contact?* Why was she even thinking about this? She forced her attention back on the map. After determining the path to get to where they'd bed down for the night, she carefully rolled the document up and slipped it into her backpack. "This way," she said, pointing.

A short time later they reached the rocky edge of the Colorado River, which rolled lazily down a long channel beneath a darkening sky. Two magnificent granite slopes jutted up on either side of the water, like two massive arms reaching to the heavens. In the center of the "V," lingering traces of the descending sun painted the sky crimson. It was beautiful.

Megan watched Bruce make adjustments to his camera and take pictures. Whereas, when hiking, his movements were slow and almost clumsy, while taking pictures he moved with fluidity, stepping cat-like over rocks with his eye to the lens, capturing different angles of the horizon.

But then when they skirted the river's edge toward their destination the clumsiness returned. "I don't like rivers," he kept saying. "I don't like rivers."

Soon enough they reached a group of small caves in the cliff wall, the ancient cave dwellings.

They picked the biggest one, which was about ten feet wide, and entered.

After unpacking their gear, Bruce fired up the Bruceman stove, while she opened two cans of salmon. She then heated navy beans and they sat and ate, transfixed by the river rolling languidly along in front of them.

"Isn't it wonderful?" she said softly. "There's no traffic, no television, no radio. And no helicopters! Just the sound of the river."

Bruce nodded, as he chewed.

"Siddhartha Gautama believed that life is like a river," she said, looking out at the water. "He said our physical form is a temporary vessel for the soul. When the body dies, the soul moves on to another body, and then to another and then another. And with each new lifetime, there is the illusion of a beginning, and with each death, the illusion of an end. But the river of life, the soul, never stops flowing. No beginning. No end."

She paused and looked to the sky. "Do you believe that?"

"I don't like rivers," he proclaimed yet once more. He then dug a fish bone from his mouth and said, "You're asking if I believe a person lives forever, lifetime after lifetime?"

"Yes. Do you think we come back and, you know, get another body?"

"Come back as a cow or something like that?"

"No. I don't mean . . . I'm not talking about reincarnation as in the Indian caste system. I just wonder if you think maybe we come back to live in a new human body."

He gazed out at the black river. "I'm not sure."

"Do you believe in heaven?"

He scratched his head. "I don't think anyone *really* believes in heaven."

"Why?"

"Because everyone's so afraid to get in, especially the people who preach about it. If heaven exists shouldn't they be rushing to get there?"

"I never thought about it that way."

"Imagine there's no heaven; it's easy to do," he said.

"And just live for today?"

"Something like that."

Megan found herself staring at his soft blue eyes in the flickering light of the stove. Part of her felt uncomfortable being alone with him—so far from civilization—in the night—in such a secluded place. While another part of her was unable to unlock her gaze. He did it for her, turning away seemingly without effort.

After finishing their meals, Megan gathered the skillet and the used paper plates into a plastic bag and then stuffed it in her backpack. Bruce rolled out two sleeping bags and lay on top of his. She sat down on hers and gazed out at the river.

Night had fallen, and bright glints of moonlight danced like fireflies on the water's surface. She allowed herself a moment to absorb its beauty. She had doubts about what they were doing, but knew she had to stay the course. There were many truths in life, she supposed, but the one that stuck with her, the one she'd reminded herself of daily since the death of her colleagues, was that just showing up was ninety percent of the battle. If nothing else, she was doing that.

And so was Bruce, lying there face up, staring at the cave ceiling.

Megan thought about the deaths of her friends, hoping Buddha was right about life being a river that never ends. She thought about her own life and how insignificant it was. Whatever value it now had would be measured by her success at finding Jensen and remembering what they'd excavated at Re's Cavern.

The excavation records stated exactly what we found.

Were the records taken by the murderers? If not, did the FBI find them when they arrived at the scene? How stupid she'd been not to look for the records herself on the morning she'd found the bodies. Another truth about life: hindsight is twenty/twenty.

She turned out the Colman stove making the dwelling pitch dark, and crawled into her sleeping bag.

"Goodnight Bruce."

In response, he began snoring. Loud snoring. She had herself to blame, she supposed. It's not easy to breathe through a swollen nose.

She rolled onto her side and closed her eyes. *Tomorrow we will arrive at Re's Cavern,* she thought. *I hope I'm doing the right thing.* She had her doubts. Serious doubts.

Her mind started to drift and she heard the angry, snorting sounds of helicopter engines. Her body jolted.

She slept.

SIXTEEN

They awoke at sunrise, left the cave dwelling, and spent the better part of the day hiking over ankle-bending terrain en route to Re's Cavern. By late afternoon, Bruce was sunburned, exhausted, and hungry. But mostly he was surprised—surprised they'd made it to their destination without a hitch. They hadn't seen even one human being since entering the canyon yesterday morning, and only the two helicopters had flown overhead during the entire trip.

For the final mile, they'd hiked in from the south along a dry valley. They climbed a moderately low ridge, and on the other side descended onto level ground, where they ended up behind a city-block-long pressure ridge, about two hundred yards from the campground. Crouched behind the ridge, they viewed the excavation site.

Through the binoculars, Bruce saw four tents: three smaller green ones, with the fourth a large, yellow, geodesic-domed tent where the bodies had been found. Two strips of yellow tape stretched around the perimeter of the campground, designating it as the crime scene.

"I can't believe all the people. Do you think they're all reporters?" Megan whispered next to him.

"Not sure," Bruce said, keeping the binoculars to his eyes.

About a dozen people wandered around outside the yellow tape, some taking pictures, others with video cameras. *How had they gotten down here?*

A chubby man in a uniform sat parked in the shade of an umbrella, reading a book. Just beyond the campground was the open mouth of . . .

"Re's Cavern," Megan whispered.

Another strip of yellow tape stretched across the cave's massive entrance. A blue sign read:

Restricted Area. Authorized Personnel Only
Federal Bureau of Investigation

Bruce counted three men guarding the area: the ranger under the umbrella near the tents and two men in white T-shirts that said "FBI" talking to each other near the edge of the taped-off area.

It suddenly struck him how completely he and Megan had failed to plan for this moment.

"Maybe we should wait until night before we go in," Megan suggested.

Leaving would be a better idea, he thought. Then something caught his eye: an old man hiking briskly around the edges of the campground taking pictures, his feet scurrying like a squirrel collecting nuts. Seeing him gave Bruce an idea.

Minutes later they backed away from their position behind the pressure ridge. As discussed, Megan went one way and Bruce the other.

Bruce clandestinely entered the campground from the north side, casually approached the man who was taking pictures and placed a gentle hand on his shoulder.

"It's good to see you, Dillon."

Dillon turned on his heel. He stared at Bruce for several moments before his bushy white eyebrows jumped on his forehead in recognition. He grabbed Bruce's extended hand.

"Good to see you, man—Bruce Brackin, right?" He tilted his head slightly, studying Bruce's face. "What the hell happened to your nose?"

"Long story."

"I didn't see you get off any of the river rafts with the others," said Dillon.

"I hiked down," Bruce whispered.

Dillon frowned. "Hiked? By yourself?"

Bruce avoided the question. "You river-rafted?"

Dillon shook his head. "The others river-rafted." He looked around to be sure no one was listening. "I had another way of getting here."

Bruce didn't bother asking him how, as there wasn't time. He led Dillon by the arm away from the park ranger sitting under the umbrella.

Being intimately familiar with the 'conspiracy mindset,' Bruce figured what he was about to reveal to Dillon would hit him right where he lived.

"Dillon, remember how you told me there is always a story behind the story?"

"Of course."

"You're right."

Bruce relayed an abbreviated version of everything that had happened to him since the press conference: he explained how he'd met Megan, how she told him she'd found the dead bodies, claimed she wasn't involved in the murders, and why they'd hiked back into the canyon—to see if the floor of Re's Cavern was caved in and to hopefully trigger her memory of what the archeologists had excavated in the cave.

"In fact," Bruce said, "Megan Eastwood is hiding behind a crag right now not fifty feet away, watching us."

As Dillon's tiny eyes darted around the campgrounds, Bruce said how his plan involved Dillon's participation. He almost hoped Dillon would laugh at the absurdity of it, and advise him to forget the whole thing and turn Megan over to the FBI.

But the old man said no such thing. Instead, he listened intently, nodding his white head and agreeing with every word.

Damn.

Megan's heart hammered in her chest. All her hopes rested on seeing the caved-in floor and remembering what they had excavated from the cavern, but first she had to get in there without being seen. If Bruce's plan failed, she'd either be killed or carted off to jail. If the plan worked, the guards would be drawn away from the cave's entrance, allowing her access. Once inside, she'd at the very least take pictures. And hopefully she would *remember*. What would happen next, no one knew.

"You have ten minutes. Get in and get out," Bruce had told her.

She tightened the Velcro straps on her boots, removed her backpack, and hid it behind a boulder. Then she ran to another boulder closer to the cavern's entrance. From there, she dashed to a granite pillar, hid briefly behind it, and then scurried to a towering stone column not fifty feet from the mouth of Re's Cavern.

Bruce and Dillon drifted apart, with Dillon strolling within sight of the two FBI agents standing near the back of the excavation tent. He took pictures for a few moments, and then suddenly collapsed on the ground.

Both agents looked curiously at the old man lying near them, but at first they did nothing.

Then Dillon started gyrating like a fish out of water. It looked so bizarre, Bruce hoped it wasn't overkill. Yet it worked. The agents dashed to Dillon's side as if acting out their parts in a play.

"Bud, get me some water over here!" the bigger one barked at the ranger lounging under the umbrella.

The chubby ranger filled a gallon container from a larger jug of water and lumbered over to the agents.

"Probably heat stroke," Bud said, handing the container to agent.

The agent sprinkled water on Dillon's face. Dillon just lay there, now as still as a dead dog. The agent kept sprinkling water on Dillon, but to no avail. With mounting anxiety, the agent finally emptied half the jug. Water splashed off the old man's slumbering face, yet Dillon still showed no reaction.

Bruce was impressed. He had positioned himself precisely between the two agents who now knelt over Dillon and the entrance to Re's Cavern. He was taking pictures of everything. After all, that was his job.

With the three guards' attention riveted on Dillon, Megan slipped into the cavern. She rolled under the yellow tape, flipped on her flashlight, and raced down the black corridor with bounding strides.

A patch of light lay ahead.

The corridor narrowed. She flew past the many passages that branched off from the main corridor until she reached the one she wanted. She turned left into it, and dashed down the passageway. Fifty feet later, it opened out into a yawning cavity: chamber C. To Megan's eyes, the chamber was like a majestic

Precambrian palace. Stone gargoyles molded by ancient lava flows stood guard in its entranceway, and stalactite chandeliers hung from its arched ceiling, while below Megan's feet lay a stone floor of Tapeats sandstone.

The gas generator that powered the lights reverberated loudly off the cavern walls.

Megan trotted forward until she reached . . .

A hole in the cave floor, a gaping puncture caused by the cave-in. *Yes!*

She found her breath. Spotted a wooden ladder fastened to the lip of the hole. *Did the crew build it?*

Ignoring the emotions that welled up inside her, Megan scrambled down the ladder.

The air was much cooler in the lower cavern. When she hit bottom, she rotated her body slowly, taking in every inch of the space, playing her flashlight off the walls. It was bigger than she had imagined, about seventy feet in diameter, she guessed. But it wasn't symmetrical at all. The lower cavern had no distinctive shape. There were nooks and crannies and jagged fissures and dark corners. The walls were like alligator skin, rock that had been compressed into strata by billions of years of wind, water, and heat.

It looked so *unfamiliar!*

The lower cavern floor was fairly clear. Whatever debris had been there from the cave-in had obviously been cleared away.

She closed her eyes and brought to mind the memory that had fired the night before last. She saw Karen Stoltz staring over her shoulder. "What is that?" Karen had asked.

What happened next? Surely, Megan had turned around to see what Karen was referring to. *What was it?*

What????????

Megan saw nothing in her mind's eye. NOTHING!

The pressure of having so little time to remember didn't help. She took several deep breaths and tried to relax. Eyes open again, she moved around the cavern, touching walls, touching the cold floor, hoping the tactile sensation would trigger a memory.

It didn't.

She directed her light to a corner of the cavern. There was an opening in the wall about three feet wide. She crossed to it and entered a narrow passageway. Several feet later, the passageway opened to a tiny, capsule-like cavern. A pool of black water lay at her boots. An extension of the Colorado River?

Suddenly she got a picture of someone entering the water. *Who?* Robert Krakow, one of the crewmembers. He had swum through the water into an underground tunnel and come out the other end, into the river.

She remembered! Yes, she remembered Robert doing this.

But, try as she might, she couldn't remember anything else about it.

Megan turned on her heel and ran back through the passageway to the center of the cavern. There had to be something in there that would spark her memory. *Something.*

She had a sudden impulse to look up, and pointed her flashlight above her. She played the white dot off the ceiling along the outer perimeter of the hole. Pink fragments of broken stalactites hung from a section of it. *Why were they broken? Had they cracked and then separated and fallen to the floor naturally?* Inspecting the floor, she saw nothing that would indicate the broken rock formations had landed there. Then again, they would have been carried off with the rest of the debris.

She again illuminated the stalactites with her flashlight. There were three extending down from the ceiling. *What were the chances that all three had broken off naturally? Not a chance,* she thought. Something must have forced them to break off simultaneously—something outside Mother Nature's influence.

Suddenly she heard Karen's voice again.

"What is that?"

Megan had a sudden feeling something was creeping up behind her. She whipped her head around.

The memory was knocking on the door, trying to get in. Megan's pulse quickened. She closed her eyes, and tried to relax . . .

Fragments of pictures flashed in her mind. Trying to corral them was like trying to catch butterflies without a net.

Just let it happen, she thought. *Let go . . .*

The scattered mental pictures began to settle down. Began to form into a logical sequence.

A large metallic structure began to crystallize. A metal object.

Megan realized the object had been here, here beneath Re's Cavern!

Her breaths grew rapid. The memory disappeared.

"Nooooo!"

She didn't have much time. Bruce would be able to divert the agents' attention for only so long. Ten minutes, he'd told her. She *had* to remember what they'd found. *Now!*

She turned off her flashlight, and stood as still as she could in the black cavern. She decided she would either remember, or die here.

Let it happen, Megan. Just . . . let it happen.

She saw flashlights prowling the silver-black surface of the metal object and realized they were coming from the crewmembers who had been standing on the rim of the open hole above the lower cavern that she and Karen were in.

"Breathe. Relax . . ."

The flashlights from the crewmembers above reflected off the metallic object's silver-black surface: a surface that looked like char-baked titanium. Megan remembered rejecting its existence as fast as she could take it in, like incorrect data being entered into a computer. ERROR! ERROR! The metal object's presence down here in this Precambrian cavern, a mile below the rest of the world, was utterly incomprehensible.

It looked like a vessel of some sort, designed to transport something, not through space, but through time.

The vessel was about twenty feet high and perhaps twenty feet in diameter. It was shaped like a giant bullet that stood upright, with a flat bottom that rose to a cone-shaped top. Frozen by time, a trio of amber calcium carbonate stalactites draped over a section of the object's top—a geologic formation that would have taken hundreds of thousands of years to manifest.

Hundreds of thousands of years! And the rock in which the vessel was surrounded by and partially encased in was millions of years old!

"What is it?" Karen asked again while struggling to her feet.

Megan didn't have a clue. It certainly wasn't an Egyptian artifact. She also stood up, and from her new perspective spotted something even more unusual. She unclipped her flashlight from her utility belt and cast the beam forward. Emblazed on the surface of the vessel was a large, golden circle. Under the radiance of the light, diamond flecks glittered within the gold almost making it appear alive. Along the circle's perimeter, four black, wavy lines extended outward: one at twelve o'clock, one at three, one at six, and one at nine. It was a symbol of some sort!

Suddenly the end of a thick rope, flew over the edge of the newly opened hole on top, and dangled a foot above the floor next to them.

Within moments, Jensen had worked his way down the rope. Mendelssohn, the remote viewer, followed. The remaining crewmembers lined the edge of the rupture and looked down, their roaming flashlight beams continuing to illuminate the lower cavern.

Awestruck, Jensen gazed up at the vessel.

"Jesus," Mendelssohn gasped.

Jensen inched toward the object as if caught in the pull of some otherworldly light. Megan reached out and took his arm. About a quarter of the vessel was encased in rock. They moved slowly toward the backside, sliding their bodies through a narrow gap between the cavern wall and the object. Karen and Mendelssohn followed. A round sealed portal came into view.

A terrible feeling of foreboding came over Megan. A dreadful premonition that they had stumbled on to something utterly poisonous to the human condition, something that had been planted deep in the earth, far from human life, for a good reason. But, by whom? And when?

Jensen retrieved a mini-recorder from his jacket pocket and started talking into it:

"We have discovered something buried in a hidden cave below Re's Cavern. Its presence here—a mile beneath the Earth's surface in the Grand Canyon—is inconceivable. It appears to be something from the future, yet it is lodged in five-hundred-million-year-old Precambrian rocks. The object is perhaps twenty feet tall and made out of a pitted, metallic

substance. There is an icon emblazoned in the surface in the shape of a golden circle. Inconceivable . . . as I said . . ."

There was a concave notch in the portal door with a flat lever extending over it. Jensen hit STOP on the mini-recorder, slipped it back in his pocket, and squeezed his fingers into the notch. With a grunt, he jerked the lever outward. A tremendous whooshing sound issued forth from the outer edges of the door as the vacuum seal was released and air was sucked into the object. Megan could even feel her hair being pulled forward and the strain on her ankles to stop her body from getting sucked into it!

Then the round door rose slightly upward by itself. Mendelssohn gave Jensen a hand, and the two pushed it high enough to permit access.

Before entering, however, Jensen allowed a moment's hesitation.

"Shouldn't we check for poisonous gas before we go in, or for radiation with a Geiger counter?" asked Megan.

"We don't have a Geiger counter," replied Jensen. He then took a step forward.

And so did Megan. She did what she had been enthusiastically doing for the last six years: she followed Dr. Jensen Reinhardt—in . . .

Megan was jolted into the present by a sound behind her. She turned and flicked on her flashlight.

Bruce jumped off the ladder on the floor. He gazed around momentarily, looking surprised that the lower cavern even existed.

"Dillon's got the guards in the palm of his hand," he announced. "He came to and babbled for a while, then pretended to pass out again. But we have to go now."

He paused and stared at her. "Did you . . . ?"

"Yes. I remembered," she said. But she hadn't remembered everything. She was sure there was more. So much more.

Bruce quickly took several shots of the lower cavern with his camera.

"Let's get the hell out of here, Megan."

She followed him up the ladder to the upper cavern. But she didn't see much in front of her, as she was trying to keep the movie playing.

"With any luck, Dillon will still have the FBI captivated," Bruce said. "Hopefully, we will be able to get out of here without being seen."

But as they left chamber C and headed down the long corridor toward the cave's entrance, a curtain fell on whatever good luck they'd had. It came in the form of a man standing at the cave's entrance, his body silhouetted against the fading daylight.

"I knew things were going too good," Bruce said.

SEVENTEEN

Agent Downer was not a fool. While he and Agent Maconi tended to the old man with heatstroke, someone could have sneaked into the cavern.

"Stay with the old man," Downer told his partner. "I'm checking the cave." As he entered, a shadow flitted past an opening ahead of him. Looking closer, he thought he saw a dark figure slip from the center of the cave's long entranceway into the shadows. It appeared to be about a hundred feet in front of him.

"Hey!" he shouted.

There was no reply. Maybe his eyes were playing tricks on him, still adjusting to the darkness from the bright sunlight. He quickened his pace down the passageway and saw movement again. A human form ran off deeper into the cave. *Fucking media. You turn your back for one minute, and the bastards sneak inside to get pictures.*

When they saw the agent in the cave's entrance, Megan bolted down the corridor, obviously expecting Bruce to follow her. Instead, he ducked in the shadows along the cave wall, contemplating his situation.

He was at a crossroads. One signpost pointed into the dark cavern, the other toward the sunlight at the cave's entrance. He was torn between learning what she'd remembered and taking the road out of this cave and back to his sorrowful life in New York.

A sorrowful life—yes, but all the same a *secure* life. Maybe he'd sell his condo, with all the memories of Rachel in it, and move to a nice house out in the suburbs. Maybe he'd take up gardening. Maybe he'd write a book. He'd always wanted to write a book. Maybe he'd . . .

"Bruce!" Megan snarled, just loud enough for him to hear.

He couldn't see her in the darkness. She'd obviously stopped running and backtracked toward him. He looked again toward the cave entrance and saw the silhouette moving swiftly down the long corridor toward them.

"What are you waiting for?" she growled.

The tapes of Megan's story were in his backpack, which he'd left with Dillon before he went into his heatstroke act. Bruce could walk out of this cave right now, get the tapes, and give them to the FBI. *Would they believe Megan's story if they heard the recordings?*

"B-r-u-c-e!"

Oh, what the hell.

He tucked his camera, hanging around his neck, under his shirt and took off running toward Megan. She jumped out of the shadows to meet him. They ran past the light generator and bounded down the ladder into the lower cavern.

"This way," she whispered as they scrambled over the lower cavern floor.

She grabbed his arm and yanked him through a narrow opening in the wall.

"What did you find down here?"

"I'll tell you later."

They followed the bouncing beam of her flashlight through a stone passageway that was barely wider than his shoulders. Megan slid easily between the jagged walls, but twice, a razor-sharp outcropping ripped through Bruce's shirt and drew blood from his upper arm. He ignored it and kept moving forward.

"We left a raft on the other side of the underwater tunnel," Megan gasped. "Once we get through, with any luck it will still be there."

Underwater tunnel?

"We have to swim underwater to get out?" Bruce asked.

"A short distance."

"How short?"

"I'm not sure, but one of the crew did it and said it was easy."

"You're sure of this? You remember it?"

She didn't answer.

"Where does it end up?" Bruce demanded.

"The river, of course."

Just hearing the word "river" made his knees want to buckle. "I don't like rivers. Feet? How many feet?"

"Not far. I'm sure of it."

They emerged from the narrow tunnel and came to an abrupt halt. By the beam of the flashlight, Bruce saw they were in an isolated, dark, subterranean section of the cavern. A pool of black water trickled along at their feet.

Bruce could hear a rustling in the passageway behind him, but his eyes didn't leave the black water. He was trying to picture himself swimming through it into an underwater tunnel.

He looked up at Megan and realized he wasn't breathing.

"There isn't rapids on the other side, is there?"

"No. No. It's calm. I think."

"Think? Do you remember or not?"

Her eyes grew liquid in the beam of the flashlight. She swallowed hard and said, "I have no right to ask more of you. If you stay here, I'm sure they won't harm you. Write the story and get the truth out. I have to find Jensen and the metal object we discovered in the cavern. Yes, Bruce. I remembered. It was a large silver object. I need to find out what was inside of it." Her eyes hardened. "I'm going to find out who took it, and get it back!"

Large silver object? What in the hell was she talking about?

"Good-bye, Bruce."

Megan jumped into the water. Bruce was dumbstruck. He could do nothing but watch the blackness swallow her. It happened so fast. Too fast!

Mere seconds later, a voice barked behind him. "Don't move!"

Bruce spun on his heel. The FBI agent had emerged from the passageway and stood no more than ten feet from him. The agent's eyes darted to the water. Concentric circles still rippled outward. He looked again at Bruce, and then back to the water.

"What is this?" the agent demanded.

"Looks like water to me," Bruce said.

The agent reached behind his back then stepped forward, a pistol in his fist.

"Comedian, are you?"

He surveyed the length of Bruce's body. His eyes stopped at the bulge in Bruce's pocket.

"Take your left hand and very carefully remove whatever is in your right pocket."

It was the Walther. Bruce didn't argue. He snaked his left hand into the pocket and wrestled the gun out.

"Place the weapon on the ground and kick it over here."

Bruce did as he was told. The gun skidded across the stone floor and stopped near the agent's feet.

"Hands in the air!" the agent growled.

Bruce obliged.

"Who jumped into the water?"

"Oh, just another journalist," Bruce said.

"And who the hell are you?"

Bruce was tongue-tied. He couldn't think of a lie fast enough.

The agent's eyes narrowed. In the shadows, his face looked gray and lumpy, like it was made of Play-doh. "Look," Bruce said. "I'm just a reporter getting a story."

"Where does this water lead to?"

"The Colorado River."

"How long of a swim is it?"

"I don't know, really."

"What's his name?"

"Who?"

"Don't fuck with me."

"Oh, the reporter. His name, ah, Keith is his name. He's from the *American Times*, too."

The agent frowned. "Why did Keith jump into the water?"

Bruce couldn't believe the agent had bought it. The thought occurred to him that Mr. FBI Man wasn't the sharpest tool in the shed. Then another thought occurred to him, as it had about ten times in the last minute: he already missed Megan. Not *her*. He missed the game. He'd been left hanging . . . left wondering what she meant by large metal object with something inside it and what she was going to do next. *Where was she going to go? How would she find Reinhardt?*

He wondered if the water was cold. *It sure looked cold.*

Screw it. What do I have to lose? My life? No great loss. She said there weren't rapids on the other side. Right?

106

Bye!

Bruce took a giant gulp of air, stepped backwards, and fell into the drink. His body hitting the icy water, convinced him he had done something really stupid.

Cold, no. Freezing! The sub-zero shock knocked most of the air out of his lungs. Yet somehow he managed to hold his breath, what there was left of it. Trying to put as much distance between himself and the agent as possible, he kicked his feet and punched forward into the inky water.

A bullet whistled past his head. *Swoosh!* Then another. *Swoosh!* Bruce hadn't expected the agent to actually shoot at him. *Control your emotions*, he thought as he pressed forward. *Energy expelled can't be replaced.*

Another bullet *thwonked* the water behind him.

SPLASH! The sound sent tremors through his already taut body. He couldn't believe the agent had enough balls to dive into the water. *Have to move fast. Stay calm. Even strokes. Move!*

Seconds passed with Bruce stroking ahead in the water, thinking he'd gotten away cleanly. Sudden pressure began to build in his ears, terrifying him, as he realized he was swimming *down* in the water! He stopped kicking and held his body as still as his nerves would permit. Slowly, very slowly, he rose upward.

Two hands suddenly clasped his left ankle.

Bruce frantically kicked his right leg. His heel connected with the agent's face. The grip on Bruce's ankle loosened enough for him to jerk his leg free.

He swam with all his might. Seconds seemed like minutes. He had expended a lot of energy, and already his lungs were starting to burn. Several strokes later, he reached toward the water's surface, praying he was through the passageway. His fingers smashed against the ceiling of the underwater tunnel.

He continued to push through the blackness while running his hands along the gnarled ceiling, searching for a pocket of air. The attempt was futile. He was trapped in a universe devoid of oxygen.

His lungs burned. His chest muscles tightened around his rib cage. He drove himself forward, trying to get the most distance from each stroke.

The water grew warmer. *Is this a good sign? Where is the end? Megan said it was a short distance. Where the hell is it?*

He found himself picturing water filling his lungs. He thought about the night before in the hotel room when he had choked on the Perrier. Only a trace of water had entered his lungs, and he couldn't breathe. *What would gallons of river water feel like?* Suddenly he was eleven years old again in the Hudson River, rushing water sucking him downward. Fighting. Heart pounding. No air. End of life . . .

His father saved him then. Dad's dead now.

The veins in his neck felt like paper straws collapsing in a vacuum.

Lights started exploding in his head.

He couldn't feel his arms or legs any more. His insides shook. His lungs burned. *Must breathe now!*

He was suddenly out of his body. He watched it kick and slash through the water. He knew this out-of-body feeling. It's what had happened when he had attempted suicide.

Is that a light ahead? It grew brighter. *Is it real, or the light you see when you die?*

Rachel's face appeared before him.

Keep going! she ordered.

He did, and his body catapulted out of the tunnel like a human missile. He flew several feet through the air and crashed into the river below. Through blurred vision, he saw the beautiful, flaming sun hovering in the sky above him. Towering stone buttes jutted up from either side of the Colorado River and soared into the blue sky.

He heard himself sucking in precious air.

Giddy from lack of oxygen, he thought the entire scenario was "kinda cool." He had escaped from the agent and survived the underwater tunnel. It was like being in a Spielberg movie!

The river dragged him downstream.

Where's Megan? The thought was a scream in his head.

He tried to call her name, but he had gone too long without oxygen, and his vocal cords were like dried twigs.

Carried downriver by the swirling water, he scanned the passing shoreline for any sign of her. *Did she make it through the tunnel? She's in better shape than I am. Surely she must have.*

Though he wanted to swim to the river's edge, he was too weak. There was no choice but to lie back, try to relax, and let the river take him.

The canyon walls narrowed, and the current quickened. Bruce was pushed around a bend. Waves of froth bubbled in his face. Foaming crests of water pounded over wave-beaten rocks. The noise was like thunder.

The sopped hair on his neck stood up. White foam crashed all around him. Black rocks flashed by. Just moments ago, the ghastly underwater silence had engulfed him. Now a raging river roared in his ears.

Rapids!

Water crashed against protruding boulders and sprayed diamond crystals of mist into the air. Spires of rock flashed by that could easily tear him in two.

Suddenly the river fell out from under him. His stomach lurched as he plummeted down a small waterfall into more churning water. His right foot hit the top of a rock, and he somersaulted headfirst. White foam that tasted like watery spinach sloshed into his open mouth. A wave hit him crossways and spun him around. He raced downstream, backside first.

Another wave arched over him and punched him on either side of the head. He saw stars. Was yanked under by the raging river and tossed about like a leaf in the wind. Just like when he was eleven years old.

Yet instinct kicked in. He fought to keep his head above water. Down the river he went. With no more fight in him, he mentally prepared for the worst.

I'm coming, Rachel . . .

Then, as quickly as it had begun, the current slowed, and the raging water eased to a velvety roll. The rapids were suddenly behind him. It was strange; it had all happened so fast. Exhausted, he lay back in the water and concentrated on letting his frayed muscles relax. The sun stared down, a gawking, golden eye laughing at him.

He laughed, too. Even though he could barely breathe, like a nitwit he laughed out loud. He'd almost bought it for real that time, yet he was alive—and he *felt* alive. He'd made it through the tunnel. He'd beaten the rapids and conquered his childhood demon! Well, almost . . . *ha ha ha*. He heard Hendrix's "Voodoo Child" playing in his head.

He hadn't realized how fast the current was still carrying him until his left shoulder collided with a stone pillar jutting out of the water. Searing pain shot down his arm, instantly turning it numb.

Bruce thrashed to the river's edge with his good arm and dragged himself onto the rocky shore. Every muscle in his body ached. He had a splitting headache from oxygen depletion. His lungs felt sharp pinpricks of pain bursting throughout them like being pierced by flaming needles.

He had to find Megan, yet all he could do was lie there like a fish washed ashore. And when the darkness rushed in, there wasn't a damn thing he could do about it.

EIGHTEEN

Bruce regained consciousness sometime later, but didn't recognize the time or place. His head felt like it was wrapped in wet plaster that was quickly drying and constricting, making his brain swell. That sound—the lapping reverberation in his skull, sloshing, wet, churning—that sound made the pain worse—the agonizing pain.

Water?

He blinked open his eyes. Blinding white light rushed in. His eyes shut involuntarily, but he kept forcing them open until the world around him began to come into focus. A shoreline stretched before him. Water lapped on rocks that quivered in the heat of the sun.

Lying face down on the rocky shore, he rose to his knees and assessed his surroundings. Bronze cliffs rose sharply on either side of him, slanting jaggedly up from the shores of the river.

A horse kick to the head could not have hurt worse than the pounding in his ears. And why was his left shoulder killing him? His lower back stubbornly locked up when he tried to stand. He fell back to his knees, hammering them sharply on the granite bank.

"Ahhhhhh!"

Then he remembered—Re's Cavern, the FBI agent, the underground river, the rapids, the redhead . . .

Megan.

He had jumped into the water after her, swam through the underground tunnel, and landed in the Colorado River.

He struggled to his feet again. The rocky shore whirled around him. He rested his palms on his throbbing knees, grabbed a couple of gulps of air, and waited for the dizziness to subside. Ignoring the pain, he scrambled up a low-pitched furrow in the cliff wall to get an elevated view of the landscape. At the top of the mesa, he cast his gaze over the river, searching.

Not far from where he stood, a dried-up gulch branched off from the river at a forty-five-degree angle. It was here, where the gulch intersected the river, that something got his attention. He squinted and used his hand as a visor to shield his eyes from the sun. Something lay at the river's edge—something that made the sweat on his face turn cold with horror.

"Megan!"

He scurried down the cliff wall, lost his footing, tumbled into a roll, and got up running. Ignoring the pain in his knees, he splashed along the river's edge, leaving a wake behind him. As he drew closer, his worst fear was realized. Russet-colored water lapped on two bare legs extending out from behind an outcropping along the river's edge.

Megan laid face up, her eyes closed. Her hair was brittle orange seaweed, dried in the sun. Her skin was pasty white. A large crimson blot of blood soaked her T-shirt on the right side.

Bruce fell to his knees next to her. Cursing aloud, he desperately pressed a forefinger to her carotid artery. Her skin was clammy, but he felt a rhythmic tick in her neck. He listened to her chest and heard quick spastic breaths.

She must have collided with a rock while going through the rapids, as he had, and gotten knocked unconscious.

She stirred, and her eyes blinked open and connected with his. They were a sickly lime green, pale with little pigment.

Christ.

Then her eyes rolled up into her head.

"Megan? Megan?"

She was out.

He had to assess the damage under her shirt. Grabbing the fabric, he peeled it away from her skin, exposing her blood-soaked abdomen. Scooping river water into his hands, he poured it over her stomach. The blood washed away just enough for him to see a large gash just below her ribs on the right side. Purple blood oozed from its center. The skin around the edges was stark white.

Searching his fuzzy memory, Bruce vaguely remembered that blood coming directly from the liver would be deep, dark purple. And that's what he saw—deep, dark purple liquid.

He ripped off his shirt, folded it over the wound to absorb the blood, and then stretched her blouse back over his shirt and tucked it into her pants to hold everything intact.

A sudden gunshot echoed down the river channel!

Bruce spun in the direction of the sound. Peering over the outcropping his eyes focused on the agent he'd encountered in Re's Cavern. He stood on a mesa across the river pointing a rifle in the air with the other agent standing next to him.

"Come out from behind the rock." The agent's voice carried over the water.

Thank God. They could get Megan to the hospital where she belonged. He looked at her face, and was grateful she was unconscious. She couldn't argue with what he was about to do.

The moron FBI agent and his partner were about to discover that "Keith" is actually Megan Eastwood.

He eased her off his lap and onto the rocky shoreline, and then stood up from behind the outcropping, arms in the air.

"I'll do whatever you say," he shouted over the river.

"Is your friend with you?" the agent yelled back.

"It's Megan Eastwood. She needs a doctor."

The men looked at each other.

"Bring her into the open. We'll call for assistance."

Bruce crouched down and scooped up Megan in his arms, but hesitated before lifting her into full view. *The agents won't harm her, will they? They'll get some kind of FBI trophy for bringing her in alive, won't they?*

He peered over the outcropping at the two men. He saw the agent's right thumb slide against the butt of the rifle. Something was brewing in his squinted eyes.

Bruce shouted across the river, "If you want Megan Eastwood, lose the guns!"

The agents appeared to discuss his request for a few seconds then to Bruce's surprise, the moron agent laid the rifle on the ground in front of him.

Feeling a bit more confident, he began to lift Megan into the open while keeping his eyes on the men. Suddenly a shared thought rippled across the space between him and the agent. Bruce's heart seized.

A gunshot thundered as Bruce fell to the ground behind the outcropping. Megan tumbled from his arms onto the rocky shore. A bullet buzzed through the air just inches above his head.

Two more blasts followed.

How...?

Why...?

He needed to find an escape route, fast!

Crouched behind the outcropping, he could now clearly see the agent brandishing a pistol Bruce hadn't seen before. He saw something else, too. The second agent was angrily shouting at the moron who'd fired.

Bruce craned his neck around to check out the terrain behind their position. The dry gulch was twenty, maybe thirty yards away. If he stayed low to the ground, making himself less of a target, he might be able to reach it. Lots of river flowed between the agents and him. He figured once he got to the gulch, he could turn the corner and be out of firing range.

It was chancy, but he didn't see any other option.

But first—he pulled the strap around his neck with the camera on it over his head. Thank God, he had put the Tetra underwater casing on his camera a couple of days ago.

This is gonna be worth a thousand words!

Agent Downer was annoyed with Maconi bitching at him for firing at the reporter. He wasn't even sure if he'd hit the man or not. If he had, he wouldn't mind the verbal abuse. But since he didn't yet know, Maconi was becoming a distraction.

A glint of light from the outcropping across the river caught his attention. He squinted.

"What is he doing?"

Maconi looked around. "Son of a. . . He's taking our picture!"

Downer raised his rifle, got the camera in its scope, and fired.

Bruce had set the shutter to automatic, so the camera snapped five pictures.

The gunshot came after the third one.

He snatched the camera from its perch as bullets drilled into the rock.

Slinging the camera back around his neck, he lifted Megan in his arms. Ignoring his sore shoulder, he started duck-walking painfully toward the dry gulch behind him. He prayed his back wasn't an easy target for the agents.

Another gunshot sounded, and a bullet drilled into the black granite, scattering sparks near his heels.

To hell with it.

He stood straight and stormed toward the gulch. He hit the dry mud while gunfire thundered behind him, bullets still coming dangerously close. His feet pounded the clay like a horse's hooves. He snorted like a horse, too, as he ran.

The FBI wants Megan dead so she won't talk. They're covering up what happened at Re's Cavern!

Bruce turned the corner and ran his ass off with Megan still limp in his arms.

"If you hadn't fired, he would have given up!" Maconi yelled at Downer. "He would have delivered Eastwood right to us. Why the hell did you do that?"

Why? Downer thought. *Because it's my job to kill Eastwood. She must be killed for what she and Reinhardt found in Re's Cavern, which we took. You think I work only for the FBI? You ignorant bastard. You have no idea what organization I really work for. You know nothing of our mission. If I had allowed the reporter to surrender with Eastwood, everyone in the Bureau and beyond would know about what the archeologists found. That cannot happen.*

Now, because of the river between them, there was no quick way Downer could track the couple down. Helicopters would have to do it. But once they were caught, Downer would have no control over how they would be dealt with. He had only one option left. While Maconi continued to rebuke him, he whisked toward the slope leading down to the river.

"Where are you going?" Maconi demanded.

Downer didn't answer. He needed to put some distance between him and Maconi. Downer stopped at the edge of the mesa, about fifteen feet from Maconi. Another foot, and Downer would tumble down the steep cliff wall to the river. He faced the agent.

"What the fuck are you doing?" Maconi barked, and stepped forward. Agent Maconi had just taken his last step.

Downer reached into his pocket and grabbed the reporter's gun he'd retrieved in Re's Cavern. He aimed the weapon directly at Maconi's chest, and squeezed the trigger. This time, Downer didn't miss.

It was nightfall when Downer got back to the campground. He had to act quickly and decisively.

Bud Arnold, the park ranger, was there stuffing a banana into his mouth.

"Did you catch up with the reporter?" Arnold asked, a banana string hanging from his lip.

"Maconi's been shot and killed," Downer said.

"My God—"

"The reporter shot him, and Eastwood was with him. What happened to that old man who passed out?"

"After you and Maconi left, he came to. He looked okay, so I didn't pay him much mind." Arnold swallowed hard. "I got busy guarding the cavern, just like you told me to."

This wasn't good news. Downer suspected the old man was in cahoots with Eastwood and the reporter. *Does he also know what the archeologists had excavated in the Grand Canyon?* All three had to be killed before they had a chance to tell *anyone.*

Downer's first step was to call his superior, Agent Pittman, to report the episode. Pittman would want to get some helicopters in the air, and Downer had to make sure he was on one of them.

Hours later, Bruce stared into the night sky, holding Megan in his arms. Rain clouds had rolled in, hindering his view of the helicopters in the distance. He only knew they hovered above the canyon by the two beams of light that extended down from their hulls.

He'd anticipated they would search along the gulch first, so after waiting out of sight for a short time, he doubled back to the river. He'd followed the water's edge for several miles before climbing an escarpment to higher ground, where he now stood. The abundant greenery in this area of the canyon at least offered some hope of shelter.

Bruce laid Megan on the ground and touched her forehead. Her skin felt like hot coals. The laceration had become infected and Megan needed medical attention. Yet without her to guide them, he didn't have a clue which direction to go. And even if he did, how in the hell would he carry her out of the canyon?

Slow down. One thing at a time.

Traveling in the dark was impossible. His first priority was to get through the next several hours until daybreak. They had to find shelter to bunk down for the night.

Low hanging branches at the edge of the wooded area next to them broke off easily, so he was able to fashion a crude lean-to against the base of a nearby tree. He could only hope they would provide enough cover to hide them from a helicopter's sight.

He settled Megan under the large branches and slipped in with her. The pitch-blackness of night within the confines of the leaves was not unlike that wretched underground river. He felt Megan's cheek with the back of his hand. The fever seemed even worse. Her body shook, and her breath was a shallow, gasping wheeze. She couldn't die on him. He wouldn't allow it. He wrapped his arms around her, using his body to warm her the best he could.

The sound of helicopters was an ominous drone in the distance. He closed his eyes, and his mind dealt up pictures from the press conference. He remembered seeing the bodies lying lifeless on the tent floor and the reaction of the media. They were shocked, not at the deaths, but by the fact that they had struck journalistic gold. They had a story. It was good business: one man's death is another man's profit.

Raindrops began to pummel the leaves above them. Thunder roared a few moments later, and their green shelter flashed white from the lightning.

Megan mumbled incoherently. Bruce drew her face close to him, settling it into the crook of his neck. Her hot panting brushed lightly against his skin. He prayed the helicopter pilots would opt not to fly in this weather. Then he tried to sleep for a short while.

NINETEEN

Megan woke to icy needles pricking her face in the damp morning air.

Drip . . . drip . . . drip . . .

She shifted her position, trying to avoid the pain. Her body shivered like a foreign object not under her control. *Hot. Numb.*

Opening an eye, she saw the silver needles falling from a green sky. It rustled, and she realized the sky was made of leaves that arched slightly above her as a ceiling. *Tree? Branch?*

Drip . . . drip . . . drip . . .

The needles were droplets of water falling from the leaves. She shielded her face with a shaking hand. *Cold. So cold.*

As she tried to sit up, a rapier of pain stabbed her between the ribs and she slumped back to the damp ground, nauseated, holding her burning gut.

Something stirred beside her. Megan turned over to see a man's face just inches from hers. A raindrop struck his plump nose, exploded, and slithered down his skin. His eyes opened— aqua blue eyes with slivers of green. . . *like the sky.* They blinked, making the pupils swell.

He bolted to an upright position as if seeing a ghost.

Am I a ghost?

"You're awake," he said.

Or am I dreaming? This man . . . she tried to remember his name.

His hand found her forehead. Fingers like icicles against her skin.

"How are you feeling?"

Bruce?

"You have a fever."

Thanks for the news flash.

"Are you in pain?"

I feel like I've been run over by a truck—maybe two trucks.

"Can you talk?" he asked.

"I am talking," she said. *Where are we?*

He looked up at the leafy ceiling.

Megan drifted. When she opened her eyes again, she was vaguely aware she had fallen unconscious. *How much time had passed? I am very sick.*

Bruce parted the leaves with his fingers and looked out.

She stared up at his naked back.

"There's a hanging cliff about a hundred yards away," he said. "We might find a dry spot under it."

As he towered over her, she wondered why he wasn't wearing a shirt. He faced her and beads of water trailed down his naked chest. A camera hung from his neck.

He said something about needing a doctor, got to his feet, and hoisted the leafy shelter off them. With the branches on the ground next to her, Megan was completely exposed to the freezing rain.

She tried to stand, but her intestines spewed liquid fire. The spicy, hot liquid rushed up her throat. Vomit streamed from her mouth and formed a yellow puddle on the muddy ground. *Oh God. . .*

Bruce fell to his knees beside her and gently wiped her mouth with the bottom of her shirt. Then he scooped her up in his arms and began lumbering through the downpour toward the overhang.

With her arms wrapped around his neck and her face against his naked chest, she gazed up at him. Raindrops stung her eyes as she examined his unshaven jaw and the glistening strands of ebony hair clinging to his forehead. *So tired.*

The last thing she remembered was diving into the water in the lower cavern. She had said good-bye to him moments before. *Yes?* What had transpired . . . after that?

A distant drone suddenly filled the sky.

Bruce looked up.

"Son of a bitch!"

Even without seeing it, Megan could tell by the sound that a helicopter was flying low, approaching them from behind.

Bruce began to run, slogging through puddles of water, splashing mud on her bare legs. The pain in her side was unbearable, and she fought to keep from vomiting again.

The roar of the engine grew louder. Closer.

Bruce picked up speed, his arms like knotted ropes arched under her back and legs. She held on to him for dear life as he ran with long, galloping strides.

The helicopter roared even louder. It sounded like it was above them now. Hovering.

Bruce made a sudden cut to the right, and Megan choked back the bile in her throat. She caught a glimpse of the helicopter just before they reached the bluff. The aircraft was slowly descending. Its underbelly had a bright yellow phone number painted on it.

It touched down a hundred feet or so away. A door swung open, and a one-armed man climbed out, shielding his eyes from the downpour.

"Dillon!" Bruce shouted. He sped to the helicopter, Megan bouncing in his arms, and ducked under the spinning blades. Dillon directed them on board and helped Bruce lay Megan down on the bench seat. *Am I dreaming?*

"How did you find us?" Bruce gasped, trying to catch his breath.

"What's wrong with her?" Dillon asked.

"She has a wound in her liver area. It's infected, and she's got a fever."

Dillon kept his eyes riveted on Megan. "You are in good hands now, dear."

"Better strap her in. The storm is gathering wind," the pilot shouted from the front of the aircraft. He wore bright yellow aviator glasses and a shirt that read, "Bird's-eye View." At least that's what Megan thought it said. Everything was a feverish blur. *Exhausted.*

"This is Parker Taft," Dillon said. "Parker's been flying over the Grand Canyon region for twenty-five years. No one else would dare fly under these conditions. He'll get you to safety."

"Not if we don't hurry," Taft grunted.

Megan's teeth chattered. The taste of bitter bile lingered in her throat.

"She needs medical help," Bruce muttered. He sounded nervous.

Megan didn't like that. He avoided looking at her too. *Do I look that bad?*

Then a tear-drop fell from Bruce's eye duct, landing on her.

It happened in slow motion . . . no, it was just sweat . . . yes, just sweat . . . the fever . . . *I'm so cold.*

Dillon sealed the cabin door shut, flung open an overhead cabinet, and pulled out a blue blanket to cover her shivering body. Then he felt her forehead.

"May I take a look?" Dillon asked her.

Megan nodded.

Bruce parted the blanket back as Megan pulled her T-shirt toward her head. She tried to touch her stomach, but felt another garment.

"My shirt," Bruce said, and helped her pull it out. It was soaked with black blood.

My blood!

Dillon examined her abdomen. She tried to get a view of the wound herself, but when she bent her neck up to look, Bruce's hand gently pushed her head back down.

"Relax," he said.

She didn't like Dillon's concerned look.

"I lost my spleen in a car accident years ago," she said breathlessly.

Dillon nodded. "That explains the infection. Are you allergic to penicillin?"

She shook her head.

"I'll have to give you a shot of an antibiotic first, then a shot of anesthesia so I can sew up the laceration."

"*You* give her a shot?"

"Are you a doctor?" asked Megan.

"A paramedic. Used to do volunteer work for the Red Cross. We have to move fast," Dillon said forcefully.

"Over here," Parker shouted from the front seat. "There's a first aid kit inside the cabinet behind me."

Bruce stepped to the front of the helicopter, rummaged through the cabinet, and pulled out a large metal case with the familiar Red Cross emblem on it.

"There's a couple of shirts in there too," Megan heard the pilot say. "Grab one for yourself."

Bruce slipped a blue denim shirt over his shoulders, returned to Dillon's side and handed the first aid kit to him.

Megan watched as Dillon dug into the contents and came out with a fistful of clear bottles and a syringe sealed in plastic. He handed a bottle to Bruce. "Hold this still, please." As Bruce did so, Dillon tore open the plastic wrapping with his teeth. He took out the needle and plunged it into the rubber cap, pulled back on the stopper, and filled the needle with the liquid. Then he asked Megan to turn on her side so he could give her the shot. She did as requested. Dillon pulled down her shorts just enough to insert the needle in her derrière. *So much for vanity.*

"Prepare for liftoff," the pilot shouted from the cockpit. "The storm is getting worse, can't wait any longer."

"What about the FBI?" Bruce yelled to the pilot. "Won't they be looking for us?"

Parker shook his head. "There's no radar over the canyon. They'd have to be in the air themselves to spot us, and they aren't crazy enough to fly in this weather. It's going to be a rough ride until I get above these rain clouds."

The helicopter engines revved, and Megan's body tensed as she felt the tremble of the machine beginning to lift off the ground. The aircraft bucked, eventually ascending into a billowing mass of black clouds. A brilliant flash of lightning exploded in the canyon sky, causing the helicopter to shudder wildly, and the remaining contents of Megan's stomach lurched upward.

Bruce saw it coming, quickly dumped out the items in the first aid kit and held the empty tin to her mouth.

She retched into it, not knowing which was worse—the physical trauma or the embarrassment in front of her companions. She could handle knocking on death's door, but having Bruce see her this way . . .

Sick as she was, her mind still wandered into a what-if scenario; *had we met in different circumstances, would he have . . . might he have . . . found me desirable?* Then she vomited again.

Bruce dabbed a cotton swab over her lips to clean her mouth.

On her back again, Dillon's head again appeared above her. "Now," he said, "let's get these wet clothes off you."

TWENTY

The news had sent a wave of fury through Special Agent Pittman. He continued to stand in his makeshift office in the Grand Canyon, staring out the window at the rain.

"Damn rain."

He shoved a stick of Big Red gum into his mouth and chomped down. Spicy cinnamon warmed his mouth as it gushed against his cheeks. Megan Eastwood had been spotted in the Grand Canyon with a man—a man who'd said he was a reporter, a man who'd shot and killed one of his agents.

Damn it to hell. Pittman worked the gum as he ran the grim details through his mind yet again.

Almost ten hours ago, Agent Downer had called him, reporting that Eastwood and the news reporter had snuck into Re's Cavern and fled through an underwater tunnel. According to Downer, he and Agent Maconi pursued the couple and found them behind the cavern near the Colorado River. It was there the reporter shot Maconi in cold blood. Then the couple ran through the brush, escaping the pursuit of the experienced FBI agent.

Why? Why did Eastwood return to Re's Cavern? What was she looking for? And who was this "reporter" who shot Maconi?

The agent said he'd momentarily encountered the man close-up in a dark section of Re's Cavern before he escaped through the underwater tunnel, but the details of his features were barely discernable.

Pittman inserted yet another stick of gum in his efforts to relax. There did appear to be one saving grace in this entire mess, he mused. Two days ago a Mexican immigrant named Chumo Emesto spotted Eastwood at a service station just outside Flagstaff. The FBI office had received the call just minutes before Downer spotted Eastwood in the canyon. Pittman had sent an artist to the Emesto residence hoping to get a better description of the fugitive. Maybe something would come of that.

The charcoal drawings had been received by fax late last night. He lifted them from his desk and took another look—one of Eastwood, the other of the man with her. The reporter, if that's what he *really* was, had two distinguishing features: a thick crop of black hair and a big nose. *A nose swollen perhaps from a fight?*

Pittman's assistant, Agent Kowalski, had worked into the early morning hours on the computer looking to match the artist's drawing with other drawings and photographs of known criminals, but to no avail. Kowalski was now viewing the video clips of the press conference trying to spot a reporter in the audience who matched the artist's drawing. No luck yet, but something would evolve—it always does. Criminals make mistakes and they'd be there to take advantage of those mistakes.

The previous night, Pittman had arranged for a helicopter to pick up Agent Downer in the Grand Canyon and to do an air search for the refugees. It was a good idea, but the chopper, had to abandon the search until weather permitted it to fly safely. No use losing more agents. They were short enough on personnel as it was. The air search had resumed less than an hour ago.

For a place that doesn't rain much, it sure the damn hell rains a lot around here!

Pittman turned toward the footsteps behind him. He allowed himself a slow smile when he saw Kowalski holding a videotape in his hand, and walking swiftly down the corridor toward him.

"Tell me some good news," he ordered.

Kowalski slipped the videotape into the VCR. "I'll show you instead."

TWENTY-ONE

They were about to enter the vessel they'd found in the cavern below Re's Cavern.

Finding this otherworldly object buried so deep in the Grand Canyon was like discovering an ancient sea-faring vessel beneath the sands of a great desert. It made absolutely no sense. And when they stepped through the portal door to enter it, any fear Megan had dissolved, and she felt as if she were entering a holy sanctuary, built so very long ago, by a once great civilization.

She had no rational reason to feel this way. In its physical appearance the vessel was nothing but a twenty-foot high metallic structure. Yet it seemed to possess a mystical aura, which made the hairs on the back of her neck stand alert in reverence.

It was as if the bouncing beams of their flashlights had stirred the dark interior into consciousness. This. After how many years of sleeping? Millions? Impossible. She still couldn't grasp its apparent age. Neither would anyone else, she thought. Men and women of archeology reject anomalies as if they were unwanted guests at a dinner party. Finds that don't fit their model of the world don't exist. But this was the last of her concerns.

Jensen first pointed his flashlight at the ceiling bringing to view six rounded and sealed, "Port holes," he whispered.

"What are they for?" Megan asked.

"Inert gas was probably pumped through them at one time to preserve these," Mendelssohn said. His flashlight riveted on four objects before them: four metallic pods lying on the floor.

The pods gleamed bright silver in the radiance of their flashlights. Jensen and Mendelssohn stepped toward them, but Megan stood frozen, held in the clutches of two opposing realities; the reality of what is, juxtaposed to the reality of what couldn't possibly be.

The pods were perfectly round. Three of them were each about four feet in diameter. The fourth was more than twice as large, at least ten feet in diameter. Each pod sat on its own concave indentation in the floor.

Megan became aware of Karen's heavy breaths, as Karen stood next to her. Finally gaining a smattering of courage, both women moved toward the objects, inching up next to Jensen and Mendelssohn.

Megan watched Jensen's bearded mouth curl into a smile. Did he know more about this dig than he'd previously revealed? They were supposed to be searching for "Egyptian artifacts," but could he have known that something this unexpected—this astounding—might be down here? Just the thought made Megan feel she was betraying her mentor; yet, she'd learned long ago not to ignore a gut feeling, as at times she was cursed with an uncanny sense of intuition. She feared this was one of those times.

Yet ignore the intuition she did. Regardless of Jensen's previous intentions, the objects, and the vessel, were truly a new archeological reality. Based on their location, they extended in time from the very ancient past, millions of years before man walked the earth. Yet, they had the technological composition to be something from the future!

Jensen spread his arms and burst into laughter that echoed throughout the cavern. It was contagious, and though Megan could barely breathe from the excitement, she found herself laughing, too, as did Karen and Mendelssohn. Yes, a new archeological reality was here. Soon they would discover what was inside the orbs, and perhaps even learn where they came from.

At least that's what she had thought at the time.

TWENTY-TWO

While Megan slept, the event had kept playing in her mind. At first, it came in the form of a fevered dream, a mishmash of non-sequential images. But when she awoke, the fever had broken, and the images melded into a logical account of what they had discovered in Re's Cavern: time capsules left behind by an ancient civilization. Now she knew, and she would never forget.

Bruce and Dillon sat in front of her in two helicopter seats, with their backs to her. She lay silently for some time, replaying the memory in her mind. Finally, after she was positive what had transpired in the Grand Canyon, she let her friends know she was awake.

"I'm b-a-a-c-k."

Both men turned toward her, unclipped their seatbelts and were instantly at her side. Two hands reached for her forehead, but Dillon knocked Bruce's hand out of the way and got there first.

"Fever's gone." He smiled.

"How long was I out?"

"About two hours," Bruce said.

"I cleaned out your wound and sewed it up," Dillon proudly announced.

She was lying face up on the helicopter bench, bundled in a blanket with three seat belts wrapped around her. Physically, she felt like hell: weak and her abdomen burned. But her spirits were high. She was alive, and she *remembered*.

"Dillon and I listened to the tapes of me interviewing you while you slept," Bruce told her. "He now knows everything you had told me."

Megan yawned. "Want to know more?"

"Not sure," Bruce said, honestly.

"Absolutely!" declared Dillon.

And just like that, she told them what she'd just remembered: about finding the vessel in the sub-cavern below Re's Cavern, about venturing inside it and finding four time capsules there.

The men listened, with Bruce occasionally giving her a quizzical look as if to suggest her memory still wasn't right, or that maybe the fever had done some damage, while Dillon seemed to accept her every word.

"When did you find these 'time capsules' in relation to—"

"About three days before everyone was killed," She told Dillon.

The men looked at each other.

"I have no doubts about this," Megan said. "It's all there. I remember everything now."

"How old were they, and where did they come from?" Dillon asked.

Megan explained how the vessel that housed the time capsules was partially encased in rock, a stratum that was about five hundred million years old, rock strata called the Great Unconformity.

"The Great Unconformity is unreadable strata caused by erosion," Bruce said. "It's about a billion years of missing Earth history. Right?"

Megan smiled. "You listen."

Dillon scratched his head. "Whoa. You're saying these time capsules are five hundred million years old, and they came from a time when Earth's history is missing?"

"By all outward appearances, that would seem to be the case."

Dillon was still shaking his head. "But intelligent human civilization has only been around for a few thousand years."

"Theoretically," said Megan. "*Homo sapiens* started evolving about two hundred thousand years ago. We've existed in our current civilized form for around ten thousand years. But there's another way to look at it."

In her quiet time before signaling the men that she was awake, Megan had carefully reviewed certain facts.

"Think of it this way," she said. "The Earth is about five billion years old. This means that in the history of our planet, there's been enough time for millions of evolutions of humans.

Just as it is unrealistic to think we are the only intelligent life in a universe with billions of planets, it may be just as absurd to believe we are the first intelligent life on a planet that is billions of years old."

Now Bruce was shaking his head. "But the planet's environment wasn't even inhabitable millions of years ago, right? How can you possibly believe human life existed?"

Megan felt awkward looking up at the men from her lying position, but suspected that sitting would be too painful. She stretched her body under the covers and her suspicion was instantly confirmed. She let out a yelp from the ache in her stomach.

"Maybe you need to rest more," Dillon suggested.

"No. I'm okay." She looked at Bruce. "You asked how human life could have existed millions of years ago. Scientists today believe that about eight hundred to six hundred million years ago, the biggest ice age the Earth has ever known occurred. After that period, planetary oxygen levels were high, and it is believed a new growth in life began called the Cambrian explosion. It's thought that animal life started at that point and evolved very slowly over the next five hundred million years. In other words, some scientists believe that it's taken half a billion years for humans to evolve. But Dr. Reinhardt didn't subscribe to that theory, nor do I."

"Why?"

"There's evidence that intelligent life existed on Earth millions of years ago, even before the Cambrian explosion."

"What kind of evidence?"

"Archeological finds."

Bruce was confused. "Are you now talking about the time capsules?"

Megan closed her eyes. Still queasy, she took a deep breath, coughed, and then said, "There's been many archeological finds that suggest intelligent life existed on this planet millions of years ago. Finds made before—"

"We got company!"

They all looked toward the pilot.

"Behind us, about eight o'clock," Parker shouted from the cockpit.

Bruce ran to the nearest window and looked out. He saw nothing but the endless blue sky and the dark floor of clouds below them.

"Over here!" Dillon shouted from the other side.

Bruce crossed the cabin and leaned his head next to Dillon's to see out his window. Another helicopter loomed in the distance behind them.

"Maybe it's just a tourist helicopter."

"Not in this air space," shouted Parker from the cockpit. "The radar must have picked us up when we got outside the Grand Canyon region.

"We were safe over the canyon," Parker further explained. "No radar there. We'd be safe anywhere if we stayed below five hundred feet. Normal radar can't pick up anything at that low altitude. But we had no choice other than to get above the rain."

A scratchy radio voice interrupted.

"This is the Federal Bureau of Investigation. Please identify yourself. Over."

Parker picked up the handset.

"This is Parker Taft, Bird's-eye View Helicopter Service. Over."

"How many passengers do you have aboard your aircraft? Over."

Parker hesitated a moment and then said, "I'm flying with a couple of friends. Is there a problem? Over."

"Please identity each of your passengers by name. Over."

The FBI helicopter was quickly gaining on them, and as it did, its unfortunate details came into view. It was dark gray with silver windows and had chrome hinges and other attachments that reflected sharply in the sun. A lump gathered in Bruce's throat as he could now make out a rack of gun barrels protruding from the undercarriage.

Dillon looked through binoculars. "There're three men aboard," he said. "Two in the cockpit and one in the backseat."

"Let me see," Bruce said and Dillon handed him the glasses.

He focused on the men, and his heart jumped. The man in the backseat was the one who had shot at them in the Grand Canyon.

"Repeat. Identify all the passengers onboard by name. Over."

"If you tell them Megan is aboard, we're history," Bruce shouted. Of this, he had absolutely no doubt.

Parker eyed Bruce for a moment, and then brought the handset to his lips. "I am licensed to carry passengers over this airspace. How do I know you are the FBI? Over."

There was no response for a beat, then, "This is the FBI, and this is your last warning. Identify each of your passengers by name. Over."

Parker stabbed the talk button on the handset. "Clarify what you mean by *last warning*? I've done nothing illegal. Over."

The tension in the cabin grew as they waited for a response.

Parker barked into the headset again. "Provide proof that you are the FBI. I see no visual—"

Suddenly a starburst of fire appeared in the sky accompanied by an ear-shattering explosion. Parker's helicopter recoiled from the blast, and Bruce was thrown to the cabin floor. His stomach lurched as the helicopter took a roller-coaster dip and began to fly out of control. The FBI chopper was blown clear out of the sky, and they were caught in the backlash of the explosion.

Cussing, Parker fought with the joystick as he tried to get the bird under control. The helicopter did a three-hundred-and-sixty-degree rotation. The engines strained.

Continuing to wrestle with the stick, Parker began to get the helicopter back on course. Yet all was not good. A strong smell of gasoline filled the cabin.

Rising to his knees, Bruce did a visual sweep of the small space. There was no structural damage that he could see. Megan was staring at the ceiling, held securely in place by the seat belts. Dillon, too, looked okay, still anchored in his seat and gawking out the window.

What happened? Why did the FBI helicopter suddenly blow up?

"My God!" Dillon cried.

Bruce looked out Dillon's window again. He expected to see stray debris, what was left of the FBI helicopter floating in the sky. Instead . . .

Several hundred feet above where the FBI helicopter had been was yet *another* helicopter. It hovered in the sky like a giant pterodactyl, wings and all.

"Who is that?"

Black smoke trailed up past the window from the wounded bottom of their helicopter, allowing Bruce only sporadic clear views of this new predator.

His stomach jumped to his throat as their helicopter once again dipped in the sky.

"I'm losing fuel pressure!" Parker shouted.

The rotors strained.

"I can't maintain altitude." Parker snorted, yanking back on the joystick. "The explosion must have severed the fuel line!"

Bruce managed to take a picture of the monster chopper just before Parker's helicopter plunged into the leaden clouds. It descended both gradually and erratically, dipping and leveling off, then plummeting again. Bruce crawled back to his seat and strapped himself in. He wondered, just how high up they were? One mile? Two miles?

"Are we going to crash?" Megan asked.

There was no response.

TWENTY-THREE

The image was surreal.

And as their helicopter soared recklessly downward, Bruce couldn't shake it from his mind: the winged chopper that had shot down the FBI helicopter.

Having grown up the son of an Air Force officer, he knew something about helicopters; at least he knew what a military helicopter looked like. And the monster he'd momentarily seen in the sky, if not itself a military helicopter, had been built by a military manufacturer.

In addition to the overhead and rear tail blades, it had rocket launchers suspended under each wing. *Rocket launchers!* And instead of a round bubble cabin, it had a sleek, rectangular-shaped fuselage, cut with sharp lines for aerodynamic efficiency. And it was black, designed for night flying. *Stealth night flying!*

Did the winged chopper shoot down the FBI to rescue us, or capture us?

Either way, their plan seemed to have backfired. *Because we're going to end up dead!*

Ever since the FBI helicopter had been blown to smithereens, Parker's helicopter had been sinking in the sky with reckless abandon. The rotors were coughing and the blades sputtering. Bruce and Dillon were strapped securely into their seats, incapable of doing anything, while Megan was lying on the bench seat gawking at the ceiling. The smell of gas lingered in the cabin. It didn't take a genius to figure out what would happen if—when—the helicopter collided with the ground.

"Do you see any trace of that winged chopper out your side?" Bruce shouted over the faltering engine.

"Lost it in the clouds!" Dillon shouted back.

The helicopter continued its sporadic nose-diving descent, making Bruce's stomach jump to his throat every few seconds. Parker cussed from the cockpit, fighting the joystick. Eventually the craft rolled into a less vertical path. Which at least, Bruce hoped, slowed its race toward the inevitable.

But soon enough the ground rose up to meet them. Parker managed the craft so they were descending somewhat parallel with the earth, like an airplane approaching a runway. The helicopter sputtered over rocky terrain, then a heavily wooded area; then they were above an open stretch of land.

"Hold on!" Parker shouted, wrestling with the controls. He had only a small window in which to set the machine down.

Bruce clutched the armrests and felt his toes curl. Sweat coated his face. He didn't understand. Didn't understand how he could crave death, yet fear it so. Then it dawned on him that this paradox was what made life so crazy: the continual fight of our fractured minds desiring one thing, yet fearing the consequence. Eat the cake. Not good for you. Buy that car. Can't afford. Take a sick day. I'll get caught. Make love. No time.

He glanced at Megan and was surprised to see her head tilted toward him, her piercing green eyes reaching out. They showed no hint of fear. Instead they held a fix glare of dedication, as if silently announcing to him, and the world, that she wasn't going down, no matter what happened. She would survive. *She was a fucking survivor!*

Suddenly the helicopter practically came to a dead halt in the air. The abrupt cessation of forward motion caused Bruce's seat belt to rip into his midsection. Megan let out a scream.

They were only about thirty feet above the ground, and for a hopeful moment, Bruce thought the helicopter might descend evenly and land on its wheels. No such luck. The chopper sputtered. Then lurched forward headlong and hit solid earth, nose first.

A shattering crash—another scream. Bruce's body flung forward. His bladder felt cleaved by the seat belt.

Then silence. He opened his eyes, gawked out the window to see the world sitting sideways. The helicopter stood upright on its nose. Then a slow creaking sound, as the chopper toppled over onto the blades, and then rocked for a few moments.

Bruce hung upside down in his seat, as did Dillon. From his perspective, he couldn't see Megan or the pilot.

But he sure the hell could still smell gas! To make matters worse, the helicopter engine hadn't stopped sputtering. The cabin was a virtual time bomb that could blow at any moment! Not a second to waste.

Some feet existed between his head and the cabin ceiling. He held his hands above him to absorb his fall. Unbuckled his seat belt. Dropped to the ceiling. Landing upside down, he quickly got his knees under him and scrambled to Megan.

She was gasping for air, being strangled by a seatbelt cutting into her throat. Her fingers frantically clutched at it, trying to find the buckle.

"Parker!" Dillon called to his friend, with no reply.

Bruce set his shoulder under Megan and pushed upward to lessen the pressure on her neck. Over her hacking and coughing, he heard her belt buckle release with a click. The weight of her upper body eased onto his back.

Another click of Dillon unbuckling his seat belt, and he too crashed onto the cabin ceiling. Turning upright, he unbuckled Megan's other two belts, releasing her from the bench seat.

"Parker!" Dillon cried out to his friend once more.

With Megan riding on top of him, Bruce could hear short breaths sputtering in his right ear.

"Let's get her out first," he told Dillon.

Dillon reached for the latch on the helicopter exit and yanked it back. Kicked the door open. The smell of half-baked gas from the straining engine streamed in from outside. Megan slid off Bruce's back and unraveled herself from the blanket. She wore only a bra and panties. Earlier, they'd removed her wet clothes to keep her warm. Bruce did a quick scan of the mangled cabin, looking for where Dillon hung them to dry, but didn't see them.

"Go," he commanded Megan.

"The pilot," she started to say.

Bruce pushed her out of the cabin into the open. "You, too," he commanded Dillon.

"But— "

"I'll get him. Now go!" Bruce shouted, surprised the cabin hadn't already burst into flames.

Dillon appeared as if he was going to argue, but then thought better of it. He grabbed the first aid kit and slithered on his belly out the door. Outside, Megan slung her arm around him. They hobbled away from the aircraft.

Bruce spun on his knees and, ignoring the pain, crawled over sharp shards of glass to the cockpit, where he found Parker still in his seat. The sight confirmed what they all seemed to know. The pilot's face was buried in the helicopter's console.

Bruce grabbed a fistful of Parker's hair and heaved his head back.

Dear God . . .

Parker's face was a bloodbath, his right eye socket a dripping void. Bruce turned away and suppressed the gag reflex in his throat.

He thought about working the body loose and pulling it from the aircraft but there wasn't time.

Wincing, he quickly framed Parker's mangled face in his camera's viewer, and snapped a picture. Knowing the power of photographs, if he made it out of this mess alive, he'd have that power to use.

Turning from the pilot to bolt, his eye caught Parker's bloodied cap lying on the ceiling. An emblem showed the American eagle with its claws perched on two rifles. It read, "National Rifle Association."

Was a gun stashed somewhere in the helicopter?

"Bruce, get out of there!" Dillon's voice funneled in from outside.

He noticed a vertical door panel in the wall next to the pilot's seat. Yanked it open.

A closet. Everything upside down was in disarray. A couple of shirts; He grabbed them. A pile of stuff on a shelf; He swept his hand over the shelf, flinging everything onto the ceiling.

A flashlight.

Federal aviation regulations book.

Bottle of aspirin.

Electric razor.

"Bruce!"

Sunglasses.

Holstered handgun!

He snatched the weapon along with the flashlight and scrambled out the cabin door, leaving a trail of blood from the razor-sharp glass digging into his palms and knees.

He launched himself through the door, got his legs under him, and made a mad dash from the wreckage. Then an earsplitting explosion and he felt his feet leave the earth as he was catapulted into the air by a hurricane of intense heat and force.

He collided with the ground and skidded on his stomach. His chin scraped over rock. He saw stars. Fought to stay conscious. Seconds later, he felt a hand tugging on his arm as Dillon helped him to his feet.

Bruce felt liked he'd been mauled by a bear. He looked down at himself to see his shirt shredded and knees bleeding. Lifting his shirt, he examined the "claw marks" on his stomach. Dozens of hairline scratches caused by ground.

"Come," said Dillon pulling on his arm. He led Bruce and Megan away from the burning furnace for about a hundred feet before a second explosion rattled the earth.

They didn't look back for another fifty feet, where they stopped and turned toward the roaring fire. Besides his body being battered and cut, Bruce bled inside. The pilot hadn't even known him and Megan, and had obviously helped only as a favor to Dillon. This was Parker's reward.

Dillon's lip quivered as he stared at the angry flames consuming his friend.

"I'm so sorry," Megan said to him.

"He was a good man. How will I explain this to his wife and kids?"

Bruce wondered if Dillon would ever have the chance to explain anything to *anyone* again. How they'd survive out here in the wilderness without drink and water, he had no idea.

"Give her a shirt, eh?" Dillon told Bruce, tilting his head toward Megan.

Staring into fire, Megan didn't seem to notice that she was half naked, wearing only her bra and panties, and her pink socks.

Bruce draped the shirt he'd taken from the cabin over her shoulder. Its tail fell to midway down her thighs. She inserted her arms in the sleeves and buttoned it up. Even with her eyes blood red from tears, she looked a hundred percent better than she had a while ago.

Dillon dug into the first aid kit, grabbed a bottle, jiggled out a couple of pills. "Take these for the pain."

Megan took the pills and forced them down her throat.

"You're a popular girl," Dillon said. "That other helicopter obviously shot down the FBI so they could get you for themselves."

The three looked skyward. "But where are they?" Bruce said.

"You can bet they're up there somewhere," said Dillon.

"And the longer we stay in the open, with black smoke billowing upward, the easier it will be for them to find us," warned Bruce.

"Where are *we*?" Megan asked, taking in the vast landscape.

"A couple of hundred miles east of the Grand Canyon on a Navajo Indian reservation in Arizona," Dillon informed her. He gazed off into the distance. "We were headed to Farmington, New Mexico. Somehow we'll have to find our way there."

"We better move before we run out of daylight," Bruce suggested.

Dillon nodded. "We'll find shelter for the night. Tomorrow we'll see if we can locate the main road leading to Farmington." He shielded his eyes and looked toward the sun. "I believe Farmington is due east. Once there, we'll find Ron Gray's operation, the place Parker was going to land. He'll help us."

"There's a wooded area that way." Bruce pointed. He could see the line of trees a few miles away and remembered passing the greenery overhead in the helicopter.

"Can you walk?" Dillon asked Megan.

She nodded.

Bruce secured the handgun he'd taken from the helicopter under what was left of his belt buckle. The three hobbled away from the blazing fire in the direction of the wooded area. As they crossed the open space, Bruce kept compulsively glancing upward. They all did. The clouds had now broken apart, offering a generous view of the sky—*and a clear view of the ground. . . from the sky.*

TWENTY-FOUR

It was early evening as Murdock Collier gazed out the twelfth-floor window of his *American Times* executive suite. Below him, New York City pulsated like some kind of living organism. Vivid memories sprang to mind—a summer evening he'd dined at Rockefeller Plaza, a holiday show at Radio City Music Hall, the times he'd strolled down Broadway at night or knelt in St. Patrick's Cathedral at midnight mass on Christmas Eve. He saw Yankee Stadium on a brilliant October afternoon— the stands rising into the blue sky filled with tiny specks of people dressed in colorful autumn clothing. Beer, hot dogs, peanuts and popcorn, pleasant odors; he could hear the crowd, too, as they roared in thunderous waves.

Murdock loved New York City. And he would miss it terribly when he was gone.

He had decided not to tell his son, Seth, of his illness until it weakened him beyond his ability to keep it a secret. The doctors said the cancer would spread quickly. He had a year at the outside. One tumor might have been operable, but two grade III tumors in his right lung and one grade II tumor in his left made surgery impossible.

Since getting the news, his quiet moments had been filled with contemplating his existence. What had he achieved in his life? What did he have of value to pass on to his soon-to-be-orphaned son?

Of course, Seth would get his father's $7.3 million estate in New Jersey, his small collection of classic cars, and the fifty-one-percent share of stock he held in *American Times*. Material things. By-products of something far more important. He realized his whole life had consisted of making money, losing it, and making it again—the same with the people in his life. They came and went. At one time, he had been married to a woman he truly loved. Now he heard from her only when the alimony check was late. The men he'd served with in World War II had

139

been his blood brothers in a quest to stop a madman from overtaking the world. *Where were they now? The one true statement concerning life is that it's just a passing parade.*

Neither money nor people last. But knowledge—knowledge can acquire money and people. Knowledge can accomplish one's goals. That's important.

After forty-six years in journalism, Murdock possessed an abundance of knowledge. And now he'd spend his final days passing that knowledge on to his over-ambitious and sometimes knuckleheaded son.

The old man shifted his gaze to the brightly lit billboard across Fifth Avenue. Earlier that day, workers had pasted on a new sign. The changing of the *American Times* billboard had been a ritual for—how long had it been? Fourteen years?

This was a banner week, he remembered. The introduction of the new advertising slogan: *"American Times Magazine. The Stories Behind the News." It took the advertising department months of brainstorming to come up with that?*

They'd told him the slogan represented their new UMP— Unique Marketing Position. They'd said it was no longer good enough to promote the magazine as being number one. They'd told Murdock that "We are the best" and "We are number one" were clichéd statements.

How things had changed.

When he'd first started in journalism, every story didn't have to be about sex, murder, or money. Most often, a solid human interest story, backed by facts, was acceptable. Murdock sighed. Forty-six years ago, the market wasn't flooded with dozens of national news programs and thousands of magazines and local newspapers. There was no talk radio, talk television, or Internet. Today, the competition was stifling. Market glut necessitated that every story have a sensationalist angle. People were numb to the news. Today, high-impact headlines were a must, even in the shortest articles. But *American Times* went beyond the quick-hitting headlines of newspapers, television, and radio. What made the magazine different was its in-depth reporting, its published insight behind every story. People couldn't get that on the nightly news. That was the *American Times* Unique Marketing Position. Maybe the new slogan wasn't so bad.

American Times Magazine. **The Stories Behind the News**.

Murdock heard the door creak open behind him. He turned to see Seth enter. Earlier, his son had called and requested that Murdock meet him at the office at this unusual hour, but he wouldn't say why. "Trust me. It's a surprise you'll like."

Now Seth plopped two pictures down on Murdock's desk. "Madeline sent us these. She's going to call any moment. You won't believe what she's on to."

Seth directed his father's attention to the first picture. It showed an FBI agent in the Grand Canyon holding a clipboard while other agents were hoisting dead bodies into wooden crates near a helicopter. Then Seth pointed to the second picture, which was a super-enlarged and rather pixilated photo of the agent's clipboard. Although it was blurry, near the top Murdock could make out a logo of a blue feather.

"Look familiar?" Seth asked.

Murdock studied it. "It looks like G. C. Overmeyer's logo."

"It is!"

"So?"

"You don't think it's strange an FBI agent has G. C. Overmeyer stationery at the crime scene?"

"Maybe his wife works at Overmeyer, or a friend. There could be a dozen reasons."

"That's what I told Madeline. But you know what a bloodhound she is. She started sniffing around and—"

The telephone rang. Murdock picked up the receiver. His secretary announced Madeline Nelan was on the line.

Seth pushed the speakerphone button. "Mad Madeline, it's me. Seth."

"I never would have guessed," an irritated voice returned. "Please don't call me that. And pick up the receiver."

"The speakerphone is okay," Seth said. "No one can hear you but my father and me."

"What's happening at the Grand Canyon, Madeline?" Murdock asked.

"Absolutely nothing. That's why I'm in Illinois."

"You're at the offices of G. C. Overmeyer?"

"Me and about fifty other reporters."

"I take it they're all holding the same photograph. What does

Overmeyer have to do with all this?"

"Anyone who owns a camcorder is here trying to answer that question. It's crazy."

"And . . . ?"

"Overmeyer's official position is they don't know anything about it."

Of course, Murdock thought.

"They have over seven thousand employees nationwide. Their PR director says they can't keep track of where their stationery ends up."

Seth leaned toward the telephone and spoke in hushed tones. "Okay, Madeline, you don't have to bury the headline. Tell him."

A low, sexy laugh bubbled forth from Madeline. It prompted another memory for Murdock—the short affair he'd had with her, years earlier. Even now, the thought awakened a male craving. He wasn't dead yet.

"Are you sitting down, Murdock?" Madeline asked.

"Yes," he lied.

"I've got a Deep Throat."

You certainly have. But then Murdock guessed she probably had something else in mind.

"Who?" he asked.

"A fellow who says the Overmeyer stationery is more than a coincidence."

"Really?"

"They weren't suicides, Murdock. Those kids were murdered."

"Your source told you this?"

"That's right."

"How does he know?"

"The guy's a chemist by trade, but he's also a closet detective. A 'Columbo' type, you know. His hobby is playing with electronic surveillance equipment. He's spent the last two years investigating Overmeyer."

"He works there?"

"No."

"Then how—"

"I'll get to that, but first, you have to understand the

connection. Overmeyer, in the main, is a marketing company. They look for new prescription drugs that might sell in the marketplace. They do this with market research. You follow?"

"Go on."

"Once Overmeyer decides on a drug, let's say something to help with acid indigestion, they hire a manufacturing lab to develop a prototype. After that, the drug goes to a testing company that does a double-blind placebo study to see if it's effective. If the drug makes the grade, then Overmeyer commissions the manufacturing lab to mass-produce it."

"Yes, yes. How's this guy involved?"

"He's the head chemist at one of the manufacturing companies Overmeyer hires for this purpose—Omnilab, Inc."

"And . . . ?"

"And he became suspicious a couple of years back because of the strange drugs Overmeyer commissioned them to develop."

"Such as?"

"Tiny tubes made out of calfskin containing antidepressant medication that can be inserted into the brains of babies to time-release the medication. Other things that, in his words, are the 'Antichrist.'"

The Antichrist?

"So he started his own little investigation of Overmeyer?"

"That's correct. He's hacked their computer network, quite illegally, and has access to their e-mails and internal memos."

"Fine. What's the connection to the Grand Canyon?"

"According to our man, people with ties to Overmeyer orchestrated the Grand Canyon murders."

Murdock lowered his bony bottom into the chair. "Who, Madeline?"

"I don't know. That's what he wants to tell us."

"Has he talked to anyone else?"

"Just your friendly *American Times* reporter. He contacted me last night."

Seth, with an asinine smile on his face, paced in front of Murdock.

"Sit," Murdock growled. Then he said to Madeline, "What does this Deep Throat know, exactly?"

"He knows who murdered them, and he knows the location of

one Jensen Reinhardt."

What?

"Where is. Reinhardt?" Murdock asked.

"Deep Throat will gladly tell us when we meet with him in person."

"Has he talked to *anyone* else?" Murdock asked again, his breathing becoming labored.

"No."

"What makes this guy legitimate?"

There was a long pause.

"Madeline?"

"If we don't move on this, he goes to *Newsweek,* or CBS, or whoever. He gave us the first shot, but we can't divulge him as our source under any circumstances—even in a court of law. It'll go down as a blind interview."

"Madeline, I've gotta know what makes him legitimate."

"I had him checked out. He's got no record, has an MS from North Carolina State, graduated third in his class. He looks like he strolled straight out of a Norman Rockwell painting. This guy is clean, and he's scared. He's got a family, so he wants to remain anonymous. He's been on a massive eavesdropping campaign, has e-mails, the works. He says when we hear the story and the facts surrounding it, we'll know it's true. Right now, he can't live with himself knowing the truth about what happened in the Grand Canyon. He's a balloon ready to burst, and I believe him. If he doesn't tell us, he's going to tell someone. This guy's for real, Murdock."

"Madeline, if we print a story the FBI doesn't yet know about, and we don't disclose our source, we could get nailed as co-conspirators in a cover-up."

"I've thought a great deal about that. It's our right under the First Amendment to print the story. We protect ourselves by disclosing the story to the FBI, but we do it after it's printed. According to Deep Throat, once the FBI learns the truth, they'll do their own investigation, and they won't care who our source is because the story will lead them to the murderers."

"Why doesn't he just go to the FBI?"

"He thinks the FBI might be in on it."

"He thinks the FBI might be in on it?" Seth chimed in.

"He doesn't know that for a fact, but he suspects there is a chance. And one more thing—he wants to be compensated for the story."

"Compensated?" Seth said. "He wants us to pay him for the story? That's unethical."

"Murdock, please," Madeline implored.

Murdock understood her implied request. She wanted him to keep Seth from interfering in their conversation. The boy didn't yet understand how *American Times* might handle this sort of situation. Normally, Murdock would never consider purchasing a news story from a non-journalist, especially a person who could indeed be fabricating the very story he was trying to sell. Yet there were exceptions. Paying for such a story wasn't unheard of, if the story could be proved to be true. And in this case, Madeline obviously thought Deep Throat's story could.

Murdock said, "Stay out of this for now, Seth." He asked Madeline, "How much does he want?"

"One million dollars."

"That's a lot of money, Madeline."

"He says when the story's printed, he'll have to leave his job and leave town with his family. He wants insurance."

"He understands I pay him nothing until after I hear his story?"

"Understood."

"We will negotiate at that time," Murdock said firmly.

"I'll tell him and hope he agrees."

This is a no-brainer. The Grand Canyon suicides were the hottest thing in the news. If this Deep Throat had something legitimate, gold dust would fill the air.

"If it works, you know who's going to be the hero in all this?" Madeline asked.

Murdock leaned back in his soft leather chair. Of course he knew who would be the hero: *American Times*, the publishing empire he'd spent most of his life building. Why else would he do it?

"'*American Times Magazine*. The Stories Behind the News,'" Murdock quoted. "And one more thing, Madeline."

"What's that?"

"This conversation never happened."

"Goes without saying," Madeline said and then hung up.

Seth was pacing the office in circles. "I can't believe you would pay for the story."

Murdock coughed. There was so much to teach his son about journalism. Murdock just hoped he would live long enough to do it.

The phone rang again. Murdock picked it up.

"It's Special Agent Pittman from the FBI," Murdock's secretary said uneasily. "He says it's urgent he talk to you."

That didn't take long. Does the FBI already know about Madeline's source? So much for an exclusive interview!

"I'll take it."

"Here he is," Nina said and made the transfer.

"This is Murdock Collier. May I help you?"

"This is Agent Pittman with the Federal Bureau of Investigation. I'm leading the investigation of the Grand Canyon suicides. Did you send a male representative to the Grand Canyon to cover the story?"

"Yes," Murdock replied and then quickly added, "but he is not one of our employees. He was hired freelance to—"

"What is his name?"

"Bruce Brackin."

"Black hair, mid-thirties, over six feet tall?"

"That sounds like him. Is he in some kind of trouble?"

"Have you had contact with Mr. Brackin in the last twenty-four hours?"

Murdock covered the receiver and looked at Seth. "Any word from Brackin in the last day?"

Seth shook his head. "Last I talked to him was Thursday."

"We talked to him three days ago," Murdock informed Pittman.

"Is he the only person your magazine sent to the Grand Canyon?""Yes. We have a girl on the story, but she's in Illinois. Can you please tell me what's going on?"

"Yesterday, Bruce Brackin shot and killed one of my agents."

TWENTY-FIVE

They had escaped from the FBI in the Grand Canyon and in the air only to end up stranded on an Indian reservation in the middle of nowhere. They'd trekked miles into a forested area, thinking it was safer under tree cover, but as nightfall threatened and they were without food or water, Bruce was starting to think they'd made a mistake. He had no trouble envisioning the three of them starving to death, never to be seen again.

Yet what choice did they have?

And what were the chances that *he*, an ex-advertising copywriter and not-quite-wannabe reporter from New York, would end up here? However, as he'd thought, it started to make sense. Ever since he'd tried to off himself a few days ago, even though he'd failed, his death wish had become woven into the karmic fabric of the universe. In essence, his desire to die took on a life of its own—and it was now playing itself out like an eighteen-wheeler racing downhill without brakes. He couldn't do a damn thing to stop it.

Trucking toward death himself without brakes didn't bother him too much, but having passengers along, namely Dillon, Megan, and the now-deceased Parker, did.

They needed a way out of this mess. But after several hours hiking, the exhaustion intensified. All they could do was rest. They settled under a large tree on the edge of a clearing. From the shaded vantage point, they would not be visible from the sky.

Dillon rubbed peroxide on cuts and bandaged lacerations on Bruce's body and extremities. Bruce adjusted his back against the scratchy bark and closed his eyes. Dillon claimed the spot to his right with Megan to his left. With luck, they'd all think clearer after some rest.

He awoke sometime later with something tugging on his arm.

"Bruce," a voice hissed. "Bruce."

"Huh?"

"Come with me."

Bruce squinted to see Megan kneeling next to him, her finger over her lips.

"I have to tell you something," she whispered.

How long had he been out? Minutes? Hours? Bruce looked to his right to see Dillon lying on the ground, sound asleep.

"Please," she whispered, continuing to pull on his arm.

"Tell me in the morning." He tried to brush her off.

"No."

Fine. Bruce slowly rose to his feet. And followed her as she led him about thirty yards into the murky woods.

"Wait here," she said, ducking behind a tree.

Bruce stood on the other side.

"Cover your ears."

Yawning, Bruce obliged. *She couldn't go alone?*

A minute later, Megan came out from the behind the tree. Bruce unplugged his ears. "Can I go back to sleep now?"

"I have something to tell you," she said, irritated.

He was so tired, and she—she didn't look so good. She was slightly bent over, nursing her right side. He'd learned to heed that extra edge on her usually edgy voice. She was going to say what was on her mind, pain or no pain.

She crouched down to the ground and leaned back against a tree. Yanking her coverlet, created from Parker's oversized shirt, under her bottom, she tucked the front shirttail between her bare legs and stared at Bruce sitting on a bulging tree root next to her.

"What's going on?"

"My memory—it's just been spilling out lost fragments of time. I remember we opened one of the time capsules."

"You opened just one? But there were. . ."

"Four time capsules," she said. "But, I remember—so clearly now. We only opened one."

He slid off the bumpy root onto the ground closer to Megan, ignoring the burning sensation in his palms and knees, and his aching muscles.

"What was in it?"

"A computer was inside," she whispered.

What? "A computer was in the time capsule?"

"I remember perfectly."

Unable to resist, he said, "Was it an Apple?"

She smirked. "Didn't look anything like our computers, no keyboard, no mouse. It was just a screen with a computer pen and writing pad attached to it."

"Did you turn it on?"

"Indeed."

"You just flipped a switch, and a five-hundred-million-year-old computer just fired up? No way."

"Must you question everything?" She sighed. "Yes, it turned on. It took a couple of days. It didn't operate on electricity."

"Then what powered it?"

"Solar energy. It had a silver plate—a solar panel—attached to its top. We believe the time capsules were buried during a period when the ancient civilization was in grave danger. They foresaw a future without technology. So they built the computer to function using only the sun as power."

The ancient civilization; Megan had spouted the words as if describing a type of people everyone already knew existed, like the *Chinese civilization*, or the *Roman civilization*. . .

"So you stuck the computer in the sun and—"

"It took exactly thirty-eight hours to start up."

"The computer wasn't damaged?"

"The time capsule kept it perfectly preserved."

He couldn't imagine how that was possible, and told her so.

"You have to think beyond the limited technology of our culture," she replied. "The vessel and time capsules were constructed of a type of metal we'd never seen before—similar to titanium, but not titanium, exactly. Each time capsule was an impenetrable compression chamber designed to protect its contents for millions of years from the extreme temperatures and pressures caused by shifts in the Earth's crust."

The tapes. They went up in a fireball with the helicopter. *Damn!* He'd been so concerned with getting out of that time bomb before it blew, he hadn't even thought of grabbing them. Now he had nothing to record Megan's memories.

"Do you remember the sun-like symbol on the vessel I told you about?" she asked.

"The yellow circle with the four lines extending out of it?"

"We referred to it as their 'icon.' It flashed on the computer screen when it powered up."

"Like a Windows logo?" It was the first thing that came into his mind.

"Well, sort of, only I doubt it represented an operating system since the icon was also on the wall of the vessel." She took a deep breath and placed her hand over her wound.

"Then what was the icon about?"

Another long breath. "We believe the icon has some deep meaning relating to their culture. After a few seconds, it disappeared, and another screen appeared with a message written in an alphabet we'd never seen before—half circles, dots, and arcs with beautiful symmetry—their language. The computer recognizing that we couldn't read the message, went into its next phase and showed a picture of the moon on the screen."

"A photograph of the moon?"

"A drawing. Every few seconds, a new picture popped up—a rock, a star, a plant, a tree, the ocean—things of nature."

Why nature? Bruce wondered.

"When a lake appeared on the screen, Jensen wrote the word *lake* on the writing pad attached to the computer. Then the word *lake* appeared on the screen, in Jensen's handwriting, next to the picture on the screen. The computer showed more drawings of nature after that—grass, leaves, flowers, a lot of fruit we'd never seen before. As pictures appeared on the screen, Jensen wrote names on the pad for all the things he recognized."

"The computer was connecting English words with the pictures?"

"It was decoding the English language so it could communicate with us. It even figured out how small words were used. After it learned the name of a tree, for example, it showed the tree falling to the ground, which prompted Jensen to write, 'The tree fell to the ground' on the writing pad. Simple. In this case, the computer learned about the words *the*, *fell*, and *to* and how they were used. It generated hundreds of such drawings, and for each one, Jensen wrote a sentence describing the action. After several hours, the computer was displaying sentences with almost one-hundred-percent accuracy."

She turned, facing him in the dark.

Wincing in pain, she said, "The last picture it showed, just after sundown, was a drawing of a man and a woman—a naked male and female. Jensen wrote 'man and woman.' It was a picture *representing the race that lived at the time.* Then it powered down."

Megan's head was already nodding an affirmative before Bruce could ask the next question:

"The picture of the man and woman, did they look anything like today's people or—"

"It could have been taken last month."

"When you turned the computer back on, did it give you a message?"

"We never turned the computer back on. The next morning I went to take photographs of Edwin Falls; that's when they were killed."

"So you don't know?" he said.

"Know what?"

"Why they buried the time capsules—the people who did it; you don't know what message, or information, or whatever, they preserved in the computer?"

"No." She stared blankly at him.

"What information do you *think* they left in the computer?"

She shrugged. "A cure for disease? How to control the weather? A political system? Technology to build weapons?" She gritted her teeth. "I don't know, but I *am* going to find out."

Bruce stared at her.

"What?" she said.

"Nothing. I just—" He didn't know what to say.

"What?"

Here was this woman half his size, and having almost just died, yet she was filled with hope and passion—passion that he could feel burning in his own chest. It made him almost ashamed of his shortcomings.

"I have to admire your persistence," he said truthfully.

Her eyes softened under the moonlight that sifted through the tree branches. He wished she'd stop staring at him.

"Thank you," she said.

"For what?"

"Saving me life."

No. No. He didn't want her thanking him. He did what any person would do in that circumstance. *Stop looking at me.*

Her face drew closer to his.

Closer . . .

He pulled his head back.

But it was too late. Perhaps their mouths touched for seconds, maybe only one, but for that brief moment he tasted her salty lips, and felt a male yearning stir inside that he hadn't felt since Rachel's death. He had no right to feel it.

He wiped the wetness from his mouth with his sleeve.

Megan's eyes fell away.

"I'm sorry," she said. "I . . . I don't know why I did that."

Suddenly a scream sprang out of the darkness.

Bruce's breath froze in his lungs.

Another scream.

Dillon!

TWENTY-SIX

Bruce and Megan rushed through the darkness toward the sound. Staying in the shadows, they got close and hunkered down behind a shrub.

Dillon wasn't next to the tree where they'd left him. Instead, he was in the clearing adjacent to it.

Under the generous light of the moon, Bruce could make out three shadowy figures wearing black, skintight bodysuits with hoods covering their heads.

What the hell?

Two of the men forced Dillon up against a tree. The third held a gun to his head.

Where did they come from? Had the winged chopper dropped them? Of course it had. . .

Two of the men wrapped a rope around the tree and then around the old man's neck, pinning him to it.

The man with the gun said something to Dillon. Dillon said something back and the man punched Dillon in the face! The old man's head snapped back and then drooped forward toward his chest, as his neck had turned to rubber. He was out.

Megan's hand landed on Bruce's thigh and her fingernails dug in.

Dillon regained consciousness. With blood trickling down his chin, his attacker brandished a knife, and started waving it demonically in the old man's face.

Bruce's pulse pounded in his ears. His mind raced for a solution, yet he knew they had to be careful. No doubt the hooded freaks were after Megan. They had to be smart. . .

What's he doing?

The black-hooded freak slowly inserted the knife blade a quarter of an inch into Dillon's bicep, while another man, with the help of the rope, held Dillon's writhing body immobile. Dillon let out a bloodcurdling scream.

"No!" Megan burst out. She didn't shout it, but was loud enough . . .

Bruce clamped his hand over her mouth.

Knifeman froze, still holding the blade in Dillon's arm. Knifeman's head rotated in their direction. The whites of his eyes peered outward from the hooded mask.

Cold sweat coated Bruce's face. The men were obviously torturing Dillon so he'd reveal Megan's whereabouts. Or maybe they assumed she was watching, and the torture would lure her in. Bruce clutched the graphite handle of the pilot's gun lodged under his belt buckle. He slipped the firearm out, held its barrel vertically to his lips, and whispered, "Shhhhhhh."

Megan nodded.

"You stay here," he said. "If anything happens to me, run."

"But—"

"No. Don't show yourself under any circumstances. We know it's you they're after."

Bruce reached behind his neck, grabbed the camera strap, pulled the Nikon over his head, and handed it to her. "Hang on to this. It's your proof."

Megan took the camera and embraced Bruce's arm. "Be careful."

He nodded, turned from her and gulped in some air. The leaves blanketing the ground would be a problem. He eased forward, slipping each foot under the dead foliage so it wouldn't make a sound. He inched toward the clearing with cat-like form—something he had learned in martial arts classes years earlier. He crouched behind a tree ten yards out and assessed the situation.

Dillon was talking to Knifeman. Bruce strained to hear, but still wasn't close enough to make out his words.

Bruce noted that all three men had guns, but now only the man who was at a distance from Dillon had his drawn from his holster. He stood guard, his eyes scanning the perimeter of the clearing.

Bruce tightened his grip on the pistol. He had a clear shot at the guard. But if he fired, he might only have time to get off one shot before the others would react by killing Dillon.

Bruce saw no alternative but to hang low and hope an opportunity would present itself to make a move.

With knifeman's blade still inserted in Dillon's arm, the

hooded freak was talking to him. It was obvious he was telling Dillon if he didn't reveal the whereabouts of Megan he'd slice his arm open.

Bruce craned his neck to look behind him. He could see only a few feet into the darkness. Even if he were to somehow rescue Dillon, where would we go? *Who's to say an army of black-hooded freaks aren't lurking out there?* He returned his attention to the clearing to see. . .

Knifeman's blade digging deeper into Dillon's arm! Blood spurted into the night air, and a red river trailed down the old man's quivering limb.

Bruce started shaking with rage as he watched knifeman's blade, so, very, very, slowly, carve its way down toward Dillon's elbow. The old man's skin parted like a bloody steak.

Then knifeman turned toward the man standing watch and said something to him, which prompted the man to holster his gun, reach into his pocket, and produce a little black case. Watchman moved toward Dillon, and for the first time all three men had their guns holstered—with their backs to Bruce.

Blood trailed the knife as it continued to move slowly down Dillon's trembling bicep. The old man bit his lip and swiveled his tortured eyes toward Bruce, as if he knew Bruce was watching. Without any outward signs on Dillon's face, Bruce still got his message: He couldn't hold out much longer, and Bruce and Megan should escape.

No way. . .

Bruce released the safety on the gun, rushed forward, and leaped into the clearing.

TWENTY-SEVEN

Hoboken, New Jersey

Peter Brackin awoke to a loud sound.

Beep . . . beep . . . beep . . .

Disoriented, he sat up in bed in the darkness.

Rubbing the sleep from his eyes, he quickly discerned it was the security alarm. Not the *main* security alarm, but the *secondary* system that monitored the electronic outlets in the house, designed to protect against power surges.

He parted the window blinds with his fingers and peered outside to see the streetlights were out. Yet it wasn't raining. No lightning. No thunder. Gazing skyward, he saw stars, not a cloud in the sky. Not a hint of a storm out there.

Maybe a storm knocked out a power grid a few miles away?

He yawned. *Damn.* He'd have to turn off the surge protector alarm in his office, all the way at the other end of the house. He slid into his wheelchair and pushed himself to the bedroom door, where he sat for several moments, listening, before venturing into the dark hallway.

Beep . . . beep . . . beep . . .

Could an intruder have set off the alarm? After all, he was a jeweler, and always had a few thousand dollars' worth of jewelry in the safe. But a burglar would've triggered the main security alarm from a window or door being forced open, not the surge protector—unless the burglar cut off the electricity . . . but on the entire block?

For a few thousand dollars? No way.

Nevertheless, Peter listened intently to the silence between each beep of the alarm, trying to detect any unusual noises. It was an old house, and one could hardly walk anywhere in it without the wooden floors creaking.

Beep . . . beep . . . beep . . .

Satisfied, he pushed his wheelchair into the dark hallway,

rolled down it, and swung into the dining room. His right hand moved the wheel of his chair forward while his left ran along the edge of the dining table, using it as a guide in the darkness. The oak floor moaned under the rubber wheels.

Beep . . . beep . . . beep . . .

He reached another hallway entrance, swung into it, and traveled a few feet toward his office.

Then something grabbed him.

Two gloved hands ringed his neck. Instinctively, Peter launched his chair forward with all his might, ramming the footrests into the intruder's shins. But the impact only caused his assailant to tighten his grip, sealing off all the air from Peter's lungs. Desperately clawing at the intruder's hands, Peter tried to lessen the pressure. The fingers were like iron thongs bearing down on his Adam's apple. A couple of seconds more, and he'd be out.

Beep . . . beep . . . beep . . .

He remembered the shelf built into the hallway wall. On it were picture frames, vases, and other knickknacks.

Can't breathe!

In desperation, Peter flung his right hand toward the wall, clawing for anything to use as a weapon. Objects crashed to the floor. His fingertips felt something solid. The baseball trophy he'd won as a kid. A batter standing on a solid marble base. He clasped the batter in his fist. . .

Hefted the trophy and swung the marble base toward the monster in front of him. A fine vibration traveled up his arm, like a bat connecting with a baseball. Yes, he remembered that beautiful feeling from all those years ago. Warm blood sprayed Peter's face. The grip loosened on his throat. The intruder slumped onto the floor in front of the wheelchair. *Homerun!*

Peter gasped for air. "Take that you shit head!"

Did he kill the man, or just knock him unconscious? Either way, he had to call the police fast. He tried to wheel around the body, but there wasn't enough space in the narrow hallway. Then he heard loud stomping footsteps from somewhere else in the house.

Peter dove out of the chair, hit the floor, snaked over the intruder's body, and hauled himself down the hallway using just his arms and shoulders, his legs dragging uselessly behind him.

He heard a crash.

He glanced over his shoulder and saw the murky outline of a dark figure rising from the floor. The new intruder had tripped over the wheelchair in the dark.

These aren't neighborhood burglars. What in God's name do they want from me?

His office was only a few feet away. Had to get there, lock the door, call 911. His palms frantically slapped the wooden floor as he dragged his body down the hallway.

He cursed his crippled legs. In a single instant, the years of counseling and therapy he'd received dissolved. Love your challenge. Don't be a victim. Accept your condition. Love it. Use it. Screw it—if he had legs he could run. If he didn't have MS he'd know jujitsu like Bruce did, and he'd wrap this new intruder into a ball and stuff him into the garbage can out back. If he didn't have MS. Why him? *Why are these men in my house?*

His eyes had adjusted to the dark enough to see the office door was open. He slid into the room and went to slam the door behind him. But a foot snaked through at the last moment, preventing the door from closing all the way.

Peter tried to muscle the door shut, but was losing the battle with the man pushing against him on the other side. The door inched open, slowly shoving Peter's body backward along the wooden floor.

"What do you want from me?" Peter shouted.

No answer. What did he expect? Peter pivoted his head to see behind him. Spotted the electrical cord hanging from his workbench. Stretched his arm toward it.

Can't. . .quite. . .reach. . .

But the goon on the other side kept pushing. Inching Peter closer. . . closer.

Peter lunged for the cord. Only managed to knock it farther out of reach. The ever-opening door slid him even closer. Arm out. Fingers stretching.

Closer . . .

Got it!

Peter yanked the cord, and his Black & Decker soldering gun flew off the bench. He reeled it in and gripped the trigger with a sweaty finger. The tool fired up, its tip glowing red in the darkness.

The intruder was unrelenting. Now his leg was entirely through the gap, wedged between the door and the frame.

Peter stabbed the fiery tip of the soldering gun against the intruder's calf.

"Take this, shit-for-brains!"

A coil of smoke rose from the burning pant leg. The crimson tip sunk into flesh like a searing knife into butter. A high-pitched scream arose.

A woman!

She tried to yank back her leg, but Peter pushed all his weight against the door, wedging it solidly in place. He directed the glowing red tip at her knee this time. Thrust the steel into her flesh. Skin sizzled. The pungent smell of burning flesh stung his nostrils.

Beep . . . beep . . . beep . . .

The leg squirmed like a dying snake, trying to withdraw. Peter wouldn't allow it. He stabbed the other side of the knee. Another scream. He waited a beat then eased up on the pressure, allowing her to wiggle her leg back through the doorway. He slammed the door shut, reached up, and twisted the deadbolt into place.

He wasted no time. Dragged himself to his desk, found the telephone, and punched in 911.

The phone was dead!

Of course. They cut all the electric *and* the phone wires.

He heard other voices.

Then a loud crash against the door.

What do these people want from me? Who are they?

The answer had become frightfully clear. He, Peter Brackin––the conspiracy theory guru—had become too visible. On his Internet site, www.conspiracyrat.com, he'd taken thorough steps to ensure his identity remained a secret. He used a fake name in his blogs, and had purchased the domain name under a fake identity. But the recent conspiracy meetings he'd held at the library—these must have exposed him. He'd thought that addressing a local audience wouldn't be a problem. After all, he was a fucking nobody! A cripple with a big mouth. But now they had arrived—arrived to shut him up for good.

Beep . . . beep . . . beep . . .

He watched as a sledgehammer punched a hole in the office door. Then an arm snaked through the hole and reach for the deadbolt.

Peter tried to attack the hand with the soldering iron, but was too slow.

Two people wearing black masks barreled into the office.

The larger of the two pointed a rifle at Peter and pulled the trigger.

Beep . . . beep . . . beep . . .

TWENTY-EIGHT

Bruce jumped into the clearing and thundered a gunshot into the air.

"Freeze! I'll shoot the first motherfucker who moves!"

He panned the gun from one man to the next, hoping the weapon didn't shake out of his nervous hand.

"Arms in the air!"

With their backs to him, the hands of the three men slowly rose up over their heads. Dillon slumped against the tree as he was released. Only the rope around his neck held him upright.

"Turn *slowly* toward me," Bruce ordered.

The three hooded freaks complied. One man was still holding the small black case in his fist. Bruce ordered him to throw it to the ground. The man complied. Bruce then focused on the freak with the knife in his fist. Blood dripped from the blade onto his hooded head.

"Toss the knife to the ground in front of you."

Knifeman didn't budge. He defiantly held onto the blade.

A trickle of sweat roll down Bruce's face into his right eye.

"Put down your gun, and no harm will come to you," Knifeman said calmly.

Bruce glanced at Dillon's bloodied arm. Had they planned to cut off his only arm?

Knifeman seemed to smile beneath the hood.

"If you do not drop your gun, we will all draw *our* guns at once. We will kill you and then your friends. Tell us where Eastwood is, and no harm will come to you."

Sweat dripping into his eye, Bruce blinked frantically.

"Are you prepared to die?" Knifeman asked, anticipating the upper hand, and sounding like he was reading a damn script. His black eyes glimmered behind the hood.

Bruce ran the scenario over in his mind. The three of them, spread out, would draw their guns and fire. He'd have a second, maybe two, to react. There was only one thing he could do. He inched closer to Knifeman, and aimed the gun directly at his chest.

"You're right, asshole. I'll only have time to get off a couple of shots. And the bullets are going straight to your heart. The question is, are *you* prepared to die?"

Even under the hood, Bruce could see the self-righteous smirk drain from Knifeman's face. Or was it his imagination? With the sweat in his own eye, everything was a blur.

"Now," Bruce barked at the men, "using two fingers of your left hand, take your guns from your holsters and toss them to the ground."

Knifeman tossed his gun to the ground.

Bruce could hardly believe it was working. Knifeman had been so much in control before. He'd seemed like an automaton.

"You, too!" he barked at the others.

Each slowly removed a gun from his shoulder holster and dropped it to the ground as directed.

Bruce took the opportunity to rub the sweat from his eye.

"Hoods off," he ordered.

They looked at each other, seeming to share the same thought.

Bruce directed the gun at Knifeman's feet and pulled the trigger. A bullet plugged the ground, just inches from his toes.

Knifeman slowly lifted his black hood. The others followed suit.

They all had bald, shaved heads, as if they had been cloned from the same DNA strand.

What in God's name am I dealing with here?

He ordered the men to lie face down with their arms and legs spread-eagled. They did exactly as he said. It was almost too easy. He wondered if they had something up their sleeves.

Then he heard a rustling. His eyes strained to see behind him without taking the gun off the men.

Megan had entered the clearing, running toward them. Hadn't he told her not to show her face? *Ah.* Bruce quickly returned his attention to the men.

She scooped up the guns from the ground.

"Remove the bullets," Dillon said, weakly.

She nervously fiddled with the guns while the men watched

her, like wolves eyeing a lamb. She figured out how to remove the clips for each gun and then tossed them into the woods behind the tree where Dillon was tied.

Then she dropped the weapons, untied Dillon, and started tending to his bloody arm. "I have a hanky in my back pocket," he told her.

"Your life is no longer your own," Knifeman calmly said to Megan. "Surrender now, and no harm will come to you."

"Where is Dr. Reinhardt?" Megan asked while she wrapped the handkerchief around Dillon's arm as a tourniquet to stop the bleeding.

Knifeman didn't answer.

Megan finished tying the knot, left Dillon, and stormed over to Knifeman.

"I said, where is Dr. Reinhardt?" She stood over him with her fists clenched.

"Get back, Megan," Bruce said. "I'll handle this."

She spit on Knifeman, and crossed back to Dillon's side.

"Who are you?" Bruce asked the man.

"Cooperate, and no harm will come to any of you," Knifeman said.

"No harm? You just sliced his arm!"

"He did not cooperate."

Bruce had had it. He dug his foot into Knifeman's back between his shoulder blades and pressed the barrel of the gun against his head.

"I'll blow your fucking brains out if you don't tell me who you're working for."

"Shoot me, and I will be replaced by two."

Bruce pushed the gun even harder against the man's skull. It ripped open the skin, producing a trickle of blood.

Knifeman was unaffected.

"There is not a city or country in the world where you will be safe. Your only hope is to give up now," Knifeman said.

"The black case," Dillon interrupted. "There, on the ground."

Megan picked up the small leather box and opened it. Inside were three syringes filled with clear liquid.

"I think it might be Sodium Pentothal," Dillon said. "Truth serum."

Megan removed a syringe from the box and, without the slightest hesitation, stabbed the needle into Knifeman's shoulder.

Bruce held his breath to see what would happen. Nothing. Knifeman looked exactly the same. Bruce asked, "What's the name of the organization you work for?"

"No name."

"What is your name?"

"Smith. Gary Smith," Knifeman answered.

Was he telling the truth?

"What do you want to do with Megan?"

"Apprehend her."

"And bring her where?"

Knifeman started to say something but gagged on his words. He squirmed on the ground as if he were in pain. Even stranger, the other two men on the ground reacted in exactly the same fashion.

"Where were you going to take Megan Eastwood?" Bruce demanded.

Incomprehensible sounds poured out of Knifeman's mouth like verbal vomit. A sheen of sweat coated his bloody head. He seemed to be two people—one person who tried to answer the question and another who was being invisibly electrocuted just thinking about it. The others squirmed simultaneously.

Bruce changed the question. "What would you do with Megan?"

"Observe Megan Eastwood," he said robotically.

"Observe her for whom?"

There was no response.

Bruce dropped down next to Knifeman and dug the gun barrel into the back of his neck.

"Who do you work for? Who?"

Knifeman went into some sort of seizure, flopping on the ground like a beached fish. His head turned so red, Bruce thought it was going to explode.

"Wait!" Dillon said. "I think I know what's happening here. He answered the questions about himself and about Megan. But every time you ask him *who* he works for or where they're located, he reacts like that. They all do."

No kidding. "But why?"

"Their subconscious minds have been programmed. I think."

"What do you mean?"

"When he tries to talk, he feels pain. These men have been implanted."

"Implanted?"

"They've been mentally programmed—either subconsciously or through a computer chip implanted in their brains—to destroy themselves or their interrogator if questioned about their associations. It's right out of the CIA's brainwashing manual."

Dillon asked Knifeman, "Why can't you tell us the name of the organization you work for?"

"Initiation rites."

"Name one person in your organization, just one."

Knifeman and the other two went into another fit.

"I understand you can't say the name of the organization," Dillon said, "but you must think of it in certain terms. When you think of your organization, what comes to mind?"

"Friends of Earth."

"Are they a branch of government?" Dillon asked.

Knifeman hissed like a rattlesnake.

"Those who govern men are not those who are elected." His voice rose in intensity. "We do not live in a world of ideologies. The world is business, always has been."

"What's he talking about?" Megan asked.

Dillon was pale, his skin sickly white. He sighed. "I have no idea."

"Enough of this," Bruce said. "We have to get Dillon to a doctor."

"What about them?" Megan asked. "We don't have anything to tie them up with."

She was right. Then Bruce remembered something he'd once seen in a movie. He could tie them up with their clothes.

"Strip," he ordered the men.

Suddenly one of the two other men rose to his feet. Panic surged through Bruce. He aimed his gun at the standing man.

"Get back down."

The man stood calmly, hands in the air, showing no threat.

"I want to help you. I will answer your questions."

With Bruce's attention diverted to the man standing in front of him, Knifeman spun his body on the ground, flinging his legs into Bruce's and sweeping him off his feet. Bruce landed flat on his back.

Megan gasped as Bruce hit the ground. She knew he wasn't much of a fighter, having wrestled the snot out of him herself. He was going to need help. Fast.

But Knifeman was already in full control. He quickly straddled Bruce and sat astride his chest. Then he reached for the gun in Bruce's right hand.

The standing man dropped into a crouched position, ready to help Knifeman if needed. But it was the other man with whom Megan was concerned. He made a mad dash away from them, out of the clearing and into the woods. She could do nothing to stop him.

Back to Bruce, Megan watched as he seemed to purposely allow Knifeman to grab the wrist of his gun hand. *What was he doing?* But just as Knifeman took hold, Bruce grabbed Knifeman's wrist with his free hand, threw his hips upward, and twisted his body so that he somehow ended up on top of Knifeman.

Now having the top position, Bruce shoved the gun into his pants pocket and, with his mouth set in grim fury, pounded Knifeman's face with both fists.

Megan couldn't believe her eyes. Bruce seemed to be taking some sick pleasure in beating the man's face. Bruce continued to pummel Knifeman. And Bruce was . . . was he . . .

Laughing?

The thought struck her that Knifeman was the victim and Bruce was the mad man. She never could have imagined. . .

The standing man moved toward the fight, ready to pounce on Bruce.

"I'm getting the bullets," Megan heard Dillon say. Out of the corner of her eye, he staggered behind the tree into the wooded area where Megan had earlier tossed them.

Still on the ground, Bruce stopped punching long enough to notice what Dillon had done. Then Bruce quickly snatched Knifeman's arm. He swung his body perpendicularly so his legs were over Knifeman's face and chest. With Knifeman's arm

166

extended between his legs, Bruce jerked the arm straight outward and down toward his own chest, hyper-extending it.

Megan heard the loud crack of bone breaking. Knifeman let out a high-pitched scream.

The other man dove at Bruce like a torpedo. But Bruce saw him coming. Twisted out of the line of fire and kicked the man in the side of the head as he went flying by.

The man rose to his feet to charge Bruce a second time, but Bruce had retrieved the gun from his pocket. Two shots exploded. The man's body jerked back, but he kept trudging forward, growling like a bear. Bruce fired two more shots, and the man went limp. He finally collapsed, first to his knees and then facedown.

Bruce jumped to his feet and spun like a trained solider, the gun still in his hand.

Megan stood not ten feet from him, gawking, frozen in disbelief.

A voice bellowed behind them. "I'll shoot him!"

Megan spun on her heel to see the third man standing in the shadows behind the tree holding a gun to Dillon's head. Her eyes shot to the ground where she'd earlier placed the weapons and realized he had grabbed one before running from the clearing. Once he reached the wooded area, he must have circled around behind the tree to the bullets Megan had thrown there. But did he actually find them? Was the gun loaded? He couldn't have found a clip in the foliage that quickly in the dark. *Could he?*

"Toss your weapon over here beyond the tree, or he's dead," the voice ordered.

Megan's eyes met Bruce's. *Was he bluffing?* They were caught in the open. If the man wasn't bluffing, and Bruce didn't surrender his gun, the man would put a bullet in Dillon's head.

Bruce didn't hesitate. He tossed the gun to the ground near the tree. As the freak reached for the weapon, he momentarily removed the gun from Dillon's head.

"Run! Now!" Dillon shouted. Then the old man, now functionally armless—who instantly became Megan's hero—pounced on the man. But the attempt was futile. The man had already scooped up the gun.

Megan knew Dillon's life was about to end, and they were

helpless to stop it. But the old man had bought them a few seconds. If they didn't take advantage of his ploy, it would be in vain.

Bruce grabbed Megan's hand and pulled her from the clearing into the woods.

Running, she heard something above them. Looked skyward, through a fissure in the overhanging branches, she saw the faint underbelly of a looming black helicopter. But there was no roar from its engine, no loud churning of whirling blades. She detected only a slight *whoosh* of air, not unlike the hum of a large household fan.

Bruce also saw the helicopter. "What the hell?" He pulled on her arm. "Come on!"

Once out of the clearing, she heard two gunshots behind them, and her knees buckled. Bruce slowed down just enough to haul her back to her feet. The gun blast rang in her ears and exploded in her heart. She stumbled forward as her mind questioned what they'd just done. Should they have at least tried to overpower the freak? So what if they got killed? At least Dillon would have lived. Yet if they had stayed, those in the helicopter would have captured them, and the truth of what happened at Re's Cavern would probably forever remain a secret. The time capsules would never be found. Nor would Jensen.

She became aware of Bruce dragging her away from the clearing, the constant strain on her arm, her legs awkwardly falling forward. Her side burning. . . burning.

"Stay with me," he commanded. "Stay with me!"

It was as if his will had entered her body. Megan found herself running in stride with him. They pushed deeper into the woods, led by nothing but their instincts. The dark forest was void of any sound other than the crackling of leaves and twigs underfoot. They had no choice but to progress slowly, cautiously, as they didn't know what kind of terrain might lie ahead of them. They didn't even know where they were going.

They ventured farther into the dark, constantly glancing upward to ensure they stayed beneath the protective overhanging branches, hoping they weren't visible from the sky.

TWENTY-NINE

Peter Brackin smelled something awful yet familiar.

It was of great importance to him that he identify the smell. He was blind, deaf, and immobile, so his sense of smell was all he had.

A cloth was wrapped around his head, covering his eyes. His mouth was taped shut with duct tape—he recognized it by the smell. His hands were tied tightly behind his back. So tight that both of his hands were numb. His ankles, too, were tied. To top it off, they had plugged up his ears. The only sounds he heard were his own breathing and the pounding of his heart.

Peter was scared. He felt sick to his stomach, and he had a horrendous headache. He sniffed. Beyond the duct tape it smelled like newly dry-cleaned clothes, only a hundred times stronger. He knew he was traveling because he felt the continual swaying sensation of motion.

The last thing he remembered was fighting with an intruder in his house and locking himself in his office. They had crashed through the office door. There had been two of them, both wearing black hooded masks. Goddamn masks! One pointed a gun and fired. It happened so fast there was barely a moment to register that he was about to die.

Yet here he was, alive and breathing. At least, he *hoped* he wasn't dead. The only thing he could figure was he'd been shot with a tranquilizer gun.

How long was I out? Minutes? Hours? Where are they—the conspirators—taking me? Why didn't they kill me? Maybe they didn't want any blood spilled in the house. Maybe they are going to dump me in a river or bury me in the ground . . .

He was scared.

Don't they have better things to do, like killing a few million people through ethnic cleansing programs, or putting the finishing touches on their new world central bank building? That

169

smell. The thought struck him that formaldehyde was used in dry cleaning.

That was it. Formaldehyde. What else was formaldehyde used for? Carpet, wood bonding, embalming.

Embalming? They're going to embalm my body! Peter fought to steady his nerves.

The swaying motion stopped. His heart drummed in his ears. Minutes ticked by. A clanking sound. Then he felt two hands grab him by his collar. He tried to scream, but nothing came out.

The hands dragged him forward where yet more hands mauled him. They ripped the mask off his face.

A white flash exploded in his eyes. Then another flash. And yet another.

He was still blinded, not by the mask, but by the exploding white light. *Pictures?*

The flashes stopped, and then three forms materialized in front of him.

"What do you want with me?" he asked, trying to blink the light out of his eyes. But his words were just muffled grunts through the duct tape.

They wore black masks. Their heads turned to each other. The tallest of the three removed a long knife from inside his left sleeve and stepped toward Peter.

THIRTY

Why? Megan asked herself for the hundredth time. *Why hasn't the black helicopter tracked us down? Or has it followed us for miles through the black forest, invisible and silent in the night sky, and we simply didn't know it? Is it looming overhead at this very moment, aware of our location, waiting for the right time to deliver more black-masked freaks to capture us?*

She and Bruce had traversed the woodlands, not knowing where they were going, only that they had to keep on. Finally, they reached the edge of the wooded area and saw a group of small farmhouses and stables.

The painkillers Megan took earlier in the evening had long since worn off, and stumbling, she felt unable to continue walking, not even another few steps. Bruce wrapped his arm around her waist.

They chose the nearest stable, crept a hundred yards to its bulky door, slipped in, and gingerly moved past two horses. While scanning the interior, they found a ladder leading to the loft. Bruce gingerly helped her up the ladder; where they huddled on the scratchy bed of hay near the open window.

Megan guessed it would be sun-up in a couple of hours. They were in dire need of a plan. But who could predict what would happen next? At least they could count their blessings that they found some semblance of shelter. She could ease the pain in her stomach by not moving and they could get some sleep before moving on.

A dim ray of moonlight funneled in through the stable window. Bruce sat with his back against the wall, his hair a tangled mess, and the muscles in his arms sagging with fatigue. She remembered how he had moved like a panther over the man in the clearing—a much larger man—and how he had bloodied the man's face and broken his arm.

She reminisced about the first time she had seen Bruce at the press conference, looking and sounding so self-assured, yet so

very insecure. Independent, yet irresistibly vulnerable. Then
again, she recalled how he had pulverized the black-hooded man,
and found herself relishing the moment. Megan Eastwood, a
member of Greenpeace, a person who had spent three summers
doing volunteer work at the Cook County animal shelter finding
homes for lost and abused dogs and cats. Yes, that Megan
Eastwood. She was turned on sexually and emotionally at the
sight of Bruce pounding the freak's face and hearing that freak
scream.

And now Bruce clenched his fists in the muted light as if
replaying the struggle in his mind as well. Megan could see the
veins in his forearms start to swell.

He suddenly looked at her as if she had called his name
aloud. But she hadn't.

"You should get some sleep," she said softly. "I'll keep
watch. I can't sleep anyway."

He nodded.

She still lamented over what had happened to Dillon. But she
refused to wallow in it, for if she allowed herself an instant to
indulge, she would become an inert puddle of grief. Now, as
with every other moment since finding her co-workers dead, she
had to muster enough strength to continue.

She gazed out the window at the silver moon and allowed
herself a moment of reprieve. As she now thought about it, the
fact that *they* had destroyed the FBI helicopter and then came
after them—after *her*—was a good sign. It meant *they* needed
her. And that could only mean one thing: Jensen was still alive,
and *they*—whoever they were—had the time capsules.

Why *they* needed her was an aspect of her involvement that
she hadn't told Bruce about: an aspect she had remembered only
hours ago, when the last of her memory had returned. She knew
they wouldn't give up until they got her. Yet she couldn't allow
it. She had to find Jensen and the time capsules herself, without
being taken prisoner. She just had to.

She tried to get comfortable on the hay-strewn floor. She was
still wearing only the shirt Bruce had given her, and her legs
were chilled. If she and Bruce huddled together, his body heat
would . . . She pushed the thought from her mind. She shouldn't
have tried to kiss him earlier. *Stupid. Really stupid.*

The light of a new day dawned. Sounds came from nearby. Megan heard a door slam. Then voices. People talking.

Her mind sprang alert from a light sleep. She was sitting upright, leaning against the wall of the stable next to the cool, open window. Quietly, she repositioned her body and craned her neck to look out. In the drab morning light, her eyes focused on a couple exiting the back door of the house. Laughing loudly, they bounded down the porch steps and strolled toward the stable where she and Bruce had been sleeping. A cold shiver ran up her spine as she heard the bulky stable door creak open below them. Horses neighed, and hooves stomped the floorboards.

Lying on the floor, Bruce awoke. His sleepy eyes focused on Megan. She jerked her finger to her lips for him to stay quiet.

The sound of horse hooves continued to pound the stable floorboards as the minutes passed. Then the hooves fell into a rhythm; were the animals being led out of the stable? Bruce crawled to Megan's side. Through the window, they watched the couple leave the stables, horses in tow, and head toward the open pasture where they mounted and rode off.

"Let's get the hell out of here," Bruce said, pulling Megan to her feet.

She became dizzy and nearly passed out as blood drained from her head.

He slid his hands under her armpits and pushed her body against the wall, preventing her from wilting to the floor.

Megan's head drooped on his shoulder. She was so tired. And famished. His arms slipped all the way under her arms and wrapped around her back.

"Let your weight fall on me," he said with his body pressed against hers.

She waited a moment for her head to clear. Then she waited another moment, allowing the warmth of his body to permeate hers. Finally she lifted her head. His face was inches from hers, his eyes crystal and alert now.

"We have to hurry," he said and unraveled his arms from around her.

Favoring her right side, Megan followed Bruce over the hay-strewn floor to the ladder and mounted the rungs after him as

173

they made their way down. Before leaving the stables, they stood in the shadow of the doorway and peeked outside to assess their surroundings. The stable was situated behind a large, three-story white house where a silver RV and a Dodge Ram were parked in the driveway,

"Are we on a Navaho Indian reservation?" Bruce asked. "That's what Dillon told us, right?"

"Yeah," Megan muttered. Dillon had told them that. But who knew? She hadn't gotten a good enough look at the couple to tell what ethnic group they belonged to. The ranch obviously didn't fit Bruce's preconceived idea of American Indian life.

"Do you think anyone else is in there?" he asked.

The house looked still enough from the outside, Megan thought, but there was no way of knowing if anyone was inside. Blinds covered all the windows.

"What are you thinking?" she asked.

Bruce's eyes shifted to the cars.

"I'm thinking we can't exactly walk to the nearest town, and I don't expect a taxi cab will be coming our way anytime soon."

"We can't steal a car."

"You got a better idea?"

She didn't. And he was right: the way she felt, there was no way she could walk any distance at all.

"You check to see if the keys are in either of them," he said. "I'll look in the house."

Bruce bolted from the stables toward the backdoor.

Megan cautiously crossed the driveway to the cars. She checked the RV first and found it was locked. However, the Dodge Ram was open, and she slipped inside. Checked the ignition. No keys. She glanced above the visor and in the glove compartment. Nothing. A screen caught her eye on the console. She looked back toward the house. Bruce had managed to open a window and was slithering through it headfirst.

Megan glanced nervously around. There were no signs of life anywhere other than a few squirrels scurrying about gathering breakfast. The nearest homes in sight were across a field, maybe a half-mile away.

Moments later, Bruce exploded out the backdoor waving his fist proudly in the air. He scampered up to the Ram and jingled a set of keys in Megan's face. She quickly slid to the passenger's seat, and he jumped in. He started the truck and backed out of the driveway.

"Wait," Megan said. "We have to get the address."

"Why?"

She picked up the GPS remote on the center console, found the power button, and turned it on. The screen lit up.

"Nice," Bruce said.

"Mail," Megan suggested.

"Right." Bruce jumped back out of the Ram, ran to the mailbox on the porch, grabbed an envelope and ran back. "We're in Shonto, Arizona," he said breathlessly, looking at a promotion for a satellite dish company.

Megan punched the city name into the unit and selected GET MAP. A detailed color map filled the screen with a red circle showing Shonto. Their original designation had been Farmington, New Mexico, which, according to the map, was one hundred and seventy miles east.

"It's too far to drive in a stolen car," she said.

"We'll have to figure it out as we go. We gotta to get out of here, before they come back."

Bruce threw the car in gear and pressed on the accelerator.

Driving over the bumpy, gravel road that lead away from the house, Megan had an idea. She zoomed out on the map until it showed Colorado. The reason they had been headed to Farmington in the first place was because Parker had a friend with a helipad where they could have landed. Although Megan remembered the man's name, Ron Gray, neither Bruce nor she personally knew him, so trying to find out where he lived and paying him a visit didn't make much sense.

She had a different place in mind. Not long after graduating from college, she had struck up a relationship with a Chicago architect who had a vacation home in Durango. Megan had spent a week there with him last fall. She happened to know he had a job in Moscow, and his house was now empty for the summer; she also knew the lockbox combination and security code to get in. She punched Durango into the GPS unit. It was a little over two hundred miles away from their current location. If she and Bruce were to make it there, they could safely hide out, write the article for *American Times* magazine, and decide what to do next.

But Durango was even farther away than Farmington. She looked for the nearest city to Shonto most likely to have rent-a-car stores. Page, Arizona? It was about sixty miles west of them, in the opposite direction of Durango, but she saw no choice but to head there first.

She pushed the MENU button on the GPS remote, and then GET INFO. A variety of lists appeared on-screen for Page, from parks to hospitals to hotels—and yes, four car rental agencies.

She told Bruce her idea about driving to Durango via Page. He was nodding his head. "Yeah. Sounds good."

Once away from the house and on the street Bruce stopped at the first parked car he saw and switched license plates with it. They spent the next hour driving to Page, compulsively looking behind the Ram, expecting a posse of highway patrol to arrive any minute. But they never did.

In Page, Bruce first stopped at a Bank of America and withdrew a thousand dollars cash. They rented a Ford Taurus at an Avis dealer and dumped the Ram on a secluded street a few miles north of town. Next stop, hopefully, was Durango.

When finally headed toward their new destination, Megan leaned the passenger seat back until it was almost horizontal and positioned her head so she could see out the window. But instead of sleeping, she just stared into the blue sky for the longest time. She kept expecting to see a black helicopter, hovering. Why had they been allowed to escape?

THIRTY-ONE

Madeline Nelan and Murdock Collier met Deep Throat at Bernstein's, a small deli in Greenwich Village. The three huddled together at a round table in the corner. Deep Throat, who claimed to know both who was behind the Grand Canyon murders and the whereabouts of Dr. Reinhardt, had insisted they meet in a public place.

"It's safer here than in our own living rooms," he whispered.

His real name was Charles Gabaree. He was short and portly with a large round face. He wore tortoiseshell eyeglasses, sweated profusely, and had an irritating habit of loudly smacking his lips when he was thinking. Murdock didn't like him right from the get-go.

"Try to look like ordinary customers," Gabaree said as the waitress approached.

Madeline ordered a garden salad with lemon wedges, Murdock a bagel with lox and cream cheese, and Gabaree a corned beef sandwich with chicken dumpling soup.

When the waitress left, Madeline poked PLAY on her micro-recorder with a red-tipped forefinger. She leaned back and smiled warmly as if to say, "You're among friends now." The gesture even helped calm Murdock. It never ceased to amaze him how the female gender possessed the power to melt stress right out of a man, even with just a smile.

But as Gabaree smacked his lips like some sort of monkey, Murdock shot Madeline an icy glare. *This was the guy we were paying a million dollars for a story?*

She just kept right on smiling. Besides being in full possession of her feminine melting powers, she was the only person at *American Times* Murdock could not intimidate with a glare.

Gabaree leaned his mound of a face closer to Murdock and explained how G.C. Overmeyer was one of the many subsidiaries of Truss Industries, a global conglomerate that

177

owned several enterprises, including pop CD companies, book publishing companies, communication enterprises, medical technology interests, and pharmaceutical drug companies such as Overmeyer, to name a few. According to Gabaree, Truss Industries was a small nation unto itself.

Although Murdock didn't mention it, he was intimately familiar with the breadth and power of Truss Industries.

Their food arrived. Gabaree bit into his sandwich. A string of corned beef hung from his mouth. He slurped it up.

"You think the American government governs its people? Financial party contributors and professional lobbyists run the government. Big business runs this country, Mr. Collier. Truss Industries has more power than any ten presidents in our history."

"What does this have to do with the Grand Canyon murders?"

"There's a secret organization within Truss, specifically within Overmeyer, that masterminded the Grand Canyon murders."

Murdock quickly scanned the restaurant to be sure no one had heard Gabaree's comment.

"Overmeyer manufactures paramedical drugs," Murdock said.

"Correction," Gabaree shot back. "Overmeyer doesn't manufacture drugs. They market them."

What's the difference? Murdock's main interest in the company was that it was a major advertiser in *American Times*.

"Why would a legitimate company like Overmeyer be the least bit interested in an excavation in the Grand Canyon?" Murdock asked, not bothering to curb his sarcastic tone.

Gabaree smacked his lips. "You have to understand the entire scope of what Overmeyer is trying to accomplish.

"See, Mr. Collier, I became a biochemist not only because it was up my alley as far as, well, being a scientist, but because it was also the right thing for me to do as a good Christian. I was born and raised a Southern Baptist, and I grew up wanting to help people. That's why I went into medicinal drugs in the first place. But they've gone too far with their practices. G.C. Overmeyer is involved in more than marketing drugs."

Murdock sighed. "It's obvious you think that."

"You won't read what I'm about to tell you in any of their PR reports or on their website. They're into some really weird stuff."

Madeline squirmed in her chair. Murdock figured she knew her source was swiftly losing credibility.

"Define 'weird stuff,' Charlie," she urged.

"Orwellian weird." He looked squarely at Murdock. "The field of medicine exists for the purpose of making sick people well, right?"

"Of course."

"If they did a good job, a really fine job, they would rid the world of sickness, right?"

"Not attainable. But theoretically, I suppose."

"But if they got rid of all the sickness in the world—if they actually accomplished their purpose—they would run themselves right out of business because they'd have no more sick people to treat, right?"

"Charlie—" Madeline interjected.

Gabaree cut her off. "Hear me out. The medical profession has two purposes that are at odds here. One is to rid patients of their illness, but the other is to acquire more business. These objectives are antithetical. The purpose of medicine is to cure illness, but the purpose of business is to bring illness. And, believe me, the pharmaceutical end of medicine is run by businessmen, not concerned doctors. Do you think these boys would applaud themselves if their medicine actually alleviated illness altogether? They'd be out of a job! Is it any wonder the rate of cancer has increased since the war on cancer began? Do you understand what I'm saying, Mr. Collier?"

"I'm in the news business, Mr. Gabaree. I, too, became a journalist to help people, and I am also a businessman."

"As you know, Mr. Collier, G.C. Overmeyer is one of the largest drug companies in the world. They were the first to mass-market penicillin after Alexander Fleming discovered it in nineteen twenty-eight. During World War II, Overmeyer rose to a prominent position in the marketplace as the major distributer of penicillin for war injuries. After the war, they damn near had a monopoly on antibiotics that lasted for years. Trouble was, they got lazy and fat. Eventually, other drug manufacturers like Walters-Ridder and Merrick Laboratories entered the marketplace with more aggressive sales strategies and captured Overmeyer's dominant market share. Merrick knocked them off as the number one seller of antibiotics. By the late nineteen sixties, Overmeyer hit the skids and went into major reorganization. Then, instead of trying to regain their position with antibiotics, they decided to enter the swiftly growing field of psychotropic drugs—what I call 'mental medicine.' It was the sixties. We'd just gone through the Korean War and were involved in Vietnam. The pace of life was getting more frantic, and religion in general was declining in popularity. The age of stress and anxiety had arrived."

Murdock started coughing. *Damn.* He shoved a napkin against his lips, hoping the searing pain in his lungs wouldn't last.

"You follow, Mr. Collier?"

Murdock followed all right, and he didn't like where this conversation was headed. He hacked some more. Though he'd quit smoking two years ago, he could taste the forty years of Lucky Strike cigarettes in his mouth. Madeline's hand squeezed his. The coughing eased.

"You should have that looked at," Gabaree commented.

Moments were too valuable to spend on this moron. Murdock, regained his composure and set his eyes back on Gabaree.

"I'm a busy man, Mr. Gabaree. I need to know only two things—what Overmeyer had to do with the Grand Canyon murders and where Dr. Reinhardt is. Now if you don't—"

"The deal was for me to provide you with that information and for you to publish it in your magazine. The reason I'm telling you all this about Overmeyer is because you must also publish *this* information. It's key to understanding the entire scenario."

Madeline said, "Please let him continue, Murdock. He'll soon tell us what you want to know."

Fine, Murdock thought. He knew he held the high card anyway, because in the end, he'd publish what he wanted to.

"Go ahead, Charlie," Madeline urged.

Gabaree took another bite of his sandwich and started talking with a lump in his cheek.

"Psychiatry used to be regarded mostly as treatment for the insane. But in the sixties, baby boomers were starting to graduate. This meant more psychiatrists coming out of college and not enough 'insane' people to fill their empty offices. To survive, they had to expand their market. Basic supply and demand. At the same time, psychiatry was discovering that Freud's theories—all that stuff about the id and the superego and Oedipus complexes—well, basically they didn't work."

He paused to swallow the lump of corned beef in his mouth.

"So the stage was set," Gabaree continued. "Psychiatry needed new customers, and they needed a therapy that worked, or at least something people would buy. Modern medicine had experienced great success with antibiotics and was regarded highly in the public eye. Overmeyer was in need of a new direction. A new drug. A profitable new drug!

"A paradigm shift began developing in the field. If modern medicine was so successful treating physical illness with antibiotics, then why couldn't modern medicine develop drugs just as effective for mental illness? After all, wasn't the brain a physical organ just like the lungs or the kidneys? Wouldn't it hold true that, if you altered the chemical interactions in the brain with drugs, you could effectively treat mental illness? Made sense to me. It's one reason I became a biochemist." Gabaree leaned close to Murdock and whispered, "Did you know that in the early sixties, there were only about a hundred mental illnesses listed in psychiatric books, Mr. Collier?"

"No."

Gabaree frowned. "Psychiatry used to deal in terms such as psychosis, manic-depressive illness, and schizophrenia. Today the *Diagnostic and Statistical Manual of Mental Disorders* lists almost four hundred mental disorders. The person who can't give up smoking may have a 'nicotine disorder.' A child with a low math score has 'developmental arithmetic disorder.' Kids having problems writing have 'developmental expressive writing disorder.' People who are happy all the time may have 'chronic happiness syndrome.' People who are afraid to be happy have 'cheer-a-phobia.' Yes, indeed, Mr. Collier, psychiatry has successfully broadened its market. Their definition of mental illness has grown to include anyone anywhere who has a problem. They are perfectly happy to 'treat' every man, woman, and child living in this country. And, today, that 'treatment' is with drugs."

Gabaree fetched a handkerchief from his pants pocket and patted the sweat on his forehead.

Murdock, too, was beginning to sweat.

"Okay, going back to the sixties, the emphasis in psychiatric treatment was swiftly moving from behavioral therapy to drug therapy, which meant drugs were needed to treat all these new and upcoming mental illnesses. Not only was this a godsend for Overmeyer, but they helped orchestrate it. It's no coincidence many of the stockholders of Overmeyer are also psychiatrists.

Soon Overmeyer became the leading marketer of Nalium, something psychiatrists and other MDs alike prescribed by the truckload in the early seventies, only to later discover it was practically worthless in improving lives, yet highly addictive in ruining them. Moving forward in time and today, with Reozac and MindPro for depression, and Vipro for attention deficit disorder, G.C. Overmeyer is the number-one marketer and seller of mental drugs."

"Charlie, are you suggesting psychiatry created all these new categories of mental illnesses just for marketing purposes?" Madeline asked.

Gabaree chuckled. "That's not the right question, Madeline. The right question is, has psychiatry created an illusion of mental illness? As just one example, psychiatrists say, 'just as arthritis is a disease of the joints, depression is a disease of the mind.' They claim depression is a pathological disease.

"But there are two problems with this line of thinking, Madeline. First, to say depression is strictly physical in nature denies that personal problems, such as the breakup of a marriage or the death of a friend or the loss of a job, would even remotely cause someone to get depressed. Second, if depression is a disease of the brain, why can't they see the disease on an x-ray or MRI the way we can see arthritis, or cancer, or every other pathological illness? Or, how about in a blood test? Does the blood show pathological evidence of mental depression? Of course not. But if you were to even question the psychiatric profession about the labeling of problems as mental illness, they would put the burden of proof on you."

Gabaree turned to Murdock.

"Look at it this way, Mr. Collier. The premise underlying theology is the existence of God. People of faith can't define God, nor can they prove His existence. Yet they believe those who deny God's existence are mistaken. They put the burden of proof on the nonbeliever to prove the nonexistence of God. They say, 'Prove there is *no* God.' I've even done it myself. That's religion. But we expect something different from science.

"The premise underlying psychiatry is the existence of mental illness. Psychiatrists can neither define mental illness nor prove its existence *in terms of physical structure*. Yet they believe those who deny the existence of mental illness are mistaken. The burden of proof is on the critic of psychiatry to prove the *nonexistence* of mental illness. This isn't science. Do you know how new mental disorders are labeled as such, Mr. Collier?"

"No."

"At their American Psychiatric Association meetings, psychiatrists literally vote on what constitutes a mental disorder by rising their hands. There is no medical evidence presented— no x-rays, blood tests, or any other medical tests are needed to add a disorder to the *Diagnostic and Statistical Manual*. Their procedure is about as scientific as voting on their favorite movie.

"And, by the way, once a 'disorder' is listed in the *Manual*, the psychiatrist can look forward to collecting an insurance check when he treats an insured patient for that newly labeled disorder. And listen to this: presently there are one hundred and seventy-nine psychiatrists who are responsible for the *Manual*. Every last one of those birds has financial ties to the very paramedical companies that sell the drugs corresponding with the 'mental diseases' they put in the *Manual*!"

"People do have problems," Murdock said. "That's why they seek help in the first place."

"Now, Mr. Collier, having a problem is one thing. Labeling that problem a mental illness or disorder and prescribing a drug for it, then secretly making a profit on those drugs, is something else. Over six million kids are on Overmeyer's drugs in this country alone, to say nothing of their infiltration into other countries."

Gabaree looked like he'd been running nonstop for an hour. He produced the handkerchief again, removed more sweat, and caught his breath.

Madeline gently patted Murdock's hand, obviously sensing his continued impatience.

"Why are you so against these medications, Charlie?" she asked.

"We haven't even begun to scratch the surface of what causes our emotions. I didn't know the depth of the problem until I was immersed in it as an associate doing work for Overmeyer. They are using our society as one big drug experiment, just as they did with Nalium in the seventies. One big, *profitable* drug experiment! Did you know the children involved in almost every major school-shooting incident in this country were on psychiatric drugs?"

"You'd better get to the point pretty damn soon," Murdock finally demanded.

Gabaree's voice rose. "Did you know, today more than seventy-five percent of all drugs sold are because the patient saw an advertisement? More than seventy-five percent! It's all business, Mr. Collier. It's all about money."

Does this jerk think I fell off a turnip truck yesterday? The man was intelligent, but not very smart. Didn't he know he was talking to the managing editor of the nation's leading magazine?

Does he not know I'm a major stockholder in all American Times interests, including Online America Internet service and Times/People television station? Does Gabaree not even have a clue that, according to last year's financial report, the magazine alone received a large percentage of its advertising revenues from the very drug companies he's referring to?

"Where does this leave us, Charlie?" Madeline asked.

Gabaree slurped some coffee and said, "If you can control someone's mind, you can control their actions. I've come to believe that's what Overmeyer is really up to on a broad scale—controlling people's minds under the guise of mental health."

"Prescription drugs for the purpose of controlling people?" Murdock had to struggle to keep from laughing. "To what end, sir?"

"To what ultimate end, I'm not sure. What I am sure of is the 'end' of making money. Drugs are the perfect business. Any type of drug can be addictive, or at the very least, become a crutch people keep reaching for. Reorders are what it's all about. You can't believe the economic stability a drug company enjoys when they get a kid on Vipro at ten years old and can count on him taking the drug for the rest of his life. Multiply that times millions, and I think you get the picture."

Murdock got the picture all right. Every business tries to create repeat customers. It's what businesses do. Overmeyer was committing no sin. Murdock had heard enough.

"Now that we've been enlightened as to Overmeyer's wicked practices, show me proof they're involved in the Grand Canyon murders, or I'm walking."

Gabaree's eyes widened. "Here's the mother lode: Overmeyer has been experimenting with implanting electrodes in the brains of animals to provoke certain kinds of behavior by stimulating brain centers with electrical charges. That's just the beginning. They've also been implanting tiny tubes in the brain that time-release drugs to change the activity of brain centers and behavior. And get this—they've developed a way to set up a direct line of communication from a brain to a computer and back to the brain, so the computer influences the brain. There is a word for what these boys are doing. And that word is *evil!*"

Murdock shifted in his chair. Madeline put a hand on his arm to stop him from leaving.

"You can rest assured, Mr. Collier, Overmeyer was interested in the excavation Reinhardt and his crew were on because they discovered something there that controls people."

"Tell us," Madeline insisted.

Gabaree smiled. "You want proof, Mr. Collier? Well, here it is." He pulled a sheet of paper from his briefcase and slid it under Murdock's nose.

THIRTY-TWO

"This e-mail was sent June fifteenth, just three days before they found the dead bodies at the Grand Canyon," Gabaree said.

Murdock put on his glasses and read the e-mail.

From: <ceo@gcover.com>

To: <bones@IntNet.net>

Subject: The Afflatus Artifact

Wave's up. 115/00 - 35/00

Investigate.

Murdock looked up. "Explain."

Gabaree pointed to the e-mail's sender, ceo@gcover.com.

"As you know, 'CEO' stands for chief executive officer," he said. "'gcover' is short for G. C. Overmeyer."

"So it's from the CEO of Overmeyer?"

"It was sent from the CEO's e-mail address," Gabaree quickly pointed out. "Although I can't verify he is personally involved."

"Involved in what?"

Gabaree pointed to the phrase *wave up* on the e-mail.

"I believe the word *wave* stands for some sort of electronic wave, perhaps radio waves or frequency waves. I believe *wave up* simply means the waves are up in the air. But here's the interesting part."

Gabaree pointed to the numbers following the "wave up."

Murdock read them out loud. "One one five slash zero zero and thirty-five slash zero zero."

Gabaree said, "One one five slash zero zero is a latitude setting, and thirty-five slash zero zero is a longitude setting."

"Which is somewhere in the Grand Canyon," Murdock guessed.

"Re's Cavern, to be more precise. In other words, some kind of wave was sent up from Re's Cavern *two days prior* to the Grand Canyon deaths. Whoever sent the e-mail from Overmeyer was telling the party on the other end to investigate the wave."

"Who is the party on the other end?"

Gabaree shrugged. "Don't know for sure. It's a generic e-mail address for the administrative division of Truss Industries. Any number of people could have used it."

Murdock examined the e-mail again. The subject line at the top of the page said, "The Afflatus Artifact." *Afflatus.* That certainly wasn't a word you heard much these days. He was surprised how clearly he remembered first hearing it from his college days at St. Paul's Seminary.

My body is turning to shit, but my mind is still sharp.

"*Afflatus* means a creative impulse, usually resulting in a message of wisdom," Murdock said. "So what the hell does that have to do with the Grand Canyon?"

"Tell him your theory, Charlie," Madeline said.

Gabaree smacked his lips and wiped his mouth with a napkin.

"I believe Dr. Reinhardt discovered an artifact at Re's Cavern of considerable value to Overmeyer. An artifact that others wanted badly. An artifact that others had been trying to find for a long time. An artifact, Mr. Collier, that carried a message of ancient wisdom.

"And when Reinhardt discovered it," Gabaree added, "that's when the wave went up. The other guys were notified of his find."

"The other guys?" Murdock asked.

"The murderers."

"They rushed into the canyon, took the artifact, killed everyone, and made it look like a mass suicide," Madeline concluded.

"The wave was some sort of signal that prompted the murderers to show up with a jug full of poisoned apple juice?" Murdock asked sarcastically.

Gabaree swallowed. "Damn right they did. Reinhardt found the artifact, and some sort of electronic flare shot into the air."

He again reached for his briefcase and pulled out two more sheets of paper.

"Take a look at these e-mails. This first one was sent as a reply to the e-mail you just saw, the request to investigate Re's Cavern."

From: <bones@IntNet.net>To: <ceo@gcover.com>
Subject: RE: The Afflatus Artifact

A college archeological expedition led by one Dr. Jensen Reinhardt has uncovered the third afflatus artifact. Must act fast to retrieve goods and dispose of evidence. Details to be worked out in person.

Murdock read the e-mail and said, "It says Reinhardt found the *third* afflatus artifact. It sounds like Reinhardt was working for Truss. When he found what they wanted him to, he alerted them with some kind of signal, or wave as they call it."

Gabaree shook his head. "Look how the e-mail is written. It says, 'a college archeological expedition led by *one* Dr. Reinhardt.' Does that sound like they're talking about an associate?"

Murdock wasn't sure what it sounded like. He was getting nervous about the mounting evidence that Truss and G. C. Overmeyer were involved in all of this.

"How did you get these e-mails?" Murdock asked.

"I have my means." He handed Murdock the third one.

Murdock looked it over. It verified that the expedition members had been disposed of, the afflatus artifact had been retrieved, and Reinhardt had been abducted.

Well, there it is, as black-and-white as a zebra's ass. This wasn't good news. Again Murdock reminded himself he was in control. He would get exclusive rights to run Gabaree's story, or *not* run it. There was one question left to answer.

"Where is Reinhardt?" Murdock asked pointedly.

Gabaree reached into his case once again and brought out a map. A world map. He produced a fountain pen from his white cotton shirt pocket and drew an arrow in the middle of the Pacific Ocean. It pointed to absolutely nothing.

"I don't understand," Murdock said. "There's nothing on the map but water."

"Is there an island?" Madeline asked.

"There is no island. Just international waters, Mr. Collier. Not governed by the laws of any country."

Murdock realized that Gabaree had failed earlier to list one of Truss Industries biggest subsidiaries, South Pacific Oil.

"Are they holding Reinhardt captive on an oil tanker?"

Gabaree rested his elbows on the table and leaned forward. Murdock and Madeline leaned in as well. Their heads almost touched.

"Damn right they are."

THIRTY-THREE

"Megan."

"Earth to Megan."

She blinked open her eyes.

"We're in Durango." Bruce's voice nudged her awake.

She glanced at him in the driver's seat, and then gazed sleepily out the car window. Rich green pine trees and snow-white aspens covered a mountainous landscape. Rubbing her eyes, she couldn't believe they were there already, could hardly believe they'd made it at all. How long had she been sleeping?

"Where do we go?" Bruce asked.

Getting her bearings, Megan realized they were only a couple of miles from her friend's house.

"About a mile up," she said. "Turn right on Valley Road."

"Who again is this guy who lives here?" Bruce asked.

"I told you—he's an architect I dated in Chicago."

"I see. He must have a lot of money. I mean if he lives in Chicago *and* owns a home in Durango."

Megan yawned. "You're surprised I would date someone with a lot of money? You don't think I'm worth it?"

He gave her a sidelong look but said nothing. She was being cranky. She had a right to be cranky. Her stomach ached, and she hadn't showered in days.

Besides, the subject of Michael was a sore spot with her. *Relationships* were a sore spot with her—too many, too dull, too bad. Her time was better spent doing what she loved to do, which was archeology. All that mattered now was that Michael had a house they could stay in. That is if he hadn't changed the locks, a definite possibility she'd failed to mention to Bruce.

He turned on Valley Road.

"Two blocks down on the right, number three sixty-five," she said.

Bruce brought the car to a crawl as Michael's home came into view, a two-story A-frame with cedar siding and large picture windows that, she remembered fondly, offered a gorgeous view of La Plata Mountain. Megan couldn't wait to get inside and settle in.

She suggested they park a block away and walk over so the neighbors wouldn't see a strange car in the driveway.

Bruce obliged.

Outside Michael's front door, she punched numbers into the lockbox. She'd only visited Michael here twice, yet easily remembered the combination, which was his birthday: 041260. The box opened, and she retrieved the key. Bruce followed her through the door into the foyer, where she went to enter a different set of numbers to disengage the security system, but paused.

"What's the matter? You don't remember?"

"I remember," said Megan. Still drowsy from sleep, it took some concentration to arrange the numbers in her head—his birthday backward. Finally she entered 062140. The red light on the system panel blinked then turned green. Megan breathed a sigh of relief.

They stood in the front entranceway for a moment, allowing their eyes to adjust to the dimly lit space. All the blinds were closed, and only the skyboxes over the kitchen provided light.

The gorgeous details of the interior began to take form. Michael was an award-winning architect, and his home was one of his works of art. Megan didn't miss the man much, but she did miss this house. It looked like a picture out of *Metropolitan Home* magazine.

"Not bad," Bruce muttered as he stepped past her into the open room, a vast space with a gorgeous red oak floor. Knotty pine wooden posts supported a sloped tongue-and-groove wooden ceiling. In the east corner was an open kitchen with crosscut travertine countertops and beautiful maple cabinets. Two brass ceiling fans hung above a serving bar that also had a travertine top. The west corner of the room held an entertainment area with a large flat-screen TV, computer, and a wall of other electronic gadgets Megan didn't know much about.

Bruce had already made a beeline to the refrigerator. After finding no joy there, he scrounged through the kitchen cabinets but stumbled on only a few stray cans of food, a bag of chips, and other no-interest items.

He turned to her. "How about I get some food while you get things settled around here?"

"There's a grocery store just a couple of miles away."

She drew him a map how to get there, and told him there was a shower in the first-floor bedroom he could use when he returned.

Bruce left and Megan couldn't wait to take her own hot shower. In the second-floor bathroom, she removed her Sphinx necklace and the shirt Bruce had given her: the pilot's shirt—a dead man's shirt. After turning on the water to get it warm, she examined her stitches in the mirror. A crooked line of crisscrossed thread ran for about five inches just below the ribs on her right side. It reminded her of Dillon. She imagined it wasn't easy for a one-armed man to sew her up during a turbulent helicopter ride. She removed her underwear, stepped into the shower, and angled her body so the water didn't run over Dillon's handiwork.

Up until now, she hadn't allowed herself a moment to dwell on what had happened to Dillon—the stranger who had saved her life. But now she couldn't stop the memory, or the tears. She fell against the cold, tiled wall as her mind dealt up images of Dillon's arm being sliced with the knife. Then other pictures flooded in. One by one, she recalled her friends' dead bodies she'd found at Re's Cavern. Her heart clutched with every reminiscence, but she didn't try to stop them. She let them come so that they could wash away, could flow into the drain along with her tears.

Yet there was a lingering sentiment that wouldn't wash away, the feeling that, despite outward appearances, she was utterly alone in this world. Sure, there was Bruce. He saved her life too, hadn't he? Yet. . .yet he seemed so distant; one minute there with her, at other times absent, at least in spirit. She supposed he had a right. As he'd once pointed out, he owed her nothing. So why should she expect more? Why did she *always* expect more from people? Why did few match her passion, her drive, her zeal for life? Especially men?

Get over yourself.

She grabbed the bar of soap and washed her face and neck,

trying to scrub away the emotional pain. *Life goes on.* She had to muster enough strength to continue. Water streamed over her stitches and it burned like hell. She jumped out of Harm's Way and cried some more.

After finishing her shower, she dried herself off and went to Michael's closet to find something to wear.

It was empty. Did Michael take *all* his clothes to Europe for the summer? Maybe he gave them away? Whatever. She had no choice but to wear the pilot's shirt again. Back in the bathroom, she washed her panties in the sink and dried them with the blow-dryer. Then she heard the door close downstairs. Bruce had returned from the store. She slipped on the warm panties, and thought about Michael's wine cabinet in the living room.

When she came downstairs, she could hear the other shower running through the open bedroom door. She checked out the wine cabinet and found it well stocked. Michael was a bit of a connoisseur, which, at the moment, she was grateful for. She grabbed a bottle of Pinot and a teardrop glass—two teardrop glasses.

In the kitchen, she filled the glasses and opened the refrigerator to see what Bruce had bought: a wrapping of turkey breast, bacon and eggs, whole wheat bread, and some assorted vegetables. On the counter was plenty of fresh fruit. Not bad.

The house was almost dark now. As much as possible she wanted to keep it that way for fear a light might draw attention from a neighbor. At the entertainment center, she found a candle and lit it. Then she retrieved the two glasses of wine from the kitchen along with an apple. On the sofa, she folded her legs under her, bit into the apple, and flicked on the TV with the remote.

A stately looking man with snow-white hair sat at a news desk. Creases on his face were set in a frown of fatherly concern. Behind him on a large screen was a picture of Re's Cavern.

Megan took a gulp of wine. At first, she couldn't believe what she was seeing. Then it dawned on her that TV stations had probably been running specials about the incident since it had happened.

She turned up the volume.

"What does it take for a group of young people in the spring of their lives to commit suicide?" the man asked.

The screen behind him showed Jim Jones, then dissolved into David Koresh, and then into Jensen.

"What kind of man was Jensen Reinhardt? What power did he hold over the thirteen individuals who took their lives at his command? How do we identify the Joneses, Koreshes, and Reinhardts of the world? We are hoping Dr. David Horowitz, a psychiatrist from the UCLA School of Medicine and behavioral expert on group suicides and aberrant social phenomena, can shine some light on this rather complex issue."

The camera pulled back and revealed Dr. Horowitz alongside the host at the news desk. He had a long fleshy nose and ash-colored eyes set in deep sockets below bushy white brows.

Megan was aware Bruce had entered the room, but kept her eyes glued to the TV.

"Well, Hugh," Dr. Horowitz began, "to say Dr. Reinhardt is delusional is both an understatement and too simple an explanation. We could state, however, that a man such as Reinhardt operates under an elaborate system of grandiose delusions that are complex, as well as rooted, we must assume, in a childhood craving for attention. Add to that the self-aggrandizement of his chosen status as God's hand and his obvious intelligence—being a scientist—and we can conclude that Dr. Reinhardt is an egomaniacal despot suffering from disassociative superiority complex."

Huh?

Bruce was standing next to the sofa now, watching.

"This is like a *Saturday Night Live* skit," Megan bemoaned.

The host cleared his throat. "How then, Dr. Horowitz, can people be alert to dangerous cults led by men such as Reinhardt? Are there guidelines that can be used to assess a group, or leader, before someone gets involved?"

Megan wanted to barf.

Dr. Horowitz said, "We are all susceptible to cults. However, there are six warning signs of a cult a person or parent should be on the lookout for."

Six numbered sentences appeared on the screen superimposed over Reinhardt's picture. Dr. Horowitz read them aloud.

"One: Total commitment to the leader's interpretation of the

Bible or the creation of life.

"Two: Belief that the leader is seldom wrong.

"Three: Belief in continued revelation that contradicts previous religious beliefs.

"Four: Strong belief that we are in the times prior to the end of the world.

"Five: A 'we-they' mentality.

"Six: Pressure to conform to the dictates of the group."

Megan envisioned millions of people around the country listening to this cretin. He sounded so sure of himself, so *official*. She'd probably believe him, too, if she didn't know better.

She looked up at Bruce. "They aren't talking about Jensen and the rest of us. We were on an expedition, not a church retreat!"

"Wine. Nice," he said, reaching for the second glass of wine on the table.

"Sensationalism," she spouted, stewing about the TV program.

"You should be honored," he said.

"About what?"

"Those six points the shrink said pretty much describe Christ and his early followers. Next thing you know, your man Reinhardt will be deified."

He smiled down at her. His hair shone in the candlelight, a mass of sable strands combed back Elvis-style. She shut off the TV with the remote. "You're an expert on Christ, are you?"

"I know enough to recognize that Christ started a cult, which eventually grew into a world religion. Several world religions."

"Every major religion in the history of the world started as a cult."

"Well then, there you go." He plopped down on the chair across from her and sipped his wine.

How strange it was to be with this man without danger lurking around the corner. No helicopters, no police, no FBI— just the two of them securely settled into this house. Yet, being alone with him made her nervous—and she wasn't sure why.

He swirled the wine in his glass. A pretty reflection of the candle flame danced on the crystal surface.

"Were you brought up on any specific religion?" she asked.

"Catholic. You?"

"Fortunately, my parents didn't push me into any one belief," she said. Growing up, her parents always encouraged her to have an open mind and seek out her own answers. And that's exactly what she'd done.

But as the years passed, most knowledge she'd attained about the world's religions was gathered more from an archeological/historical perspective than out of personal need. Not that she would have minded learning some spiritual truths along the way, but she found most of the beliefs she'd studied to be too wrapped in superstition and ritual for her liking. She'd have to bend herself into something she wasn't in order to accept them.

Yet the deep questions did intrigue her: Who are we? Where did we come from? Why are we here? In truth, she secretly yearned for answers, answers that made sense to her. Answers that, for her, the Bible did not sufficiently provide. The teachings of Buddha made some sense, but even those left her wanting . . . wanting answers that *she* could more relate to.

"Back in the Grand Canyon, you told me you don't believe in heaven, so I'm assuming you're no longer Catholic," said Megan.

"That would be correct."

"You don't seem fond of any religions."

He rested his elbows on his knees and leaned forward in the chair. "I have nothing against anyone's beliefs. I just resent it when religions that are man-made try to ram down your throat that they exclusively represent the 'word of God.'"

Megan was pleased to see she'd hit a hot spot. Starting to relax, she scooted to the edge of the sofa and watched him take in the resulting added length of bare thigh. She quickly tugged her shirttail back down her legs, covering them the best she could. Then she casually sipped from her glass, pretending nothing happened. The wine's bitter bite felt good on her tongue. What *did* happen? She liked his eyes on her. Pretended not to.

He changed subjects. "There was something you said on the helicopter, just before we were hit, about ancient archeological finds."

Megan remembered the conversation well. "*Super*-ancient finds," she corrected him. She'd first become interested in the subject years ago when she'd read a quote by Henry Ford. He'd said something to the effect that if the oceans of the world were dredged, we'd find evidence that intelligent civilizations had built cars and other high-tech machines in the past.

Fascinated with this prospect that advanced civilizations may have once existed on earth, she dove into research and even wrote an essay on subject.

"There are records of many archeological finds suggesting human life existed on earth millions of years ago," she said.

"Like what?"

"So many," she said, starting to mentally corral the facts she'd once memorized. *Where to start?* She sipped her wine. *Human skeletons.* "Okay. At the turn of the century a rock collector in Utah found halves of two skeletons while digging around his farm. A professor of anthropology later verified they were human skulls and dated them as being three hundred million years old."

An eyebrow rose on Bruce's brow.

"And then there was a guy named Dr. Booth who operated an iron ore mine who found portions of what looked like a human skeleton resting on a layer of iron ore. It was dated at over four hundred million years old."

Bruce started shaking his head.

Megan was used to this sort of reaction from anyone that she ever told about these finds.

"I'm not making these up," she said and took yet another sip of wine. She was already starting to feel giddy. What a lightweight she was. *Okay Mr. Skeptical. . .*

"And then there was a five hundred million year old footprint archeologists found encased in coal, and an iron pot discovered by a utility worker in Illinois, also in a coal seam, dated at three hundred fifty million years."

Taking in more wine, she gasped and described a one hundred and fifty foot human manufactured wall that had been dug up—it, too, encased in coal—that had been preserved for more than three hundred million years. Sensing she was impressing him, she pressed on: told Bruce about a man-made, cast-iron cube found in Australia that scientists had determined to be sixty million years old. And about a woman in Illinois who was shoveling coal into her furnace when a chunk fell and broke open. An exquisitely made gold chain was sealed inside. "The coal," Megan said, "was dated over two hundred million years."

"How do you know about these finds?" he asked.

"It's no secret. There are books on the subject, such as *Forbidden Archeology* by Michael Cremo and Richard Thompson. Anyone can learn about them."

"Can they be found in museums?"

"Oh God, no. Museums, like school classrooms, are dedicated to the accepted chronologies for human evolution, that is; the basic premise that life started in a sea of ammonia billions of years ago and has taken all this time to evolve to its present condition. Museums would be the last to change their thought paradigms." Megan loved talking about this stuff. Loved it.

"Thought paradigms?" he asked and took a drink.

"Sure, it's what science basically is; it's human perception of what we *believe* reality is at any given time. We package these beliefs into thought paradigms so they make sense to us. Throughout history there's been many thought paradigms that scientists and leaders promoted as absolute truth, which were later discovered to be false theories that sounded reasonable at the time, based on the available technology and information.

"People once believed the heavens was a place populated by angry gods, and that the earth was the center of our universe. . . When Newton first proposed the law of gravity scientists of the day thought he was some new age freak spewing an occult belief: an invisible energy that holds matter to the ground. Absurd!"

Whew, the sudden burst of air made Megan light headed. She gulped more wine and continued: "Today, many scientists are relegating the theory of evolution to a 'has been' thought paradigm. Unfortunately, schools and museums will be the last to catch on."

"So, today scientists believe—"

"Many subscribe to catastrophism."

"Which is?"

"That there's has been no billion year journey of evolution. That throughout earth's history life has come and gone and catastrophic events such as earthquakes, volcanoes, floods and meteors hitting the earth, have drastically changed the environment and wiped out species of animals, such as dinosaurs, and even advanced civilizations."

"That doesn't explain where life came from in the first place."

"No, it doesn't," Megan agreed. "But neither does evolution. If life started with a mono cell in a sea of ammonia, and lightning struck it and caused a chemical reaction, which through billions of years evolved into intelligent life, *who* or *what* created the mono cell, the lightning, the sea, and the earth? Even evolution doesn't negate the reality that life of some sort was created, rather than evolved. " It felt so wonderful to just sit and talk—talk about the subject she loves.

And Bruce, with his misty blue eyes staring at her, made a good audience—*his beautiful misty blue eyes*. The swelling had gone down on his nose and he was looking better, much better. The wine certainly helped in this respect. She stood up, wobbled, and then went to the kitchen. She was starting to feel no pain. Well, almost. Her stitches still burned, but it was turning into a good burn. She grabbed the bottle of wine and returned to the living room.

"More?"

Bruce checked the small amount of wine still in his glass. "Just a short one."

"One short one coming up."

It tickled her the way he said 'short one.' You couldn't have a *short* drink. You could have a little bit of a drink, or a tad, or just a wee bit in a glass, but you couldn't have a short one. He was so funny. Drinks don't come in short or tall. Actually they do. Whatever.

She filled their glasses and plopped back down on the sofa. A puff of air ballooned her shirt out. She felt her near-naked bottom hit the cushion.

His blue eyes were still staring at her, quickly disabling her defenses. No. They had work to do tomorrow. *Change of plan.* She stood right back up.

James J. Valko

"I'll sleep upstairs," she told him and quickly crossed to the staircase. She climbed the steps, not caring that the scanty shirttail offered little coverage of her bottom.

"Megan?"

"Yes?" She turned on her heel at the top of the stairs.

"How was the Grand Canyon excavation funded?"

Funded? The question threw her. "I don't know," she said. "Jensen always took care of those things."

"Did he fund it himself?"

"No, never. He would have gotten the money from an individual or an institution of some sort."

"Did he ever mention—"

"I'm tired, Bruce."

She didn't want to talk about this now. The effects of the alcohol had quickly done a reversal, flipped her from playful to sad. She hated feeling this way. She had to be headstrong. And she had to get some rest. There was plenty of work to do tomorrow.

"Wouldn't there be a record?" He persisted. "There must be a record of the funding."

"Yes, I suppose there would be."

"Where would he have kept it?"

"Why are you asking me this? Do you think whoever funded the excavation murdered the crew?" *How stupid is that?*

"I was just curious."

"I'm tired."

"Good night, Megan."

Good night, Bruce Brackin. Good night.

THIRTY-FOUR

"Rachel!"

The dark form fell back against the wall as Bruce's raspy cry cut through the blackness.

He jerked up in bed and stared with sleep-filled eyes across the room, his heart firing in his chest.

He rose to his feet, brain still muddled with alcohol and sleep, unable to orient himself to time or place.

"Rachel," he gasped. "Rachel?"

"It's me," a weak voice responded.

Oh, how he wanted to touch Rachel, feel her warmth. He had taken such joy in pleasing her, listening to her laugh, touching her . . .

The dark form stepped out of the shadows. He was jolted back to alert consciousness. He heard sniffling.

"It's me. Megan."

"What do you want?"

"I couldn't . . ."

The sniffling intensified.

"I couldn't sleep," she whispered.

What time was it? Bruce glanced at the red numbers on the nightstand next to the bed. Four twenty-one in the morning. What did she want at this hour?

"What's wrong?" he asked.

She rushed forward and embraced him. Her sobbing face fell against his naked chest.

"I . . . I'm not as strong as I sometimes act," she said.

He listened.

"I think of them, their deaths, and I die inside, too. Dillon was only trying to help us and . . ."

Bruce instinctively put his arms around her. She responded in kind.

Her body felt warm against his. Her face nestled in the crook of his neck. Tears wet his skin.

"There's something I have to tell you," she said.

He tilted his head down slightly and looked at her in the darkness.

She returned his look up and began to speak.

While his eyes watched her lips move, his hands found her face, cupping her warm, moist cheeks. His mouth explored hers and tasted the tears on her lips, felt the warmth of her tongue. He smelled her womanly youth, and the knot of encysted grief that he'd been holding inside since Rachel's death exploded within him.

Her muscles tensed as she, at first, tried to push him away. But he continued to kiss her like the starved man that he was. All the pain, all the guilt, all the sorrow began to drain from his being, brought on by the closeness of this woman.

Megan still wore the shirt—*only* the shirt that she'd had on earlier. While drinking the wine, he had forced himself not to stare at her bare legs, which the shirt had so scantily covered. He had tried not to compare Megan to Rachel—to the picture of Rachel, also wearing nothing but a shirt, one that he'd cried over just days ago with the gun to his head. Yet the comparison had been inevitable. Rachel's legs had been bronzed, soft, and slender. Megan's legs were as white as a swan, the contours more defined. Earlier, the urge to touch them had been suppressed. But now. Now his hands roamed under the shirt and over her curved hips and toward her legs. A breathless sigh escaped her lips, and he felt her muscles start to relax. He pulled her to him, both falling back on the bed.

With her beneath him, his nimble fingers unbuttoned her shirt then strong hands pinned her arms against the mattress, stretching her limbs, exposing her breasts to the light of the moon. Bruce Bracken kissed Megan like he was sure she'd never been kissed before. He nibbled along the length of her neck and the softness of each breast as his fingers ran along her inner thigh, and he felt her wetness.

Elevating his body on the bed, he started unbuttoning his jeans. A sliver of moonlight seeped through the blinds and caught her eyes—teary olive eyes that gazed up at him longingly. Lovingly. Innocently.

What was he doing? Was he using her, not just for sex, but as a lifeline to his own sanity, to prove to himself he was still a red-blooded, *normal* man?

God damn it, I'm not a normal man. I'm a broken man. Was he using Megan as a stand-in for Rachel? Did he have genuine feelings for this woman, or was she just a shabby substitute? Was he even capable of having feelings for another woman?

Locking his eyes with her moist orbs, he saw that she needed him in the same way he needed her. Pain, guilt, the loss of her friends—she, too, had the need for human intimacy.

He slipped off his pants and she rose up to meet him as he knelt on the bed. Her lips grew swollen and supple against his. The swell of her breasts pressed to his chest, as she pushed him back against the mattress.

Her lithe body mounted him, shadowing his movements, matching his passion, directing him slowly inside her with delicate fingers. Becoming erect, she straightened and tossed back her head, arching her back.

Sensing the essence of her entire body bathed in moonlight, Bruce saw her as if for the first time. Megan Eastwood was a beautiful woman. Her breasts heaved, and her hips rotated slowly. All the while, she looked down at him as if to ensure his satisfaction was equal to hers. She bit her lip, averted her eyes, and then returned her gaze to him. Her inner warmth radiated throughout his body. Down to his icy soul.

When it was over, he didn't hate himself as he'd thought he might. Nor did he hate Megan. Something had changed within him. She fell asleep in his arms. And for the longest time, he allowed her to be there.

He rose from the bed sometime later, went into the living room, and sat on the sofa in the darkness. He wasn't sure who he was anymore. In some strange way, he felt that Rachel was pleased with him for doing what he had just done. It would be just like her to want him to be with another woman, if he couldn't be with her.

She'd been dead for many weeks, and tonight was the first time, at this very moment, that he had accepted the fact she was gone.

Forever.

"Good-bye, Rachel," he said quietly. "*Shalom.*"

THIRTY-FIVE

"Good morning, Bruce."

Pause.

"Bruce?"

Pause.

"Hellooooo."

Pause.

"Get up, Bruce—you're late for school."

What?

"You're late for school!"

He groaned. *Late for school . . .*

Bruce ascended into consciousness, blinked the sleep from his eyes, and saw a body standing before him. There were specks of yellow paint on a pants leg, a bungee cord acting as a belt wrapped around the waist, then a plain white shirt. Jutting out of the shirt was Megan's head. She was looking down at him, grinning, with bright red hair falling over her eyes.

He strained to focus. "Did you say I would be late to school?"

She giggled. "It woke you up, didn't it?"

Right. Bruce smelled cooked bacon. She'd been busy. He took inventory of himself. He was lying on the living room sofa in his underwear, exactly the way he had fallen asleep the night before, after they had . . .

"Breakfast is waiting," she informed him. "We've got plenty of work to do." With that, she turned on her heel and headed for the kitchen.

Bruce rose from the sofa and lumbered into the bedroom, found his jeans and shirt, and put them on. He came back out and went to the kitchen where Megan was now sitting at the table. She kicked a chair with her bare foot, suggesting that he sit on it, which he did.

"Cream?"

Bruce nodded, and she poured some in the cup next to the plate of bacon and eggs before him. He took a sip of the coffee and studied Megan momentarily. Her skin had a rosy glow to it; her eyes were like two gemstones. She looked happier than he'd ever seen her, and he feared maybe he had something to do with that.

"Nice outfit," he remarked.

"You like? I found it in the attic. Probably better than wearing no pants."

Their eyes locked for an awkward moment. Bruce looked away.

"We have to write the article for *American Times* today," she said.

He pierced an egg with his whole-wheat toast and took a bite. "Before we write anything," he said, "I have a few questions." Actually, he didn't have any questions at all. He had a comment. He had begun to form a theory yesterday during the long car ride from Page to Durango. It was the first quiet time he'd had since meeting Megan, and he had used it to review her story. Certain parts just didn't add up. Now was the time to confront her with them.

He held her in his gaze. "I believe Reinhardt was in cahoots with the murderers who killed your crew in the Grand Canyon."

It seemed to take a moment before the words registered with her.

"That's not funny."

"It's not meant to be. I believe Reinhardt had a prior agreement with someone concerning the dig that you didn't know about. Maybe the party who funded it."

Megan's body jolted as if she'd just stuck her finger in a socket.

"I can't believe you would even—"

"Why didn't the murderers kill Reinhardt along with the others? Why?" Bruce leaned forward. "What caused the murderers to arrive at Re's Cavern? There's only one answer, Megan: *someone* in your group had to inform them of the find. It wasn't you, and from what you told me, I doubt it was one of your crew. That leaves only one person."

She violently shook her head. "And what? Jensen helped kill the crew, too? That's insane."

She was right, Bruce thought—it *was* insane. But the overall concept had some merit. "Just remove yourself from Reinhardt for a minute. Pretend you don't know him and hear me out."

"Pretend I don't know him? Pretend I don't know the most intelligent, ethical, and compassionate man I've ever met?"

Bruce held his hands up. "Please, just listen. Two days after the time capsules were found, everyone was murdered, right?"

"On the third day."

"The night before that, Reinhardt told you to go to Edwin Falls early the next morning and take pictures, didn't he?"

"I never told you that."

"That's how it went down, though, isn't it?"

"You're saying Jensen sent me away so I wouldn't be murdered with the others?"

"Stay with me. Let's just say, theoretically speaking, that the people who funded the excavation had a prior agreement with Reinhardt. The agreement was that when he found what he was looking for, he would contact them. Let's say he did that, and as a result they—or their hit men—showed up at Re's Cavern. Let's assume Reinhardt didn't know anyone would be murdered. Let's just assume, for reasons known only to him, that he just wanted you out of there when they arrived."

She said nothing.

"Reinhardt invited the murderers in," Bruce said. "It's the only logical answer." He studied her a moment to be sure she had digested the concept before he laid his next gem on her.

He continued. "And I think Reinhardt knew about the existence of the time capsules before you ever set foot in the Grand Canyon. They were the reason he decided to do the excavation at Re's Cavern in the first place."

Bruce didn't get the reaction he expected. There was no more shock on her face. Neither argument nor attack was forthcoming; in fact, she gave him a look that he could only classify as *admiration*.

She rose slowly from her chair, fetched herself another cup of coffee, and paced the kitchen floor. Bruce waited patiently. Finally, she turned back to him and said, "There are a few things you should know."

"I'm listening."

She sat back down at the table. "Do you know what the global grid system is?"

"The latitude and longitude lines of Earth?"

"That's right. The current prime meridian of the grid runs through Greenwich, England. Greenwich is zero degrees longitude. It is the dividing line between east and west. But that's an arbitrary designation. In eighteen eighty-four, there was a conference in Washington, DC, that included twenty-five nations, and they decided Greenwich would be the prime meridian. It's just an arbitrary designation, do you understand?"

"Got it."

"Before the meeting in eighteen eighty-four, there were *nine* other prime meridians at earlier times in history that we know of."

"I see."

"Jensen believed that at some point in our history an intelligent race used the Great Pyramid of Giza as the prime meridian."

"Interesting. Why did he think that?"

"If the Great Pyramid served as the prime meridian instead of Greenwich, you would get an entirely different view of the world. There exists a mathematical code system that ancient cultures used to determine where to place ancient sites and sacred temples around the world in relation to this grid."

"In relation to the Great Pyramid?"

"Yes. It's known as the Code, and it uses a number system called gematria."

"Never heard of it."

"Most people haven't. Gematria uses numbers to mask hidden truths and meanings within words. There are thousands of significant sites around the world that all relate to the Great Pyramid using the gematria mathematical system."

"What kind of sites?"

"Sacred sites, monoliths, stone circles, temples, cathedrals. Places like Stonehenge, Giza's Sphinx, Egypt's El Kula Pyramid, the Druid Mound in Massachusetts, the Oregon Vortex . . . I can't remember many of them. But I *can* tell you, they all hold great value in terms of unexplained mystery and otherworldly phenomena."

Bruce knew very little about these places. "What does all this have to do with your excavation?"

"The location of Re's Cavern has enormous mathematical significance relative to the Great Pyramid. It falls on a key nodal point of the pyramid grid."

"Which means?"

"Which means Re's Cavern had value to the ancient people who devised the pyramid grid. Jensen knew this. It's why he wanted to excavate there."

Bruce digested what Megan said. "How would the Egyptians, or the ancient people, know to place a remote cave in the Grand Canyon on their grid in the first place?"

Megan gazed out the window. "Mysteries have surrounded the ancient Egyptian cultures for centuries. I don't know the answer. Jensen didn't know all the answers. That's why we were doing the dig—to gather information. The one thing we knew for sure was that an undeniable connection existed between ancient Egypt and the Grand Canyon, for the reasons I just gave you. Jensen truly expected to find Egyptian artifacts buried there."

"Egyptian artifacts that were time capsules?"

She stared at him. "There was absolutely no way Jensen knew about the time capsules prior to finding them. No way." She exhaled loudly. "That said, there is one connection between the time capsules and ancient Egyptian culture."

"Which is?"

"Do you remember the icon I told you about that was emblazoned on the vessel in which we found the time capsules?"

Bruce remembered. "It was round and yellow like the sun."

"That's right."

"Do you know what the word *Re* means, as in Re's Cavern?"

"No."

"Re is the name of the Egyptian sun god."

Now it was Bruce who was shaking his head in disbelief. "So the vessel that housed the time capsules had a sun emblazoned on it and it was buried in the sun god's cavern?"

"Incredible, isn't it? Yet, on the other hand, as you know, the time capsules weren't directly from ancient Egypt—they were much older."

"Could they have been transported from Egypt at some point in history and put there?"

Megan smiled. "I considered that, but there are problems with that theory. Not the least of which is the vessel was embedded in rock that was millions of years old."

Bruce gathered the last bit of egg on his fork. "Why didn't you tell me all this before?"

"Hey, you were on a 'need to know' basis. You were already skeptical. I didn't want to blow you completely out of the water."

Interesting choice of words, Bruce thought. It was more like she'd thrown him in the water.

"It gets even better," Megan said. "Re's Cavern isn't the only site in the Grand Canyon named after an Egyptian god. Many of them are. "Isis temple, Tower of set, Tower of Ra, Horus Temple, Osirs Temple…and dozens more."

"And most of them are temples," Bruce commented.

Megan nodded. "Places of worship."

All interesting facts, he thought, but what did it tell him? "We have to find out who funded the excavation. That's the key."

She nodded. "I should have thought of it myself. But our first step is still to write the article and get it to *American Times*. If the truth about what happened gets published, maybe someone will read it and come forth with *something* that may give us a clue."

She stood up, walked to the entertainment center, and turned on the computer.

Bruce finished his breakfast, and then sat down in front of the monitor with her. He began writing the article starting with the initial planning of the excavation. He told the story that Megan had told him. Wrote about the pyramid grid and the group's desire to find Egyptian artifacts. About the crew discovering the time capsules, on through to Megan finding the dead bodies, and finally up to the present, of course omitting any details about their current location.

He would have liked to have the original tapes to send to Murdock Collier along with the article. Megan telling her story, in her own words, would add credibility to the piece. But the tapes had been destroyed in the helicopter crash, and they didn't have the time or equipment to recreate them. He did have pictures though, including ones of the FBI shooting at him.

It was late afternoon by the time Bruce finished writing the final draft. He printed out the pages and Megan read them. He'd written the story in the first person, from her point of view. She teased him about having written it so well. "You really had to get in touch with your feminine side for this!" She glanced at him with a hint of amorous allure. Reminiscent of the look he'd gotten the night before when she'd been on top of him bathed in moonlight.

"It's perfect," she said, smiling warmly.

Bruce transferred the pictures from his camera into the computer, the critical shots that would document what he'd outlined in the article.

Megan scooted close to his side as they looked at each shot.

"You have the e-mail address for *American Times* magazine, right?" she asked.

"I do. But I'm going to have to make the pictures smaller so they will e-mail okay. It'll take a few minutes."

"Fine. You get started while I use the washroom."

While Megan was gone, Bruce decided to write Peter a quick e-mail and let him know what was going on. He went to his Earthlink account. Twenty-nine new messages awaited him, most of them junk mail. But one from Peter was near the top of the list. This was no surprise. What was a surprise was the text in the subject line:

I need your help!

He clicked on the message, and the e-mail opened.

> *Dear Bruce,*
>
> I am being held captive. They tell me I will be physically tortured beyond my ability to tolerate the pain every day that Megan Eastwood is not delivered into their hands. Reply to this e-mail to learn where and when to deliver her to them. Hit reply now. Please help me. Peter.

What the F########! His heart froze. He clicked on the attachment. A photo of Peter filled the screen. It had been taken at night. Peter was sitting down. Silver duct tape was stretched over his mouth, and his hands looked tied behind his back.

Dear God. Is this for real?

He forced himself to reread the e-mail. Peter never used capital letters in his e-mails, yet this message had capital letters. Peter also would never start an e-mail with "Dear Bruce"—not in an e-mail. He would have just written "Bruce, or "Co," or even "Bubby."

Peter didn't write this e-mail.

Yet the e-mail had come from Peter's e-mail account, fortto30@yahoo.com.

The picture. *Was Peter really tied and gagged, or had someone taken an existing photograph of him and manipulated it?*

Having been in advertising, Bruce knew how it easy it was to Photoshop an image. Maybe they'd gotten a photograph of Peter and . . . He couldn't fool himself. Peter's eyes told the truth. He was scared. *Scared to death.*

Bruce suddenly felt like he was flying off in a hundred different directions. *Who had sent the e-mail? The FBI? Who? It had come from Peter's e-mail account, but who was behind it? Had they hurt Peter?*

He couldn't believe he hadn't seen it coming. As soon as he was spotted in the Grand Canyon by the FBI, he should have realized there might be disastrous ramifications.

He was a fucking idiot not to see it coming. He had already lost one family member because of his stupidity.

Rage boiled up inside him. He clicked on REPLY and began typing, numb fingers stabbing at the keys:

Tell me when and where to meet you. If you harm Peter in any way, you will never see Megan Eastwood, and you'll pay in ways you can't imagine.

He hit SEND.

Trying to control his breathing, he started downsizing the photographs while periodically refreshing his e-mail account. The reply to his e-mail came quickly. He went to open it when he heard Megan enter the room from behind him.

James J. Valko

"Let's do it!"
She plopped back down in the chair next to him.
"Did you send them the article?" she asked with a grin.
She looked so happy.
But Bruce felt sick to his stomach.

THIRTY-SIX

"Gotcha!"

Special Agent William Pittman stood over the computer station, working a gob of Big Red gum between his teeth. Seated in front of him was FBI computer technician Robert Minor. Standing next to him was Pittman's right-hand man, Agent Bill Kowalski.

They were in a makeshift office at the Grand Canyon information center. They had been tracking Bruce Brackin's e-mail account for the past twenty hours, ever since Pittman had verified with the managing editor of *American Times* magazine that Brackin had been on assignment for them in the Grand Canyon. Finally, an e-mail had been sent from the account.

Robert Minor stared at the computer screen in front of him, and in his usual light-speed manner of speaking, told Pittman the e-mail had been sent from Brackin's Earthlink account at 2:18 p.m. Mountain Time.

"From where?"

Minor stabbed a few keys. "According to the 'by' line, the ISP for the computer he is using is Verizon."

"Do we know who owns the Verizon account?"

"One second," Minor said. He rattled his mouse and hit some more keys.

Pittman waited impatiently, cracking his gum.

"The party who owns the account is called Henneburg & Root."

"A business?"

Minor nodded. "Yeah. Looks like they're an architectural firm in Chicago. They're at Fifteen Sixty South Michigan Avenue, to be exact."

Chicago?

"But you said the e-mail was sent at two eighteen *Mountain Time.*"

"The computer Brackin sent from is physically located in a Mountain Time zone. Henneburg & Root pays the ISP bill. Let me see if I can nail down the exact physical location the e-mail was sent from. One second." Minor clicked on the mouse and read the gobbledygook at the top of the screen, mountains of numbers and letters that looked like hieroglyphics to Pittman.

Minor shook his head. "I can't give you the physical location of the computer Brackin is at. The computer he's using is accessing the Internet through an anonymizer."

"A what?" Pittman asked.

Minor looked up at him over his glasses. "An anonymizer is a software program that prevents traffic analysis. It's designed to disguise where your e-mails are coming from and going to. Companies often use anonymizers for security purposes. I can only tell you he sent an e-mail. I can't give you the physical location."

"Is there any way to get around the anonymizer software?"

Minor rubbed his chin. "There's a way to get around any preventive software. I'll have to dig into it, make a few calls."

Pittman turned to Kowalski. "Contact this Henneburg & Root company and see if they have any offices or personnel in the Mountain Time zone."

Kowalski nodded. He crossed to the far side of the room and picked up a phone from the desk.

Pittman turned his attention back to Minor. "All right. For now, just tell me if you can read the e-mail Brackin sent?"

"No can do. I only know he was responding to an e-mail sent to him."

"From?"

The tech turned back to the computer screen. He typed and clicked some more and said, "It was sent from Peter Brackin's account."

The agency had done its homework and learned that Peter was Bruce's brother. They had already tried to contact Peter at his home and place of business, but had not yet been able to locate him.

"Did the e-mail come from Peter's house in New Jersey?"

The computer tech looked at the screen and scratched his head. "This is strange. Give me a second."

Pittman sighed. "Give me a second. Give me a second." Sometimes he hated computers. The trouble was you got used to them and expected instant results all the time, which wasn't always possible. He reminded himself that it was a miracle they had even gotten this far. Years ago, he would have had to get a search warrant to hack into an e-mail account or to pry into any private information about an individual. But today, with the Patriot Act in place, the FBI was free to investigate anyone it chose without written permission from any authority, which made his job a hell of a lot easier.

"I can't tell what physical location Peter Brackin's e-mail was sent from either," Minor said.

"Because the computer he sent from also has an anonymizer?"

"No, I don't think so. The address is just well disguised."

Minor pointed to the screen.

"See, this is the header here." His finger indicated the gibberish at the top of the page. "It's basically the record of where Peter Brackin's e-mail came from. As you can see, it has—" he counted under his breath "—thirty-seven received lines. Received lines are like links in a chain. The message is passed from one computer to the next with no breaks in the chain. The received lines indicate it ended up at jphotor@earthlink.net, Bruce Brackin's e-mail account, and it started at fortto30@yahoo.com, Peter Brackin's e-mail account. Basically, this e-mail was sent through many, many servers, and the header is designed to make it untraceable. There is no way to know what ISP or physical location it originated from."

"Enough." Pittman was getting a headache from all the geek talk.

They had to learn Brackin's exact location. In all likelihood, Megan Eastwood was still with him. Perhaps Minor could figure out a way to get around the software barrier, but getting the location directly from the Chicago company would probably be faster. He glanced over at Kowalski, who was talking to them on the phone. Hopefully, he'd get the information they needed without having to send an agent to their office.

Pittman retrieved his cell phone from his jacket pocket. He searched the menu items and found the FBI office in Denver. He needed them to be on standby. As soon he learned the whereabouts of Brackin, he would give the order for Denver to deploy a team of armed agents to the location. He gave a shout to Kowalski, who was still on the phone: "Any news?"

Kowalski looked back at Pittman, nodded, and gave him a thumbs-up.

THIRTY-SEVEN

It had taken all of Bruce's willpower to display some semblance of mental composure when Megan had walked back into the room.

"You haven't sent the article yet?" she asked as she sat next to him at the computer.

He blinked at her.

"I think we should snail mail it to them instead, Megan."

"Why?"

"My e-mail address. What if the FBI or someone else has a trace on it?"

Megan frowned. "Is it even possible to trace an e-mail address?"

"I don't know. But I would rather not take any chances."

She nodded. "Good point."

Bruce had to get her away from the computer. "Why don't you see if you can find an envelope big enough to put the pictures and the article in?" he said.

"Okay." She got up and went into the kitchen.

Bruce quickly pulled the second e-mail from Peter's captors up on the screen.

The hair rose on his neck when he read it, for it was agonizingly clear the captors knew he and Megan were in Durango. This house, which had been a safe haven for the last twenty hours, now seemed possessed by a ticking time bomb. Bruce didn't know a damn thing about e-mail hacking, but he had to assume the captors determined their whereabouts by tracing the e-mail he'd sent them.

Their instructions said for him and Megan to meet them at Greenmount Cemetery in Durango at 10 p.m. tonight. It stated that Greenmount Cemetery would be under surveillance. If Bruce told anyone, or if anyone accompanied him besides Megan, Peter would instantly be killed. If Bruce attempted to trace the e-mail, Peter would be instantly killed. Bruce racked his brain for an alternative course of action. Yet he could think of none. The rules of the game were simple: Megan for Peter.

"I found one!"

Bruce swiveled around in the chair to see Megan holding up a large brown envelope.

She picked up the *American Times* article and stuffed it in along with the pictures Bruce had printed out. Then she started mumbling something, but Bruce barely heard a word. He wanted to scream at her that it was over. A day from now, he would be nothing but a painful memory to her—*if she was still alive.*

He needed time to think. There had to be a way to divert the inevitable. He also needed to get out of this house, at least for a while. He'd mail the envelope, too. This would create a chance for him to be alone.

Megan was staring at him.

Dear God, don't look at me that way.

He couldn't believe what came out of her mouth next. "You are free to go."

"What?"

"You did exactly what I asked you to do, Bruce. You wrote the article. I don't need you anymore. You should return to New York and make sure the article gets published."

It sounded like she had been rehearsing a speech. But a tear betrayed her words. She didn't really want him to go. No way. *Then why did she say it?* Suddenly he got it. She had picked up on his anxiety and mistaken it as a sign that he wanted to leave her and return to New York. She was giving him an easy out.

How stupid was that?

He had to cement their relationship even more. She could have no more doubts about his intentions. None. Bruce swallowed hard, then reached out and took her hand.

"I'm not going anywhere until this thing gets resolved. We are a team to the end."

He aimed his words straight at her heart. Then he hugged her in a way that left zero doubt. And he felt like a big zero doing it. But it had to be done.

Please accept my promise and don't question me further.

Megan seemed to examine his response under a microscope. First, there was a look of concern, followed by a frown of consternation. Finally, a glimmer of affection showed in her eyes.

"Thank you," she said.

"I need to go into town to mail the package. I won't be long," he said.

"I need clothes."

This was true. But could he chance her being seen in public?

"I'll wait here," she said. "There's a clothing store called Top Drawer in town. Also I think I should dye my hair a different color, so I'm not so easy to recognize. What do you think about black?"

Bruce was glad one of them was thinking. "Yes. Black. Sounds good. I'll pick you up some dye. And clothes."

Megan was three steps ahead of him. She'd already decided what her new wardrobe would be, and the type of hair dye she wanted. She wrote it all down, and nestled up along side of him showing him the list.

And as she read each item aloud, he made a pact with himself. If the trade had to be done, when it was complete and he got Peter safely back to New York, he would kill himself. This time, without fail.

He moved away from her toward the front door, but before he could slip out she kissed him on the cheek and said goodbye.

It was a dark, dreary day; and while Bruce drove into town his thoughts were like hungry wolves flittering in every direction, searching for food—searching for a way to get back his brother without having to betray Megan.

He stopped at a gas station just outside the historic business district, filled up the car and grabbed a map of the Durango area. Next, he hit Top Drawer on Main Avenue and 8th Street. Inside the small boutique, a young woman slipped through a door of hanging beads from the back and asked if she could help him. Bruce simply handed her Megan's list of clothes and started pacing in circles, thinking.

Twenty minutes later, after the salesgirl gave Bruce a detailed explanation as to why she'd picked out the clothes she had, Bruce paid her cash and left the store, still with no solution in mind.

Back in the car, he drove to the post office, and slipped the *American Times* article into a mailbox. Then he went to the corner drug store and grabbed a bottle of black hair dye. Finally, he found Greenmount Cemetery, and drove slowly through the main entrance until the road veered to the left about five hundred yards in. He stopped and threw the car in park. This was the place the e-mail said they were to meet. The landscape looked like that of any other cemetery. Just being there gave him the creeps; bringing to life the last two funerals he'd attended, Rachel's and his fathers.

His father's funeral. . . He recalled the hundred and twenty-three USAF personal who had attended. Out of the sea of faces and deep blue uniforms one man in particular stood out, Major Brewster McCullen.

Bruce's father had served with McCullen for over twenty years in the Air Force. Together they had overseen the development of high-tech weapons designed to defuse enemy communication systems. While growing up, Bruce had seen McCullen often, and had often heard his father comment on how Brewster was an absolute genius when it came to electronic communications.

At the funeral Brewster had put his arm around Bruce and hugged him as if Bruce were his own son.

"Your father was the best man I've ever served with," Brewster said, handing Bruce his card. *"If you ever need anything at all, just call me. I will help you if I can."*

He threw the car in gear and raced through and out the back exit of the cemetery.

His next stop was at a pay phone back at the gas station. In the booth, he fished through his wallet until he found the card he was looking for. It was badly buckled from its trip down the Colorado. Yet he could still make out the phone number on it.

He picked up the receiver.

THIRTY-EIGHT

Bruce returned to the house to find Megan in high spirits. There's nothing like a shopping bag full of new clothes to put a hop in a woman's step he thought as he handed over the loot.

Although Bruce's spirits weren't so high, he was certainly in a better mood. The conversation with Major McCullen had gone better than he'd hoped for. *Far better.* The good major had meant it when he'd said, ". . . just call me, I will help you if I can." By all standards, he was certainly a man of his word. But neither of them was out of the woods yet, not by a long shot. At least now he had a plan that had potential for success.

In the living room, she modeled her new clothes for him: jeans, T-shirt, Polo shirt, a creamy gold tank dress, and a plain black jogging outfit. Her enjoyment of just being a woman, even for only a short period, was evident in her airy steps and sparkling eyes—a reprieve from reality, for her, but not for him.

His attempt to share her joy waned as his own reality began to sink in even more. The new plan was not a slam dunk by any means. It had to be carried out perfectly, and without Megan suspecting what he was doing. Even then it could fail.

Step One involved killing enough time to allow the same-day express envelope from Major McCullen to arrive at the Western Union station in Durango. Bruce engaged her attention by suggesting they use some of their free time to figure out what person, or group, had funded the Grand Canyon excavation.

After ending her enthusiastic modeling exhibition, Megan, still dressed in her new jogging outfit, scooted next to Bruce at the computer. For the next couple of hours they tried combinations of user names and passwords in an attempt to get into Reinhardt's online bank account and Facebook.com page. No luck there. Okay. Discovering who funded the excavation would have helped, but it wasn't crucial to the plan. More important, they had worked until six o'clock, time for the express delivery to have arrived from McCullen.

Step Two was for Bruce to get out of the house again, alone.

"How about pizza for dinner?" he asked.

"You like thick crust?"

"Sure."

"Gluten-free pizza at BeauJo's is the best. I'll call and order one."

"We shouldn't use the phone," Bruce said. After receiving the e-mail he knew the kidnappers could trace their phone calls. "I'll just go there to place the order and wait. You stay here."

Megan didn't argue with him.

He took the paper with BeauJo's address she'd found online and hurried out the door. After a quick stop to order the pizza, Bruce headed to the Western Union station. When he'd contacted McCullen earlier he'd shared every last detail about his situation with Megan.

The Major had accepted his story without question and even offered a suggestion. "I may be able to trace her whereabouts for you," he'd said and then described a high tech tracking device called "Little Ears" which the Air Force used to locate soldiers lost in battle.

Step Three was to somehow fasten "Little Ears" to Megan's clothes without her knowledge. It would be so much easier if he could just tell her the truth—tell her about Peter's e-mail and tell her that with the tracking device McCullen would be able to locate her whereabouts after Bruce turned her over to the kidnappers, tell her there was a possibility that she'd be rescued and the kidnappers would be caught—a slim possibility though it was.

But he couldn't tell her. He could not chance her being unwilling to give herself up in exchange for his brother. Peter's life was nonnegotiable. He *had* to get his brother back. *Megan's life should also be nonnegotiable.* He wished there was another way, but in the short time available, secretly implanting Little Ears in Megan's clothes seemed like the only solution.

The express mail package was waiting for him at the Western Union station as planned. Relieved, he picked it up and stopped at a convenience store to get a sewing needle, thread, razor blades, and a pair of needle-nose pliers. Then he drove back to

BeauJo's, picked up their dinner, and headed back to Michael's house where a strange woman greeted him at the door.

He did a double take.

"Megan?" he asked tentatively.

"You like?" she asked, raking her fingers through newly dyed silky black hair.

He stepped back to look more closely .

Black lines rimed her eyes, too, making them look even more emerald than usual and her lips were a deep, slick red. She was eerily beautiful.

"It smells wonderful," she said, referring to the pizza that he held in his arms. "Let eat." He followed her to the kitchen table where they devoured the pizza.

After dinner, it was time for the final step of his plan—just the thought of which made him squirm. It was the only thing he could think of to get her to remove her clothes so that he could implant the tracking device. He kept a cool exterior and held out his hand to her. She took it, and without a word, he led her into the bedroom, laid her on the bed and made love to her.

Afterwards, with her in his arms, he suggested they go for a walk.

"I'll shower downstairs and you can shower up here," he said.

Megan agreed, and went into the bathroom, leaving her jogging outfit where it had fallen, on the floor next to the bed.

Bruce quickly removed the tiny object from the envelope. He cut a slit in the waistline of the cotton workout sweats, sewed Little Ears into the lining, and stitched it back up. With the shower still running, he opened the bathroom door.

"Here's your clothes, Megan," he said, while laying them on the sink counter.

"Oh, aren't you the gentleman!"

Yeah right.

Bruce rushed downstairs and took a shower himself. When he was done, Megan was waiting for him at the front door, wearing, not the jogging outfit, but her new tank dress.

THIRTY-NINE

"We are approaching the target area now." Agent Breeden's voice vibrated in Pittman's cell phone.

Agent Breeden was heading up the FBI team that had been dispatched to Durango from the Denver office. Pittman had wanted to be there himself to capture Eastwood and Brackin, but there hadn't been time for him to fly to Colorado.

Earlier that day, they'd learned about the Henneburg & Root employee whose home in the Mountain Time zone had a computer that used the company's Internet Service Provider. But the employee was currently overseas, and the firm refused to give out his name or address without his permission.

Pittman had sent two agents from the Chicago FBI office to the firm to persuade Mr. Henneburg to call the employee, but because of the time zone difference, he was unable to make contact. After the call, Henneburg still wouldn't give out any information, despite the agent's threatening to arrest him for obstructing justice. Pittman ended up having to get a court order and search warrant, which took several hours. Finally, they'd learned that the employee's name was Michael Singer, and his house was in Durango, Colorado.

"We are in front of Singer's house now," Breeden said in Pittman's cell. "There are no cars at the curb or in the driveway. There is a faint light on the second floor."

"I'm sending four men around to the back," Breeden said. "We're going in."

"Go for it," Pittman said. It was times like this that he loved his job.

FORTY

Bruce had once read that when all is said and done, the life you've lived is the result of only one thing—the *decisions* you'd made along the way.

As he drove the car down the lonely cemetery road, he hoped to hell his most recent decision was the right one. If not, he, Megan, and Peter would likely never leave this place.

They probably have headstones planted for us already.

It was times like this that he wished he could believe in God––a higher power smarter than he to make his decisions for him. *At least then, if the wrong one was made, I could say that God did it—the one who works in mysterious ways.*

For many minutes, such stupid thoughts had been bouncing around inside his head. He looked over at Megan in the dark interior, who was fondling the gift he'd given her hanging around her neck just below her pendant of the Sphinx. It was the Star of David Rachel had bestowed on him on their third wedding anniversary.

Back at Michael's house, when he'd seen that she'd taken off her jogging outfit with the tracking device in it, he had to think fast. He told her he had a present for her, which he needed a few minutes to get ready to give her. He said that he needed to go back up to the bedroom and get it, that he thought it had fallen out of his pocket. He rushed up the stairs, found her jogging outfit, took out the tracking device, and put it in the pendant.

Using the needle-nose pliers he'd bought, he'd placed the tracking device between the star and the back plate. Giving it to her, he said that the Hebrew message on the back—the exact words of which he "couldn't remember"—were supposed to bring good luck to the person who wore it.

As he'd hoped, Megan was moved by the gesture.

He'd then told her that no matter what might happen to him, or her, she should never remove the star from around her neck. It sounded corny as hell. Nevertheless, she seemed to accept his words. Hopefully, a day from now, or a month, she'd remember what he'd said. And hopefully the tracking device would do the job lodged between two pieces of metal, rather than sewn into fabric.

The streets leading up to the cemetery had looked completely normal, with the amount of traffic you would expect at this time of night. He hadn't noticed anyone following him.

"This is where we are going to take a walk, in a cemetery?" Megan asked.

"No one will see us here," Bruce said, feeling his skin grow damp with perspiration.

The cemetery was dark, with only a few dim lamps along the narrow road. The e-mail had said the place would be under surveillance. *How?* Bruce wondered. *Were men posted in the shadows behind tombstones or around the outskirts of the cemetery?*

He inched the Ford forward until he came to the first crossroads where the e-mail had said to go, and pulled the car over. His heart drummed in his chest. He checked the clock on the dash: 10:03.

"This is kind of creepy," Megan said.

The clock clicked to 10:04.

Where are they?

She looked at him in the dark interior. "Well, are we going to get out?"

A floodlight stabbed out of the darkness in front of them. Blinding light invaded their car.

Bruce shielded his eyes.

"What is that?" Megan asked, also shielding her eyes.

He peered over his forearm. The light came from about fifty feet away. Bruce couldn't tell for certain, but he thought it was from a spotlight attached to a car.

"Let's get out of here," Megan said.

He didn't respond.

"Bruce! Let's get out of here!"

"I can't leave."

"Why?"

He turned toward Megan, but could say nothing. He remembered the first time he'd seen her in the backseat of his car, staring at him wide-eyed and nervous. She looked at him the same way now.

"What's going on here, Bruce?"

Maybe someday you will forgive me.

Movement caught his eye in front of the car. He faced forward again and saw out of the darkness, from behind the bright light, a wheelchair rolling toward him.

"Who is that!?"

It took every ounce of willpower Bruce had to face her again. He forced the words out:

"I'm sorry, Megan."

With that, he flung open the door and rushed out of the car.

"Bruce!" Peter's voice rang out.

Through tear-blurred eyes, Bruce watched his brother pushing the wheels of the chair toward him. Within moments, Peter's outstretched hand touched his.

Bruce heard Megan shout something from inside the car. He didn't understand her and didn't try. He hurled open the back door and told Peter to slide in.

Suddenly, the blinding light in front of them went out. It took a few moments for Bruce's eyes to adjust to the darkness.

Slowly, a vehicle rolled into view.

"Megan?" a husky voice called. "Megan?"

At first, Megan didn't respond, then . . .

"Jensen!" she screamed.

The Ford's lights were still on, and Bruce could see the outline of a mountain of a man standing beside the passenger side of the car in front of them.

Megan did exactly what she was supposed to do. She jumped out of the Ford and ran to Dr. Reinhardt with outstretched arms.

Bruce quickly collapsed Peter's wheelchair, chucked it into the trunk, and jumped into the driver's seat. He didn't allow himself a moment to question his decision. With Peter in the backseat, Bruce threw the Ford in reverse and gunned it.

The e-mail had guaranteed this was not a trap, and there would be no harm to either Peter or himself after Bruce gave them Megan.

"You will be allowed to leave without interference. Our concern is only with Eastwood," it had said.

Right. This was from the same people who had offed a group of archeologists.

Yet Bruce had no choice but to believe them. If they were to muster an attack, he had no defense. All he could do was try to get the hell out of there—fast!

The last thing he saw was Megan in Dr. Reinhardt's arms. She turned to watch the Ford speeding away in reverse. Her big green eyes reached out to him. They were glossed over with tears, reflected in the Ford's headlights, and grew distant as the car retreated. Bruce tore his gaze from her, threw the wheel to the right, and slammed on the brakes. The car spun around and skidded to a stop.

With the front of the car now pointing away from Megan, he stabbed the accelerator and sped out of the cemetery.

FORTY-ONE

Megan turned to Jensen, confused.

She barely had the breath to talk. "Jensen, what is happening here?"

"In the car," a voice said.

Megan looked beyond Jensen and saw a man in the back seat of the car aiming a gun at them. He wore a black hood. Two men in the front seat also wore hoods. *Are they the same men who attacked us in the forest? The same men who killed Dillon?*

"Get in the car, now!" the man ordered.

"You fucking bastards! Fucking killers!" Megan blurted out.

Jensen gasped. "Megan, stop." He tightened his grip on her arm.

Fury raged in her like she'd never experienced. "You don't even have the guts to show your killer faces!"

"Tell her to shut up and get in the car. Now!" the hooded man ordered Jensen.

Jensen's face drew closer to Megan's. "Do what they say. Don't argue with these men. Don't *ever* argue with these men."

She looked into his eyes. They darkened, and his massive fingers gripped her triceps even harder. "You *must* obey them. Don't say another word!"

She nodded as she allowed Jensen to pull her into the car. *So confused . . .*

The man in the passenger seat turned and handed her a black hood. He told her to put it over her head and not remove it. He also handed a hood to Jensen.

Megan did as she was told. The hood blinded her completely as she felt the car move forward.

She was besieged by conflicting emotions—on one hand, ecstatic to be with Jensen, on the other sickened by what Bruce had done.

Just before Bruce had spun the car around, his eyes met hers. The space between them became nonexistent, like it had the

229

night before when they made love. Megan had never experienced this with a man before, this *oneness*.

But as she'd watched Bruce race away, she now knew the oneness was only an illusion, a desire created solely by her imagination. He'd used her.

FORTY-TWO

As they had sped down the streets of Durango and on to Route 60, Peter kept one eye out the back window while clamoring on about how the *conspirators* had kidnapped him. But, why?

"Who was that woman, Bruce? What do they want from her? Dr. Reinhardt, I recognized him, but they wouldn't allow me to talk to him. What does he have to do with all this? How did *you* get involved in this? What are they after?"

Bruce didn't respond as he was too busy choking back his grief. That look in Megan's eyes when he had abandoned her: the pain and bewilderment.

And his own questions also suffocated him: What was Reinhardt's real role in all this? What side was he on? Will Megan keep the necklace around her neck that he gave her, or will she throw it away out of spite? Will the tracking device even work at one-hundred-percent efficiency? *Major McCullen told me to put it in clothes, not between a stone and metal backing. Would the signal even work?*

He could hardly believe they'd even made it out of the cemetery, yet alone out of Durango. Despite the final e-mail the kidnappers had sent that promised they would not harm his brother, Bruce had expected trouble. Certainly, Peter's captors—now Megan's—would feel compelled to rid the world of the only two people who knew of their existence who weren't now under their control. Namely, Peter and him.

And he was right. It was only minutes after they got on Route 60 when the inevitable happened:

"Look!" Peter gasped.

About a mile-and-a-half back, headlights appeared on the road behind them. A string of cars had come over a rise. Floodlights extended outward from the lead cars, searching the dark highway for prey.

It suddenly became obvious why they had been allowed to travel this far from Durango. Megan's captors wanted to do away with Peter and him on a desolate road, out of the city, where there was less chance someone would see them.

But that made no sense, either. They had been in a cemetery, for Christ's sake. Megan's captors could have killed them right there and buried their bodies—and no one would ever know.

"How many cars are there, Peter?"

"Hard to tell. Six, seven?"

Bruce tried to envision outrunning the posse. The road ahead was long and straight. He was driving a mid-sized, six-cylinder Ford. No way.

The road dipped, and the headlights disappeared behind them. Momentarily they weren't in the sights of their pursuers.

They passed an intersecting side road. Bruce thought that if he killed the lights, he could jump off the highway and on to the side road, hopefully without being seen.

He hit the brakes. Snapped off his headlights, left on the parking lights. He did a sharp U-turn. Tires screamed. He gunned it, heading back to the side road they'd just passed. It was disturbing to race *toward* their pursuers, even if the posse couldn't see them.

"There!" Peter barked. "Turn. Turn!"

Bruce shoved the wheel down and hung a quick left. The car started to skid off the road into a field. He fought the wheel. Regained control. Got both tires on the pavement. Raced forward. Without headlights, it was almost impossible to see the narrow road. Should he continue with the lights out, moving at thirty-five miles per hour, or turn them on and step on it?

He opted to keep the lights off. Being invisible was more important than speed. The road curved right. The tires jumped on the gravel shoulder. Bruce slowed. Got back on track.

Peter was gawking out the back window. "I can't see them," he said.

"Good. That means they can't see us."

They drove forward. *Slowly forward.*

For the briefest of moments, Bruce thought their luck had turned. He didn't know where this road would lead, but enough time had passed for him to believe the posse had passed the side road and was continuing to race down Route 60.

Then a sound overhead.

Peter rolled the window down, stuck his head out, and looked skyward.

"A helicopter!" he cried.

Seconds later Peter amended his statement.

"Actually, there's two!"

FORTY-THREE

The drive was long, giving Megan time to think. But her mind felt like it had exploded into a million fragments that she was groping to put back together.

Who was the guy in the wheelchair? How had these arrangements been made? And when? How long had Bruce known about this? A day? A week?

The questions were like daggers being thrust into her heart.

Juxtaposed to this pain was the unbelievable reality that she was with Jensen again.

Jensen's broad shoulder pressed firmly against her. She wanted to ask him so many things, but he had made it clear she was not to say a word. She concentrated on her breathing, trying to stay centered.

She didn't know how much time passed before the car stopped. The doors opened, and she was grabbed and pulled from the vehicle. The captors handcuffed her hands behind her back.

"Jensen!"

"Just cooperate," he said firmly.

Though blinded by the mask, Megan could tell by his voice that he was standing next to her. She recognized the sound of jet engines nearby. She was led across an open space, up some stairs, and into the cabin of the aircraft.

"Jensen?"

"I'm here, Megan."

She was told to sit next to him, and she rested her head on his shoulder. The engines roared, and the plane sped forward. Hours passed. Megan dozed in and out, but never fully slept. The plane landed. A hand clamped down tightly on her right arm and pulled her out of the cabin. She called Jensen's name yet again.

"I'm here, Princess," he said.

Princess. It was a silly nickname he'd given her long ago on their first excavation together. She had complained about everything: about getting her fingernails dirty when digging, about the food, about their not having anyone to wash the pots and pans. She was just teasing him. Nevertheless, from then on, she was Princess Eastwood.

Now she was being led away from the sound of the jet engines, through humid hot air. *Tropical?*

They were brought under the swirling rotors of what was undoubtedly a helicopter. They sat silently in the cabin. After a short flight, they landed.

They were pushed out of the helicopter, again into the heat. They stopped walking after a short distance, and Megan heard metal against metal—*a door being unlocked?* She was pushed forward into a cool, air-conditioned space.

As they walked forward, Jensen told her they'd soon be separated. He repeated that she should do whatever they asked of her *without resistance*. She hated that tone in his voice. It wasn't him—it was one of a cautious man, not Jensen. But she made a firm resolve to follow his instructions and told him so.

"Try to get some sleep. Tomorrow is a new day," he said. It was a phrase he uttered often.

Tomorrow is a new day, and the next, and the next after that.

The implication being life is always new—a potential bright future just around the corner.

"Good-bye, Megan," Jensen said. His voice already sounded distant.

The person leading Megan stopped abruptly, and she again heard metal against metal. The cuffs were removed, and she was shoved from behind. As she staggered forward, she heard a door close behind her, everything happening so quickly. She tore off the mask and found she was alone in a small room. There was a single bed and a nightstand with one lamp, but no windows. The walls were gray, the ceiling white. Too exhausted to contemplate her circumstances any longer, Megan fell on the bed.

Try to get some sleep, Jensen had said.

She turned out the light, sunk her head into the pillow, curling it around her face, and tried desperately not to think of Bruce. She lay there for the longest time, unable to sleep.

Then a pungent odor stung her nostrils. It took a moment to register. Gas vapors were flooding into the room.

Megan flew into a panic. She jumped to her feet and struggled to open the door. It was locked. Gasping for air, she hammered her fists against it. She screamed, for all the good it did.

It only took a few moments before a calm came over her. *What's the problem?* Her body fell against the wall and slid down onto the cold floor.

Life is beautiful.

Tomorrow is a new day.

FORTY-FOUR

White light seeped through her eyelids, nudging her awake. At first, her mind couldn't register what was happening. There were no thoughts, just a vague awareness that she existed.

The room was sharply lit by fluorescent lights shining down from the ceiling. No windows or pictures on the walls. The only object was a gray veneer nightstand next to the bed in which she lay.

Slowly, a sense of reality began to form. She became aware she was in a place she'd never been before. She wondered if it was a hospital, but she saw no medical equipment, no blood pressure machine, no rails on the bed.

She sat up. Leaning against the headboard, she struggled to recall how she had arrived there. For that matter, she tried to remember *anything*. But her mind offered no memories or points of reference. Her only certainty was the pain in her head, like she had a wreath of thorns wrapped around her skull. There was another pain, too—a sharp one in the back of her neck. Megan ran her fingers over the skin there and thought it felt slightly swollen, but she wasn't sure.

She sensed something else. She was not alone in the room.

She threw off the covers, found the floor with her bare feet, and stood up.

Then—a mental picture of a car.

It faded. She knew this car, but couldn't pinpoint it. *Where or who . . .*

A mental picture of a wheelchair.

Who . . .

Bruce Brackin. The dark outline of his face behind a windshield. His eyes running from her.

Then she remembered Jensen, and the hooded men he was with. Then the long ride away from Durango and the flight to this place, where gas had rendered her unconscious.

Her body was suddenly chilled. She looked down and saw she was wearing only a bra and panties. Beige panties? These weren't hers. What the . . . ? Nervously, she ran her fingers along the fresh scar on her stomach and down her thighs. Something else was wrong. She sniffed under her arms. Then she raked her fingers through her hair. The scent of the shampoo was unfamiliar. She'd been bathed. By whom?

What else had been done to her?

Feeling dizzy, she sat down on the edge of the bed. She looked over her surroundings again, this time more focused, and noticed a television camera situated at the ceiling in each corner of the room.

She rose again to her feet and moved on wobbly legs across the cold tile floor to the bathroom. Inside were two more cameras and a large closet. Not only were the clothes inside the right size, they were styles she might have picked herself—earth-colored body shirts of amber and green, cotton tops, and shorts. There were Levi's blue jeans and white T-shirts with a breast pocket, just the way she liked them. There were even shoes in her size.

She slipped on a pair of jeans, stepped into a pair of sandals, and buttoned up a blue cotton blouse. While doing so, she noticed for the first time her pendant—both her pendants—were missing from around her neck.

It was her pendant of the Sphinx that most concerned her. She'd worn it faithfully for eight years. The other pendant from Bruce—what had he said when he'd given it to her? That it would bring her good luck? What a joke. Why would he do such a cruel thing knowing he was going to turn her over to the murderers?

She looked up at a camera. "My pendants!" she barked. There was a microphone attached, which meant they could hear her. "Where are they?"

Of course she didn't expect a response.

There was a loud metallic clang from the other room. She exited the bathroom and found the door unlocked.

She plodded unsteadily across the room, through the door, and into a hallway. Small yellow circles ran down the carpeted center of the hall, not unlike a broken yellow line of a highway. She followed them.

As her balance returned, she quickened her pace. The carpet crunched beneath her step, like walking on graham crackers. She passed two doors on either side of the corridor, but both were locked. She continued forward, following the yellow circles.

Follow the yellow brick road.

At the end of the hallway, she saw a blinking red light above a door. The cherry glow beckoned her to advance. The blinking light turned solid red when she reached the door.

She slowly turned the knob. Once started, the door opened by itself.

An expansive, futuristic-looking room stretched before her. She gingerly stepped forward onto a translucent floor. Instead of shining down from the ceiling, the light radiated up from under the floor. She inched forward tentatively, moving into the open space. The air had a deafening, dark hush to it, which Megan assumed was caused by the thousands of tiny foam rubber cones protruding from the walls. Her hand grazed the cones as she passed.

Computer workstations lined one wall. Built into the opposite wall was an instrument panel not unlike something on the starship *Enterprise*. Computerized lights flickered on and off, creating a medley of dancing colors. In the center of the room was a glass conference table.

Other rooms adjoined the main room, separated from it by glass walls.

As Megan moved further into the space, spherical objects came into view in one of the adjoining glass rooms. She gasped, and a flood of emotions swelled within her.

The time capsules!

The sight of the metallic orbs sent her mind reeling back to the moment when she had first seen them in the Grand Canyon.

She and Dr. Reinhardt had entered the shadowy vessel. Jensen's flashlight had cut through the blackness and illuminated the capsules. Three of them were four feet in diameter, while the fourth one was over ten feet. They were grouped together each nestled in its own concave indentation in the floor, with dozens of tiny holes rimming the perimeter of each indentation. Jensen had speculated that at one time, an inert gas had blown out of the holes, lifting the capsules and suspending and protecting them within the vessel, the same way the white of an egg suspends and protects the yoke.

The archeological team had found six pinholes on the surface of each of the smaller capsules. The team had inserted a safety pin into each hole of one capsule, triggering the opening of a surface valve that allowed air to enter the vacuum-sealed interior. For two hours, the valves had whistled softly as the capsule took in air. Then the top section of the capsule had literally sprung open, separating itself from the bottom section by the action of two interior mechanical arms. Iridescent green liquid had oozed out and over the edge—presumably a chemical preservative of some kind. Submerged in the liquid had been a titanium trunk, and inside that the solar computer.

Then they had concentrated their efforts on the larger capsule. It, too, had pinholes, not six like the others, but twelve in a circle. When they inserted the pin into these holes, a small rectangular panel slid open. Underneath the panel were two glass plates designed to accept two handprints as identification codes to open the time capsule. They had used Jensen's right hand and Megan's left. The capsule had obviously recorded them then automatically programmed the unit to forever need the same two prints to open it.

Inside the larger time capsule had been a single chair, a metal footboard, a wristband, and a metallic headpiece—a picture of simplicity. They had closed the capsule, deciding to reopen it later once they had analyzed the contents of the other capsules.

Later never came.

Megan knew her captors had pursued her because she possessed the key that opened the large time capsule—her left hand. She never told Bruce about this larger capsule, and was now happy she hadn't.

A man entered the room across from where she stood. He strolled to the glass wall and examined the time capsules. His demeanor seemed to literally take ownership of them. Then his body grew rigid, like a deer alert to changes in its environment. He turned and faced Megan. His laser-like gaze crossed the open space and took ownership of her as well.

She ran to Dr. Reinhardt. He folded her into his arms.

"Are you all right, Megan?"

"Doing okay," she whispered, notwithstanding her aching head.

He held her to him for many moments. Then she stepped back and looked into his face. He looked different today. It wasn't physical as much as—as what? There was a radiant glow about him, a youthful vitality. His russet eyes, alive with energy, studied her as if inspecting her for any broken parts.

"What is this place, Jensen?"

He said nothing, only looked over Megan's shoulder and focused on something behind her. She turned to see what he was looking at. It wasn't a something but a someone.

"Hello, Megan," the man said with a grin.

FORTY-FIVE

Megan rushed forward and threw her arms around Dillon.

"I thought you were . . ." she stopped herself from saying the word.

"Dead? I wouldn't miss this for the world." He grinned.

She stepped back to inspect him. He looked so different from the last night she'd seen him, as his eyes were bright and color had returned to his cheeks. His arm was encased in plaster from wrist to bicep. He even wiggled his fingers for her to demonstrate they still worked.

"What happened that night after we . . ." Again the words got caught in Megan's throat—*after we abandoned you?*

Dillon told her that while the man in the forest had had a gun aimed at his head, another gunshot had rung out from above them. Two men rappelled down ropes from a helicopter. They had fired a warning shot, apparently to stop their accomplice on the ground from killing him. A net fell over Dillon, and they hoisted him into the aircraft. The next thing he knew, he'd woken up in this place.

Megan was happy to see Dillon, yet she didn't understand. She assumed she was here because her handprint was needed to open the time capsule. But why had they brought Dillon to this place? She didn't have the answer, but for the time being it didn't matter. He was alive. They were all alive.

"We'll start with a tour," Jensen said.

He turned on his heel and headed toward a door.

Tour? Megan scurried beside him "What about the time capsules? Aren't you going to show us what's in them?"

"They are off-limits to us at the moment, Megan."

"But they're right there," she protested, and pointed at the glass wall. Plainly visible on the other side were the otherworldly artifacts Megan yearned to examine.

"We don't have access to that room."

"Why not?"

Jensen stopped to face her.

"They do what they want for reasons known only to them."

"But you *have* viewed their contents, haven't you?"

"I've done little else since I've been here. But right now, the time capsules are off-limits."

As an archeologist, Megan knew Jensen was aware of the torment she was experiencing. The treasure chests were in view, yet she wasn't allowed to see inside them. She wanted to protest even louder, but a threatening glare stopped her.

"Come," Jensen said. He shoved a door open and stepped through.

Dillon and Megan followed Jensen down the carpeted hallway. He led them through a door into a room complete with Stairmasters, a dozen weight machines, treadmills, upright bicycles, and other exercise equipment. He walked to the back-mirrored wall and lowered his bulk on an exercise bench.

"Where are we?"

"A workout room."

Megan frowned, while Jensen's bearded mouth arched into a smile. "I know what you meant. However, we can't discuss our whereabouts. Besides, I don't know where we are." The smile disappeared.

Jensen took her free hand and gently squeezed her fingers, a gesture for her to listen very carefully to what he was about to say.

"The rules here are simple: we don't ever discuss *who* our captors are, we don't talk about *where* we are, and we never discuss how we might *leave* this place. Never. Do you understand?"

Megan understood perfectly. They were prisoners. She looked up at the ceiling. As in her room, cameras were situated in each corner. Their captors were watching their every move and listening to their every word.

"Megan?"

"I understand," she said. Then she asked the question that had been burning inside of her for the last six days: "What happened to the crew at Re's Cavern? How did they die?"

Jensen's expression grew dark. He seemed caught off guard. Yet surely he had to have known the question was coming. "I have much to tell you," he uttered softly. "Follow me."

Megan and Dillon trailed Jensen back into the hallway.

Jensen pointed at two wooden doors as they passed.

"Saunas," he said. "Use them any time."

At least it's a white-collar prison, thought Megan. And there was something else unique about it. She felt a slight and constant swaying—a subtle motion similar to being on an ocean liner.

She scooted up alongside Jensen and intertwined her arm with his. A good foot taller than she, he had a Paul Bunyan-sort of presence—a lumberjack persona that any woman would find appealing, not in a sexual way, not for Megan, but in a *survival* way. She felt protected in Jensen's presence. It wasn't just because of his physical size either but because of his intelligence. Megan had once told him he should run for president. But Jensen didn't see himself that way, as he had told her he was just an archeologist and a teacher. His modesty made him that much more appealing.

They passed through another door into a beautifully decorated library with rows of varnished wood bookshelves. The group gathered around a table and sat down.

Jensen removed a handkerchief from his pocket, dabbed his brow, and told Dillon and Megan what had happened that morning in Re's Cavern.

They learned how Jensen had found all the crewmembers in the main tent stumbling about with saliva dribbling from their mouths. They learned about the men who had entered the tent wearing helmets, chaining Jensen up, and putting a helmet on him. They learned about how the men had handed out cups of poisoned juice that the crewmembers willingly drank. They learned how Jensen had only been able to helplessly watch as each crewmember died.

"What was the helmet they put on you?" Dillon said.

"It made the negative feelings disappear," Jensen said. "My coordination returned, and I was able to think logically. They wore helmets, too."

Listening to all this, Megan was consumed with one thought: she should have been there with Jensen and the others that morning. Instead, she'd been off taking pictures of Edwin Falls.

"Reinhardt told you about Edwin Falls, didn't he? He was the one who suggested you take pictures that morning, wasn't he?"

The night before the murders, Megan and Jensen had stayed up late discussing how the time capsules would challenge one of the most cherished beliefs of modern man: the theory of evolution.

Just before midnight, Jensen had handed her a map.

"I want you to take pictures of Edwin Falls, first thing tomorrow morning," he had said.

At the time, Megan had wondered why he'd given her such short notice, especially as she would need a partner. Traveling in twos was the first rule of hiking over unknown terrain.

Stop being paranoid. Jensen had simply wanted pictures for the record book. He probably assumed she would wake someone the next morning and make the person go with her. *I should have made the entire crew go with me!*

"Why did they drink the apple juice?" Dillon asked.

"They had no choice. They were like robots all following the same internal commands."

"No one told them to drink it?" Megan asked.

"Not outwardly. I think they were following the commands of someone from outside that somehow got into their minds."

"These internal commands *caused* them to act that way?"

Jensen was shaking his head. "I don't know." His eyes swiveled to the camera in the room as he seemed to debate whether to linger on this subject.

"Psychotronic weapons with subliminal voice capabilities," Dillon muttered.

Surprised, they looked at the old man. "What did you say?" Jensen asked him.

"Psychotronic weapons might have been used on your crew," Dillon said. "The technology has been around for years. But I've never heard it used for anything like *this*."

Jensen adjusted his bulk, causing the chair to creak. "Tell me what you know, please."

Dillon gathered his thoughts. "I wrote a piece about psychotronic weapons several years back. I'm not an expert on the subject, but this I can tell you: the purpose of such weapons

245

is to bring a person into a submissive state. A machine broadcasts extremely-low-frequency electromagnetic waves that have mind-altering potential. These waves travel through the air and are able to permeate brain tissue and affect the nervous system of the target person. Governments have been experimenting with such weapons since before World War II. The Russians especially tested psychotronic weapons in the eighties. It's believed the U.S. military has advanced the technology since then, but no one can prove it because the government keeps it a secret."

"How is it possible for psychotronic weapons to alter someone's mental state?" Jensen asked.

"The theory is that the low-frequency waves can carry emotional signatures within them."

"Emotional signatures?"

"For some time, scientists have been able to identify and isolate different emotions in the brain by studying computer-enhanced EEG scans. They call them 'emotion signature clusters,'" Dillon said. "These clusters can be synthetically reproduced by duplicating their wavelengths and storing them in a computer. The clusters can then be encoded into the electromagnetic radio waves that are broadcast by the psychotronic machine. The recipients experience the emotional signatures being emanated at them."

"So if the emotional signature being emanated is one of severe depression, let's say, the recipient would then experience depression?" Jensen asked.

Dillon nodded. "That seems to be what happened to your crew. But as I said, I've never heard of a case this extreme."

"But how would these electromagnetic waves cause everyone to drink the apple juice?" Megan put in. "Jensen said it was as if everyone were ordered to do so."

"In all likelihood, subliminal synthetic sounds were also encoded in the electromagnetic waves. These are high-pitched commands that can't be detected by the human ear. It sounds like your crew was put in a depressed emotional state and then subliminally commanded to drink the apple juice. Security systems in shopping malls have been utilizing subliminal synthetic commands for years. Along with the musical broadcast that you hear in stores, there are hidden subliminal messages that issue threats against shoplifting."

"They must have set up a machine near the campgrounds," Megan said. She watched Jensen rub the back of his neck, noticing her own neck was starting to itch.

Dillon turned to Megan. "In the interviews I did, I was told psychotropic weapons were used on one person at a time, with a machine set up right next to him or her. I've never heard of a group being subjected to them. From my understanding, low-level frequency waves don't travel great distances through the air." Dillon paused to massage his neck. Beads of sweat had begun mounting on his brow. "I'm not sure where the machine, or machines, would have been set up in relation to your crew."

The tingling on the back of Megan's neck was turning into burning heat. Then she remembered . . . remembered how she felt when she awoke that morning. She had a headache, and the back of her neck was sore. Something had been done to her during the night. *Something had been placed in her neck that was now coming to life!*

She watched Jensen and Dillon start to squirm in their chairs. Jensen held up his hand, palm out, as a signal for them to stop talking. But it was too late. A hot tremor trailed down Megan's spinal column, and a thousand razor sharp needles stabbed her back muscles. *Was she being electrocuted?*

"No!" Jensen pleaded to a camera, but the sickening current only grew stronger.

Megan's coordination faltered as she tried to stand up; the searing heat ravaging her muscles caused them to spasm forcing her back into the chair. Out of control body tremors left her eyes rolling back into her head then swiveling in place while she tried to focus on her friends, a blur of quivering bodies before her.

The pain was unfathomable. How long would it last? How long could she take it? She looked at her quaking left hand, the key that opened the door to the larger time capsule. She lifted her trembling fingers for the camera, hoping their captors would get the message—*if you want the capsule open, you need me alive! Or did they? Could they use her handprint, along with Jensen's, even if they were both dead?*

247

Megan's insides shuddered violently. Unable to breathe, her surroundings faded, growing darker. Her last memory was of Bruce Brackin. *What a waste!*

FORTY-SIX

Every day of the week for more than thirty years, Murdock had arrived at his office to find a stack of ATP news releases sitting on his desk. Today was no different, except there were two additional items next to the ATP articles—a thick envelope from Bruce Brackin and a rough draft of an article written by Madeline based on Charlie Gabaree's briefing the night before.

Murdock was anxious to read Brackin's correspondence, but the headline of the top ATP article caught his eye.

EASTWOOD SPOTTED—FBI AGENT GUNNED DOWN!

According to the article, Megan Eastwood had been spotted in the Grand Canyon. She'd reportedly entered Re's Cavern with a man. A chase ensued and ended in a confrontation during which the man shot and killed an FBI agent. It said the man, Bruce Brackin, was an employee of *American Times* magazine!

Brackin was just a freelancer, Murdock thought, not a Times employee. *They should get their damn facts straight.*

Murdock eased into his soft leather chair, tossed aside the ATP article, and picked up Brackin's package. He slid the papers and photographs out of the envelope and spread them out on the table. Cradling his chin on his bony hand, he looked over the article. The pages were cluttered with red ink.

The *American Times* copy editor, Ed Mattingly, arrived at six o'clock each morning to edit articles before they came to Murdock. He had left a mass of comments in the margins of this one: "Wow!" "Impossible!" "Must substantiate!" Murdock looked past the red scribbling and began reading.

Brackin's article matched the e-mails Gabaree had shown him the night before, except for one notable point: according to Brackin, the FBI had chased him and Eastwood in Re's Cavern and "tried to kill both of us."

Brackin had included photographs of various sections of the Grand Canyon: a picture of Eastwood climbing an escarpment, another of her smiling for the camera with her red hair glistening under the sun. She looks like any other tourist, Murdock thought. She also looked like his first wife, Kathleen—bright Irish eyes with milky, sunburned skin.

Another photograph showed two FBI men—one pointing a finger at the camera, the other a rifle. The letters "FBI" were printed boldly on their shirts. A Post-it note on the picture read, "The FBI agents as they fired at us."

Of course, Brackin made no mention of him killing an FBI agent, as Agent Pittman had told Murdock in their phone conversation. Indeed, Brackin's article said he and Eastwood were unarmed when the agents fired on them.

Brackin's article went on to say a "friend" had helped them escape from the Grand Canyon by helicopter. An FBI helicopter had tracked them down, but it had been blown out of the sky by yet another helicopter. Murdock didn't like what he was reading. He glanced at the corresponding pictures, one of the FBI helicopter and another of its conqueror, a savage-looking chopper replete with heavy artillery. Murdock's chest started to tighten. Had Overmeyer or Truss Industries been involved in shooting down an FBI helicopter?

Murdock finished reading the article, and then read it again. Whatever doubts he'd had on the first read-through dissolved on the second. Bruce Brackin might be an inexperienced reporter, but he was an ad copywriter with a reputation for integrity and an eye for detail. The truth was evident on these pages. He'd have no reason to make up, or even exaggerate, the story.

The new pain in Murdock's chest, which had started the day before, now clawed at his insides for the third time that morning. It felt like an alien creature with razor talons scratching its way out from under his ribs. He tucked in his chin and took tiny, shallow breaths. Short of doping himself into a stupor with Demerol, it was the only way to ease the pain. *I'm going to die a slow, painful death. . .* When the burning lessened, he read Madeline's rough draft. It was written in the old journalist manner, masculine and powerful in style.

When done, he held Brackin's article in his left hand and Madeline's in his right. Both read like fiction, yet there were enough similarities and "hard facts" to make them believable.

No other media source had these stories, making them tickets to publishing prosperity. If Murdock chose to print one of them—or both—*American Times* wouldn't be just reporting news: they'd be making it. The Grand Canyon story could do for *American Times* what Watergate had done for *The Washington Post* in the seventies.

And the timing couldn't be better: the Grand Canyon stories would run just as the new promotional campaign was being launched.

American Times Magazine. The Stories Behind the News.

If only life were that simple.

He let his mind wander, thinking for a moment of the gorgeous blonde he'd seen in a restaurant that morning. She had crossed her legs the way women do, and a bare thigh parted the slit in her skirt, exposing a long, beautifully tanned leg. Just a glance had invigorated him. Half-dead and headed south, he still dreamed of love—that insatiable desire that had driven him his entire life. As an old fuck, he still wanted it. Not to be loved as much as to love. Body and soul, he wanted to give—to *own* someone from head to heel. Taste her young sweet juice. He could do it. He knew he could still do it. Just the thought lessened the pain in his cancerous chest. A young woman would make him feel alive again. He could steal back some of the years. Imagine that—at his age, still looking for love.

Murdock knew his excursion into dreamland was an act of avoiding the task at hand.

Madeline's article implied that G. C. Overmeyer was involved in the Grand Canyon incident. That was a problem.

He lifted his weary eyes to gaze at the east wall of his office. Several covers of past *American Times* issues hung in gold-leaf frames. They dated all the way back to the 1930s, showing the stellar history of the honorable magazine. There was a cover showing soldiers raising an American flag on a battlefield, representing American victory in World War II. There was Elvis, the Beatles, Richard Nixon, Ronald Reagan, Neil Armstrong, O. J. Simpson . . .

Over the years, before he gave the final okay for the publication of any *American Times* cover, Murdock had developed the habit of mentally picturing that cover hanging on the wall. He now tried to imagine a cover showing the two FBI agents who shot at Brackin and Eastwood next to the other best-selling covers.

Instead, what came to mind was a scene from late yesterday afternoon—Harlan Butterworth staring at Murdock menacingly from across his desk. Butterworth held no title at any company. He held no office in any government. He signed no paychecks. His name was not part of the public consciousness, if that even was his real name. Yet, by association alone, Butterworth was possibly one of the most powerful men in America, for he was the right-hand man of famed multi-billionaire Nelson Dilworth. The same Nelson Dilworth who was the majority stockholder of Truss Industries. The same Nelson Dilworth whose family had started the Dilworth Foundation almost ninety years ago to provide grants to those groups and individuals who could advance the well-being of mankind throughout the world. The same Nelson Dilworth who had funded Dilworth University, a medical research center dedicated to medical science. Dilworth had written the book on how to protect wealth by giving it away to humanitarian causes. The more money he gave, the richer he became.

Nelson Dilworth owned a financial empire—an empire on which *American Times* magazine depended.

Murdock had known of Harlan Butterworth for more than twenty years, but yesterday was the first time the man had ever set foot in Murdock's office. It was in response to a call Murdock had made concerning his conversation with Gabaree. Butterworth had arrived with two bodyguards who had stood just inside the door like two armed knights guarding their king. Murdock had told Butterworth everything Gabaree had said the evening before. Harlan's deep-set eyes had seemed to sink farther into his skull when Murdock had presented copies of the e-mails sent from the CEO of Overmeyer concerning the Grand Canyon incident.

"Gabaree thinks Dr. Reinhardt is being held prisoner on a South Pacific oil tanker," Murdock had concluded.

Butterworth responded with a vile laugh but had quickly caught his breath. "Who else has Gabaree told about this?"

"He verbally agreed to an exclusive contract with us. He says outside of his family, we are the only ones who know."

"And what do you plan on doing with this information?" Butterworth had asked.

"I had planned on telling the story only once, and that was to you."

"Do you have a way we can contact Mr. Gabaree so we may set the record straight?"

Both Murdock and Butterworth knew there would be no "setting the record straight." But Murdock had given Butterworth Gabaree's contact information.

Murdock now looked down at his watch. It was time for a meeting of his editorial staff. He began to formulate what he'd say, hacked up some phlegm, and spat it into a Kleenex. He stood and slowly moved his decaying body to the conference room.

Inside, his editorial staff was sitting at the same redwood table that had been there for years, four people on either side. Murdock tossed both Madeline's and Brackin's articles onto the table.

His assistant crime editor, Douglas B. Jarrett, handed him a third article. It was the story *American Times* magazine had been assembling all week.

"What's the premise?" Murdock asked Jarrett. Although Murdock already knew the answer, he wanted to hear it again to see how it struck him.

"Genius college teacher obsessed with the occult carries out delusional apocalyptic vision on innocent students."

Sounds just like what everyone else is writing. He looked down at the three articles. Different stories. Different viewpoints. Which was he to run? The decision had already been made—a decision based not on truth, but on reason.

253

FORTY-SEVEN

The electronic onslaught had stopped as fast as it had started. For several minutes afterward, the three had sat slumped over in the library chairs, gasping for air.

Jensen blamed himself: "You should have known better. Damn fool!"

"What did they do to us?" Megan asked, barely able to talk.

"An electric relay is implanted at the base of your skull," Jensen wheezed. "They put it there last night while you slept. They've done it to all of us, obviously."

He caught his breath. "I should have known better. At their discretion, they can flip a switch that triggers the transmitter to send an electrical charge to the implant, which in turn directs the charge to the nerves running from your brain down your spinal cord."

Megan didn't know how much electricity it would take to kill a person, but as far as she was concerned, the three of them had almost bought the farm.

The electronic onslaught had obviously been instigated by Dillon's talking about psychotronic weapon technology, the method of subversive control they had speculated the murderers had used to make the crew at Re's Cavern commit suicide. No doubt their captors' goal was to induce prevention through pain, and it worked. Psychotronic weapons would not be a topic of discussion in the future, not in this place. Megan never wanted to experience that hell again.

After they regained their strength, Jensen led them out of the library and into the dining room, where he directed them to a computerized serving bar. He placed their orders by touching pictures displayed on a screen. Megan ordered a smoked salmon sandwich and a cup of French roast coffee. Their meals arrived through a portal in the wall. The equivalent of food being slipped under prison bars, she thought.

The Find

As they sat around a fine glass table eating, Megan had to admit the contrast of going from near death to eating a delectable lunch was almost humorous. Although she certainly didn't laugh. And she felt something else, too—the place was definitely, if ever so slightly, rising and falling. She had no doubt now they were on a ship, which made her feel even more distraught over their situation. What possible chance did they have of ever being rescued on a ship? How would anyone even find them? Would their captors toss them overboard after they were done getting what they wanted out of them?

What exactly *do they want from us?*

"Jensen . . ."

His hand rose, palm out, intended to stop Megan. "I have an assignment," he said, as if reading her mind.

"An assignment?"

"My job is to teach you what I've learned from the time capsules. Nothing else will be tolerated."

"That's why we're here?" Dillon cocked an eyebrow. "To be your students?"

"They want to observe how you react to the information." Jensen's eyes flicked to a camera on the wall, but quickly focused back on them. "I must tell you what I've learned."

Having Jensen as a teacher was old hat for Megan. She'd been his student for years, although in college, she'd never had an electronic implant in her neck ready to fry her brain if the wrong word was uttered. She glanced at the camera, whose lens looked like an ogre's eye gawking at them. She pictured their captors sitting in a room watching them on a monitor, taking notes, maybe drinking beer, maybe taking bets on how the captives would act. They were like Pavlov dogs about to be given stimuli so their reaction could be measured.

"This is a social experiment, eh?" Dillon struggled to tuck a napkin in his collar, his fingers hindered by the cast. Megan helped him.

"From their perspective, I'm afraid so," Jensen said.

As Megan helped Dillon with his napkin, she could feel her lungs tighten in anticipation. Despite the looming danger, despite all that they'd been through, archeology was what she lived for. Finally, they were going to enter that realm—the world of the ancient civilization that had lived on this planet all those millions of years ago.

"The people who left the time capsules behind were highly advanced," Jensen said. "Their culture was on the brink of destruction, and they built the time capsules in an attempt to preserve their most cherished knowledge for the benefit of a future race."

Megan already suspected this much.

"And what was that knowledge?" Dillon asked pointedly.

"The time capsules carry the ancient people's spiritual beliefs concerning the creation of life and the universe."

It took a moment for Jensen's words to register. When they did, Megan felt foolish for not having predicted the answer beforehand. Of course, she thought, almost every culture in the history of the world deemed its spiritual or religious beliefs to be its most valued knowledge.

"And those beliefs were?"

Jensen silently looked inward. He again began speaking, slowly issuing forth the words as if pounding each with a stamp of approval before uttering it. His baritone voice resonated in Megan's chest.

"The Ancients who left behind the time capsules believed a higher power existed in the universe, and all their efforts went toward manifesting that power within themselves. Their goal as individuals was to become what we would probably call today supernatural beings. The wisdom they left behind in the time capsules is the system they used for achieving this goal."

Megan's pulse quickened. *The Ancients used a system for becoming supernatural beings?*

Dillon leaned closer. "What power did they believe in?"

Jensen quieted momentarily, his dark brown eyes closed, as he contemplated his response. "To understand the power," he finally said, "you must understand that the Ancients held a different view of reality."

"How so?" Megan asked.

"They believed that two opposite realities existed, the reality of matter, or *phantom reality*, and the reality of *antimatter*."

"Antimatter?" Dillon asked.

"The opposite of matter. While matter is a somethingness made of atoms, etc, antimatter is a nothingness in terms of physicality. It's pure consciousness."

Jensen fished a pen out of his shirt. "The Ancients represented the matter/antimatter relationship with this symbol." He drew a circle on a napkin, then four lines extending out from it: one at twelve o'clock, one at three o'clock, one at six, and another at nine.

"Their icon," Megan informed Dillon. "It was the symbol on the outside of the vessel."

Jensen pointed to the circle with the tip of his pen. "The circle represents antimatter. The four wavy lines that extend out from it symbolize the four parts of the material world." He pointed to the line at the top. "This first line represents *space*." He moved the pen to the next line in rotation. "The second line represents *time*. The third, *energy*. And the fourth, *matter*. These are the things of which the material world is constructed.

The Ancients believed the antimatter—represented by the circle—was the source that created these things: created the material world of space, time, energy, and matter." He continued to point at the lines, moving from one to the next. "As you can see, each of the lines that represent the material world *starts* within the circle and extends outward. This antimatter is really a representation of the Ancients' true, spiritual self. It symbolizes their belief that the material world was created by *them*, and stemmed from them as an illusion they called phantom reality— the universe."

"So they believed they created the universe?" asked Dillon, knitting his brows.

Jensen nodded. "They believed they were a higher power that created matter. The material world, they considered, extended from them. Oddly enough, the way the computer translated the words from their language to ours; if you take the first letter of each word—space, time, energy, and matter—it makes the English word *stem*. The material world *stems* from the higher power—from them."

Dillon frowned. "But what you're describing is God."

Jensen pushed himself away from the table, stood up, and began pacing. "God," he said reflectively. "Now that's an

257

interesting subject." He stroked his beard. "When you say 'God,' are you referring to the Jewish God, Yahwah? The Indian God, Vishnu? The Chinese God, Cheng-huang? The Christian God, Jehovah? Or perhaps you are referring to the Islamic God, Allah?"

Dillon didn't answer.

Jensen continued, "Throughout history, thousands of gods have been worshiped by thousands of cultures, each god possessing his own distinct character. Men of these various faiths would tell you that *their* god alone created the world. Could it be true that thousands of gods actually did create the universe? Had all these individual gods created the individual men who believed in them? Or was it the men who had created the gods?"

"The age old question," said Dillon.

"Exactly," Jensen agreed. "Philosophers have been arguing over that one for centuries. But the idea of God aside; what's most intriguing about the Ancient's philosophy is that they believed the universe was something they were creat*ing* in the present," Jensen said, emphasizing the 'ing.' "We, of course, believe the universe was made at some point in the past."

"I don't get it," said Megan.

Jensen motioned for Megan and Dillon to follow him. As they exited the dining room, he continued. "According to the Ancients, they created the universe with their thoughts moment by moment in their present. They believed that perception wasn't a process of acquiring information, but the *act* of *creation* in and of itself. To them, the act of perception was an act of creation."

This last sentence, Jensen repeated while walking down the hall: "The act of perception is an act of creation."

Megan knew from being a student of Jensen's in the past, if he repeated something it was of utmost importance.

FORTY-EIGHT

Murdock Collier had decided it was a good time to teach Seth an important lesson about news publishing. Murdock set his living room rocker in motion and swirled his martini in its glass. Seth had just finished reading the last of the three articles about the Grand Canyon incident.

Seth held Brackin's article and, his eyes aglow, looked up at Murdock.

"The archeologists were murdered, and according to Brackin and Gabaree, G.C. Overmeyer was involved! Now *this* is a story!"

Murdock sipped his martini and swallowed hard.

"A shame no one will ever read it."

Seth's brow crinkled. He looked like his mother when she was baffled, which was most of the time. Picking up Madeline's article, he held both it and Brackin's up in front of him.

"You're saying no one is going to read these?"

"That's right."

"But we paid Gabaree all that money for his story. And Brackin's piece. I can't believe the son of a bitch is with Eastwood. We couldn't have dreamed up a better scenario!"

From practically the moment Seth was born, Murdock knew the boy wouldn't be a good journalist. His tongue wasn't sharp enough or his wit deep enough. For five years now since college, he'd been working at *American Times* as Murdock's glorified personal assistant. For the longest time, Murdock couldn't face the fact his son would someday own his majority share of *American Times* stock. Now, with Murdock's illness, that moment was quickly approaching. The boy needed a reality realignment. Murdock told him about his meeting with Harlan Butterworth.

Seth was aghast. "You told Butterworth, a representative of Truss Industries, everything Gabaree told you?"

259

"For good reason," Murdock said. "Gabaree claimed Jensen Reinhardt was being held captive on a South Pacific oil tanker and that Overmeyer was involved in the murders. I will not print Madeline's article because of those claims. I'm not running Brackin's article for the same reason. We're going with Jarrett's piece."

"But Jarrett's piece is—"

"Untrue?"

"A lie."

How many times had Murdock tried to drill into Seth's thick skull that the *American Times* did not sell truth? Discovering the truth was the job of courts of law—and even they had a hard time getting it right—not a news magazine, or any news media for that matter. The objective of *American Times* was to gather the viewpoints available on any given story and print those that were most compelling, controversial, and plausible.

And in this case, there was yet another criterion for deciding what to print. Murdock handed Seth a ledger sheet. It showed the advertising revenues *American Times* had collected from subsidiaries of Truss Industries in recent years. Seth, of course, was not completely unfamiliar with these figures. But it was obvious he, like everyone else, assumed the enormous sums of money that landed in their lap did so simply because *American Times* was a good magazine with considerable circulation. *Right. And the Tooth Fairy really does exist.*

"Subsidiaries of Truss Industry spend a lot of money with us," Seth stated the obvious as he studied the ledger sheet. He looked up at Murdock. "So what?"

"You are familiar with our publishing policies?" Murdock asked, knowing full well Seth was intimately familiar with the magazine's book of policies.

"Of course."

"There is an unwritten policy you won't find in that book."

"Which is?"

"Don't bite the hand that feeds you."

Seth frowned. "This is why we won't print anything negative about Overmeyer?"

Murdock took another swallow of his martini.

"What about our senior editorial policy?" Seth asked. "The one that says the editorial and advertising departments work separately, and the two are never to discuss the ramifications of news content on advertising?"

Murdock bit down on an ice cube, a loud crunch reverberated through his jawbone. "Our senior editorial policy is in full force," he said. "But as the future majority stockholder in *American Times*, you must never forget you are above policy. There are times when the survival of the magazine is more important than policy. This is one of those times."

"But people's lives are at stake here," Seth said. "There's Reinhardt and Eastwood, and what about Gabaree? You told Butterworth his name. What will happen to him?"

"I can't control that."

"But wouldn't running Brackin and Madeline's stories better serve us? *American Times* would be the only news source in the country running these accounts. Our circulation would skyrocket. We wouldn't need Truss Industries. We'd have the readers!"

Murdock laughed, and it hurt badly. When was the last time he even heard them called "readers"? Twenty years ago? Today they were called "consumers." Even if *American Times* ran the stories, the attention they'd receive and the increase in consumers would be only short term. It wouldn't make up for losing Truss and their subsidiaries as advertisers.

Murdock lifted the briefcase from the floor, opened it, and handed Seth a copy of an *American Times* article written in 1942. He then told Seth about the long-standing relationship between *American Times* and Truss Industries and their subsidiaries—in particular, South Pacific Oil. Murdock explained that South Pacific had been one of their best advertisers from the thirties through the sixties; without them, the magazine might not have made it. Murdock told Seth how, in March of 1942, South Pacific Oil came under government investigation for war profiteering during World War II. It was discovered that South Pacific had supplied Hitler with the secret for making tetraethyl lead for gasoline, without which Hitler could not have operated his war machine. During the investigation, Harry Truman, a senator at the time, called South

Pacific's activities treasonous. *American Times* publicly lambasted Truman.

"Without our assistance, South Pacific might not have survived," Murdock continued. "Because of our actions, they increased their advertising with us. They carried us through the war. We became their lifeboat, and they became ours. The business relationship has served us both very well over the years."

Seth quickly scanned the *American Times* article that criticized Harry Truman. Seth's reaction wasn't what Murdock had hoped for.

"South Pacific Oil gave Hitler the secret for making tetraethyl lead for gasoline?"

Murdock exhaled what tiny amount of air was in his lungs. The boy was missing the point, and Murdock needed to put it in terms Seth could understand.

"What I'm trying to say is there is a long-standing relationship between *American Times* and South Pacific Oil. Currently, G. C. Overmeyer is one of our biggest advertisers. There are a dozen other Truss subsidiaries that advertise with us as well. If we bite this hand, you may have to give up your Porsche or stop wearing four-hundred-dollar Traversi shoes, or maybe sell one of your condos. Maybe even that place in South Beach you like to hang out at with your girlfriends."

Seth considered this and grew docile. Apparently, Dad finally had spoken a language his son could understand.

Murdock said, "The media are the most powerful force in our society today. We are the eyes and ears of the world. We not only mold public opinion, we create it."

Murdock lifted his bony finger and pointed it at his son.

"Remember, Seth, an event has little power in the world in and of itself. It is the *reporting* of events that give them power and presence. We are the power, Seth. And in this case, we are doing the right thing by not abusing our power, by not publishing these stories. We aren't the bad guys for not publishing them. We didn't kill anyone. The truth is we don't know what really happened at the Grand Canyon. Our stance is simply that we are not going to print something that may unduly harm Overmeyer or South Pacific Oil. We aren't going to behead these companies.

If they are found guilty of a crime somewhere down the road, that's their problem. But we aren't going to convict them. That's not our job."

Seth stared at his father for a few moments contemplating what he had just heard. Then he looked around Murdock's finely decorated living room with its expensive collection of carved oak antique furniture—furniture Seth would soon own. Murdock it was as if Seth saw it for the first time.

"I understand," Seth said softly.

FORTY-NINE

Jensen sat across from Dillon and Megan in the library, while Megan still struggled to understand the Ancients' view of reality.

"Jensen, are you saying that if the Ancients looked at something with their eyes, they believed the simple act of seeing would be the act of them mentally creating in the present that thing which they saw?"

Jensen nodded. "They believed perception was creation. I imagine if an Ancient were here, he might say that each of us is like a movie projector casting out three dimensional illusions with our intention in the present, perceiving what we create, and calling it reality."

"Doesn't compute," Dillon said. "They didn't believe the past existed?"

"Sure, they believed the past existed. But the concept of past was one of the four illusions of the phantom reality, that of *time*. The past existed, but it wasn't what it appeared to be. The past was a memory—a phantom representation of a previous present moment. To them, to think of the past was to create a memory in the present. No matter how you twist it, the past always takes place in present time consciousness."

Megan breathed deep. "What if they found, let's say dinosaur bones, which obviously came from the past, how would they explain that?"

Jensen shrugged. "Again, the act of perception would be the act of creation; if they perceived it then they created it. They'd say the dinosaur bones were created in the present by the thoughts and intention of the perceiver."

"That's crazy," said Megan.

Dillon nodded.

"Maybe, maybe not." Jensen's manner became pensive. "Modern day quantum physicists have done experiments where they've viewed matter through high powered microscopes. Several scientists looked at the same cluster of atoms and then separately described what they saw to an artist who would draw a picture. The descriptions and drawings were drastically different, indicating that the expectancy and intention of the observer had everything to do with forming the structure of what was being observed. Today, many quantum physicists theorize that matter, when broken down to its basic core, is nothing more than infinitesimal vibrating strings of potentiality. The Ancients would argue that it is the intention of the observer that transmutes the potentiality into actuality or into what we call reality."

A stretch of silence passed as they contemplated this last statement.

Perception is creation, Megan thought reflectively. *How can we create matter without being aware of doing so? Were the Ancients aware of doing it?*

"Were the Ancients aware that they were continually the creators of what they perceived?" Megan asked.

"That's the odd part," Jensen said. "According to the computer, most of the Ancients were unaware they were the projector, the creator of life. That was the problem. The inability to recognize self as being the source of creation made life miserable. When one became aware of their own hand in creation, it followed that they would naturally be accountable for what they perceived. Conversely, a lack of awareness of self as creator bred unaccountability. They explained this paradox of being unaware of self as creator with a concept they called *echelons of awareness*."

Yet another term, thought Megan. It was like being in college again, she, the student, Jensen, the teacher.

"What does that mean?" she asked.

"Echelons of awareness were levels of consciousness that one could experience, from complete unawareness of self as a creator up to total awareness of self as a creator. At the lowest echelon of awareness an individual had no recognition of himself as a creator. Such a being, or animal, was a total stimulus response organism. An echelon up from there, awareness developed that *something* had created reality, but they wouldn't necessarily recognize themselves as that something. At the highest echelon, individuals would be aware that they were creators of their own reality—the creator of the phantom world they perceived."

"Their beliefs wouldn't make many monotheists happy, eh?"

Jensen's eyebrows rose. "I suppose not, Dillon. But even belief in one god still doesn't answer the question of whom or what created that god? A monotheist would argue that God is above space and time. He always was and always will be.

"An Ancient might ask why interpose a separate god into the equation? Why not say, 'I am immortal—I have always been and always will be?'

According to some prophets the Ancients might have had a good argument. If you are to believe the Bible, even Jesus stated, *Hasn't it been written in your laws, I said: 'you are gods?'* Didn't Jesus also say, '*The kingdom of god is within you?*' One might logically ask; how can something invisible and all-powerful be within you, without being you?

"Of course monotheists will interpret the 'true meaning' of those quotes a thousand different ways. Perhaps that's why the Ancients believed that truth cannot be understood through information alone; one must experience truth to have full understanding."

"There's something I don't understand, Megan said, still contemplating the idea of the echelons of awareness. How could a person at a lower echelon of awareness, create reality without knowing he was doing it?"

"A good question," Jensen replied. "The Ancients believed someone at the lowest echelon of awareness created reality just as someone at the highest state did. It's a matter of being *aware* of oneself as a creator. When you're aware of yourself as the source of your reality, according to the Ancients, you have both freedom and power. It's at this level that miracles happen."

"Not an easy concept to fully comprehend," Dillon muttered.

"And therein lies the problem," Jensen said. "People see the world, not according to the way things are, but according to the way *they* are. Each person views reality from whatever echelon they're on. For instance, just as it would be impossible for a blind man to visually comprehend a rainbow; it would be impossible for one at a lower echelon of awareness to comprehend a higher level. Certainly those at the lower echelons would react violently to the claim that a higher reality even existed. This is apparently why the Ancients said the only way to truly understand a higher state was to experience it."

They were right on that account. Megan didn't subjectively comprehend the highest echelon, having never experienced it. All the same, she relished learning the Ancient's philosophy.

"From what I understand," Jensen went on, "the Ancients didn't try to force their teachings on anyone. Instead, they developed a system their people could use to elevate themselves to the higher echelons of conscious awareness. This could take years to achieve, however, and since the average person couldn't envision these higher states from their present plane they were likely to give up their studies before achieving their goal.

"To circumvent this problem, the higher consciousness Ancients—referred to as the Masters—invented a machine that could lift a person to a higher state of awareness The *rising machine*, as they called it, elevated a person into the upper realms of consciousness on a temporary basis. Once people had experienced the highest echelon of awareness as offered by the rising machine, they could then see reality as it truly existed. The secrets of life were revealed to them. They would have become so moved and inspired by the experience that they would willingly study the path to achieve this higher state on a permanent basis."

Was the rising machine the large time capsule they'd opened in the Grand Canyon? Megan wondered. She looked down at her hand, remembering her handprint would be the key that would open it again.

Then a voice poured down from the ceiling. "Proceed to the main room now."

FIFTY

Murdock Collier stood at his desk looking down at the most recent issue of *American Times* magazine. The cover simply showed a picture of Jensen Reinhardt. The headline read, "The Lure of a Megalomaniac."

It had been a long, rough week. He had endured much debate among his editorial staff over the cover story. They disagreed violently about what headline to run, as well as what photograph to use. Scrutinizing the cover was not unusual, however. A magazine's cover was the glowing neon sign that attracted customers like a light attracts insects. All the bickering and last minute changes were generally worth the trouble. This week would have been no different from any other, were it not for his ailing body.

The pain was something he never could have imagined. It was so bad that at times he had to fight to even stay conscious. Yet he maintained his grasp on reality and did his job, making the five o'clock Thursday afternoon deadline just as he had every week for the past thirty years.

He hacked up a gob of phlegm, coughed some more until his knees buckled, and sank into his chair behind his desk.

It was almost eight o'clock. He was to have dinner with Seth in ten minutes at the Gaijin sushi restaurant just around the corner. It was time Seth learned the truth about the cancer. It was time they made arrangements for Murdock's departure from this world.

Nina poked her head in his office door.

"I'm headed out, Mr. Collier."

"Good night, Nina."

"Are you leaving soon? You're the last one here."

"In a few moments."

Nina closed the door. Murdock slipped his cell phone into his coat pocket. He picked up one of the several latest issues of *American Times* from his desk and placed it in his briefcase. It's a good cover, he thought. His last cover. He had spent the previous two weeks turning over his responsibilities to his assistant editor, Dewey Redman. Next week would be his final week of production at *American Times*. Soon he would clean out his office, make the announcement to the staff, and say his good-byes.

Murdock closed his briefcase and wrapped his bony fingers around the handle. He lifted it and took a last look around his office. He'd promised himself he wouldn't get sentimental. But there seemed to be no stopping the tears now blurring his vision.

Just hours earlier, he'd had a falling out with Madeline Nelan about the Grand Canyon article she had written but he'd chosen not to run. He told her *American Times* stock had taken a nosedive last April and had not recovered since. As he'd told Seth, Murdock explained that printing Gabaree's accusations about Truss Industries and Overmeyer would cause untold damage to the magazine. Murdock had never seen her so enraged, but he held his ground. Madeline had stormed out of his office, quitting the magazine after twelve years of faithful service.

I've always done things my way, and I'll go to my grave doing things my way.

He dabbed his wet eyes with a tissue and left his office. He trudged painfully through the reception area and exited into the common hallway where . . .

Two ice-blue eyes confronted him.

"We've gotta talk."

Murdock took a step back. "Brackin."

"In your office," the young man growled.

His brow was furled in anger. His jaw set. He looked like the murderer they'd made him out to be in the latest issue of the magazine.

"How did you get past security downstairs?" Murdock demanded.

Brackin didn't answer. He stabbed Murdock's shoulder with his forefinger, sending Murdock stumbling backwards through reception all the way into his office. Brackin slammed the door behind them.

"The FBI's looking for you. You're wanted for murder,"

Murdock stammered, reaching out to his desk to stabilize himself.

"I know. I read about it in the *American Times*—how I shot and killed an FBI agent in the Grand Canyon. What the hell is going on, Collier?"

"You're on your own, son. You were never anything more than a freelance hire. *American Times* takes no responsibility for you and owes you nothing. Now please leave my office."

Brackin's eyes narrowed. "You *did* get my article?"

Murdock nodded. "I got it." There was no use in lying.

"Why didn't you print it?"

"Just before I received your article, the FBI called me. They said you shot and killed an FBI agent. I told them I hadn't heard from you. I protected you. Do you think I could then publish a story you had written, especially *that* story?"

Bruce snatched the latest issue of *American Times* from Murdock's desk, held it in his fist, and shook it in Murdock's face. "Instead, you printed the same garbage everyone else did?"

This moron could be dangerous. I need to call the police.

Of course, Brackin wouldn't just let him pick up the phone and dial. Seth was waiting around the corner. *Could I call Seth on my cell phone without looking at the numbers?*

"You damn well know every word I wrote in my article was true. You still could have printed it!" Brackin's voice grew louder.

"I did what I had to do," Murdock said.

While Brackin started babbling on about Murdock being irresponsible in his reporting, Murdock slipped his hand into his jacket pocket and grabbed his cell phone. Seth's number was the first in the speed-dial list. Murdock's fingers negotiated the phone, pushing the buttons to connect with his son. He was pretty sure he nailed it. Seth would see it was a call from him and pick up. He'd hear the conversation, realize what was happening, and call the police.

"You have a responsibility to print the truth," Brackin said for the third time.

Murdock had to keep the conversation going so that Seth could hear them. That wouldn't be hard, considering Brackin was starting to piss him off.

"Don't you lecture me on responsibility," Murdock snapped. "You're not even wet behind the ears. Hundreds of employees depend on *American Times* being around next month and next year. Thousands of stockholders expect us to turn a profit. I have people who have been with me for over twenty years. They have retirement funds, kids in college, mortgages to pay. My first responsibility is to *American Times*, its stockholders, and its employees. The survival of this publication is my responsibility."

"So you publish a sensationalist story of lies when you *know* the truth?"

Murdock reminded himself there was no way Brackin could know about the connection between Overmeyer and the Grand Canyon murders. Murdock's tired eyes drifted to the gold plaque on his desk. It was a gift from his staff years ago. Engraved on it was the First Amendment: *Congress shall make no law respecting an establishment of religion, or prohibiting the free exercise thereof; or abridging the freedom of speech, or of the press; or the right of the people peaceably to assemble, and to petition the government for a redress of grievances.*

"*American Times* is a private business," Murdock informed Brackin. "I am free to print whatever *I* deem publishable."

Bruce was also looking at the plaque. "Freedom of speech means printing lies?"

"Freedom of speech means being free to print whatever the hell I wish. And may I add, young man, freedom of speech has value only if you have an audience. It is a guaranteed right under the Constitution, but there is no guarantee that anyone is listening. To be heard in this country, you have to print what people will read. You have to print whatever is necessary to keep your publication on the newsstands. Being listened to is not a constitutional right. It's an earned right. And I have earned it!"

Brackin glanced at the magazine, and then looked back up at Murdock. "You're protecting someone, aren't you?"

"Our business is done here."

"The truth would threaten your advertisers. Am I a damn fool or what?" He glanced again at the magazine. "How fitting," he said, and read aloud the new advertising slogan printed on the front cover: "*American Times Magazine*. The Stories Behind the News."

His face tightened, and his eyes met Murdock's once more. "You're going to run my article in a special edition of *American Times*."

"That's absurd. I can't do that."

Brackin stepped closer. "You're going to run an edition dedicated solely to the truth about what happened in the Grand Canyon."

"I refuse," Murdock said.

The muscles in Brackin's neck tightened.

"You need to get out of my office and turn yourself over to the FBI."

"Where's the article I sent you?"

Just as Murdock had suspected. The kid was stupid enough to send his only copy.

"I shredded it."

Brackin stepped even closer.

"You lay one hand on me, and I'll sue you and your family for everything you've got," Murdock warned.

Brackin was unfazed.

"I'm not fucking around," Murdock gasped.

"Nor am I."

Seth stormed through the office door. "Step away from my father!"

Brackin gave Seth a casual glance.

Seth ripped off his jacket. A skin-tight, nylon shirt revealed his rock-hard muscles.

Brackin, unimpressed, turned to Murdock, giving Seth his back. "How do we start?"

"I told you to back off," Seth bellowed.

Brackin's gaze stayed locked on Murdock. His voice rose in volume. "The men who killed the archeologists in the Grand Canyon are holding Eastwood and Reinhardt captive. The only chance they have is for you to make the truth known."

Seth slapped a hand on Brackin's shoulder from behind.

"Remove your hand," Brackin said without turning to face Seth. "You won't get a second warning."

Seth made a buzzer sound with his voice. "Ehhhhhhh. Wrong answer!"

I'm going to enjoy this, Murdock thought.

Seth spun Brackin around and leveled a karate kick at his thigh. Brackin hit the floor and grabbed his leg, wincing in pain. Seth stood over him, bouncing on his toes, and then unleashed another kick to Brackin's exposed face. His heel bit into Brackin's forehead. Blood trailed down his nose.

Brackin lay helplessly on the floor, covering his head with his arms. Seth slammed another kick into Brackin's stomach and brought his leg back for yet another strike. A fleeting thought told Murdock he should stop Seth. With twelve years of karate training and a third-degree black belt, his son could kill Brackin. Yet something inside Murdock—a place close to his agonized lungs, his heart—told him he should let Seth teach the asshole a lesson.

Seth's foot came forward to meet Brackin's head for one last strike. Murdock closed his eyes. Even he couldn't watch this.

When Murdock opened his eyes, he saw Brackin holding Seth's foot in an iron grasp. Brackin had caught it in mid-flight and was now rising to his feet while maintaining his hold. Seth bounced on his free foot, trying to maintain his balance.

"Finish him, Seth!" Murdock shouted.

Seth cursed at Brackin, who smiled back with a river of blood flowing between his eyes. He looked like a madman. Then he flung Seth's foot skyward.

Seth lost his balance and went reeling backward onto the floor.

Brackin drove a knee into Seth's stomach, and Murdock heard the air exit his son's lungs. Brackin kept Seth pinned to the floor with a knee and grabbed both sides of his shirt collar, drawing it tight around his neck.

Drops of blood slid down Brackin's nose and landed on Seth's anguished face.

Seth was in a terrible position. He squirmed and threw punches that bounced harmlessly off Brackin's arms and shoulders. Brackin ignored the futile attempt and bore down on Seth's neck.

"Kick him!" Murdock screamed.

But Seth's face was already turning bright red. An instant later, it turned as white as a ghost.

Seth's arms and legs stopped kicking. His body went limp.

Brackin released the collar of Seth's shirt.

It happened so fast, it took a moment to register . . .

He killed my son!

"No!" Murdock roared and hurled himself at Brackin as his aged body sprang to life.

Something short-circuited. A stabbing pain, not in his lungs, but near. He couldn't breathe. His head felt like a horse had kicked it. His chest, too. A sheen of cold sweat instantly coated his body. His legs gave way, and he fell to the floor. His world went black.

Dear God, I'm having a heart attack!

Bruce watched Murdock collapse onto the floor. *What was wrong with him?* Both Colliers lay at his feet. Bruce knew Seth would regain consciousness in a few seconds. He hadn't strangled him; he'd just momentarily stopped the blood to his brain by applying pressure to the two carotid arteries that ran up either side of his neck.

But what about the father? The old man was covered with sweat, and he was bone white.

Bruce wiped the blood from his eyes with a sleeve, and then checked Murdock's neck for a pulse. Collier's skin was cold to the touch. There was nothing. He put his ear to Collier's chest and heard neither the sound of breathing nor a heartbeat.

Bruce slowly rose to his feet. This hadn't gone as planned. Not at all! He had come to Murdock's office for a specific purpose and—now this?

He heard movement behind him and spun on his heel.

A handful of men in uniforms flooded through the office door, rifles trained on him.

The men parted their ranks, and a tall, broad-shouldered man filled the doorway. The man looked at the bodies on the floor, then at Bruce. Dismay flashed in Special Agent Pittman's silver eyes.

"It was an accident," Bruce said in defense.

Pittman kept looking back and forth between Bruce and the two bodies on the floor, shaking his head in disbelief.

FIFTY-ONE

And it just kept getting stranger . . .

The voice that had told them to proceed to the main room sounded ridiculous. It was muffled like one of those *Sixty Minutes* interviews designed to hide the interviewee's identity.

It was the first live communication Megan had heard from their captors. Although Jensen didn't mention it, she suspected he'd heard the voice before. The three dutifully followed the order, making no comment about the voice, or the man behind it. They didn't need reminding that talking about their captors could trigger another electric onslaught.

Once they were in the main room, they were directed to go to the glass-walled room that housed the "rising machine."

Megan took a moment to gaze upon its mirror-like metallic surface, allowing herself to once again become enraptured by it. The rising machine was a perfectly round metallic orb except for its flat bottom that allowed it to sit upright. There were twelve pinholes in its surface in the form of a circle. Near the holes was the identification plate with two outlines the shape of hands.

She and Jensen were instructed by the ceiling god to place their hands on the plates. They obliged, and the time capsule door opened, as it had done in the Grand Canyon.

Then the ceiling god ordered them to retire to their rooms.

FIFTY-TWO

Megan awoke the next day nervous. And why shouldn't she be? After all, today she would be transported to a higher state of consciousness in the machine. Yet upon rising, she found herself thinking about something entirely different, something she'd spent most of her life trying to forget.

When kids are abandoned by their natural mother, most are given up directly after birth. Megan learned this years after it had happened. She learned that children are scooped into the loving arms of surrogate parents or rushed off to an orphanage before they've developed enough awareness to know, or to even suspect they are unwanted. Not in Megan's case. She was nearly five years old when her mother ushered her out of their dingy apartment through the pouring rain into a taxi.

"Where are we going?" Megan had asked. The ride was long.

"Where are we going?" Megan kept asking. Her mother had never answered. Instead she just hugged the door, keeping her distance from Megan in the back seat, mumbling under her breath, "Our Father who art in heaven . . ."

Megan hadn't even realized it was a prayer until years later when she'd attended a Christmas mass and heard the congregation speak it in unison.

The driver had dropped them off at a curb in front of an old brownstone building. Holding Megan's hand, her mother pulled her through the downpour and up the stairs to the front door of the building. Eyes rimmed in red, she shoved a note in Megan's jacket pocket. Then dear old Mommy handcuffed Megan to the door and dropped the key in the mailbox.

"Mommy. Mommy. What are you doing this for? What are you doing to me?"

Her mother had faced her, tears streaming down her cheeks and said: "I don't deserve you."

She stabbed the doorbell and ran into the pouring rain. "Mommy. Where are you going?"

It was the last time Megan ever saw her mother.

Eventually she was adopted. Her parents, already in their late forties, loved and raised her as if she were their own. And she loved them back. They became her true parents. The subject of her real mother was never discussed.

Megan sometimes awoke in a cold sweat, dreaming about being left in the rain. Sometimes the memory flashed to mind while she was sitting in school, or getting dressed, or watching a movie. She'd wonder if the event ever really happened, or was it a nightmare she'd kept remembering?

But in her heart she knew her past was real, and she'd submerged the memory in her psyche, never fully viewed, yet always there, threatening to surface.

Now, as Megan walked from her room down the gray-carpeted hallway, the memory of her mother was suddenly supplanted by the recent memory of Bruce driving away, racing from her in the night. Try as she might, she couldn't shake the feeling—one feeling that bonded the two memories together—that her destiny in this world was to be disposed of. She wasn't worth the effort it would take to keep her.

Is this why I was ordered into the machine—to be disposed of, either by the machine itself or afterwards by our captors—because it's my destiny?

She entered the main room and crossed the translucent floor toward the rising machine, where Jensen and Dillon were standing. It felt like she was approaching a space capsule with members of the Houston ground crew waiting to bid her farewell, especially when Dillon said, "Ready for takeoff?"

"I think so." In truth, if they weren't in this prison, if they were still in the Grand Canyon, Megan would be the first to volunteer to try the machine. Such was her nature. Besides, she had no choice in the matter. The ceiling god had proclaimed she was the first to take a "ride" in the machine so that was that.

"You'll need this," Jensen said, handing her an ear piece.

Megan took it, hugged each of the men, and stepped through the tiny portal into the rising machine.

"Remember," Jensen said, "we'll be watching you from right outside the capsule on the TV monitor. You can bail anytime you want to."

She nodded, and Jensen closed the portal door behind her, sealing her into the capsule. The air circulation system kicked on, and she felt a rush of cool air waft over her face and neck.

The inner capsule was a picture of simplicity with round metallic walls, and in its center, a solitary metal chair that would "transport" her to a higher state of consciousness. Hanging on the armrest was a headband and wrist strap, while below the chair was a footboard. All these items were wired into a blue crystal cylinder protruding from the ceiling above the chair. There was an ON/OFF switch on the armrest. That was it.

A moment of claustrophobic panic gripped Megan, and she glanced back at the portal door handle.

You can bail anytime you want to, Megan.

She drew in a deep breath and lowered herself into the chair, trying to get comfortable in the rigid seat. She nervously fastened the metal band around her head and the wrist strap around her left wrist. The wristband became handcuffs, and the ghosts of her childhood again filled her head. She was five years old, alone in the rain.

She forced her attention back to the present, positioning her feet on the floorboard and wondered how sitting in this chair could possibly elevate her to a higher plane of consciousness. For a moment, the entire concept seemed just plain silly: levels of awareness, higher consciousness, achieving a supernatural state . . .

Give me a break. I am who I am; what can a machine do to change that?

She quickly reminded herself it was also possible the experiment might come to absolutely nothing. The machine might not even work. *After all, it hasn't been used in millions of years.*

She looked up at the only item added to the capsule, the video camera positioned above and in front of her. Even though she couldn't see them, she knew their captors, along with Jensen and Dillon, were watching her on a monitor. She waved.

278

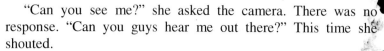

"Can you see me?" she asked the camera. There was no response. "Can you guys hear me out there?" This time she shouted.

Why weren't they responding? Was the camera microphone not working? She reached up and tapped it with a finger.

"He-l-l-o-o."

Suddenly the portal door swung open, and Jensen popped his head in.

"Your earpiece," he said, pointing to his own ear and closed the portal door again.

Megan felt the heat of a blush rise to her cheeks. She had forgotten to insert the earpiece. Fetching it from her breast pocket, she positioned it in her right ear.

"Now can you hear me?" she asked, looking sheepishly at the camera.

"Loud and clear," Jensen said. "Take a couple of deep breaths."

Megan complied.

"We'll be right here." Jensen's deep voice rattled the tiny ear speaker. "Any time you want to stop, just hit the OFF switch."

Megan nodded and bit her lip.

"Here goes nothing," she said and clicked the ON switch with her right hand then jokingly waved good-bye to them. Of course, she wasn't going anywhere. She placed both her hands on the armrests and tried to relax in the chair.

At first nothing happened. Not a hum. Not a sensation of any kind. Nothing. Moments passed, and she began to wonder if the machine was even working. Then just as she shrugged her shoulders for the camera, a cosmic quiet started in her stomach and spread through her like a gentle ripple of water. A slight tingling sensation started in her head, moved to her wrists, and feet as an invisible energy was emanating from the blue crystal stationed above her. The nervousness she'd felt all morning melted into a warm glow of security. A nice feeling consumed her. She smiled at the camera and signaled with a thumbs-up.

"I'm feeling all warm and fuzzy inside," she said.

Jensen's voice returned. "Keep us posted."

As the glow spread throughout her body, Megan's feeling changed to an emotion she couldn't quite identify. She let the feeling percolate for a minute before saying anything to Jensen.

"I feel like I'm growing." She shrugged again.

"What do you mean?"

Good question. "It's hard to explain. It's like . . ." Megan struggled for the right words. *How do you explain a feeling?* "It's like there's been noise inside me, but now it's not there, and there's more of me available. I'm getting bigger."

Megan knew her explanation fell short, but it was the best she could do at the moment. Her mind stilled—a calm, smooth lake with not a single ripple. There were no meddlesome thoughts, no fears or unsettling anticipation of what was to come. *Interesting.* She had not been aware these things were part of her normal self until this moment when they were absent.

The crystalline silence radiated outward, like light, from her innermost self.

"What's happening now?" Jensen asked.

His voice startled her, and she suddenly saw herself through Jensen's eyes as he watched her on the television monitor . . .

Through Jensen's eyes!

She was looking at her body through the monitor, sitting in the capsule with her eyes closed.

FIFTY-THREE

A cold chill washed over Megan.

She jerked open her eyes and was relieved to find the interior capsule walls before her. Yes, she was still inside the rising machine where she was supposed to be. But just ..moments before, she had seen herself—her body—from outside the capsule, through the television monitor, as if she were standing where Jensen was standing.

"What's happening, Megan?" Jensen's voice vibrated her earpiece.

"I'm really not sure."

Had she actually left her body and assumed Jensen's viewpoint?

She continued to gaze at the silver capsule walls. They sort of glowed, as if the molecules that formed them were engaged in a playful subatomic dance.

The world isn't as it is, it's as you are. Her perceptions were changing.

Even though the walls were millions of years old, they radiated newness, as if they were materializing in the moment before her very eyes. She suddenly had the startling realization she was contributing to their materialization. That is, the walls existed literally because she *thought* they existed. This startled her. The interior of the capsule looked more like an *idea* than a solid object.

She glanced down at the wristband once again, and saw her mother handcuffing her to the door of the orphanage. It struck her how thoroughly that single act had defined her existence. From that moment forward, she was secretly obsessed with proving to the world that she was worth having around. Only now did the hidden effects of that mind-set become evident to her. She saw it so very clearly.

It wasn't just her mother's action that had left the painful imprint, it was *her decision* about how she felt about that action that had granted the moment power over her life. It wasn't what had happened to her that was important; it was how she had processed it. And now that moment, like the capsule walls, was starting to disappear as a "solid thing."

Megan laughed with relief.

"Are you okay?" Jensen asked.

"Yes. Fine."

In a flash, Megan realized just how much of her daily life had been influenced by her past. A mental video camera of sorts had recorded everything that had happened to her since her birth and stored that data in a computer. That computer had constantly mixed past video clips in with present events, forcing Megan to view life through a composite reality of then and now, yesterday and today. But the computer wasn't actually her. It was her mind. A mind so intertwined with her being, she had never thought of it as something separate from herself until now. Her mind, she realized, had pulled up these past recordings as a matter of stimulus reaction, but now she was able to view the present simply as it existed, without interference from the past.

Everything exists in the now, she thought. *Even past memories and future ideas exist only in the present. The present is all there is, all there ever was, and all there will ever be.*

A warm glow continued to radiate inside her.

Heat rose to her ears, and her eyes grew moist. Shimmering ribbons of joy danced within her as she recognized all of life was new, and at any given moment, she had the power to change things.

Truth is in the moment. We always have the power to create what we want in the present.

Megan had a sense of rebirth. Each cell of her being was celebrating the realization it was free to create the moment—in the moment.

"Now what's happening, Megan?"

Her view changed to looking at her own body through Jensen's eyes again—an incredibly clear view. She saw her body sitting in the rising machine chair, her lips arched into a smile. Then, just as quickly, her perspective shifted back to normal.

"Talk to me," Jensen said.

It took too much effort to translate what she felt into words. She just gave him another thumbs-up.

What she was feeling was the continued sense of freedom in knowing the present was the only reality. She was also feeling her confidence grow. She now knew she was not just her body. She was herself, a limitless being who created her own limitations, including the idea that she was fastened to her body. At that moment, the richness of her being filled up the time capsule and beyond. Those things inside her that had previously been black-and-white began to emerge in full color, like feathers of a peacock fanning out toward the heavens.

She looked down at her hands clutching the armrests and realized she wasn't in her head looking at them, but outside her body.

"Megan?"

"I'm feeling separated," she heard herself say. Her voice sounded loud in her head.

The personality that was Megan Eastwood—the vibrant and colorful entity she recognized as herself—had definitely moved out of her body. She was surprised how natural—even familiar—it felt. She commanded her left hand to move, and from above, she watched it rise off the armrest.

Megan wondered if she could move further out. She closed her eyes and visualized being outside the time capsule.

That was all it took. She found herself hovering slightly above the capsule, looking down at the metallic orb, while her body remained inside. Her heart lurched.

This is impossible, she thought.

Just like that, she was back in the time capsule—back in her body.

"You said you feel separated." Jensen's voice rattled her earpiece. "What do you mean?"

It occurred to Megan newly that their captors were watching and listening to her every word. She didn't want them to know what she was experiencing. She smiled for the camera and gave a thumbs-up for the third time.

There was silence, and Megan sensed Jensen intuitively knew why she wasn't communicating.

283

She willed herself to move outside the time capsule again. For a few moments, she hovered there, carefully monitoring her body, which still sat comfortably inside the capsule. Not only did her body not die as a result of being separated, it felt exceedingly relaxed.

How can I not be in my body, yet still be able to control it?

Megan's urge to analyze the experience was overridden by an extreme feeling of freedom. She found herself wanting to move out farther, and she wondered just how far out she could go. *All the way out? Above the prison that houses us?*

She visualized herself in the sky, high above their location.

It wasn't like traveling through space to get there. She just decided to *be* in the sky, and she was—in the endless blue sky.

This can't be happening, she thought. And with that, she found herself back in the time capsule.

"I get it," she said.

"What, Megan? What do you get?"

She couldn't tell him. She simply winked for the camera, and then willed herself to the sky . . .

And again as though propelled by giant wings she hovered high above where her body was caged in the time capsule. Below her was a beautiful aqua ocean. Floating on that ocean was a massive hunk of steel—the ship where they were imprisoned.

Its flat green deck was vast and looked like a football field covered with machinery and checkerboard grids and barrel-shaped tanks. The oil tanker's long hull had four levels.

Sight was different than when using her physical eyes. Amazed at how she could see at all, her vision absorbed the view more clearly than anything she'd ever seen before. Instead of capturing reflected light, her senses just became aware of what was there—the colors, the material of the tanker, shapes, the solidity of the materials she saw.

Megan sensed her nearness to the ship, even the ship's age. And, of all the damn things, she was aware of ideas and decisions—the primary thoughts and agreements of the builders of the ship that brought it into existence. Like the walls of the time capsule, this piece of matter looked more like an idea, a series of ideas, than a solid object. She saw it as a thought-form, rather than a solid form made of matter.

284

Yet this sensation of truth and freedom was in direct contrast to the "reality" she was experiencing.

Any vestige of hope she may have had of being rescued dissolved into the thin air about her. Thought-form or not, they could be imprisoned forever.

How can I be trapped unless I agree to be?

It struck her as humorous to think she could ever be trapped in any circumstances. Her body could be, but not her true self.

She turned her attention to the sun falling on the horizon and realized the descent was also an illusion. The sun, of course, remained stationary, while the Earth rotated. She marveled at how infinitesimally small the Earth was in comparison to the vast universe. Yet *she* didn't feel small, knowing she wasn't bound by her body. She felt she could reach out to the sun, and if she desired, extend her being throughout the entire universe.

You are not in space; space is in you.

She gazed down at the misty clouds suspended in the sky below her. They floated with aimless abandon, not owned by anything. But this too was an illusion. The clouds were controlled by an invisible force. Air currents moved clusters of fine water droplets through the atmosphere to where they needed to go to supply rain.

The invisible controlling force was the wind. She realized her relationship to her body was similar: her intention to move her body was like the wind that moved the clouds.

A pelican sailed the skies below her. She focused all her attention on its feathery body. In that instant, her position in space changed, and she made a connection.

She felt the bird's great wings hang in the air, riding the thermals. The sensation was like a hundred dreams she'd had before, soaring through open space, feeling the thrill of every rise and fall. She was *being* the pelican! She felt a hint of anticipation growing within her—the pelican's anticipation.

Suddenly, the bird angled his wings back and swooped high into the sky. The quick ascent alarmed Megan, as she worried she'd slide right off the bird's back. It rose higher. Higher. Higher . . .

Finally the bird leveled off. Megan saw a silvery glint reflecting from below the ocean's surface—a fish flitting through the water.

The bird pinned its massive wings against its body, and with head-snapping velocity, it dropped into a nosedive. Megan's stomach caught in her throat.

Oh. My. God!

"Ahhhhhhhhhhh!"

"What's happening to her?" Dillon gasped.

As Jenson watched Megan on the TV monitor, her hands clutching the armrests of the chair, he asked himself the same question. The scream was so loud it rattled the monitor's speaker. Obviously, Megan was experiencing mental anguish. Her body squirmed in the seat as if she were on a roller-coaster.

"What's wrong, Megan?" Jensen asked.

There was no reply.

He continued to watch her on the screen. Megan's eyes were squeezed shut and her lips puckered.

Splash!

The next thing Megan knew, the pelican was bobbing on the water's surface, holding the thrashing fish in its beak. The mighty bird threw back its head, and the fish slid easily down its gullet.

Megan felt what the bird was feeling—the pride of a job well done, the satisfaction of a freshly caught meal.

Something struck her as curious. When the pelican had raced toward the water, she'd closed her eyes, and for that instant, she couldn't see. But her eyes were in her physical body, which was of course seated in the time capsule. Her true self had no "eyes." So how was she blinded for that moment when she thought the bird was going to hit the water? Was it simply because she made a decision *not* to see?

As the pelican floated lazily on the ocean, digesting its catch, Megan imagined slapping its rump with a whip. To her surprise, the bird took flight.

Her thoughts had influenced the pelican's actions.

She left it and returned to the sky above the ship. She went in for a closer look and could feel the power of the ship's massive engines as it plowed through the water.

She willed herself back into the time capsule and hovered just above her head. Then she willed herself outside the time capsule, just above where Jensen and Dillon sat watching the monitor. She was a foot above them, and they had no idea.

The reality of her situation was becoming even more apparent—she could go anywhere she focused her attention, without regard to space or objects. She simply willed herself to be somewhere, and she was there.

This is real, she thought. She truly was above space and time.

Above time is *now*.

Above space is *here*.

She suddenly felt cramped in the tiny room outside the time capsule. She sprang into the air again above the ship. She latched onto a cloud and hung onto its misty fibers.

It felt as if the world was hers, from the oceans to the stars. She was living the ultimate existence. She was free. She was love. There was no fear, no pain, and no one else's restrictions. She was her infinite self—a beautiful self.

If only others could experience this.

Then she heard the music . . .

FIFTY-FOUR

Where was the music coming from?

Megan focused her attention on the sound. It wasn't actually sound vibrations as much as a melodic, rhythmic *feeling*. Like music she'd sometimes experienced in her dreams. But there was something else, too. She felt a *presence*.

Colors started to form around her. "Thought colors" created by other beings. Each color evoked its own unique sensation as it moved through her in glorious waves. Amber, lavender, azure, affinity, serenity, love . . . with each wave came a new rush of emotion, followed by a joyful anticipation of the next one. The dream music intensified. A melody flowed on the crests of the waves, weaving sadness and splendor through her. It was godly music that made her want to cry tears of joy.

This place. These feelings. They were familiar. She thought it might be the place where all great art came from: Van Gogh's brushstrokes, Mozart's sonatas, Whitman's poems.

Then Megan realized the kaleidoscope of music and colors was manifested by the non-material beings who existed on this higher plane. They were communicating to her and to each other with music paintings perceptible only on a higher level. It was a game they played. They exchanged the paintings for each other's pleasure. Each music painting was a mental projection, and it was the intention of the artist that Megan felt. Like those wonderful dreams where you fall in love and never want to wake up, only a thousand times better.

Megan felt the presence of one being in particular. He projected a music painting with pearl pillars, like the columns of a great Doric structure. He invited Megan to enter through the pillars. She did, and he was "inside" waiting for her. She was enveloped in something beautiful, something she recognized as *him*.

"Welcome," he said. No words, as such, were spoken. No sound vibrations—just a thought from his center to Megan's center. For a breath, Megan was either too shy or too shocked to answer.

"Welcome," he said again.

"Thank you," she answered back with her thoughts.

"You're new here."

"Yes. I've never . . . ah . . . never been here before," Megan said. "It's beautiful."

She couldn't get over how she felt, as if she were in the presence of the most stunning and powerful being in existence. Her heart fluttered.

"I like what you do here," she said.

"Do here?"

"Yes. The music and colors."

She felt warmth radiate from him and realized he was smiling.

"We don't think of the music and colors as something we do, Megan. It's more that we are just *being* music and *being* colors."

"Oh."

"And as far as your being 'here,' this is not a place."

Megan of course knew that, but all this was so new to her.

"It's a state of consciousness?" she asked.

"You could call it that. We play a different game on this plane, a game without a time/space playing field. On this plane, we have other agreements. We don't agree to space and time. We sometimes make fun of those, actually. Things are as you agree they are."

"Do people arrive here, on this plane, when they die?"

He paused to consider this. "Some beings come here. But people who resided on the material plane tend to go back to it. That's what they're familiar with."

"They get another body after their body dies?"

"Beings do what is familiar to them. The unfamiliar frightens."

"Are you God?" The question just sprang from Megan.

He laughed, and a wave of dazzling colors washed over her.

"By 'God,' do you mean the force that created you?" he asked.

"Yes."

"You were not created."

"I don't follow."

"The concept of creation is a material concept. Creation and destruction are both properties of time and space . . ."

His colors darkened, and Megan realized he sensed she was confused.

"You have to think outside time and space," he said. "When you say something has been created, you are saying it has a beginning. The concepts of beginning and end are both time concepts. In your natural state, the way you are right now, there is no time. There is only being. You have always existed, and you always will exist because you are outside the laws of time. You were not created. You just are."

"So there is no God?" she asked.

"If by 'God' you mean an infinite being, who transcends space and time, I'd have to say God does exist, and you are God."

"That would mean we're all gods, and we're all infinite—but how can people of the material world not know they are infinite?"

"They have confused themselves with that which they create—material things. They have become material-like and fallen into the low, low depths of consciousness."

There was a long moment of silence. Megan felt him watching her. His gaze was like a warm light radiating affinity through her entire being.

"Who are you?" she asked.

"Just me."

"But I perceive other beings. You are the only one who is communicating to me. Why?"

"I am a guardian."

"Your job is to keep certain beings out of here. Like evil beings?"

His colors darkened again.

"Okay," she said. "I know we're not 'here,' as in a place. But you know what I mean."

The colors brightened.

"Evil could not possibly arrive on this plane, Megan. Evil only exists on lower planes of consciousness. In truth, evil is the very fabric of the lower planes of consciousness. My job is to inform those beings who arrive on this plane what and who we are. As I'm doing with you."

"Why do I feel like I love you?" Megan asked. She couldn't help herself. She felt safe enough to say what she was feeling.

"What's not to love?"

"Hmm, you even have a sense of humor."

"One could not arrive on this plane without a very good sense of humor."

"Are you a man?"

The "guardian" sighed, and his colors darkened.

"I know," Megan said. "You're neither man nor woman. You're above the whole sex thing."

"We have no need for sex as you know it. But we do partner. We create enjoyment for each other far beyond sex. It's more fun when you share."

"But since this plane is a universe of thought, it seems like everything is shared. I mean, I can sort of feel others listening in on our conversation."

"They are a nosey bunch here."

"Are all beings one?" Megan asked.

"If we wish to be. Or not."

"The music makes me want to cry."

"Shall I change it?"

"No," Megan said. "It's beautiful. Beyond beautiful. In fact, everything here is beyond beautiful." She paused. "But there are things I love about the material world, too."

Megan felt a touch of nostalgia as she remembered some of her favorite pleasures. She loved digging in the dry earth, searching for lost treasures. She loved to curl up in front of a warm fire with a chilled bottle of wine. Loved to laugh at night in bed and to hide under the covers to keep out the cold. She loved the smell of wet leaves after a rain. Overcast skies. Softly falling snow. Travel. Maps. And . . . and what was wrong with sex, anyway?

Suddenly the music intensified and swirled around her. Violins sang out colors of violet, cellos bowed waves of gold. A vast rolling countryside appeared. Fields of silvery grain swayed with the music, dancing in a legato breeze. The grain shed motes, which drifted into the sky like a thousand weightless diamonds and swirled in dizzying rhythm. They formed a billowing cloud and exploded in a thunderous drum roll over the endless fields.

Crystal droplets of rain fell with the playful tinkling of harp strings. Then a golden castle burst from the ground, its uppermost tower touching the overcast sky. Wet leaves fluttered to the ground from the trees as the smell of autumn permeated her being. One of the castle's iron doors opened with a creak.

Inside, a fire roared on the hearth. Two teardrop glasses of rosé wine sat on the granite floor and next to them, a man. Megan couldn't make out his face, but could feel his presence. Her heart did a slow tumble. All became scarlet. A cymbal crashed. Suddenly, bone-white snow fluttered gently from the sky down on the castle, inside and out. The fire dampened. The man's eyes reached out to her. Then he was gone. Flutes weaved a dark and mysterious melody, and the castle walls crumbled and fell to the earth. Drums pounded and bells droned in circular rhythm, and a thousand years passed.

The countryside transformed into an endless carpet of green. Ancient stone columns and crags and granite pressure ridges appeared here and there. Megan could see hidden caves and half-buried stone relics nestled in secret places. The man who had been in the castle appeared pushing a wooden wheelbarrow stacked full of shovels and pans and buckets and other tools for digging. He beckoned her to join him. The music exploded like golden fire and then died with a smoldering, single note of a violin.

"There are plenty of hidden treasures here for you now, Megan."

She gasped. "You just created all this with your thoughts?"

"Our thoughts, yours and mine. It's how everything is created."

"Not down there, it isn't. Not like the way you just did it," Megan said, referring to her material life. She felt dizzy.

"That's why it's called a lower plane, Megan. 'Down there,' as you call it, beings think they have to add steps between the creation of the thought and its end result—a slow and arduous process. On this plane, thought and result are one and the same."

"Could a person learn to do that while living in the material world?"

"Some have tried and failed. You're taking a chance among lower-plane beings. Those things that are unfamiliar frighten."

"I like it better here. It feels like home."

"It is home."

She felt sad.

"You can stay."

Megan considered Jensen and Dillon and . . .

"Your friends?"

"It's why we go back, isn't it?" she asked.

He said nothing at first, then, "Maybe he's not so bad."

"Who?" Megan asked.

"The one you push from your heart. After all, you wouldn't have arrived on this plane if not for him."

Megan hadn't viewed it that way before.

"You are always welcome here, Megan."

"But how—without the machine?"

Megan could tell he was thinking. When he finally spoke, his "voice" was alive with wonder and admiration.

"Those who built the machine were very smart indeed," he said. "How they got an instrument to do for you what you could already do for yourself—a stroke of genius."

At that moment, the strangest sensation came over Megan. She felt as if she was falling, and as she did, the "guardian" faded from her conscious mind as if he'd never existed. She instantly knew what was happening. Her "ride" was over. The rising machine was shutting down.

FIFTY-FIVE

On the monitor, Jensen watched Megan slowly open her eyes. She oriented herself for a moment then suddenly jumped out of her chair. The screen went black. Did she disable the video camera?

Jensen cringed, expecting the bone-rattling electric current to ring his neck. Yet there was no immediate sensation.

Dillon grabbed the time capsule latch, and flung the door open.

The camera lay on the floor next to Megan. She quickly waved them forward.

The two men squeezed into the tiny capsule. Jensen shut the door behind them.

Megan's eyes were aglow, and her skin luminous under the capsule lights

"We're out to sea, on an oil tanker," she said breathlessly. "Somewhere in the Pacific. If I would have had more time, I could have gone farther out and determined our exact location."

"Farther out?" Jensen asked.

"Out of my body," Megan said. "We have to arrange for me to do the machine again."

Jensen stared at her in disbelief. "Out of your bo—"

The door suddenly swung open. Three men stood at its entrance, rifles in hand.

"Eastwood," one said. "Come with us."

Jensen positioned himself in front of Megan, shielding her from the men. "She goes nowhere without me."

In the blink of an eye, all three men had their rifles trained on Jensen.

"Stand down," the man ordered. "Just Eastwood."

Jensen ignored the order and advanced toward the men. He held his head high. If they were to shoot him, or electrocute him, let them get on with it. He was done being a slave.

Two of the guards readied their rifles with a loud click. The third urgently mumbled into his headpiece.

Jensen's chest met the barrel end of a rifle.

"Megan goes nowhere without me."

"Let them pass," the third guard told the other two. He'd obviously gotten the order through his headpiece.

The men parted ranks, and directed the trio through the doorway.

Jensen noticed Megan walking unsteadily and held her hand. "Out of your body?" he said. Megan gave him a sidelong grin.

They were led down a series of hallways and through six doors that each needed to be unlocked. They ended up in a room where a group of men seated at a table awaited them.

Megan was having difficulty being back in her body. It made no sense that she couldn't leave it again at will, yet she was utterly incapable of doing so. Gone were her feelings of freedom, of tranquility, and the knowing vision. Her wings had been clipped. If not for the urgency of their situation, she'd probably be mourning her loss. Still, the machine gave her a truth she'd never forget—she was a spiritual being not bound by space and time. For this reason, as she took in the men seated at the table, she knew she was in control. Not them.

Jensen stood on her right, Dillon on her left.

"Welcome," one of the men said. He had a beak nose with a long protruding neck. His deep-set eyes were barely visible in the shadows under his eye bones. On the table before him sat a small black box.

"I am Harlan Butterworth," he said coldly. "These men are my colleagues."

Megan counted twelve including Butterworth. They all wore suits. Despite the bright fluorescent lights that illuminated the room, the atmosphere was dark. *There are many secrets here.*

Butterworth's mouth arched into what Megan could only guess was a smile. "It's been more than a year Jensen, and finally we meet in person."

Megan stiffened.

Butterworth eyed her. "Let's get down to business, my dear. What did you experience in the rising machine?"

"So who's oil tanker are we on?" Megan asked with a sly grin.

The question visibly rattled the men as a murmur rippled through the group. A man next to Butterworth whispered something in his ear as Butterworth's shadowy eyes remained fixed on Megan.

"What makes you think you're on an oil tanker?" Butterworth asked.

Megan shrugged. "I saw it while I was in the rising machine. I learned a lot in there. I will tell you everything… "

"Start."

She paused. "After you tell us a few things."

Butterworth's jaw tightened. His crab-like fingers opened the lid of the black box.

"Flip that switch and you'll never know what happened in the machine," she warned.

She'd be dammed if she'd tell these men what she'd experienced without at least learning something about their agenda. She'd be damned.

"Mr. Butterworth will answer your questions," a different voice suddenly cut in.

A portly fellow with a drooping double chin and pasty white skin rose in his chair. He shook his head slightly at Butterworth, who instantly withdrew his hand from the box.

"Ask what you please," said the man with a haughty English accent.

No doubt of the pecking order here. But Megan wasn't sure if the English man's dictate was good news or bad. Was she granted permission to ask questions only because they'd never leave this ship alive?

"Who exactly are you? Megan asked bluntly.

"You might say we're concerned businessmen with a world view. Our concern is the betterment of life on this planet. Our purpose is altruistic. The time capsules and what they represent have the potential for being a formidable presence in the world."

You have no idea, thought Megan.

Butterworth rose from his chair. "Our mission is to ensure this planet survives, and we're the only ones who can do it."

"By murdering innocent people?" Megan asked.

Butterworth shrugged his shoulders. "Sometimes sacrifices are needed for the greater good. We couldn't have all your archeology friends running around the country telling everyone what they found in the Grand Canyon. Now could we?"

Contrary to Butterworth's repugnant looks, he talked with an air of elegance, which made his words sting that much more. Megan said nothing.

"The average person in the world has an IQ of eighty-six," Butterworth continued. "If the masses got hold of the time capsules do you think they would actually understand the spiritual teachings of the Ancients? Give the time capsules to the world, and the rising machine would end up as a ride at some theme park."

"And what makes your kind so superior?" she asked.

Butterworth seemed to enjoy the interchange now. He started pacing. "Let's just say my colleagues and I were raised with different expectations than you." His eyes narrowed. "The human species is headed for extinction. We are simply taking steps to avert that outcome."

"Extinction?" Jensen asked. "By what means?"

"What means? By a means that you'll never hear your political leaders talk about because it suggests racism, it appears to attack family values, it strikes at the heart of religion. And, thus, like a cancer, it grows."

"Over population," Dillon piped up for the first time.

Butterworth gazed at the blank wall in front of him. "Someone has to take responsibility."

"By creating social genocide through disease, poverty and war!?" Dillon said angrily. "This is what you do, isn't it?"

Butterworth spun and fixed his gaze on Dillon. "There are over six billion people on earth today. That's more than the total number of people who've occupied this planet from the beginning of civilization up to nineteen-fifty. At the rate we're going the population will double in fifty years. The herd must be brought under control: The spics that live six families to a hut. The niggers, who collect welfare while making babies. The

297

James J. Valko

Africans who depend on shipments of food bought with your tax dollars. For every mouth the herd brings into the world, food, land, medicine, and energy are needed. If they are not stopped the herd will procreate like rabbits until we are *all* extinct."

"How, exactly, do you plan on reducing the herd?" Dillon asked. "Or are you too embarrassed to speak of it?"

Butterworth chuckled. "Embarrassed?" He glanced at the Englishman who seemed to be entertained by the exchange. He again gave a slight nod, granting Butterworth permission to continue.

Butterworth said, "Our mission is to create a world that can survive on its own remaining natural resources—*one* world."

"The new world order with a one-unit monetary system" Dillon remarked offhandedly.

"That's right," said Butterworth. "International monetary units controlled by an independent world central bank, all under non-elected leaders who don't need the permission of the herd to do what must be done to survive. Restrictions will be made on the number of children per family. There will be diseases, wars, and famine among the herd until only one billion people exist on the planet, each one of those people useful to the ruling class."

"Ruling class?" asked Megan.

"Why would we need a middle class? It's contrary to nature. We need only rulers and servants. The way it's been since the beginning of time. The way it was intended."

"Also since the beginning of time," Jensen said, "servants will not tolerate a ruling class. There will be revolution."

"Technology has changed the game, Jensen. With a micro-chip implanted in every child at birth there won't be any uprising, I can assure you. Psychotropic drugs will further the malleability of their minds. Look how easily they already clamber for relief from their own emotions. It's like shooting fish in a barrel—all in the name of help." He paused briefly seeming to admire the simplicity of the plan.

"Cash will be obsolete," Butterworth went on. "If one breaks the law, the one-world police force will deplete their card of funds. They will starve to death. The herd will not be allowed to carry firearms. There will be no revolution."

298

When Butterworth stopped he appeared unmoved by his own words, as if he'd been talking about the weather. His cohorts also looked close to indifference. *Business as usual.* If Megan didn't know better she'd think this bunch were nothing more than old men with too much time on their hands and penchants for megalomania. But she knew better. These twelve shadow men were well on their way to achieving the Orwellian reality that he described.

The elite of the elite," Dillon mumbled, almost to himself.

"What do you mean?" Megan asked.

"These men are the overlords of the conspiracy. They're probably behind all the secret societies promoting globalization: The Council on Foreign Relations, the Trilateral Commission, the Bilderberg Group. . .The 9/11 attacks, the invasion of Iraq and Afghanistan, the economic depression, the socialization of America. It's you?" Dillon demanded of Butterworth. "Isn't it!?"

Butterworth ignored the question and sat back down at the table.

"Now, my dear I have spoken as requested, and answered your questions, quite honestly I may add. Now it's your turn. The Ancients said if one sits in the rising machine, the person would experience the highest echelon of conscious awareness. What did you learn?"

With all eyes on her, Megan took a moment to reflect on her experience in the rising machine. The purpose of the apparatus was to allow a person to experience one's true, higher self—a state of being that had to be experienced to be understood. Now these men expected her to give them a blow by blow? They'd never understand.

Butterworth's fingers tapped on the black box. "We are waiting."

Megan looked at him. "Things don't exist as *they* are, they exist as *you* are."

Butterworth frowned.

Some men laughed, other sighed. The Englishman grunted. "It that it?" he asked.

While Megan groped for the exact words to say, something unexpected happened:

She heard voices in the distance. Shouting. Then loud cracking sounds echoed from somewhere outside the room. *Gunfire!*

The men jumped from their seats and headed toward the emergency exit. Butterworth hesitated for a moment, however, and glared at Megan, as if she had somehow caused this unexpected development. Then he snapped open the black box and flipped the switch.

FIFTY-SIX

The base of Megan's neck caught fire. The pain shot down her spinal column as if a poisonous snake had injected a venom into her back. Her body started to quiver.

Electric needles stabbed her eyeballs. She instantly realized the onslaught of electricity was stronger than the first time she'd experienced it.

The twelve men stood in line at the emergency exit.

What was happening?

She watched both Jensen and Dillon violently tremble, in the clutches of a *grand mal* seizure. Dillon fell to his knees while Jensen struggled to stay on his feet and took a step toward the black box on the table.

The gunfire continued. An alarm blared. Megan watched the guards try to open the emergency door, but it was jammed. The dozen men waited to get out. Butterworth was last in line.

Dillon started crawling toward the black box.

Flipping the switch off was their only hope.

Megan also tried to crawl toward the box, but her body was already a quivering mass of flesh, incapable of movement.

She struggled to leave her body, thinking that somehow she could be more effective on the outside, like she was in the rising machine.

For the life of her, she couldn't get out.

She became infuriated. The power she'd experienced in the rising machine was so real while she'd been in it, but it had already faded to obscurity. Like a dream.

Was it all just a delusion? What good is accessing a higher power if I'm unable to manifest that power now, when I need to?

Out of the corner of her eye, she saw Jensen take another step toward the black box.

The pelican. She'd made its body move with *her* intention. That wasn't a dream. She had done it.

The rising machine had stopped working the moment she had doubted it.

Megan again willed herself to leave her body.

Nothing happened.

She remembered the guardian's words: "How they got a machine to do for you what you could already do for yourself . . . a stroke of genius."

Suddenly she was out! But something was wrong. She looked down at her gyrating body lying on the floor. Her eyes were rolled up in her head. The electricity was still ravaging her flesh and bones but she no longer felt the pain. Was she . . . was her body . . . dead? Was that why she was able to leave it?

She saw Jensen lunge onto the table and reach for the black box. His fingers fell inches short.

She concentrated all her energy on her mentor. She could feel the sensation of the electricity going through him. She was aware of his despair, his emotional pain for having let them down.

She felt him go unconscious.

She commanded Jensen's quivering hand to reach the black box and flip the switch upward. She became his hand. With every ounce of life she possessed, she intended it to move. The fingers responded, jumped to the box. She directed them to flip the switch.

Jensen's body instantly stopped quivering. So did Dillon's. She saw Jensen's eyes open, then Dillon's.

Still out of her body, she turned her attention back to the men now single-filing out of room. The guards had managed to open the emergency door and were seeing to the twelve conspirators. Butterworth was still the last in line.

Megan felt hate for this man. And she felt physical movement, too. She realized it wasn't her anger or her movement—it was Jensen's. She watched him struggle to his feet, storm across the room on wobbly legs, and plow into Butterworth from behind.

Butterworth hit the floor face first and skidded into a wall with Jensen riding him. Jensen got up, stood over him and flipped him onto his back like a bear pawing a lame animal.

He then started bitch slapping the cowed man with loud fleshy strikes to the face. Butterworth tried to shield his head, but Jensen's massive hands pounded through the weak defense.

"Help me," Butterworth cried. "Someone help me!"

Megan watched the English man glance back to see the bloodied Butterworth. He made no attempt to help. None of the men did as they hurried, like scared rabbits from the room, leaving their associate behind.

Suddenly four new guards stormed through the main door on the opposite side of the room. She thought they were going to shoot Jensen. Instead, they turned toward the door they had entered and skittering backwards on their heels, fired their weapons into the hallway. One guard, backed up and tripped over Harlan, lying on the floor.

Gunfire was returned from outside the room drilling bullets into the walls. A guard went down, blood splattering from his chest. Another was hit in the shoulder, the force of the blast throwing him down flat. A dozen more bullets ripped into him. The fallen guard lay over Butterworth, dead.

Then it was over.

But something else was wrong. Megan realized she'd been watching all this still from outside her body. She became aware that Dillon was now kneeling over her, trying to revive her. Everything went black.

FIFTY-SEVEN

"Megan?"

The gentle voice resonated in her eardrums like light seeping into darkness.

"Can you hear me Megan?"

She felt a warm hand touch her forehead.

She opened her eyes and a face above came into focus. Kneeling over her, he stroked her hair with his hand. She closed her eyes and concentrated on her chest muscles. They were moving, which meant she was breathing. She wasn't dead. Was she dreaming? Hallucinating?

She opened her eyes again and once more focused on the man, on the loose strands of black hair falling onto his forehead, and his soft blue eyes looking down at her.

"You didn't think I would abandon you without a plan, did you?" he asked.

She blinked.

His hand touched her cheek. "There will be plenty of time to explain later," he said.

Jensen and Dillon appeared above him and stared down at her.

"How you feeling princess?" Jensen asked.

"Confused. Help me up please," she said.

Bruce placed his hands under her arms and lifted her to her feet. She looked around the room to take in the dead bodies sprawled out on the floor. Men in green army outfits were cleaning up the mess. The dozen men were gone, except for Butterworth who lay lifeless on the floor a few feet from her.

Her equilibrium started to falter, but Bruce wrapped his arms around her to hold her upright.

"Lean on me," he said softly.

Megan did.

She was so confused. Part of her wanted to kiss Bruce and never release him. Another part hated him for abandoning her. *But how. . .*

So many questions, yet all she could do was cry. Her legs weakened. Bruce tightened his grip. She buried her face in his chest. She'd assumed death was inevitable for her, Dillon and Jensen. The last thing she expected was to be rescued. *And by Bruce. . .*

Suddenly a jolt.

What happened next was something Megan would never forget, something she would play again and again in her mind, as if trying to reverse the outcome, but it never would reverse, for time only moves in one direction.

There had been a gunshot.

Megan felt wetness on her hand wrapped around Bruce's waist. His body went limp, and slid downward, out of her arms, onto the floor.

She turned to see Butterworth with a gun in his hand. Rifles fired, drilling bullets into his chest. He died instantly.

She fell to her knees over Bruce. Blood pooled through his shirt. He'd been shot in the side.

"He needs help!" she screamed.

"Hold on," she said. "You're going to be okay."

His eyes darkened. He gasped for air. His breaths were short and quick.

Jensen started removing Bruce's shirt.

His body trembled. His face drained of color. His eyes never left hers. His expression wasn't a look of shock., nor of fear. It was a look of peace. In a strange and indefinable way, Megan thought he looked happy, happier than she had ever seen him.

Megan was ushered onto the helicopter; two men awaited her there: one she'd never seen before; the other she had.

The familiar one worked a wad of gum. "Hello, Megan," he said, offering his hand to her. She reluctantly shook it.

"My name is William Pittman. I've been looking for you."

"Aren't you going to handcuff me?" she asked, only half jokingly.

He smiled and turned toward the other man. "This is Major

Brewster McCullen."

Megan looked to see a silver haired man with a square jaw, and leathery tanned skin. A stately looking fellow, he wore a dark blue uniform and sunglasses. He extended his arm. "It's an honor."

Megan shook his hand,

"Another helicopter will be picking up Mr. Waterford and Dr. Reinhardt as soon as we take off," Pittman said.

Megan nodded. She'd already been told this. She strapped herself into the seat next to Pittman.

The engine growled as the helicopter began to lift off the deck of the ship. She had a million questions, but would wait until they were airborne and the engines settled down before asking them. Gazing out the window, she watched the ship's green surface retreat as they ascended. She remembered seeing the ship from this perspective just hours earlier, only then she'd seen it from outside her body.

She turned back toward the men. "I'm very confused," she said. "None of the men who rescued us on the ship would tell us where they were from or who sent them."

"They had orders not to do so," said Major McCullen. "Bruce would have informed you if…"

The Major paused and cleared his throat. "Bruce had insisted he arrive on the ship with the men. I never should have allowed it."

"Was this an Army operation?" she asked.

"I'm in the Air Force," said McCullen. "But mercenaries rescued you. Former U.S. military special operatives. They parachuted from an aircraft and landed on the ship's deck. Taken by surprise, your captors were easily overcome."

Megan's head was spinning. "*You* set up the mercenaries that rescued us?"

"Yes," McCullen said. "I directed them to the ship's location. They did the rest."

"But who are you, and how in God's name did you know where we were?"

Pittman handed a box to Megan. Inside, was the bright yellow tank dress she'd worn on the ship.

"Under the dress," Pittman said.

She lifted it to find two necklaces, her Sphinx necklace and the Star of David that Bruce had given her.

McCullen told Megan how Bruce had contacted him three days ago and explained his predicament. "I express-mailed him a special micro transponder that we use in the service. He wedged it under the Star of David just before the trade."

"That's how you knew I was on the ship?"

"We would have arrived sooner, but it took a while to gather the men and resources to pull it off, as you can imagine."

Megan's eyes started to burn with tears. All those terrible things she'd thought about Bruce.

Pittman explained how he'd tracked down Bruce in Colorado shortly after he'd left Durango. "We caught him and his brother on the road heading toward Denver. Bruce told me everything that happened since he'd met you.

"He told me he'd written the entire story and sent it to *American Times* magazine. I contacted the managing editor, Murdock Collier, to verify what he'd said. Collier denied that he'd gotten any story. So I put a wire on Bruce and sent him to the *American Times* offices. I learned that Collier did in fact receive Bruce's article but didn't run it. A scuffle broke out between Bruce and the editor's son and Murdock had a massive coronary on the spot."

It just kept getting stranger. "A heart attack"? She asked.

Pittman nodded. "Turned out Collier had a weak heart, along with terminal lung cancer. A strong wind might have blown him over the edge."

"What about our captors on the ship? What happened to them?" Megan asked.

"They escaped. Left the ship, we gather, in a miniature submarine. They were long gone by the time the mercenaries discovered their escape route."

A more important question came to mind: *How had Butterworth and the captors known the time capsules were in the Grand Canyon in the first place?* She knew that neither of these men would have the answer to that one, but she suspected who might.

Suddenly the chopper's cockpit door flung open, and the copilot told them he just got word from the hospital: "Brackin was rushed into surgery."

Megan shut her eyes.

The recent memory sprang to mind: After Bruce was shot Dillon had found the ship infirmary, where he located a ventilator among the medical equipment. He'd put the mask over Bruce's face. "Short breaths," he'd told him. "No matter what happens, don't stop taking short breaths." The mercenaries had hoisted Bruce up to the helicopter hovering over the ship and flown him to the nearest land hospital.

Two hours later, Megan was picked up by a second helicopter. And then Dillon and Jensen, reportedly by a third helicopter.

"Where are we headed?" she asked Pittman.

"John Wayne Airport in Southern California. From there, a driver will take you to the hospital to see him."

She was exhausted. Pittman reached into the overhead compartment, grabbed a pillow, and handed it to her. "It will take a couple of hours to get there. Perhaps you should rest."

She thought that was a good idea. She positioned the pillow under her head and closed her eyes.

She awoke some time later to the sound of straining engines as the helicopter descended.

With some sleep, the world looked brighter. She took inventory. First, she was alive. Second, she was off that prison ship. Third, Bruce was still alive. Things could be worse. The helicopter slowly touched down at the airport.

She followed Pittman and McCullen into the terminal, and it struck her that every passing face she encountered looked so serious. The space inside the terminal felt *serious,* too. How different this was compared to how she'd felt in the presence of the guardian while out of her body.

She decided never to tell anyone what she'd experienced in the rising machine. Words could never adequately describe spiritual reality. And, like the Ancients had said, people at lower levels of awareness often try to destroy those who communicate about higher levels. She didn't need any more fights on her hands. There was too much living to be done.

Pittman turned to her. "The other helicopter is only fifteen minutes behind us. When it arrives, we've arranged for a driver to take you to Hoag Memorial Hospital in Newport Beach."

FIFTY-EIGHT

Megan embraced both Dillon and Jensen when they arrived at the airport.

"We owe you our lives," Jensen said to McCullen.

"I was helping a friend. That's who you owe your lives to. Just ensure that he makes it."

"He'll make it," said Megan. "I still have a bone to pick with him."

"The FBI is going to need sworn statements from all of you," Pittman said. "But we can handle that later. You'll be contacted."

"What about the creeps that held us captive?" asked Dillon. "What are you going to do about them?"

"Unfortunately, that investigation won't be under my control. Since the ship was in international waters, the subject of your kidnapping will be investigated by the CIA."

Dillon laughed. "The CIA? The same CIA that formed al-Qaeda in the nineteen eighties when the former CIA director, Vice President George Bush, ran the government after the shooting of President Reagan? That CIA? They probably already report directly to the one-world boys—our captors."

Pittman looked on blankly.

"Well," said Megan. "We'd better get going." She shook McCullen and Pittman's hands, thanked them both. She got into the waiting car along with Dillon and Jensen.

As the driver pulled away from the curb, she decided it was time for her own little investigation.

"Jensen, how exactly did you fund the excavation at Re's Cavern?"

Stroking his beard, Jensen gazed out the window at the passing landscape. "Keeping his identity a secret, Butterworth had contacted me by mail more than a year ago and told me both about the time capsules that had been found, and about the ones he believed were buried in the Grand Canyon. He offered to fund the dig if I were to take it on, the stipulation being that I not reveal to anyone what I was digging for."

"Are you saying *other* time capsules had been found, *before* the ones in Re's Cavern?" Dillon asked.

"Long before Megan and I ever even talked about Re's Cavern, two other sets of time capsules had been dug up in other parts of the world, near Veracruz, Mexico, and Mungo National Park in Australia. These two sets were in the possession of Butterworth and his boys. But apparently they'd been significantly damaged. Each set, however, did disclose that another set had been implanted in the earth, which Butterworth believed was in the Grand Canyon region.

"At first, I was skeptical. But Butterworth sent me photographs and revealed to me some of the information they'd learned about the ancient civilization. Eventually, I became intrigued and agreed to take the project on. After all, what was there to lose?"

As Megan contemplated the irony of the question Jensen continued talking. "The Ancients constructed the time capsules in such a manner that they couldn't be kept a secret once found. Apparently, they didn't want any one person or group to monopolize them. Unbeknownst to me at the time, when we opened that capsule in the Grand Canyon, the solar computer inside released an electromagnetic wave with encrypted information that could be detected by simple radar. Butterworth knew this might happen from the other sets of time capsules they had in their possession. They were monitoring the Grand Canyon region while we were busy doing the excavation. When they detected the wave generated by the time capsule, they went in and took what they considered was theirs, while making sure the crew would never tell anyone what they'd found."

"Why didn't they just dig for the time capsules themselves?" Dillon asked. "Why did they hire you in the first place?"

"I can only speculate that Butterworth didn't want any ties to the dig. Park officials don't just let anyone do an excavation in the Grand Canyon. A permit must be applied for, a background check done, and any items found in the Grand Canyon become the property of Grand Canyon National Park." Jensen shrugged.

"Since I'd done previous excavations in the canyon, he probably figured I was the perfect candidate. I suppose my history of involving students in alleged occult activities helped his cause as well. Butterworth probably foresaw the setup of the suicide scenario."

"So they killed your crew and got the time capsules out of there before the FBI ever showed up."

Dillon didn't state it as a question but rather a statement of fact. Jensen just nodded. The driver announced that they had reached their destination. Megan's heart raced as she and the men exited the car and entered the main lobby of the hospital.

In the anteroom outside where Bruce's surgery was being performed they were greeted by Bruce's brother, Peter. Megan had plenty of questions for him, too, but they would have to wait. No sooner did they arrive than a short balding man in green scrubs approached the group and introduced himself as Bruce's doctor.

"The bullet ripped through the pectoral muscle in his chest," he began "and lodged just millimeters from his upper left lobe, just missing the lung but causing enough bleeding to hinder his breathing. The bullet has been successfully removed and the bleeding stopped."

"Then he's going to be okay?" asked Megan.

The doctor smiled. "He's going to have to take it easy for awhile. But he should be just fine."

FIFTY-NINE

Three weeks later
FBI Headquarters
Washington, D.C.

"Thank you for coming," he said.

"Did we have a choice?" Bruce asked.

"I suppose not. But it's not all bad."

"Why didn't you invite Dillon and Jenson?" Megan asked.

"And Peter?" Bruce added.

The two sat in front of Pittman's desk waiting for an answer.

"They thought it would..." Pittman stopped and glanced over Bruce's shoulder at the two men in dark suits seated at the back of the room. "I thought it would be less complicated this way."

Megan and Bruce looked at each other. *Less complicated?*

Pittman opened his top left desk drawer and pulled out five envelopes. He reached across the surface and handed them to Bruce.

"There's one for each of you. "Please open the ones with your names on them."

Bruce handed Megan her envelope, and then tore open the one marked "Bruce Brakin." Inside was a check from the U.S. government for three hundred and fifty thousand dollars.

"I trust you will give the respective envelopes to Dillon, Reinhardt and your brother," Pittman said.

"What's this all about?" Megan demanded.

Pittman yanked a pack of Big Red gum out of his jacket pocket. "Like one?" Both declined. Pittman unwrapped a stick, slipped it in his mouth and began chewing. Bruce could smell the sugary cinnamon from where he sat.

Pittman gazed off, avoiding eye contact. "You might want to lay low for a while. Not make yourself too visible. Hopefully the money will help you do this. The others also. Just tell them to—to not cause a stir."

Megan was aghast. "You're ordering us not to discuss what happened with anyone?"

"Ordering you? No. It's merely a suggestion, for your own sake."

"What about the time capsules?" Megan asked, her voice rising.

"They're in good hands."

"Whose hands?"

Again, Pittman glanced at the two suits behind them.

"Who are these guys?" Megan turned and looked at the men.

"Like I already told you. They're just security guards."

"Yeah right," she said.

"Who has the time capsules?" Bruce reiterated.

"The government. Our technicians are taking care of them. You'll be contacted if you're needed."

"But…"

"It's already been decided, Megan."

"By who?"

Pittman bit his lip. Bruce could see him working, trying to be helpful. He gave Bruce a pleading look that silently suggested they not press the issue—*for their own sake.*

"Megan," Pittman said. "My job today is to inform you that the time capsules were found at a National Park owned by the U.S. government. Thus, they legally belong to the government. You've been compensated for your trouble. Now, I'm asking you to please leave it at that."

One of the suits opened the office door.

"Leave it at that?" Megan stood up. "How can we leave it at that when…" Bruce jumped to his feet and grabbed Megan's hand before she could say more. He yanked her toward the door. "Thanks!" he said to Pittman on the way out.

When they reached the light of day in front of the FBI Headquarters Megan was still venting; saying she couldn't be paid off like that and then just told to go away.

"I agree," said Bruce.

"Then what are we going to do?"

"I'm a little tired of fighting and running. Maybe we could just hang out for a while."

Today was the first time he'd seen Megan in three weeks, since she and the others had visited him in the hospital. At

Pittman's request she had flown to the FBI Headquarters from Chicago, and he'd driven from New York. She looked different than he'd ever seen her. Her hair was its natural red color, and she'd gotten it styled so that her bangs hung pointedly down on either side of her face, with the back cut short. Her eyes were a beautiful olive hue, the color highlighted by makeup, Bruce noticed. He'd never seen her with makeup on before. Wearing a skirt, he recalled how, back in Pittman's office, she'd crossed one leg over the other, allowing her shoe to dangle lazily on her toes, revealing the bare the arch of her foot. He had tried not to stare. But now he found himself unable to take his eyes off of her.

Megan was about to argue with Bruce when he interrupted her with a kiss. It was a beautiful, soft kiss. When they disengaged she said:

"Hanging out might not be a bad idea."

Bruce took her hand with his one working hand, his other arm in a sling.

"For how long?" she asked.

He shrugged. "New York's a fun place when you've got money." He held up the envelope with the money. And we've got plenty to spend. It could take a while."

"Hours? Days? Weeks?"

"Or longer?" Bruce smiled.

He kissed her again, which triggered that old ghost from the past. That feeling of abandonment was still prodding at her heart, but not enough to dissuade her.

She caught her breath. "I think I would like that," she said. "Would very much like to hang out with you."

Bruce handed her his keys. "You drive. I'll be in charge of the music. You like classic rock 'n roll?"

"Like Guns & Roses?" Megan said, hopping in the driver's seat.

Inside, Bruce gave her a look. "I'm talking *classic*. He examined a case of CDs, pulled one out and held it up for Megan to see.

"The Yardbirds. Most innovative guitar group of all time."

"Sweet," said Megan, starting the car.

"During different periods, the Yardbirds had three of the greatest British guitarists who ever lived: Eric Clapton, Jeff Beck, and Jimmy Page!"

"I love that Clapton song…" Megan paused, trying to remember the name of it.

"Layla?"

"Duh. Layla. Never get sick of that song."

"Clapton recorded that much later with Derek and the Dominos. He wrote it about Pattie Harrison, George Harrison's wife, who he was in love with at the time."

"Oh."

He slipped in the CD. Megan recognized the song, "For your love."

After watching him bob his head for a few moments to the music she turned the volume down and said, "I never thanked you."

"For what?"

"For not kicking me out of your car that night I snuck into your backseat at the Grand Canyon."

"That night you held the gun to my head?"

"Yeah then."

"You're welcome."

She threw the Jeep into gear.

"After this we'll listen to Moby Grape and Canned Heat," Bruce informed her, as she drove out of the parking lot.

"Okay," Megan said. She had no idea who Moby Grape and Canned Heat were. But she was happy. Happy to be "hanging out" with Bruce Brackin.

But as she drove down the winding road away from the FBI building she was already plotting how she was going to get the time capsules back.

OTHER TITLES by FIRESIDE PUBLICATIONS

- <u>THE FURAX CONNECTION</u> by Stephen L. Kanne
- <u>THE CLEANSING</u> by B.F. Eller
- <u>BLESSED: My Battle With Brain Disease</u> by Mary J. Stevens
- <u>ENGLEHARDT</u> by Gisela Englehardt
- <u>THE COST OF JUSTICE</u> by Mike Gedgoudas
- <u>TEXAS JUSTICE</u> by Judith Groudine Finkel
- <u>LOVE TAG</u> by Peter Shianna
- <u>THE LONG NIGHT MOON</u> by Elizabeth Towles
- <u>AN AGENT SPEAKS: A Primer for Unpublished Writers</u> by Joan West
- <u>THE CRYSTAL ANGEL</u> by Olivia Claire High
- <u>BEYOND FOREVER: Experiences From Past Lives</u> by Taylor Shaye

For more information or to order any of the above books, please visit www.firesidepubs.com or contact:

Fireside Publications
1004 San Felipe Lane
Lady Lake, Florida 32159

Visit the author at: www.jamesjvalko.com